BEST SHOT IN THE WEST

THE ADVENTURES OF NAT LOVE

By Patricia C. McKissack
& Fredrick L. McKissack Jr.
Illustrated by Randy DuBurke

chronicle books · san francisco

Library of Congress Cataloging-in-Publication Data
McKissack, Pat, 1944–
Best shot in the West : the adventures of Nat Love / by Patricia C. McKissack and Fredrick L.
McKissack, Jr. ; illustrated by Randy DuBurke.
p. cm.
ISBN 978-0-8118-5749-9
1. Love, Nat, 1854–1921—Comic books, strips, etc. 2. African American cowboys—West (U.S.)—
Biography—Comic books, strips, etc. 3. Cowboys—West (U.S.)—Biography—Comic books,
strips, etc. 4. West (U.S.)—Biography—Comic books, strips, etc. I. McKissack, Fredrick, Jr.
II. DuBurke, Randy. III. Title.

F594.L892M34 2011
978'.02092—dc22
[B]

2007021419

Book design by Amelia Mack, Izzy Langridge, Mai Ogiya, and Lauren Smith.
Typeset in Crimefighter.
Narration and speech panels drawn by Anthony Wu.
The illustrations in this book were rendered in acrylic and pen.
Manufactured in China in March 2012.

3 5 7 9 10 8 6 4

Chronicle Books LLC.
680 Second Street, San Francisco, California 94107

www.chroniclebooks.com/teen

To the Kummers. Thank you.
— F. L. M.

To my wife, our two boys, and my publisher and editor

who stuck with me through the hard times.
— R. D.

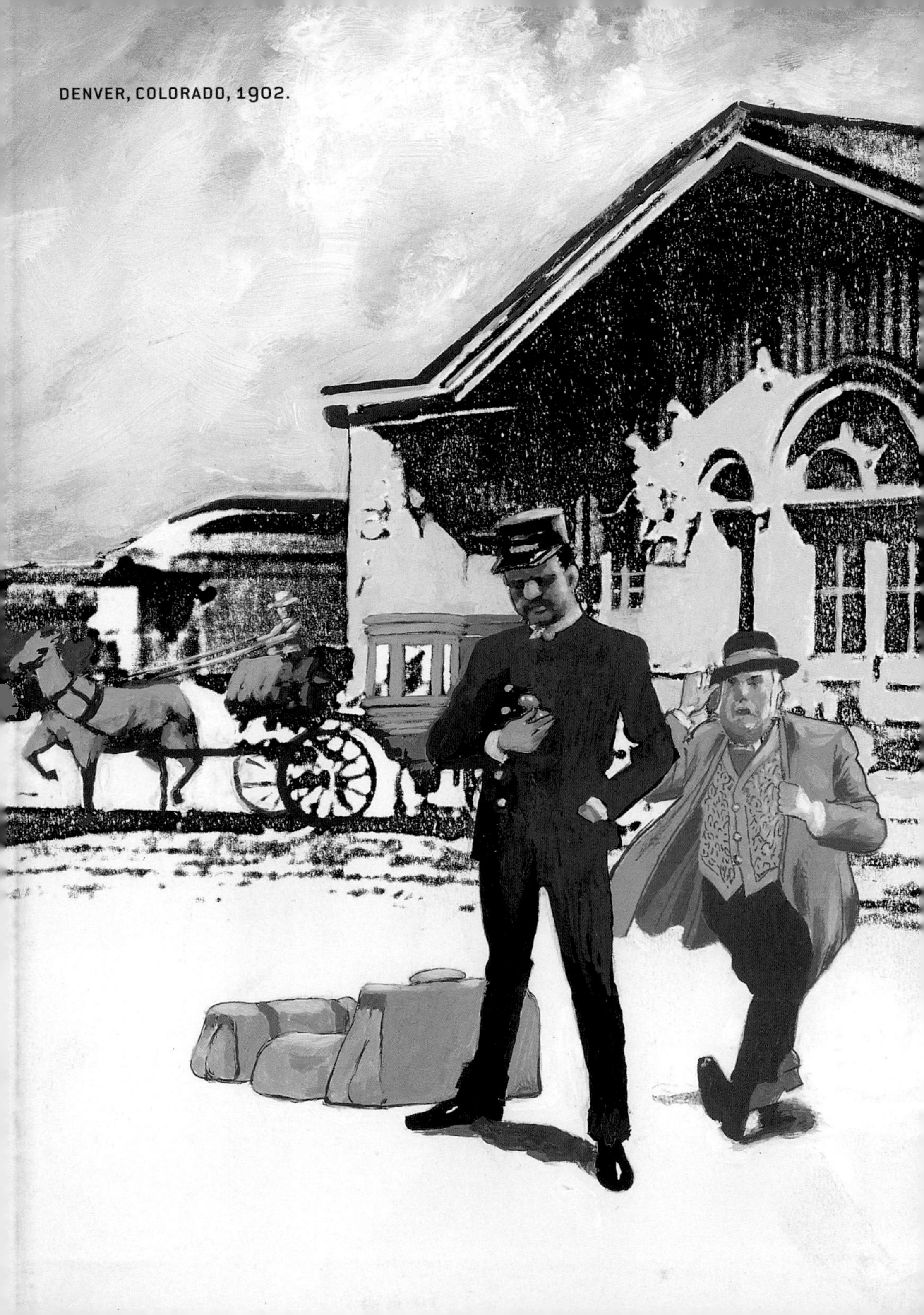
DENVER, COLORADO, 1902.

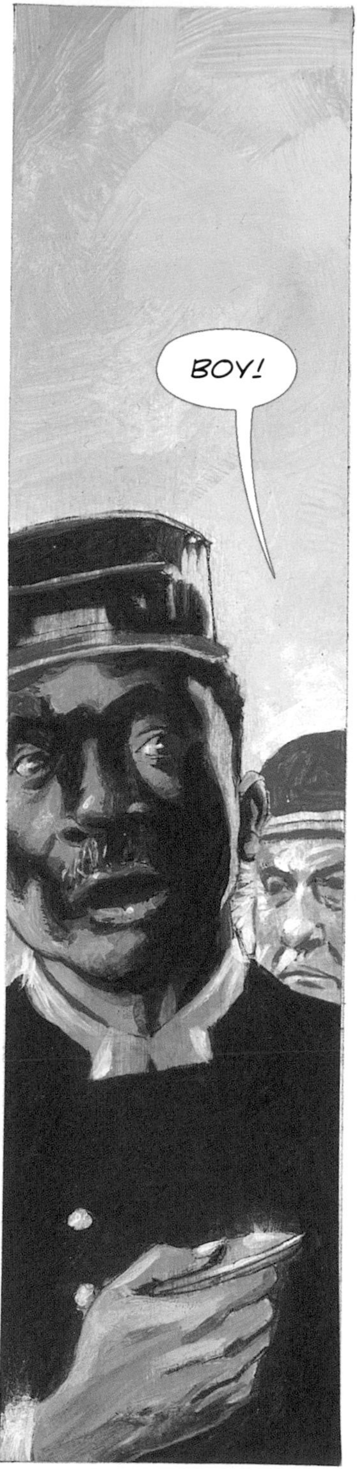
BOY!

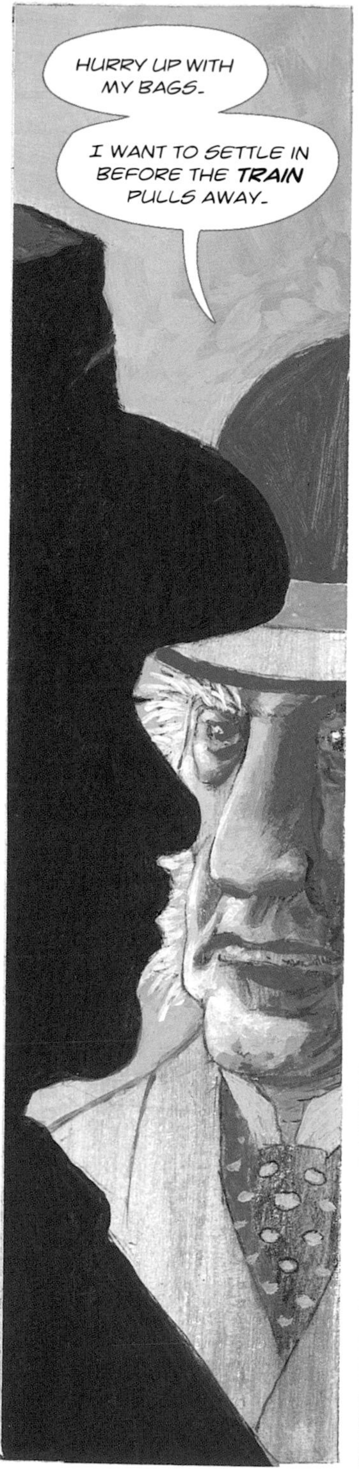
HURRY UP WITH MY BAGS.
I WANT TO SETTLE IN BEFORE THE **TRAIN** PULLS AWAY.

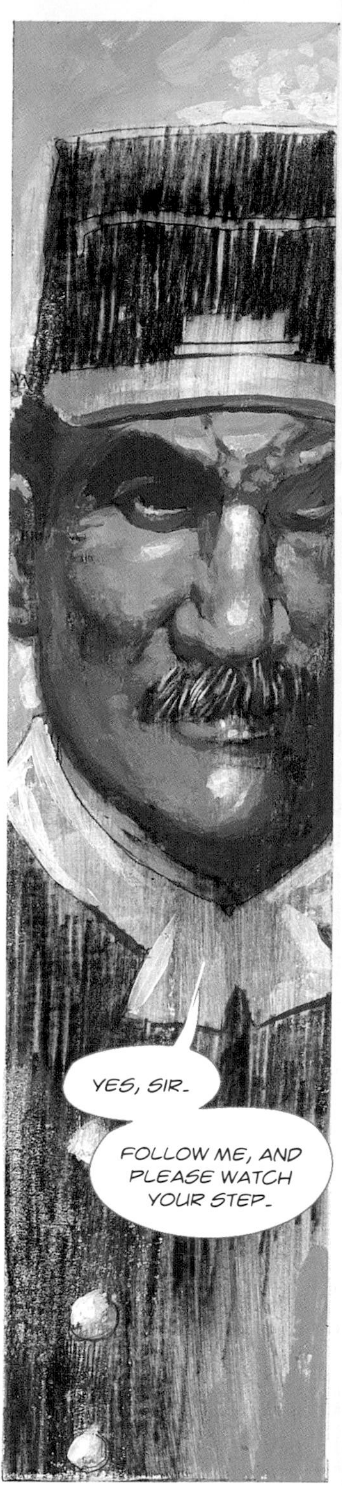
YES, SIR.
FOLLOW ME, AND PLEASE WATCH YOUR STEP.

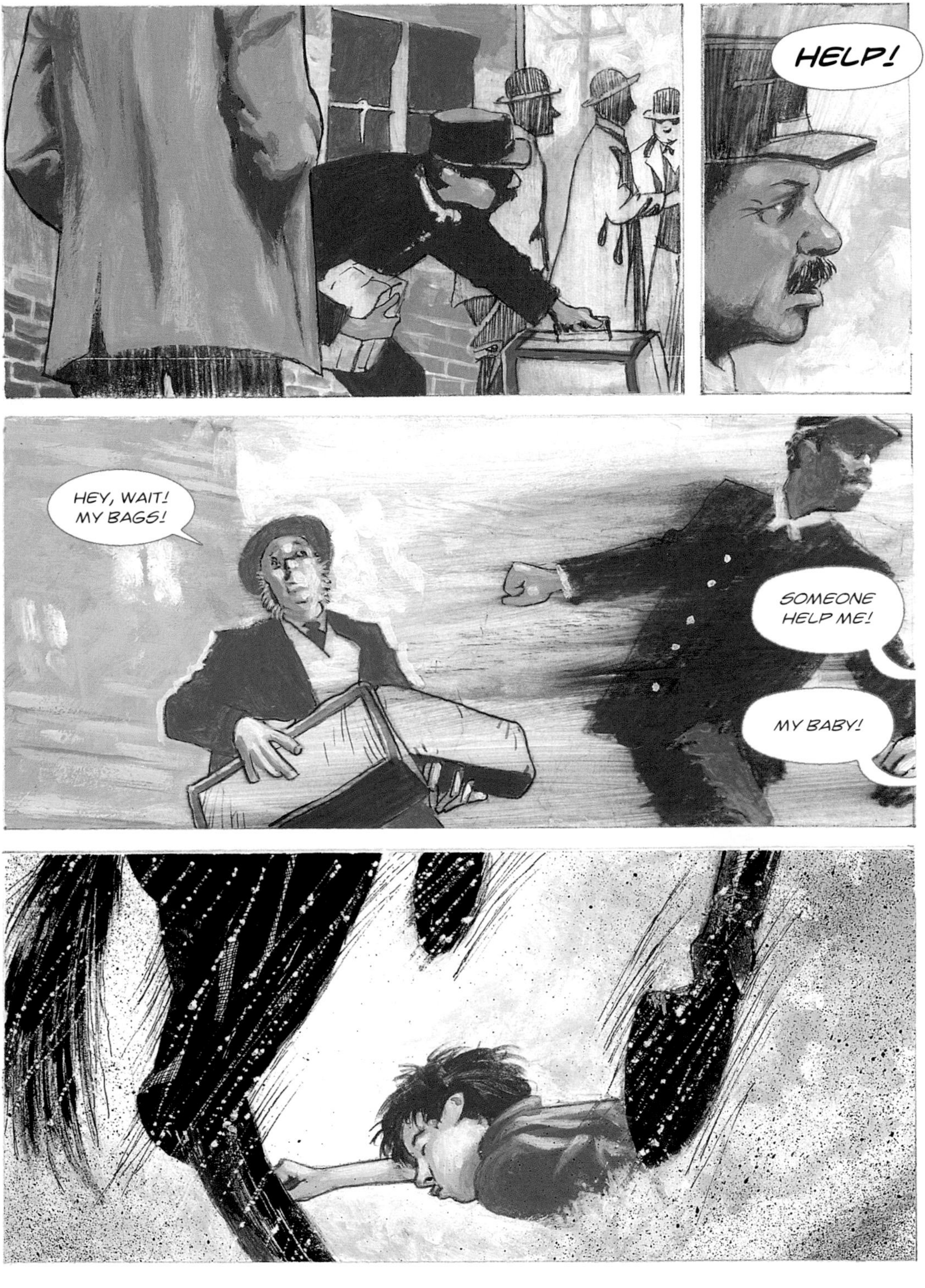
HELP!
HEY, WAIT! MY BAGS!
SOMEONE HELP ME!
MY BABY!

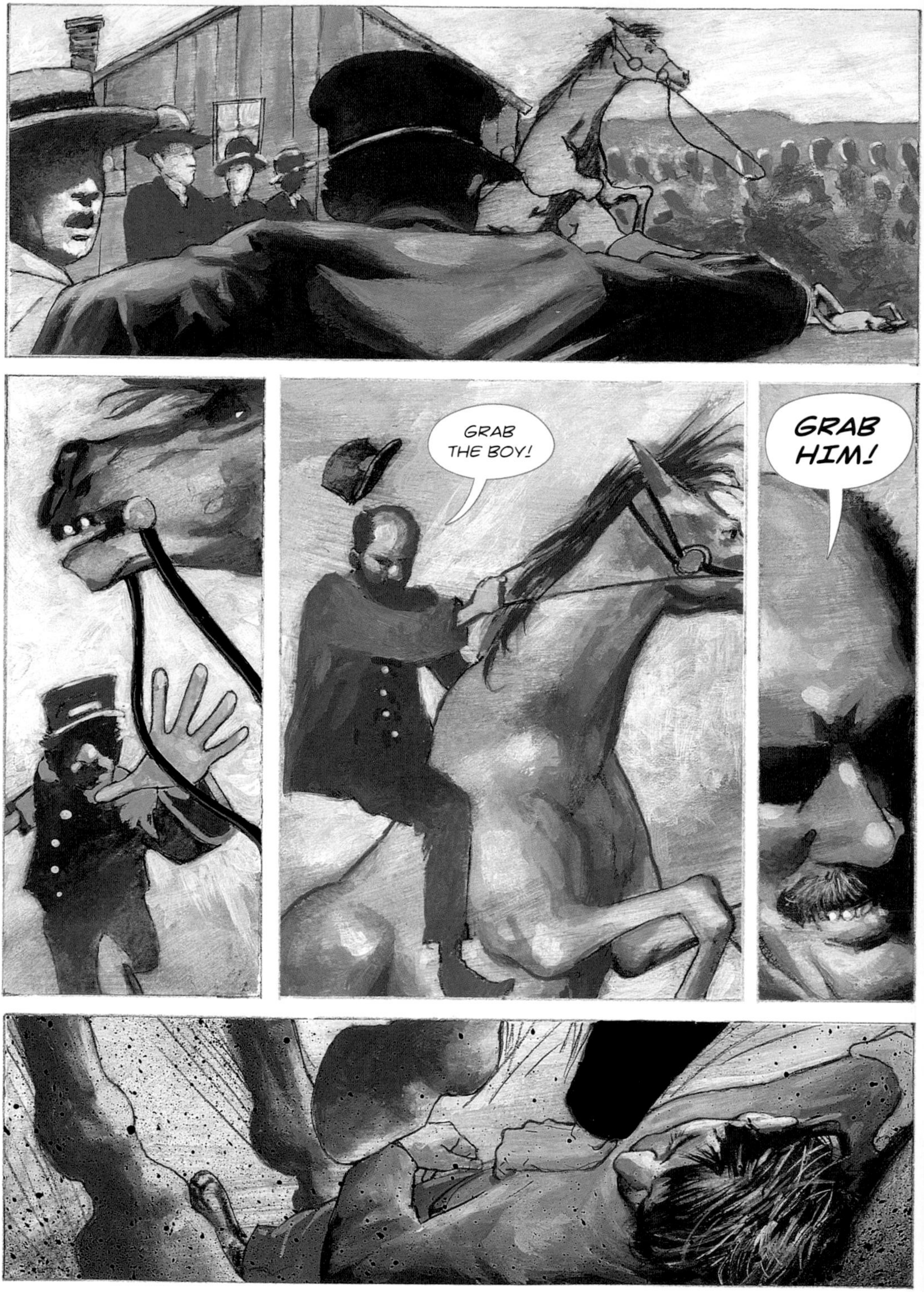
GRAB THE BOY!
GRAB HIM!

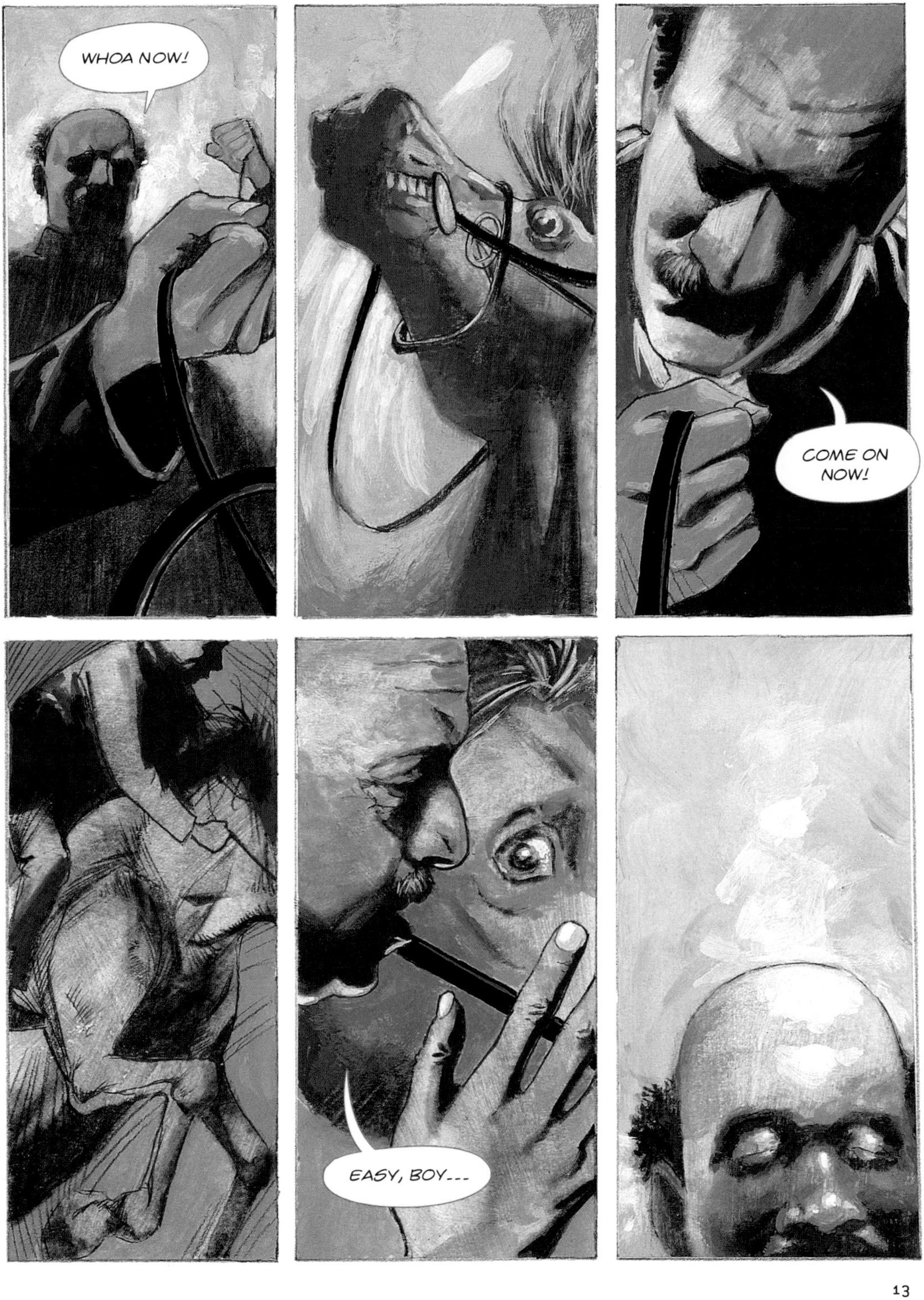
WHOA NOW!
COME ON NOW!
EASY, BOY...

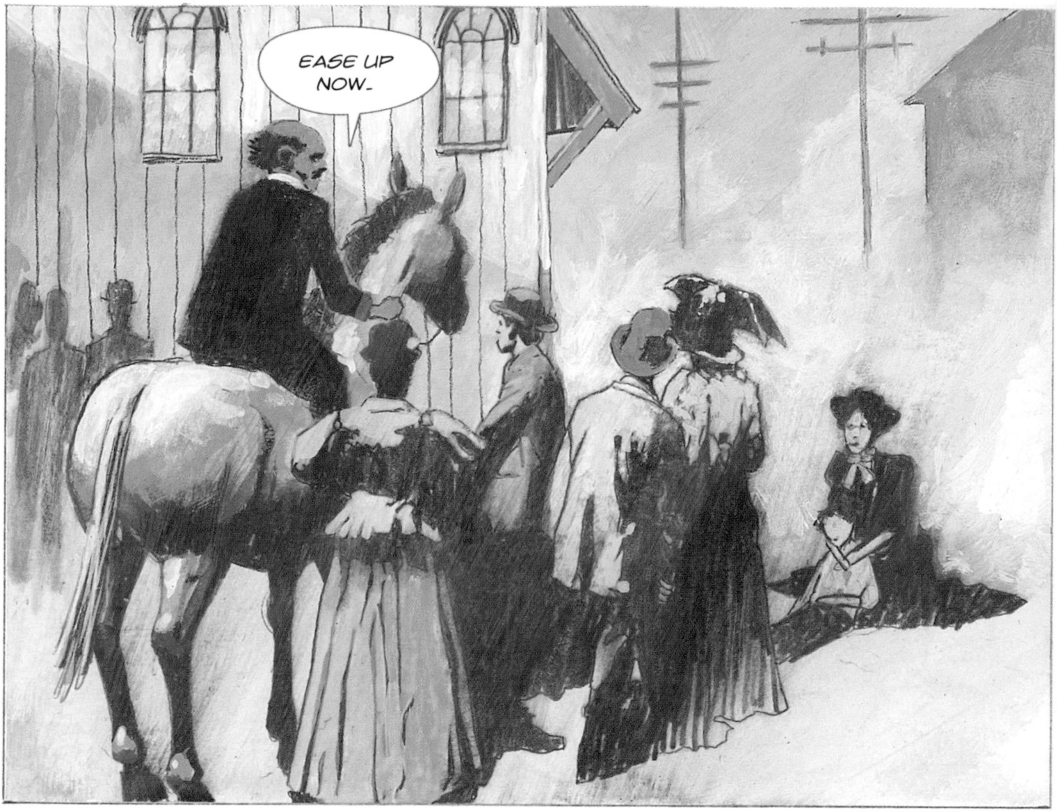
EASE UP NOW.

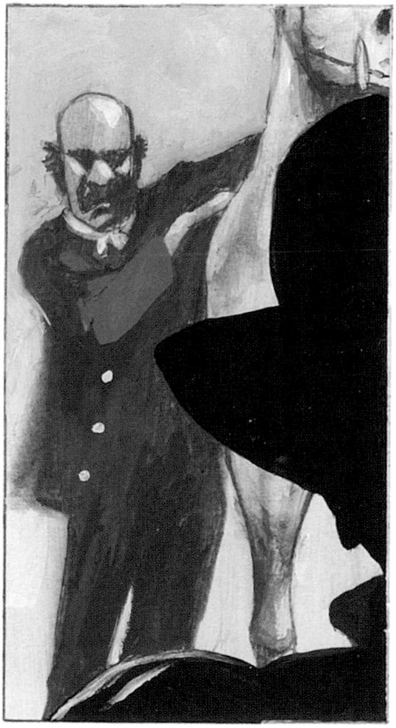

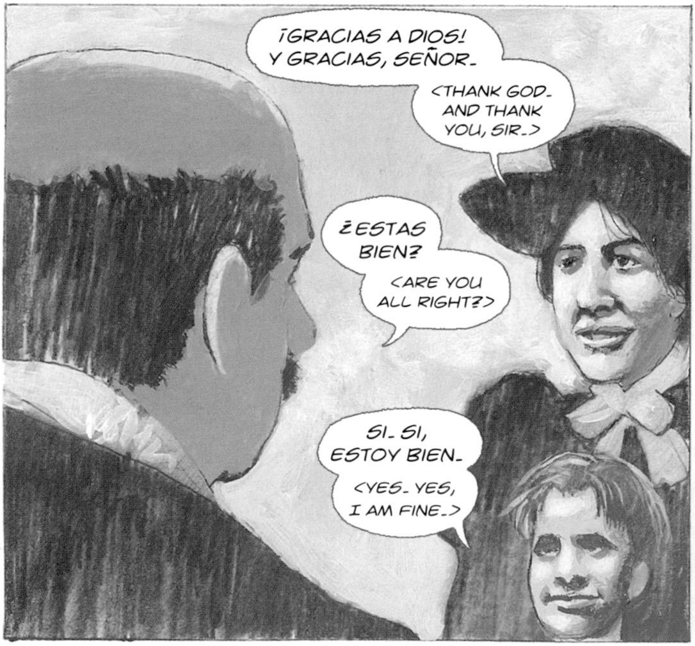
¡GRACIAS A DIOS! Y GRACIAS, SEÑOR.
<THANK GOD. AND THANK YOU, SIR.>
¿ESTAS BIEN?
<ARE YOU ALL RIGHT?>
SI. SI, ESTOY BIEN.
<YES. YES, I AM FINE.>

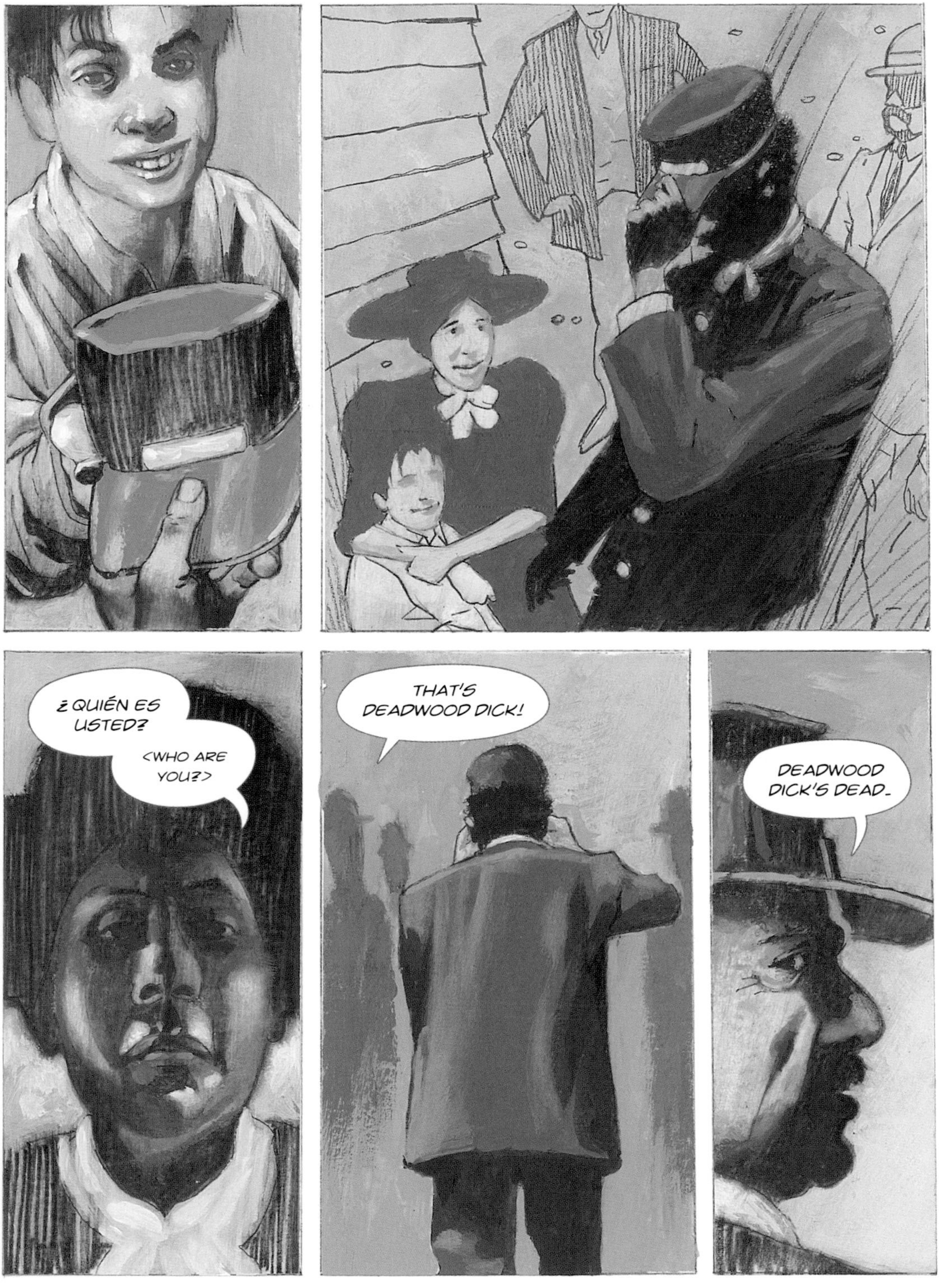
¿QUIÉN ES USTED?
<WHO ARE YOU?>
THAT'S DEADWOOD DICK!
DEADWOOD DICK'S DEAD.

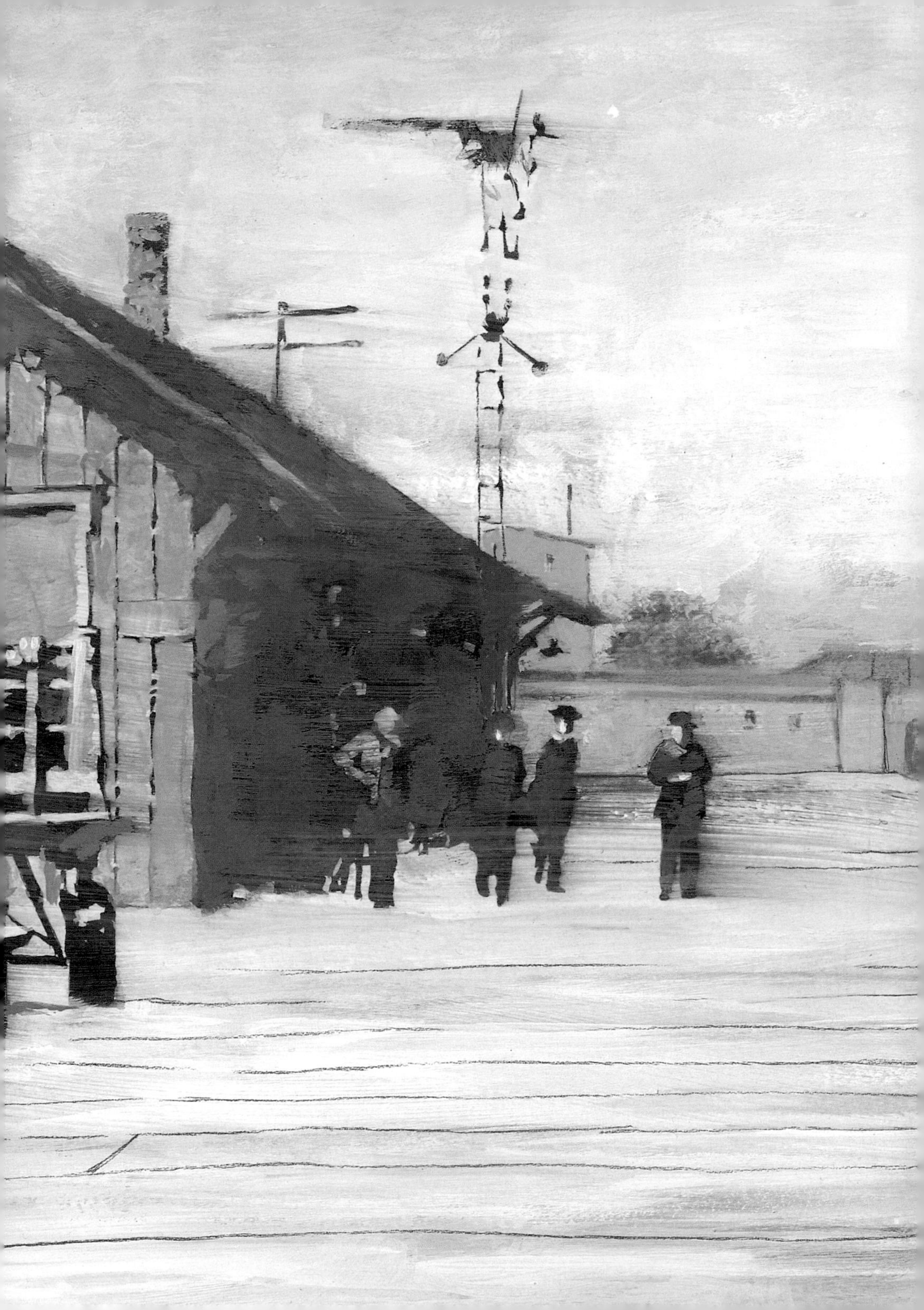

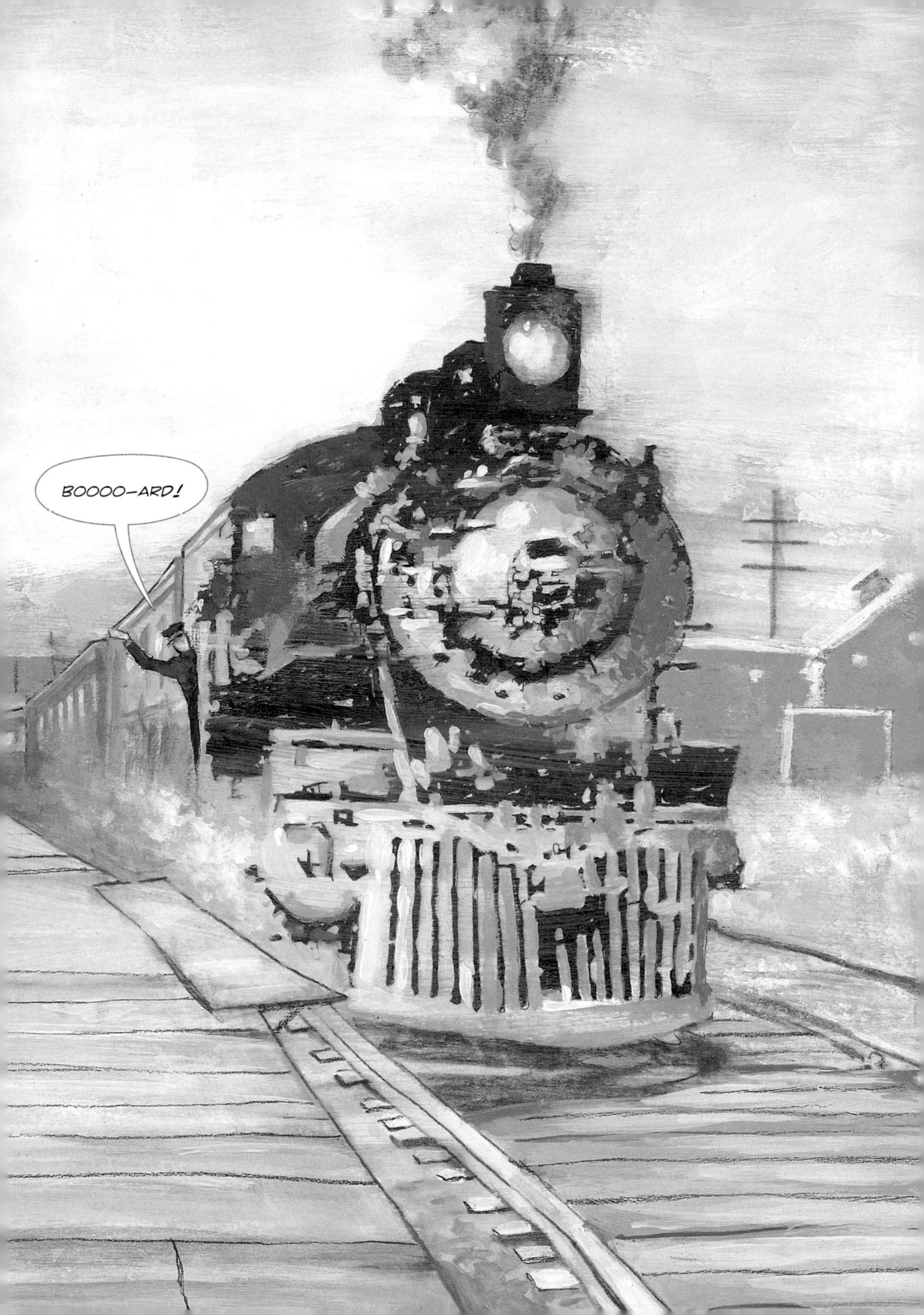
BOOOO-ARD!

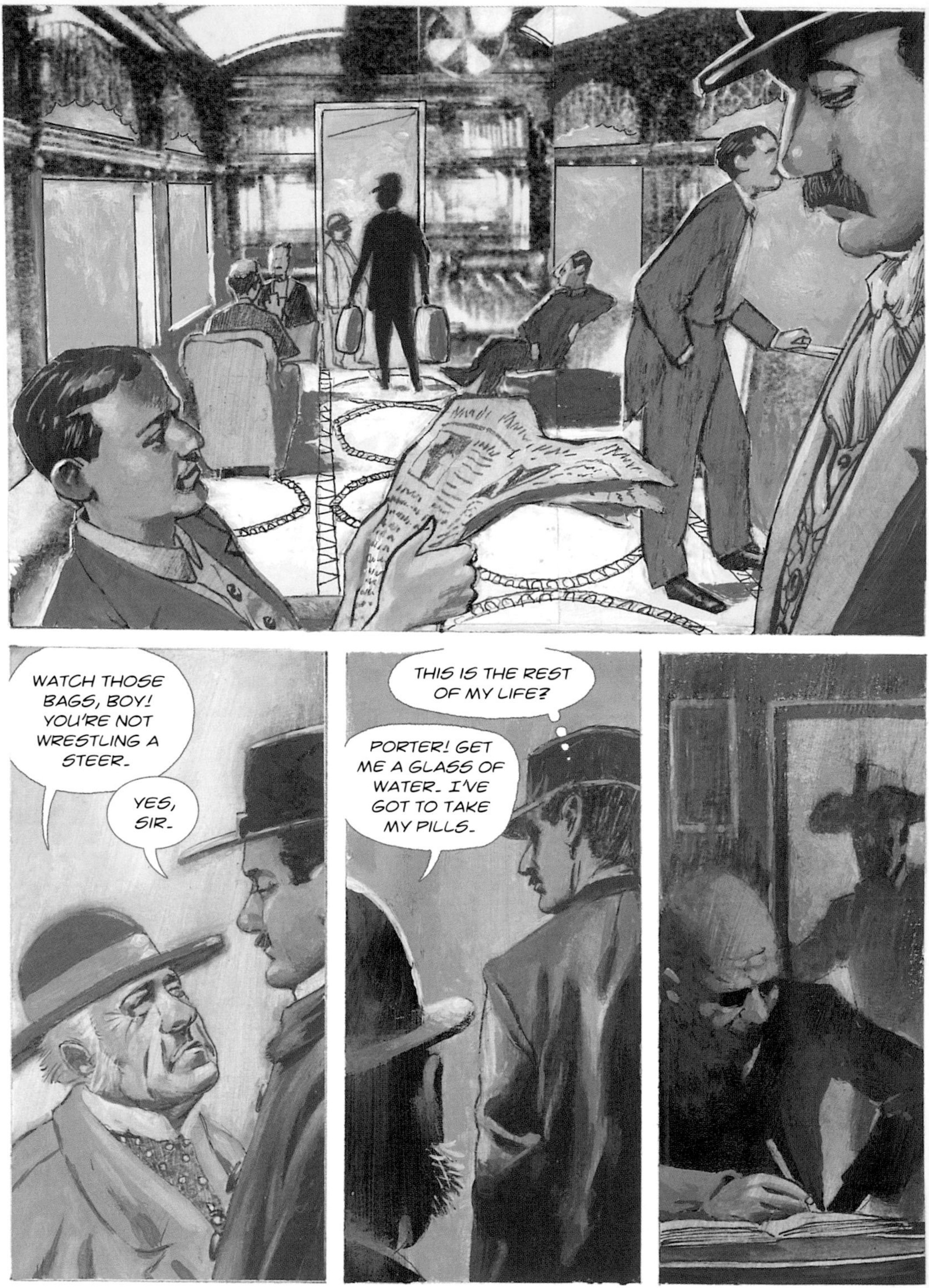
WATCH THOSE BAGS, BOY! YOU'RE NOT WRESTLING A STEER.
YES, SIR.
THIS IS THE REST OF MY LIFE?
PORTER! GET ME A GLASS OF WATER. I'VE GOT TO TAKE MY PILLS.

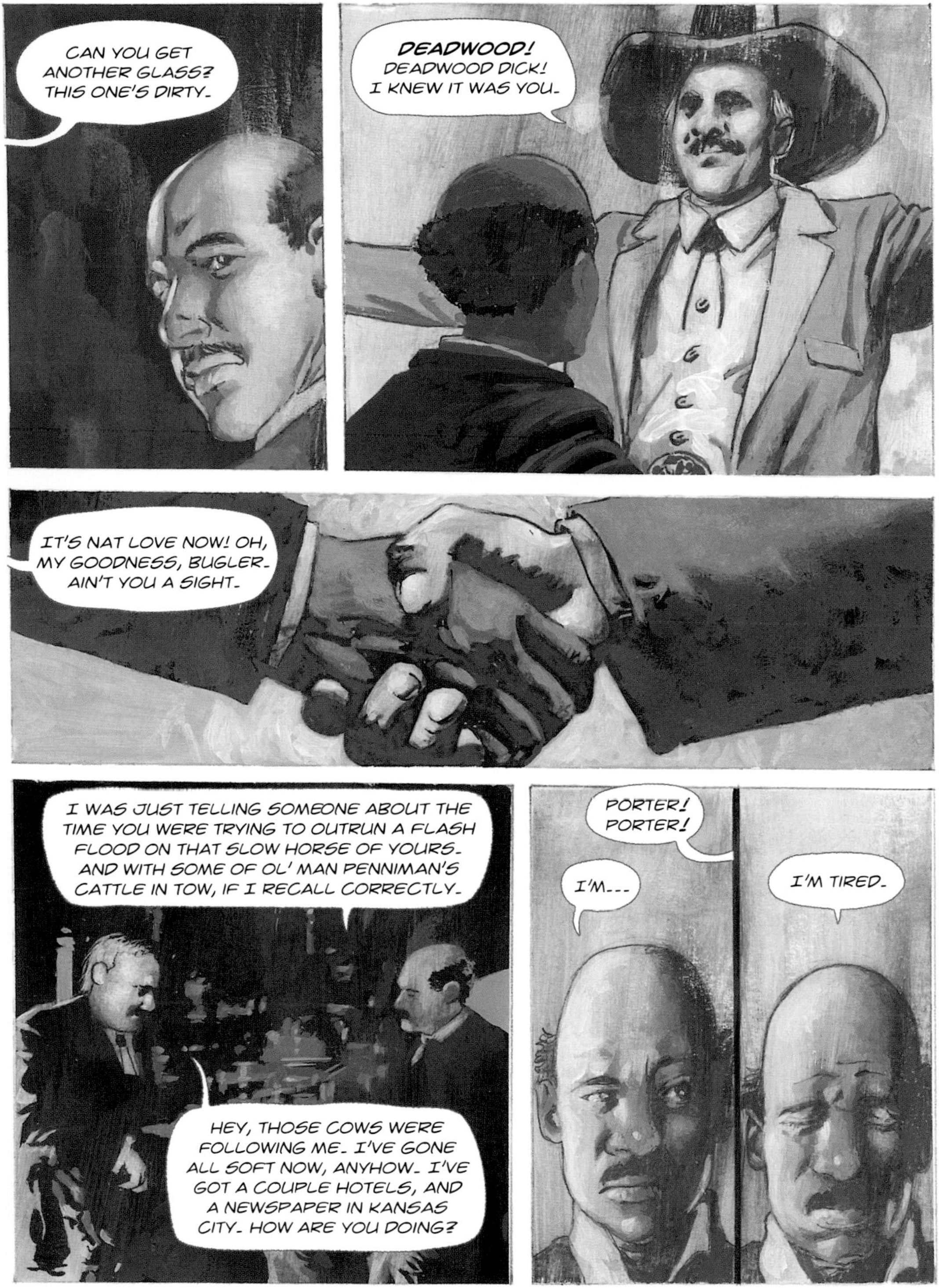
CAN YOU GET ANOTHER GLASS? THIS ONE'S DIRTY.
DEADWOOD! DEADWOOD DICK! I KNEW IT WAS YOU.
IT'S NAT LOVE NOW! OH, MY GOODNESS, BUGLER. AIN'T YOU A SIGHT.
I WAS JUST TELLING SOMEONE ABOUT THE TIME YOU WERE TRYING TO OUTRUN A FLASH FLOOD ON THAT SLOW HORSE OF YOURS. AND WITH SOME OF OL' MAN PENNIMAN'S CATTLE IN TOW, IF I RECALL CORRECTLY.
HEY, THOSE COWS WERE FOLLOWING ME. I'VE GONE ALL SOFT NOW, ANYHOW. I'VE GOT A COUPLE HOTELS, AND A NEWSPAPER IN KANSAS CITY. HOW ARE YOU DOING?
PORTER! PORTER!
I'M...
I'M TIRED.

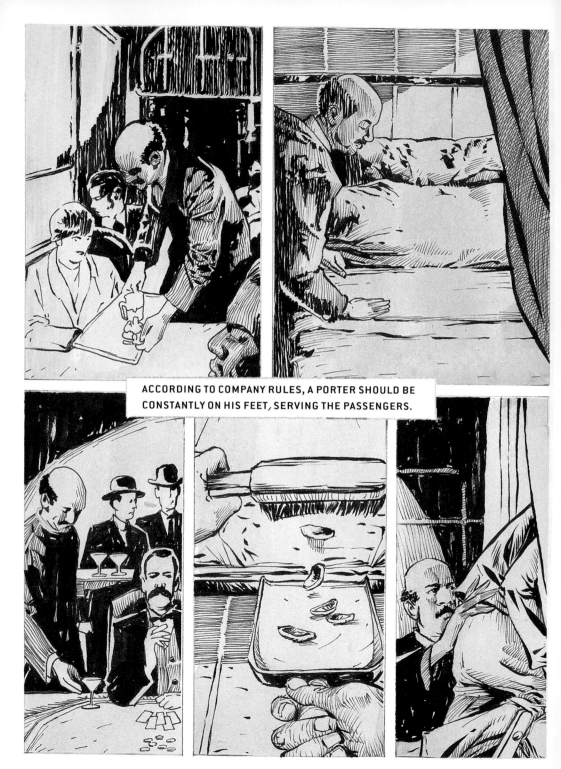

ACCORDING TO COMPANY RULES, A PORTER SHOULD BE CONSTANTLY ON HIS FEET, SERVING THE PASSENGERS.

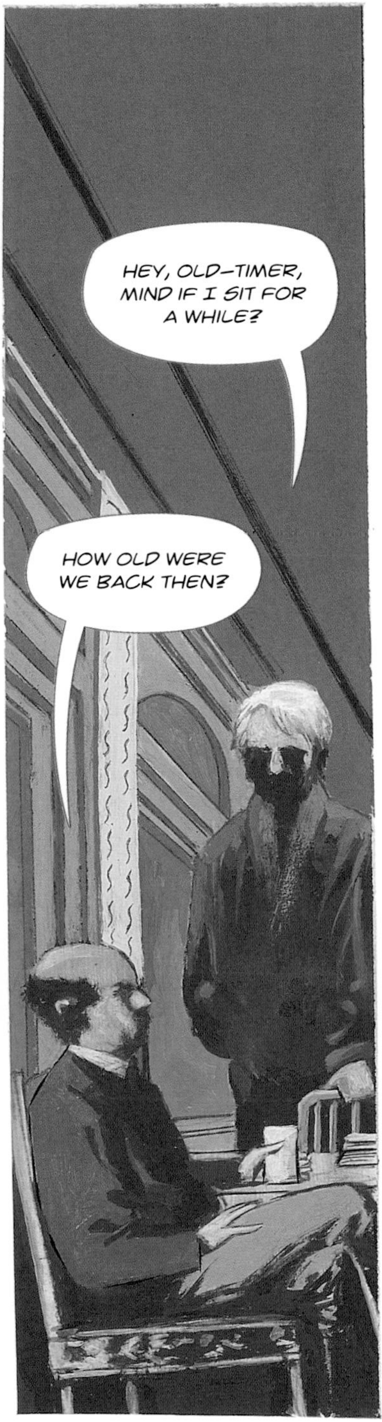
HEY, OLD-TIMER, MIND IF I SIT FOR A WHILE?
HOW OLD WERE WE BACK THEN?

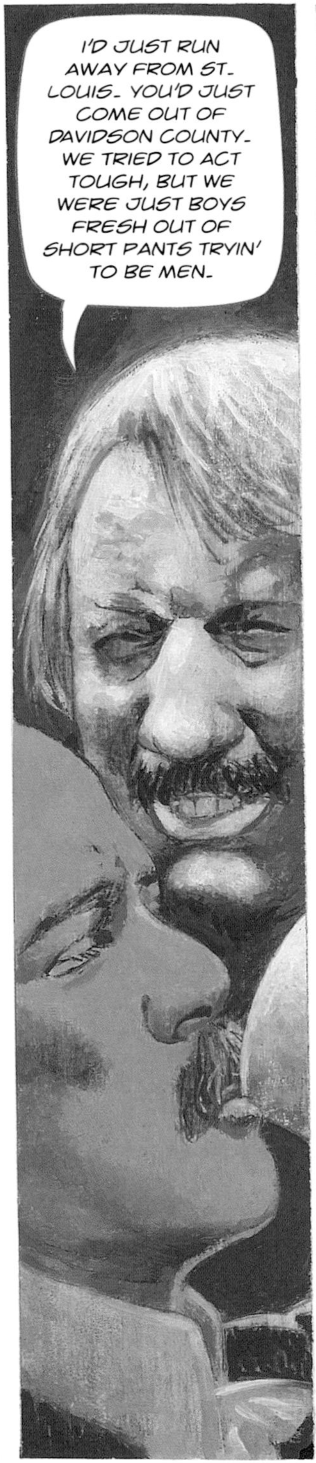
I'D JUST RUN AWAY FROM ST. LOUIS. YOU'D JUST COME OUT OF DAVIDSON COUNTY. WE TRIED TO ACT TOUGH, BUT WE WERE JUST BOYS FRESH OUT OF SHORT PANTS TRYIN' TO BE MEN.

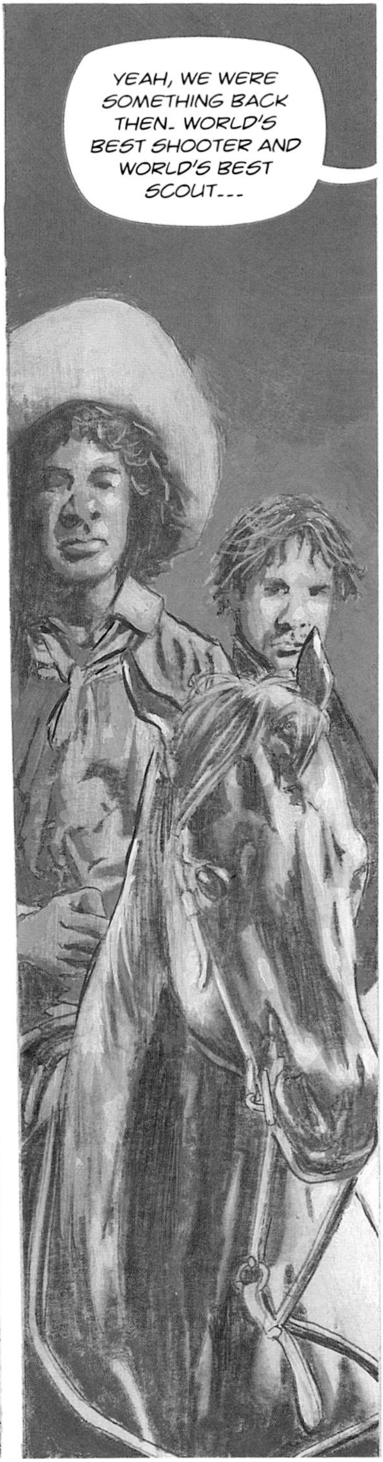
YEAH, WE WERE SOMETHING BACK THEN. WORLD'S BEST SHOOTER AND WORLD'S BEST SCOUT...

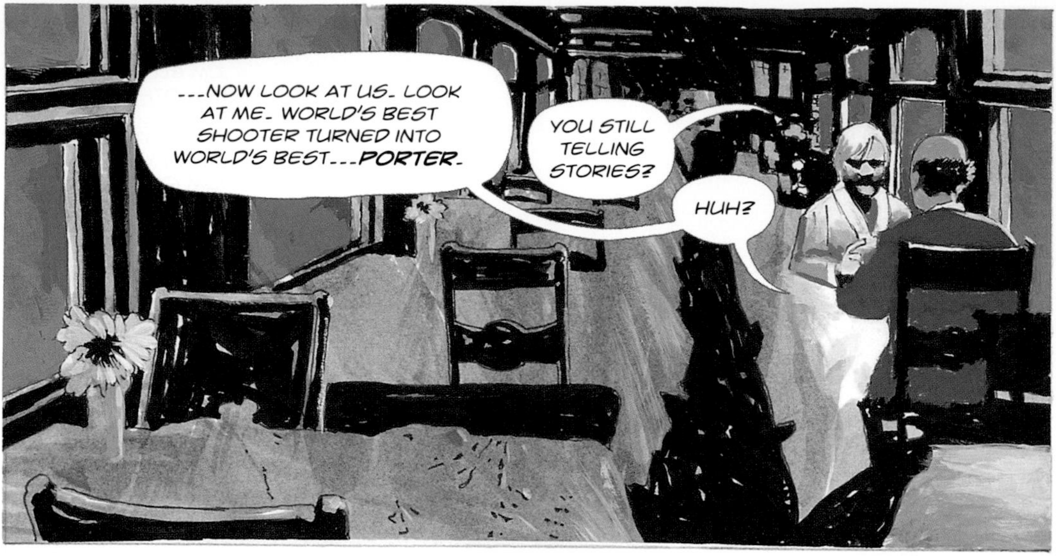
...NOW LOOK AT US. LOOK AT ME. WORLD'S BEST SHOOTER TURNED INTO WORLD'S BEST...**PORTER**.
YOU STILL TELLING STORIES?
HUH?

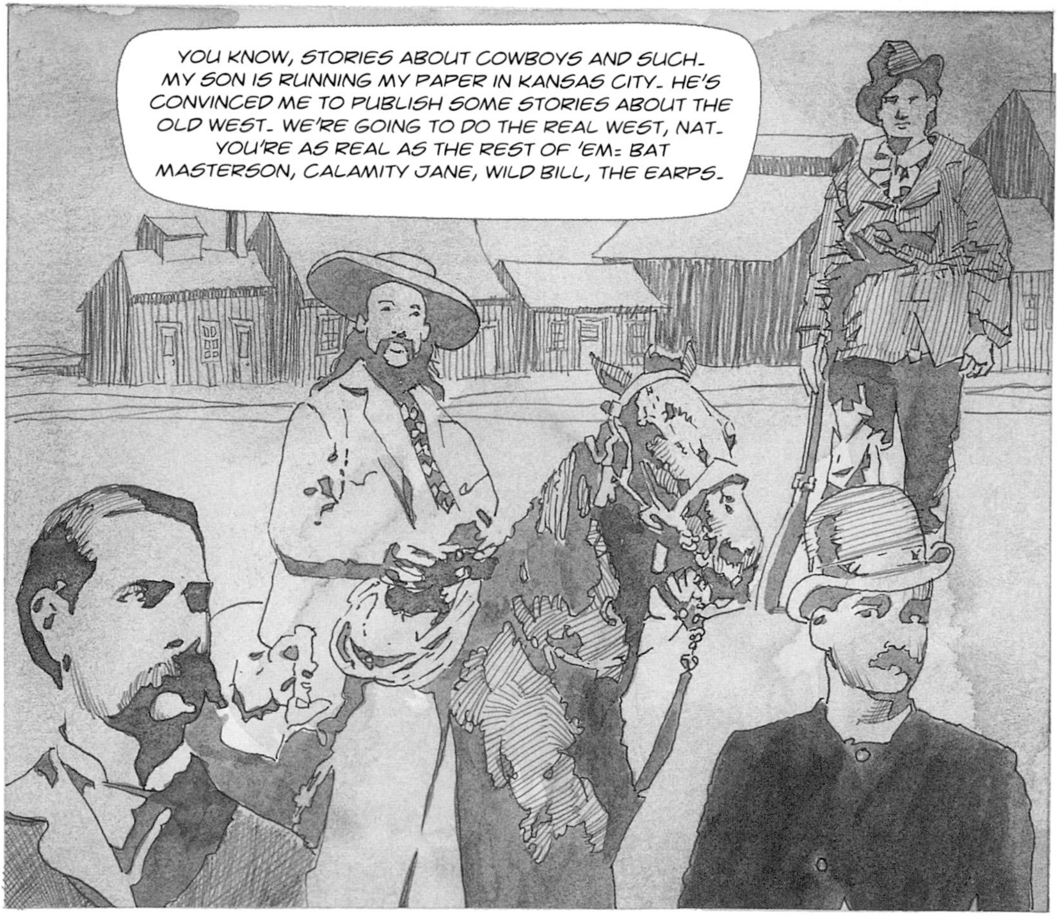
YOU KNOW, STORIES ABOUT COWBOYS AND SUCH. MY SON IS RUNNING MY PAPER IN KANSAS CITY. HE'S CONVINCED ME TO PUBLISH SOME STORIES ABOUT THE OLD WEST. WE'RE GOING TO DO THE REAL WEST, NAT. YOU'RE AS REAL AS THE REST OF 'EM: BAT MASTERSON, CALAMITY JANE, WILD BILL, THE EARPS.

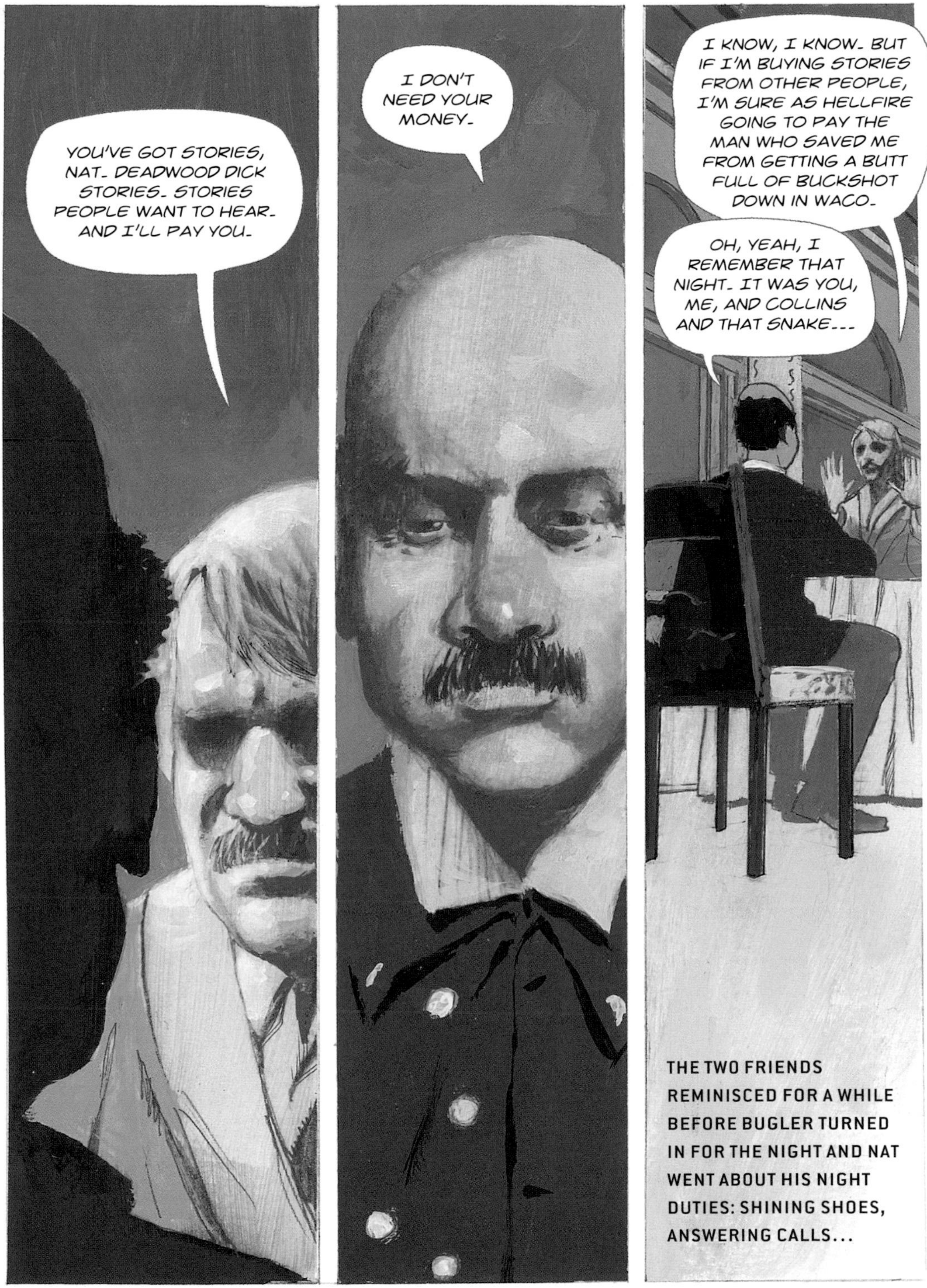
YOU'VE GOT STORIES, NAT. DEADWOOD DICK STORIES. STORIES PEOPLE WANT TO HEAR. AND I'LL PAY YOU.
I DON'T NEED YOUR MONEY.
I KNOW, I KNOW. BUT IF I'M BUYING STORIES FROM OTHER PEOPLE, I'M SURE AS HELLFIRE GOING TO PAY THE MAN WHO SAVED ME FROM GETTING A BUTT FULL OF BUCKSHOT DOWN IN WACO.
OH, YEAH, I REMEMBER THAT NIGHT. IT WAS YOU, ME, AND COLLINS AND THAT SNAKE...
THE TWO FRIENDS REMINISCED FOR A WHILE BEFORE BUGLER TURNED IN FOR THE NIGHT AND NAT WENT ABOUT HIS NIGHT DUTIES: SHINING SHOES, ANSWERING CALLS...

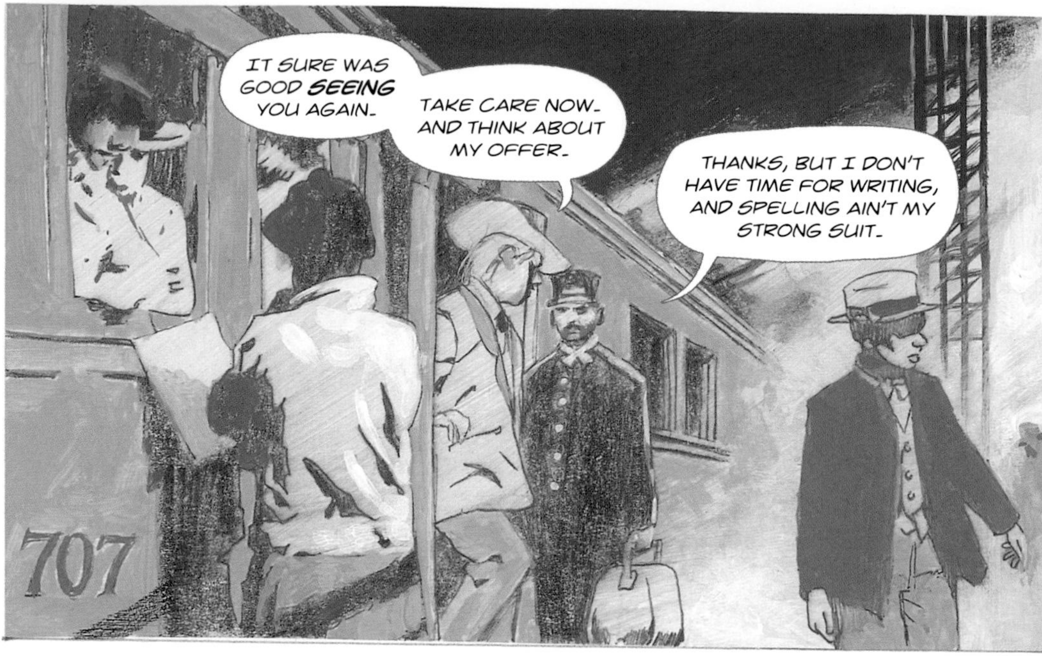
IT SURE WAS GOOD SEEING YOU AGAIN.
TAKE CARE NOW. AND THINK ABOUT MY OFFER.
THANKS, BUT I DON'T HAVE TIME FOR WRITING, AND SPELLING AIN'T MY STRONG SUIT.
707

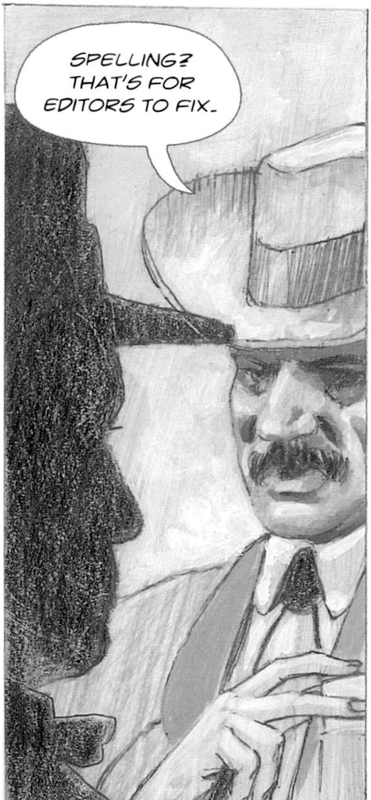
SPELLING? THAT'S FOR EDITORS TO FIX.

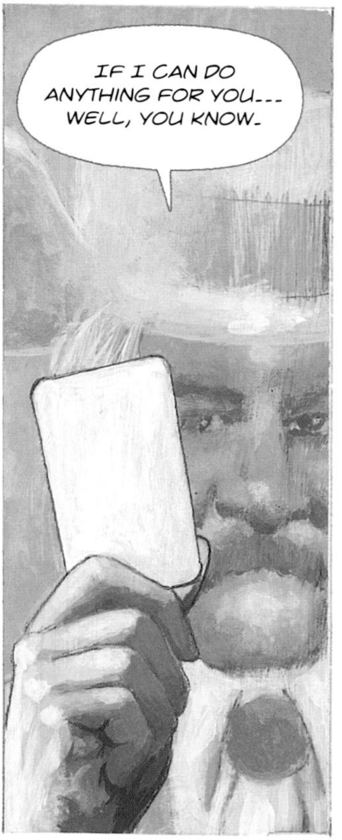
IF I CAN DO ANYTHING FOR YOU... WELL, YOU KNOW.

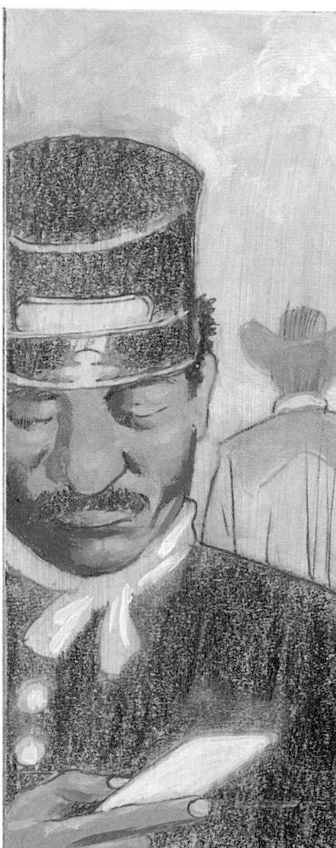

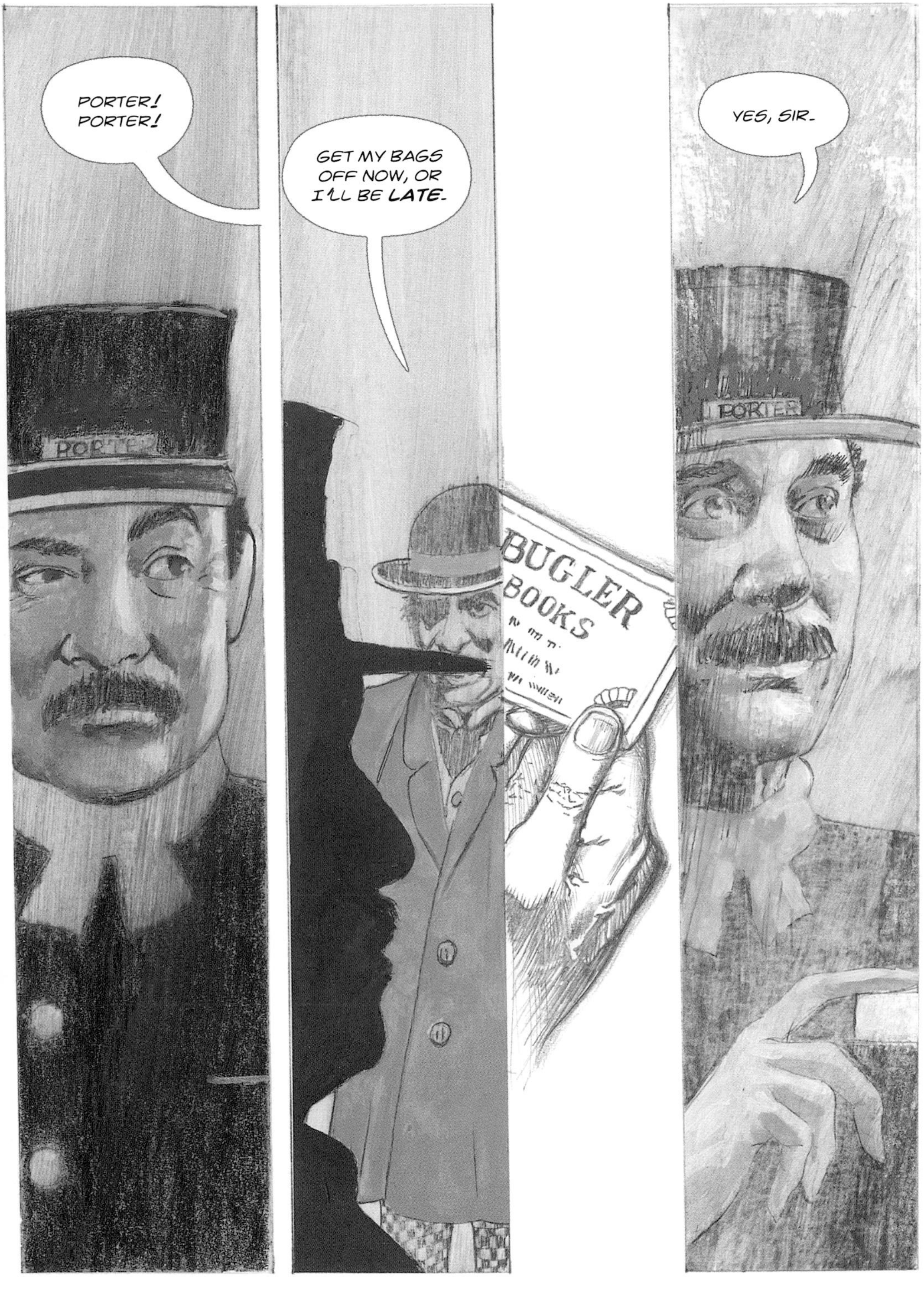
PORTER! PORTER!
GET MY BAGS OFF NOW, OR I'LL BE **LATE**.
YES, SIR.
PORTER
BUGLER BOOKS
PORTER

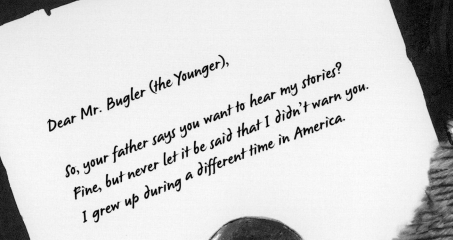

Dear Mr. Bugler (the Younger),

So, your father says you want to hear my stories?
Fine, but never let it be said that I didn't warn you.
I grew up during a different time in America.

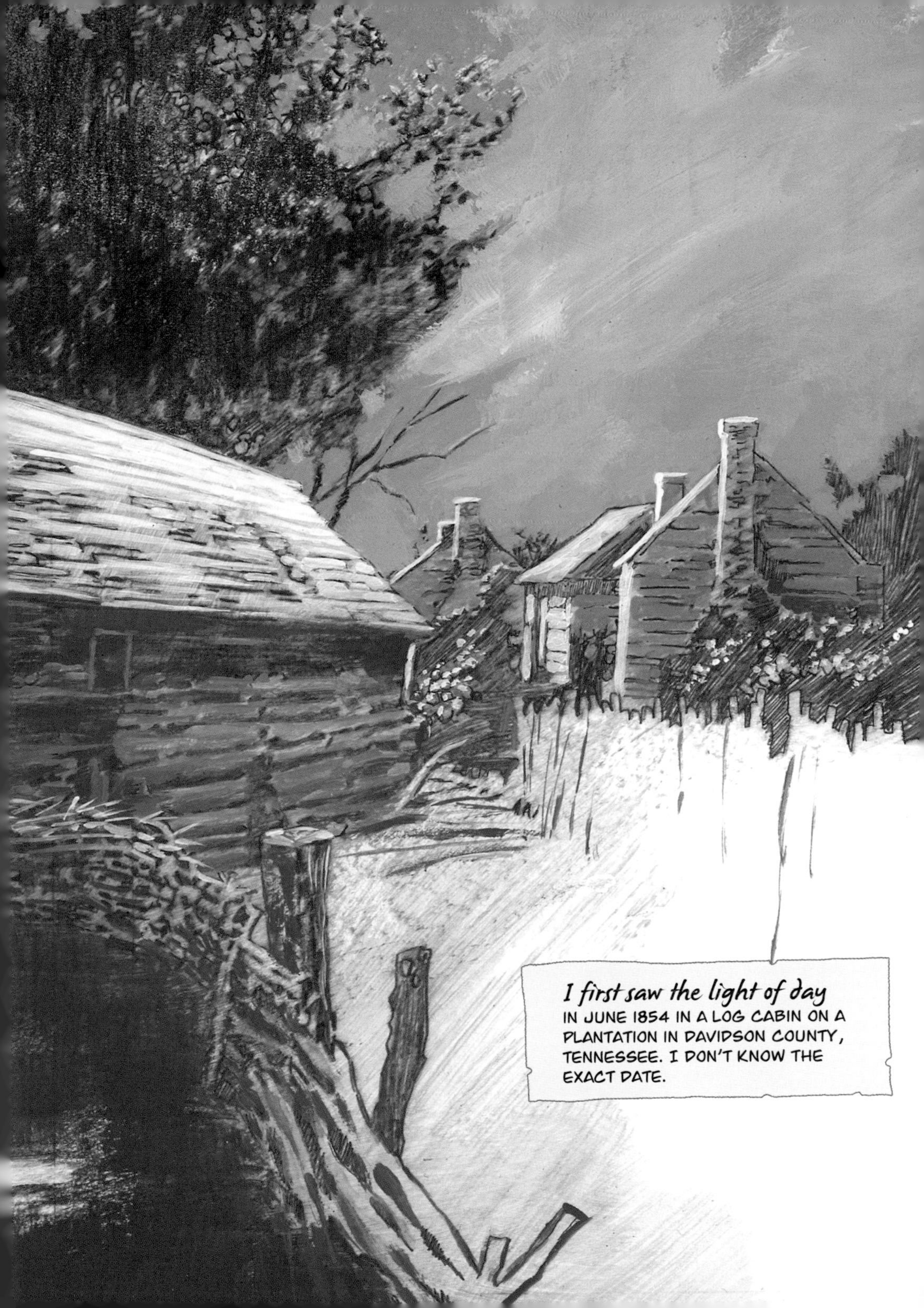
I first saw the light of day
IN JUNE 1854 IN A LOG CABIN ON A PLANTATION IN DAVIDSON COUNTY, TENNESSEE. I DON'T KNOW THE EXACT DATE.

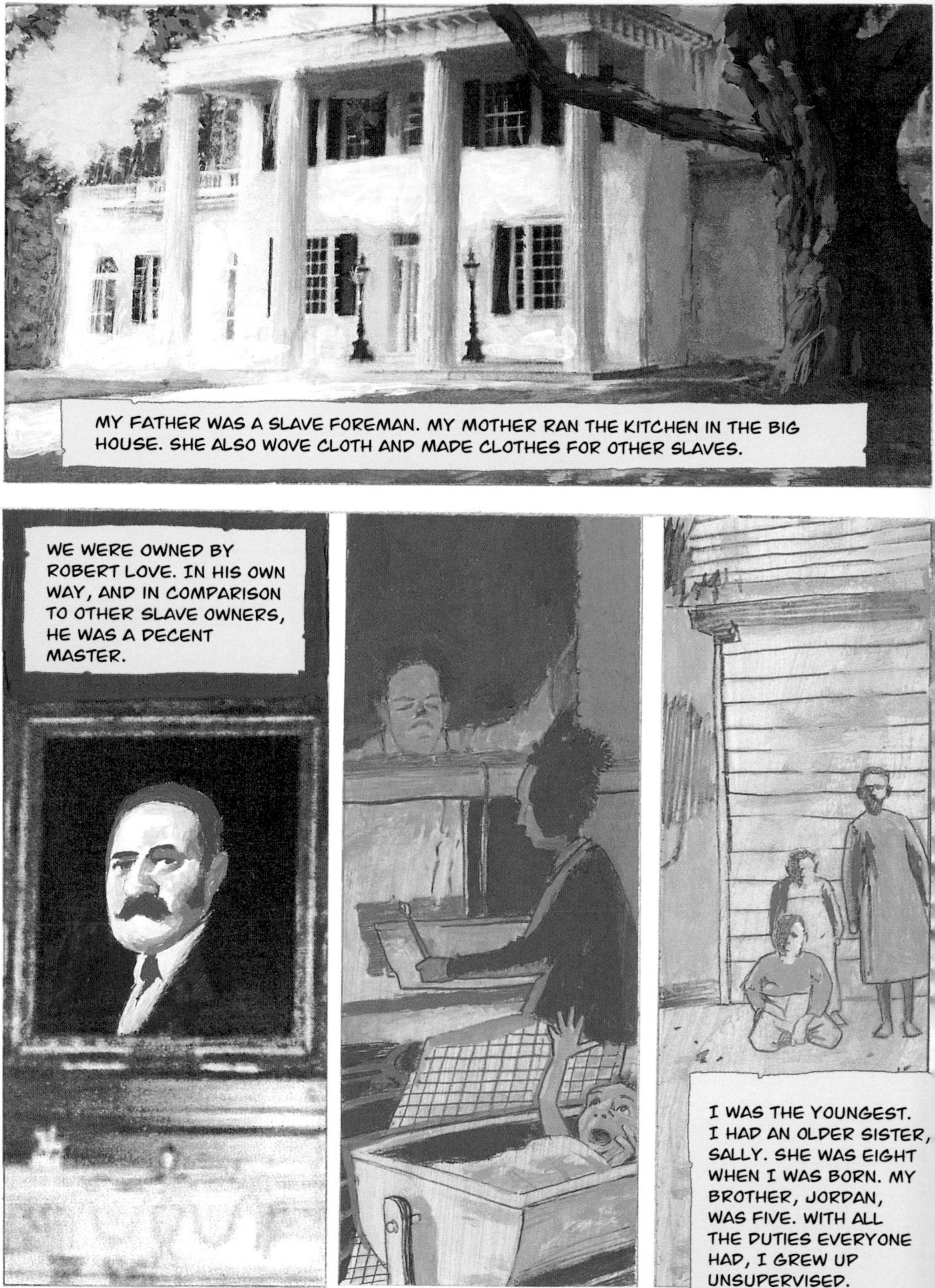
MY FATHER WAS A SLAVE FOREMAN. MY MOTHER RAN THE KITCHEN IN THE BIG HOUSE. SHE ALSO WOVE CLOTH AND MADE CLOTHES FOR OTHER SLAVES.
WE WERE OWNED BY ROBERT LOVE. IN HIS OWN WAY, AND IN COMPARISON TO OTHER SLAVE OWNERS, HE WAS A DECENT MASTER.
I WAS THE YOUNGEST. I HAD AN OLDER SISTER, SALLY. SHE WAS EIGHT WHEN I WAS BORN. MY BROTHER, JORDAN, WAS FIVE. WITH ALL THE DUTIES EVERYONE HAD, I GREW UP UNSUPERVISED.

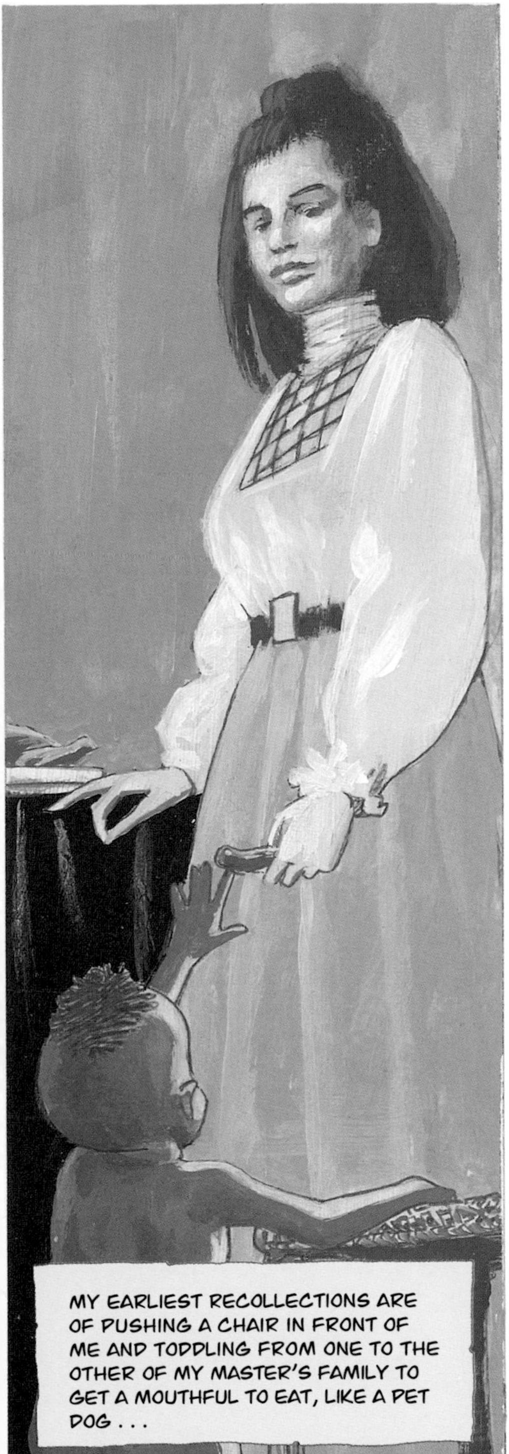
MY EARLIEST RECOLLECTIONS ARE OF PUSHING A CHAIR IN FRONT OF ME AND TODDLING FROM ONE TO THE OTHER OF MY MASTER'S FAMILY TO GET A MOUTHFUL TO EAT, LIKE A PET DOG . . .

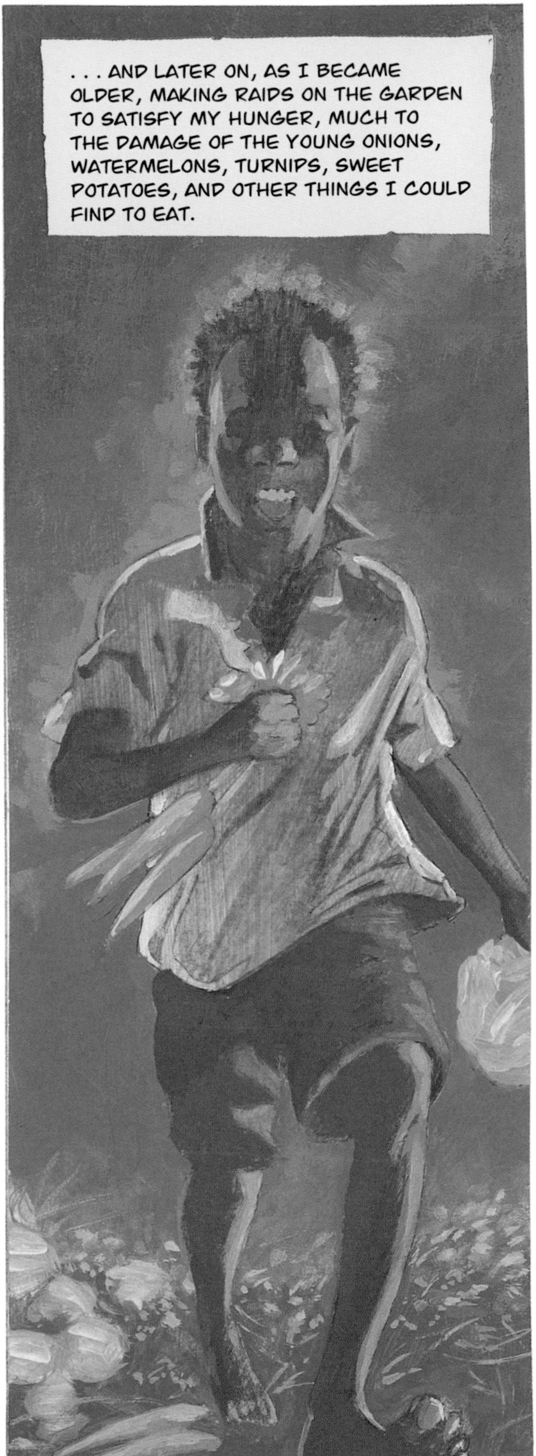
. . . AND LATER ON, AS I BECAME OLDER, MAKING RAIDS ON THE GARDEN TO SATISFY MY HUNGER, MUCH TO THE DAMAGE OF THE YOUNG ONIONS, WATERMELONS, TURNIPS, SWEET POTATOES, AND OTHER THINGS I COULD FIND TO EAT.

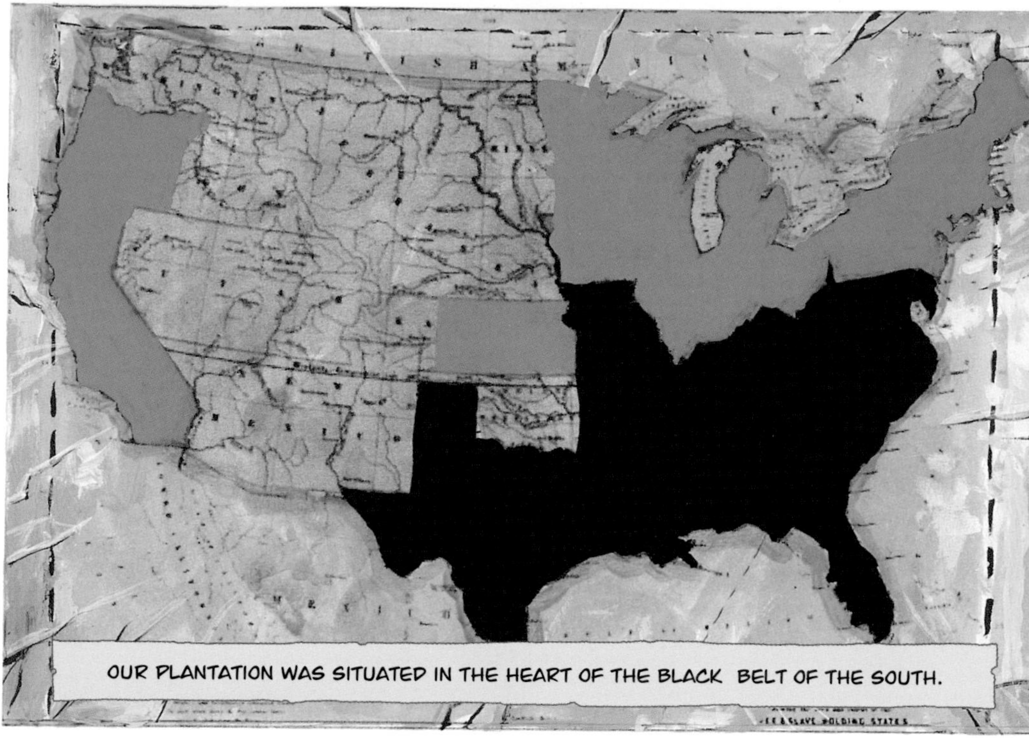
OUR PLANTATION WAS SITUATED IN THE HEART OF THE BLACK BELT OF THE SOUTH.

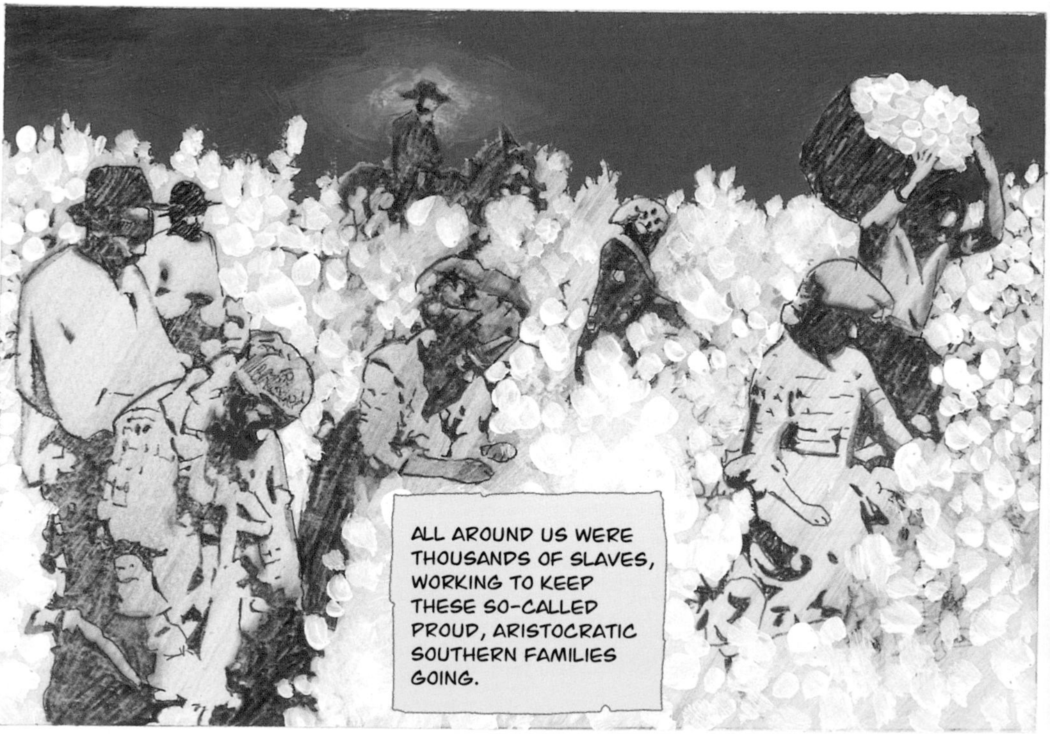
ALL AROUND US WERE THOUSANDS OF SLAVES, WORKING TO KEEP THESE SO-CALLED PROUD, ARISTOCRATIC SOUTHERN FAMILIES GOING.

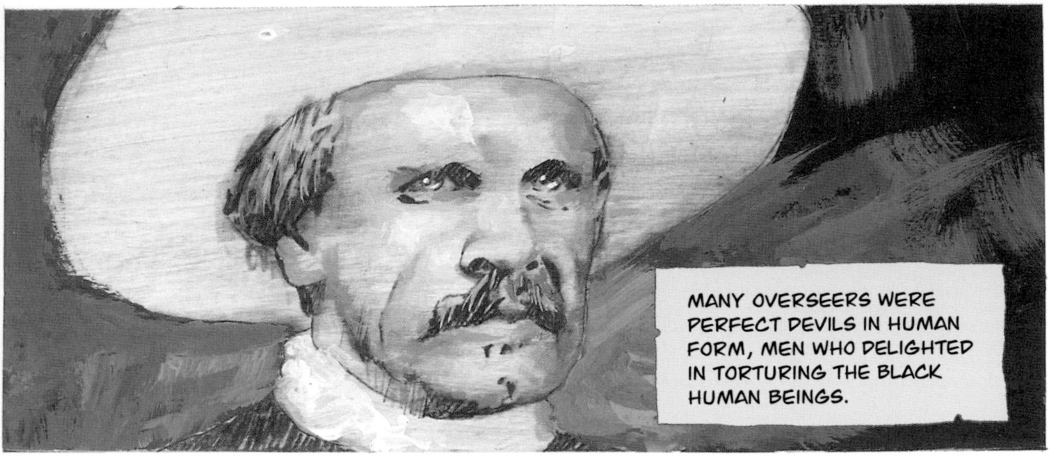
MANY OVERSEERS WERE PERFECT DEVILS IN HUMAN FORM, MEN WHO DELIGHTED IN TORTURING THE BLACK HUMAN BEINGS.

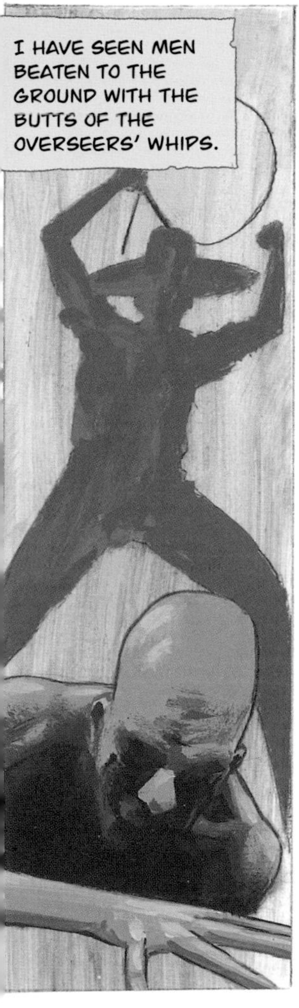
I HAVE SEEN MEN BEATEN TO THE GROUND WITH THE BUTTS OF THE OVERSEERS' WHIPS.

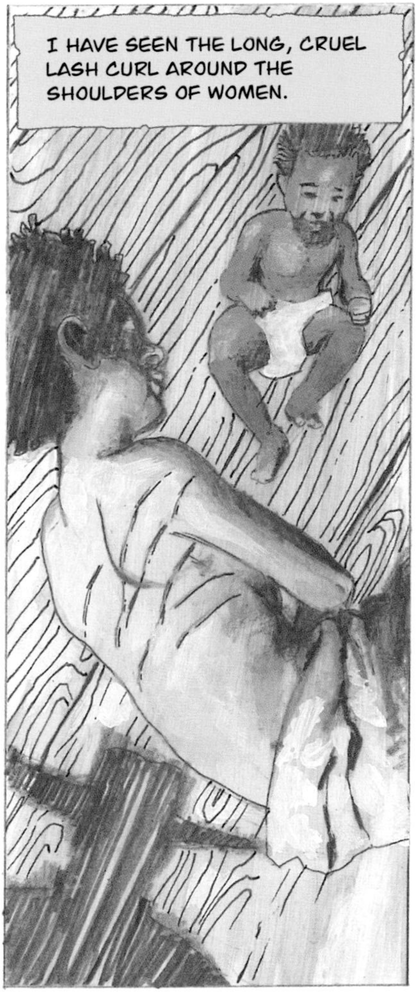
I HAVE SEEN THE LONG, CRUEL LASH CURL AROUND THE SHOULDERS OF WOMEN.

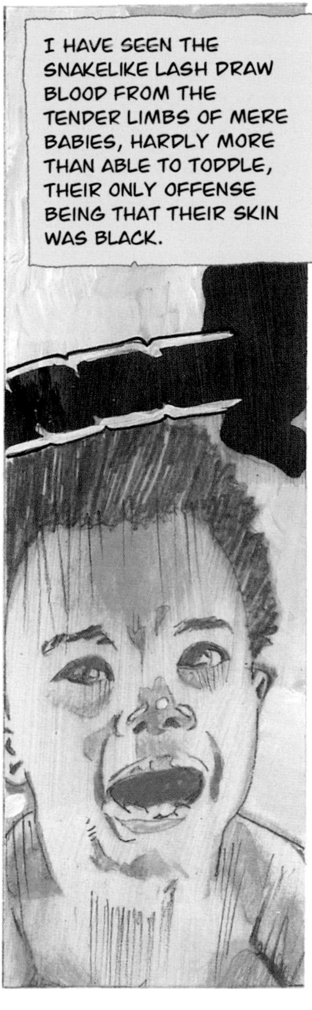
I HAVE SEEN THE SNAKELIKE LASH DRAW BLOOD FROM THE TENDER LIMBS OF MERE BABIES, HARDLY MORE THAN ABLE TO TODDLE, THEIR ONLY OFFENSE BEING THAT THEIR SKIN WAS BLACK.

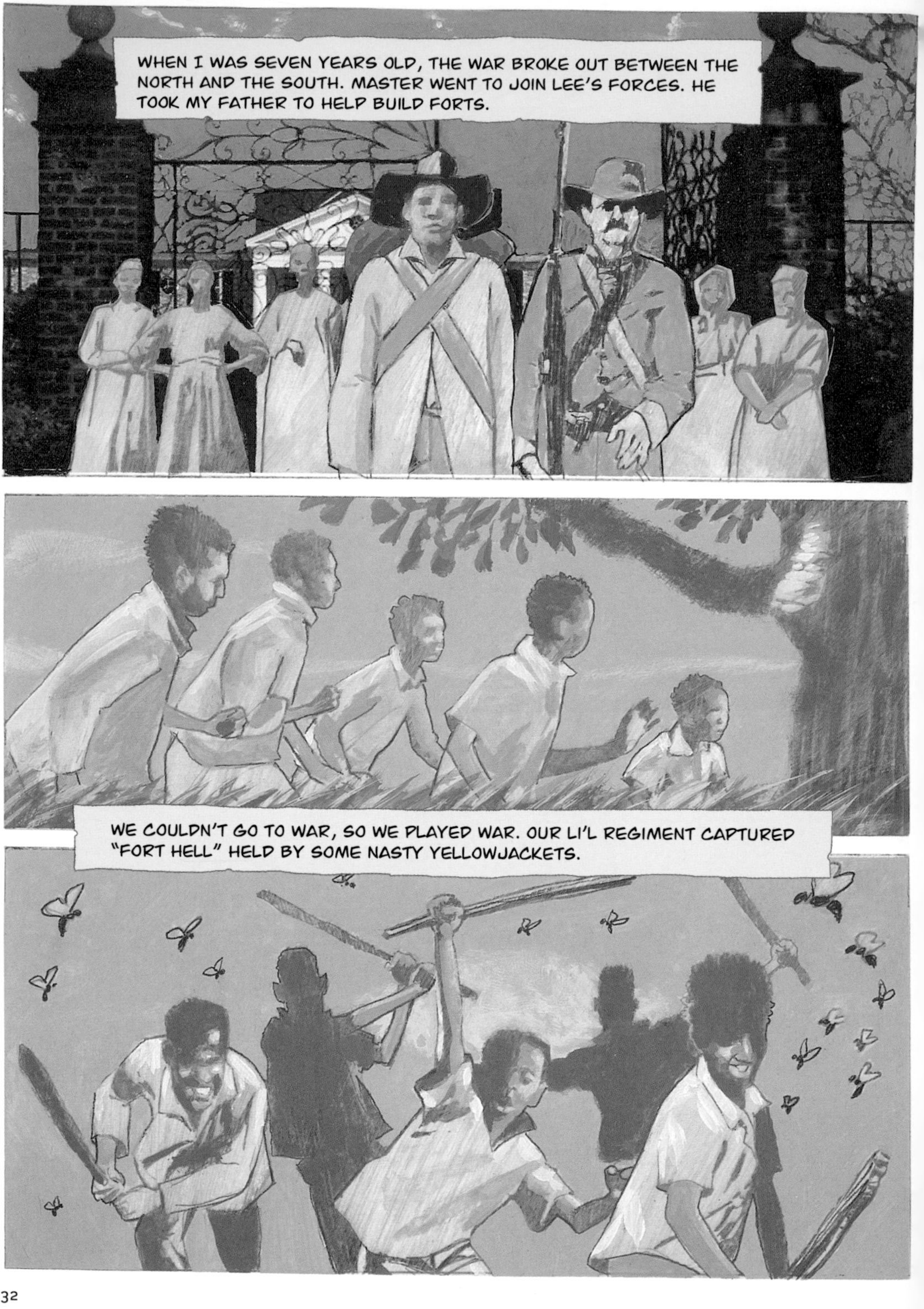
WHEN I WAS SEVEN YEARS OLD, THE WAR BROKE OUT BETWEEN THE NORTH AND THE SOUTH. MASTER WENT TO JOIN LEE'S FORCES. HE TOOK MY FATHER TO HELP BUILD FORTS.
WE COULDN'T GO TO WAR, SO WE PLAYED WAR. OUR LI'L REGIMENT CAPTURED "FORT HELL" HELD BY SOME NASTY YELLOWJACKETS.

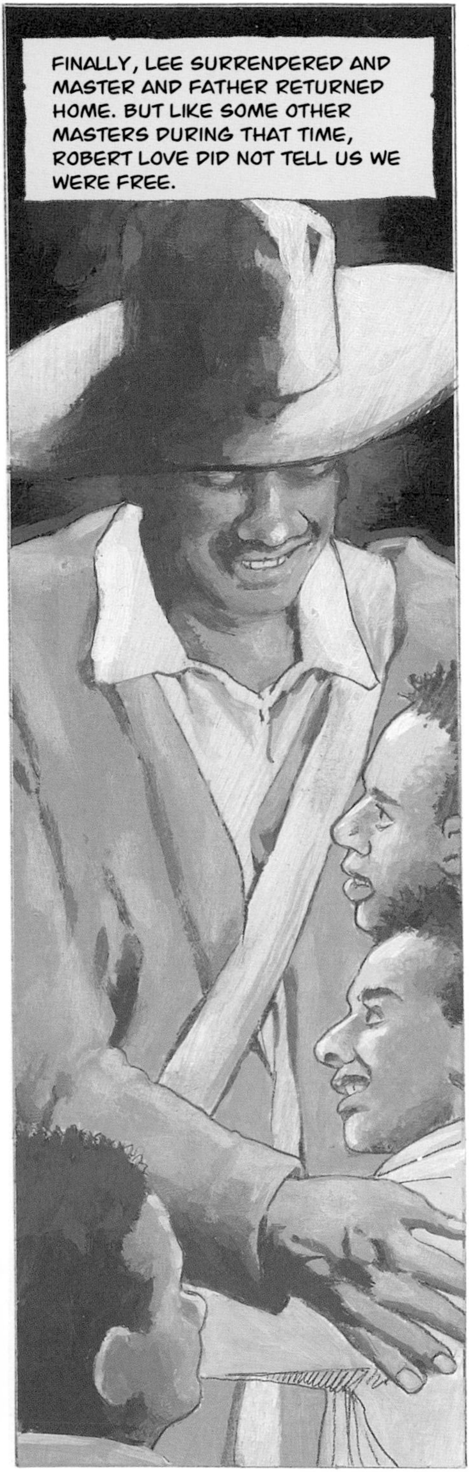
FINALLY, LEE SURRENDERED AND MASTER AND FATHER RETURNED HOME. BUT LIKE SOME OTHER MASTERS DURING THAT TIME, ROBERT LOVE DID NOT TELL US WE WERE FREE.

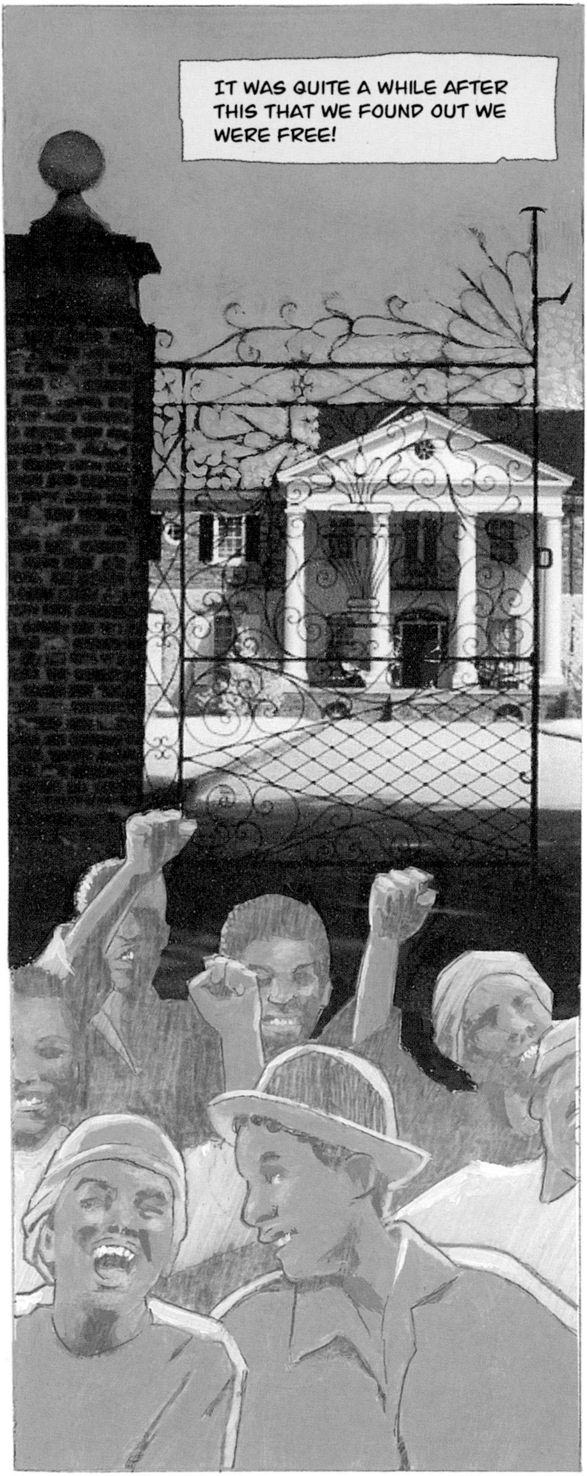
IT WAS QUITE A WHILE AFTER THIS THAT WE FOUND OUT WE WERE FREE!

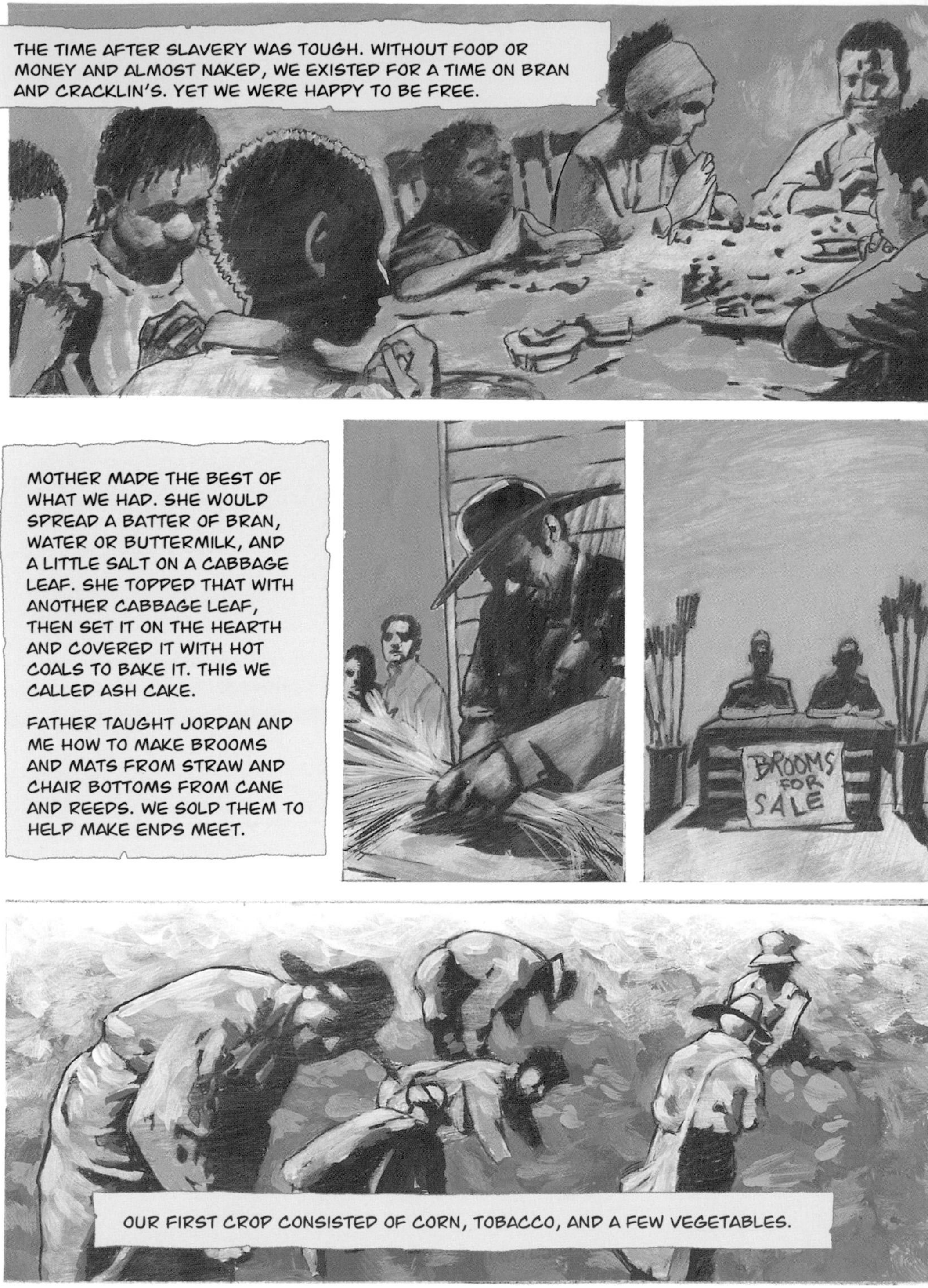
THE TIME AFTER SLAVERY WAS TOUGH. WITHOUT FOOD OR MONEY AND ALMOST NAKED, WE EXISTED FOR A TIME ON BRAN AND CRACKLIN'S. YET WE WERE HAPPY TO BE FREE.
MOTHER MADE THE BEST OF WHAT WE HAD. SHE WOULD SPREAD A BATTER OF BRAN, WATER OR BUTTERMILK, AND A LITTLE SALT ON A CABBAGE LEAF. SHE TOPPED THAT WITH ANOTHER CABBAGE LEAF, THEN SET IT ON THE HEARTH AND COVERED IT WITH HOT COALS TO BAKE IT. THIS WE CALLED ASH CAKE.
FATHER TAUGHT JORDAN AND ME HOW TO MAKE BROOMS AND MATS FROM STRAW AND CHAIR BOTTOMS FROM CANE AND REEDS. WE SOLD THEM TO HELP MAKE ENDS MEET.
BROOMS FOR SALE
OUR FIRST CROP CONSISTED OF CORN, TOBACCO, AND A FEW VEGETABLES.

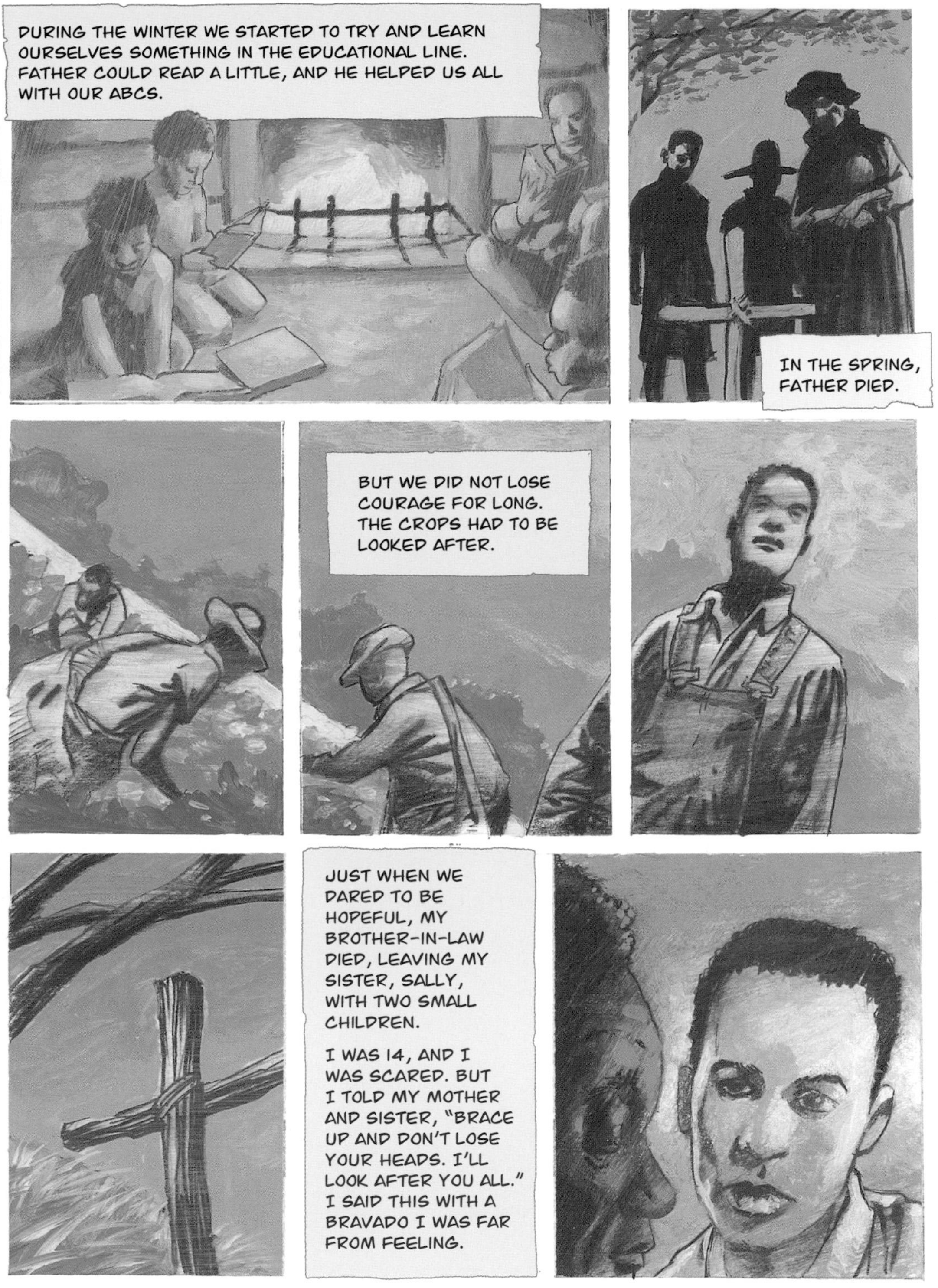
DURING THE WINTER WE STARTED TO TRY AND LEARN OURSELVES SOMETHING IN THE EDUCATIONAL LINE. FATHER COULD READ A LITTLE, AND HE HELPED US ALL WITH OUR ABCS.
IN THE SPRING, FATHER DIED.
BUT WE DID NOT LOSE COURAGE FOR LONG. THE CROPS HAD TO BE LOOKED AFTER.
JUST WHEN WE DARED TO BE HOPEFUL, MY BROTHER-IN-LAW DIED, LEAVING MY SISTER, SALLY, WITH TWO SMALL CHILDREN.
I WAS 14, AND I WAS SCARED. BUT I TOLD MY MOTHER AND SISTER, "BRACE UP AND DON'T LOSE YOUR HEADS. I'LL LOOK AFTER YOU ALL." I SAID THIS WITH A BRAVADO I WAS FAR FROM FEELING.

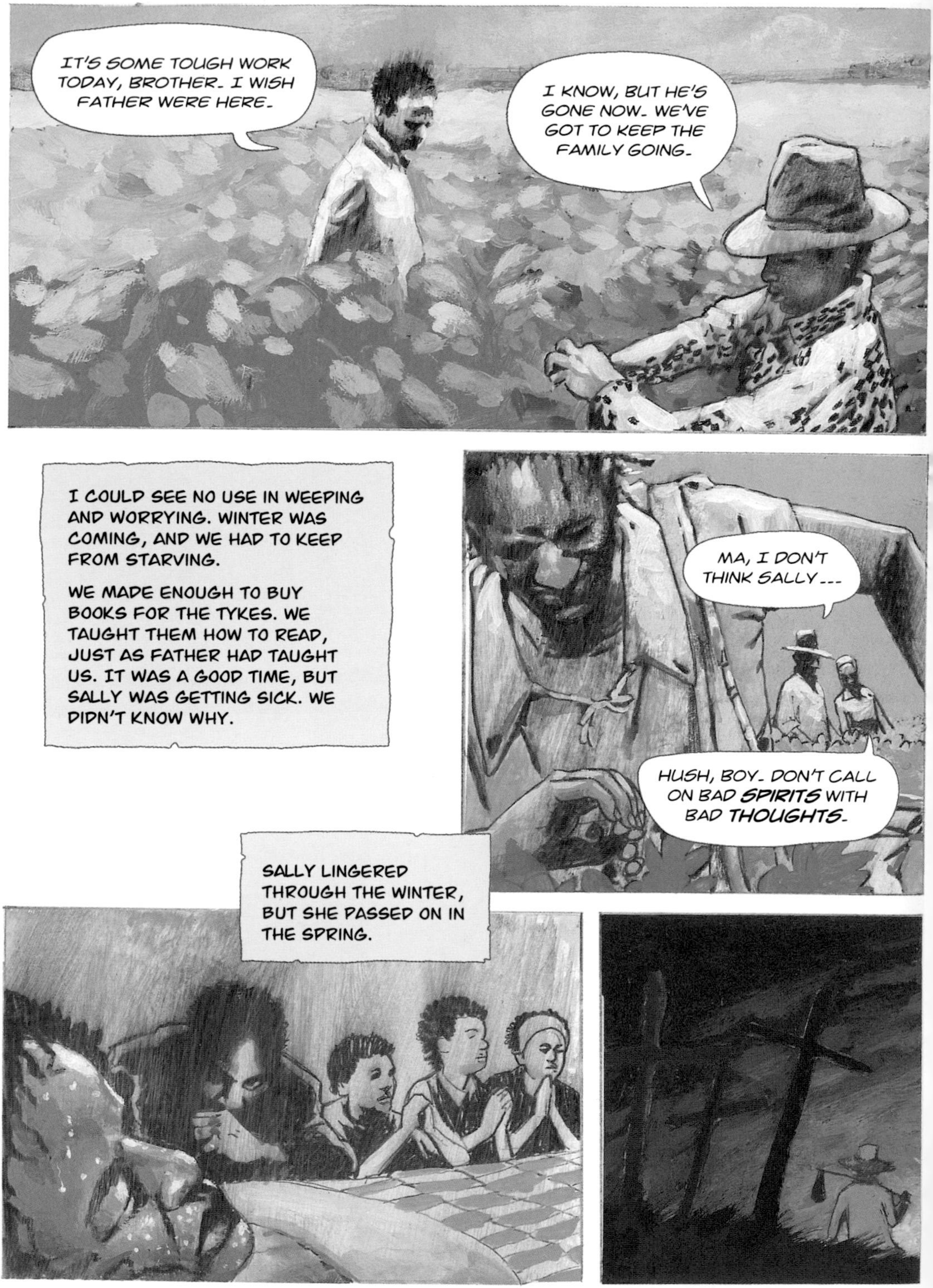
IT'S SOME TOUGH WORK TODAY, BROTHER. I WISH FATHER WERE HERE.
I KNOW, BUT HE'S GONE NOW. WE'VE GOT TO KEEP THE FAMILY GOING.
I COULD SEE NO USE IN WEEPING AND WORRYING. WINTER WAS COMING, AND WE HAD TO KEEP FROM STARVING.
WE MADE ENOUGH TO BUY BOOKS FOR THE TYKES. WE TAUGHT THEM HOW TO READ, JUST AS FATHER HAD TAUGHT US. IT WAS A GOOD TIME, BUT SALLY WAS GETTING SICK. WE DIDN'T KNOW WHY.
MA, I DON'T THINK SALLY...
HUSH, BOY. DON'T CALL ON BAD SPIRITS WITH BAD THOUGHTS.
SALLY LINGERED THROUGH THE WINTER, BUT SHE PASSED ON IN THE SPRING.

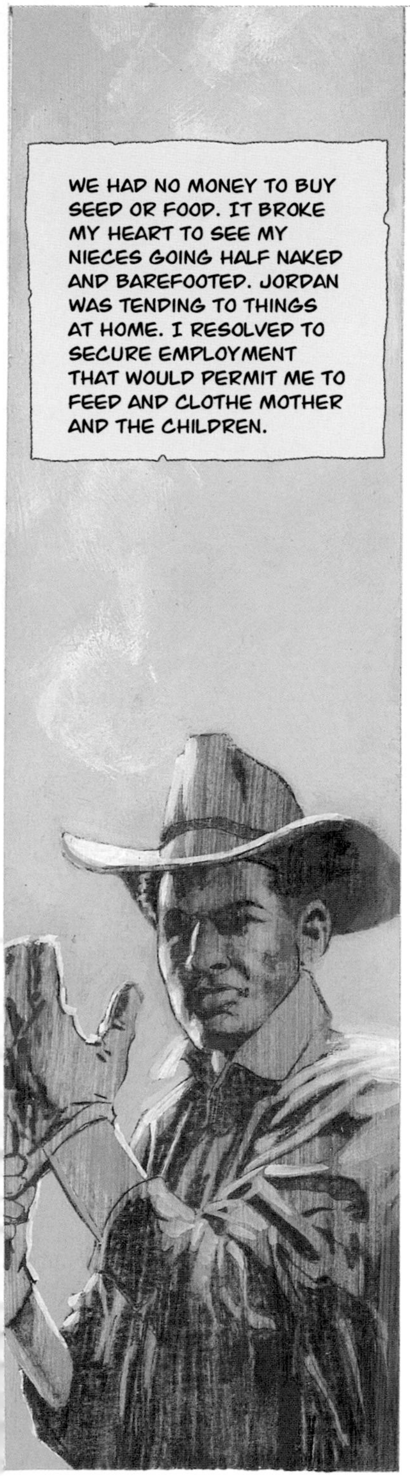
WE HAD NO MONEY TO BUY SEED OR FOOD. IT BROKE MY HEART TO SEE MY NIECES GOING HALF NAKED AND BAREFOOTED. JORDAN WAS TENDING TO THINGS AT HOME. I RESOLVED TO SECURE EMPLOYMENT THAT WOULD PERMIT ME TO FEED AND CLOTHE MOTHER AND THE CHILDREN.

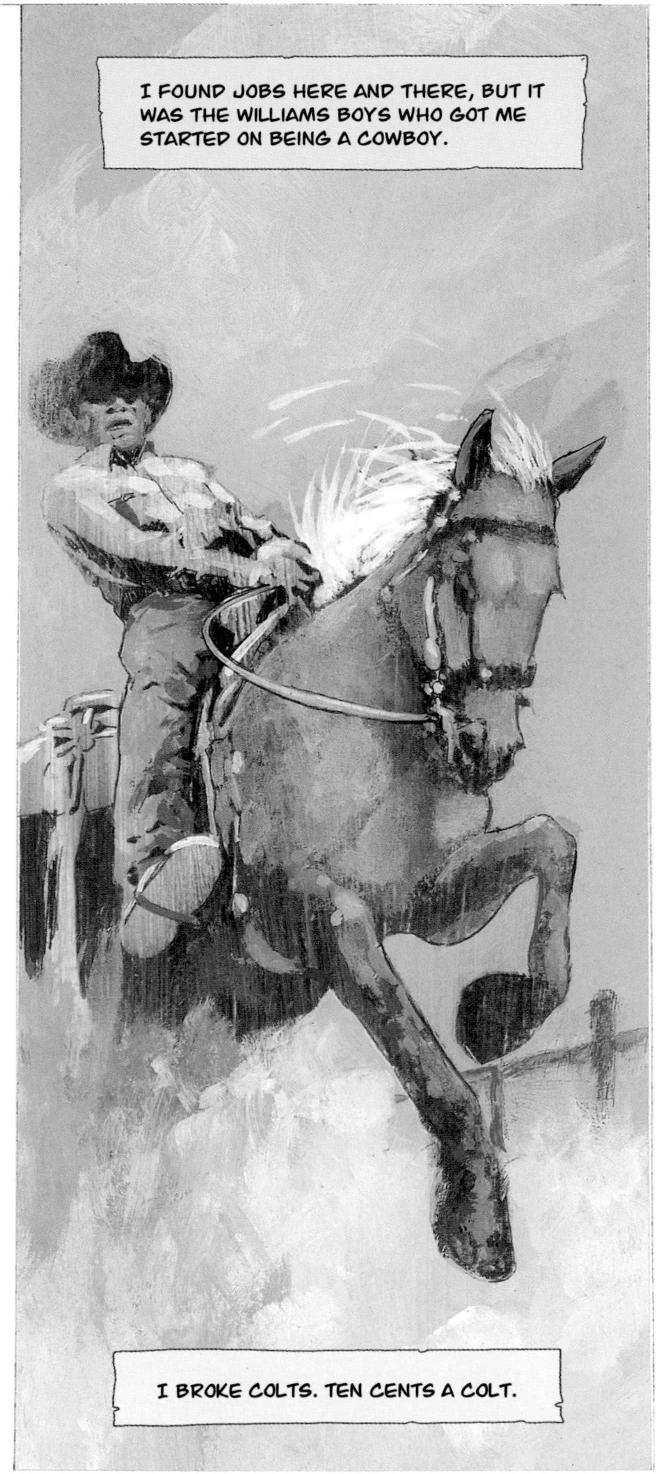
I FOUND JOBS HERE AND THERE, BUT IT WAS THE WILLIAMS BOYS WHO GOT ME STARTED ON BEING A COWBOY.
I BROKE COLTS. TEN CENTS A COLT.

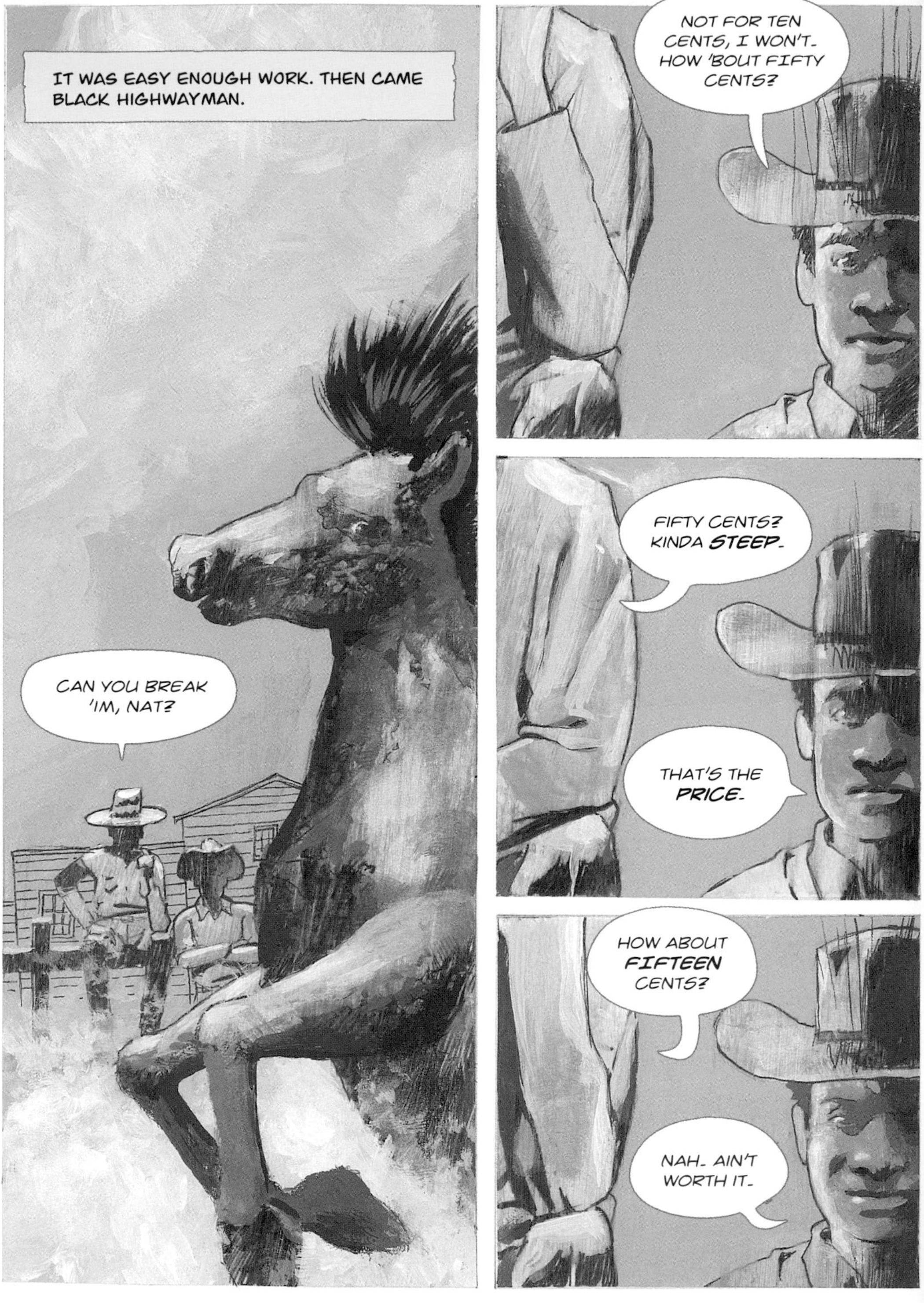
IT WAS EASY ENOUGH WORK. THEN CAME BLACK HIGHWAYMAN.
CAN YOU BREAK 'IM, NAT?
NOT FOR TEN CENTS, I WON'T. HOW 'BOUT FIFTY CENTS?
FIFTY CENTS? KINDA STEEP.
THAT'S THE PRICE.
HOW ABOUT FIFTEEN CENTS?
NAH. AIN'T WORTH IT.

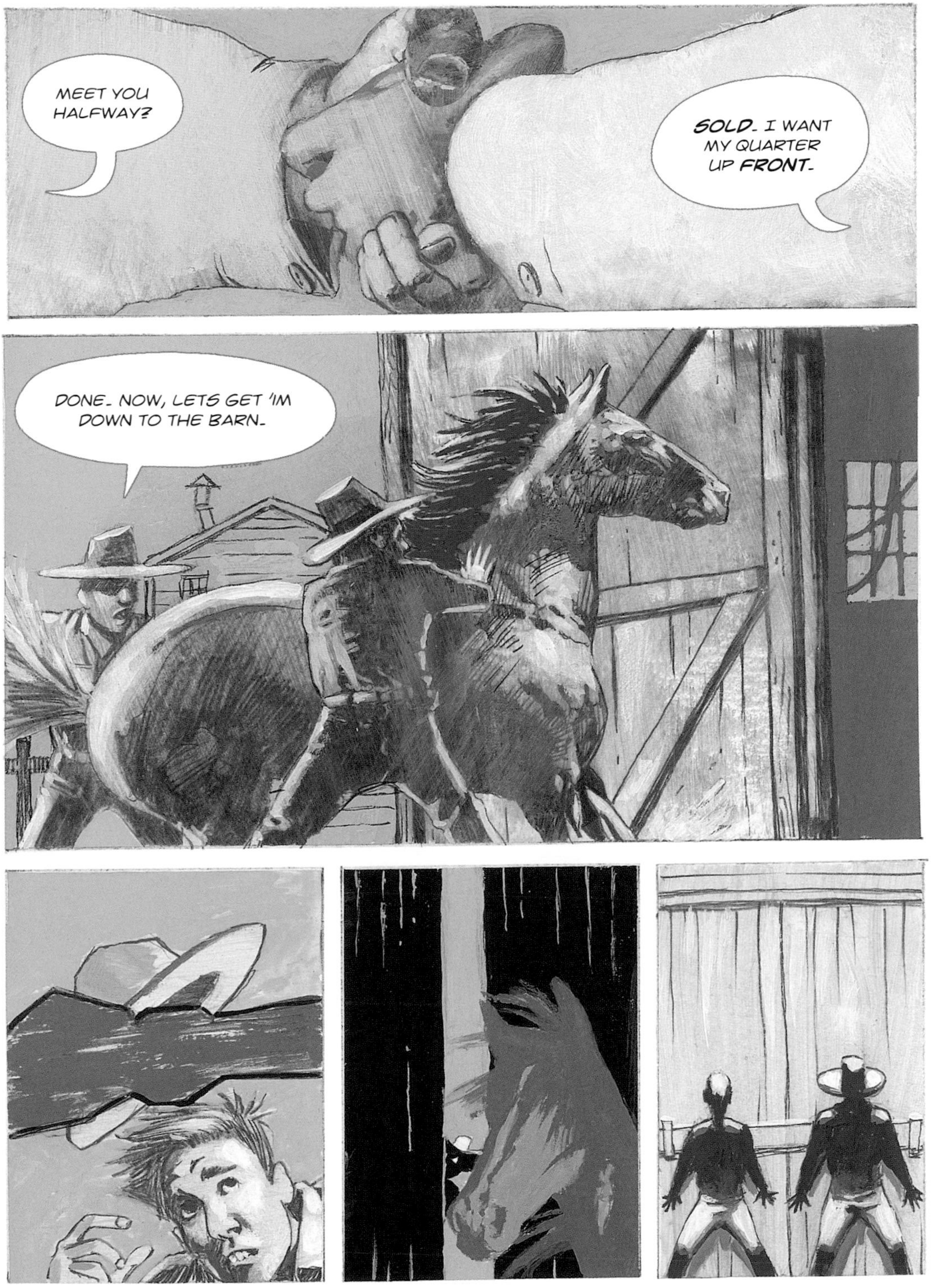
MEET YOU HALFWAY?
SOLD. I WANT MY QUARTER UP FRONT.
DONE. NOW, LETS GET 'IM DOWN TO THE BARN.

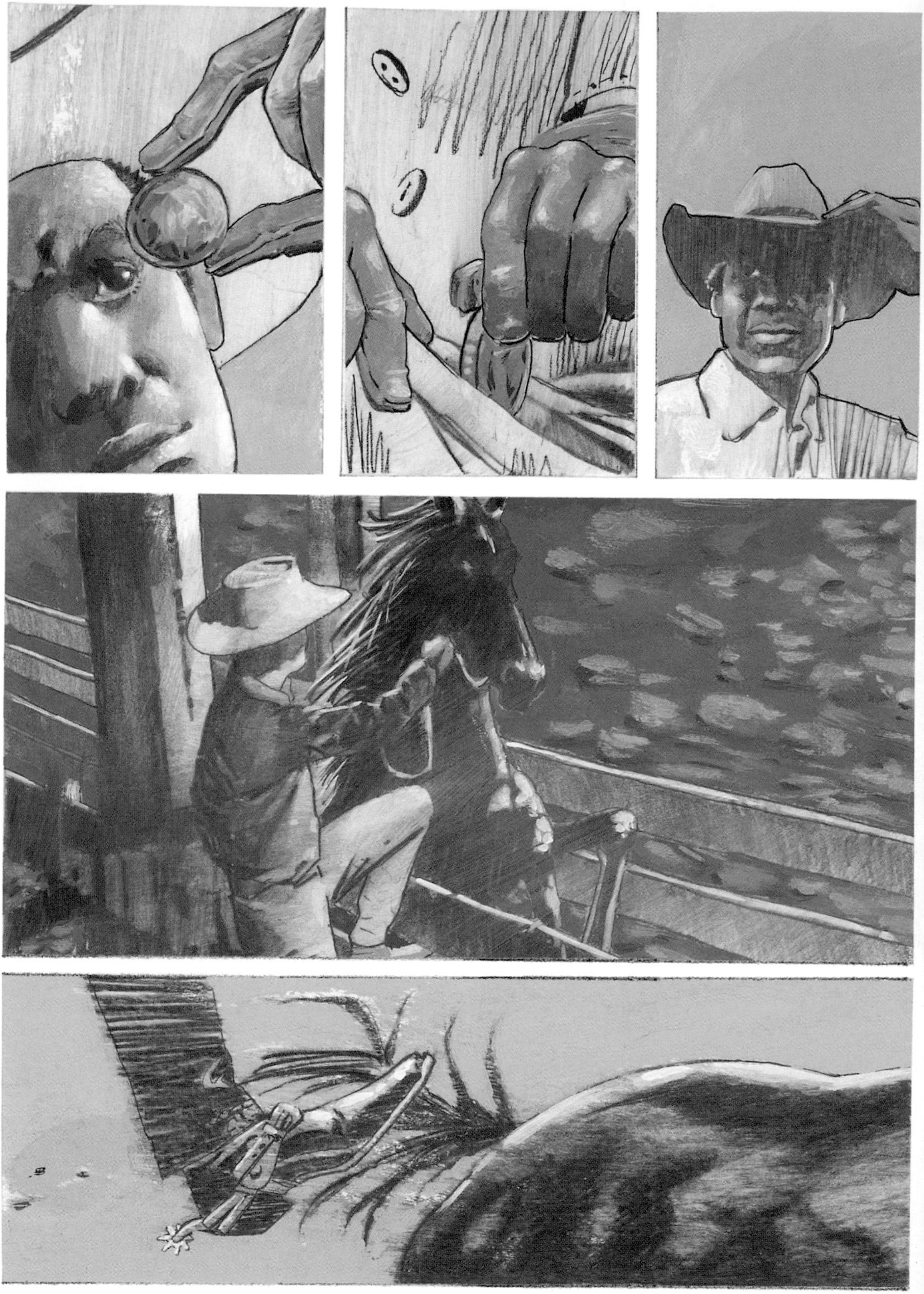

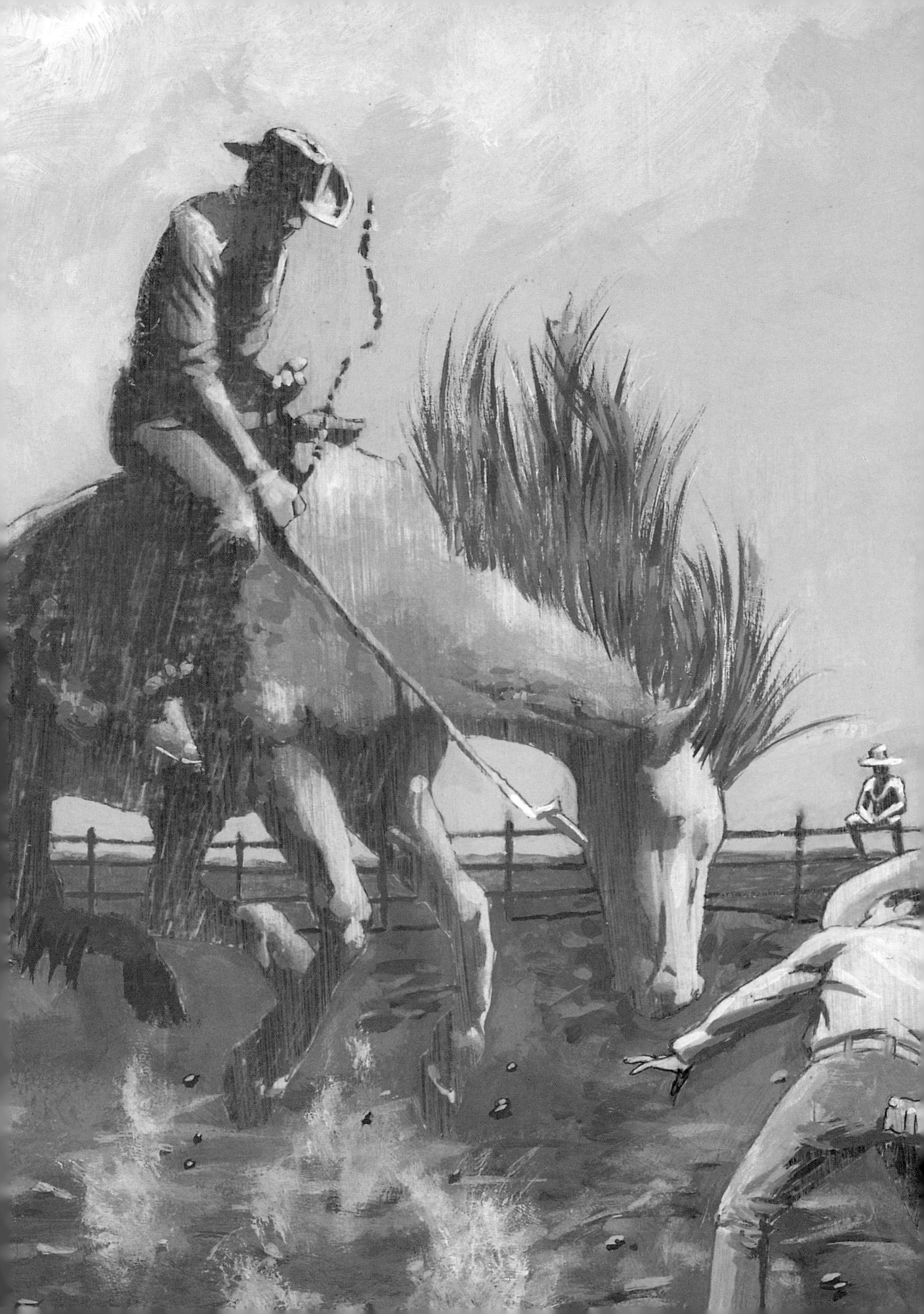

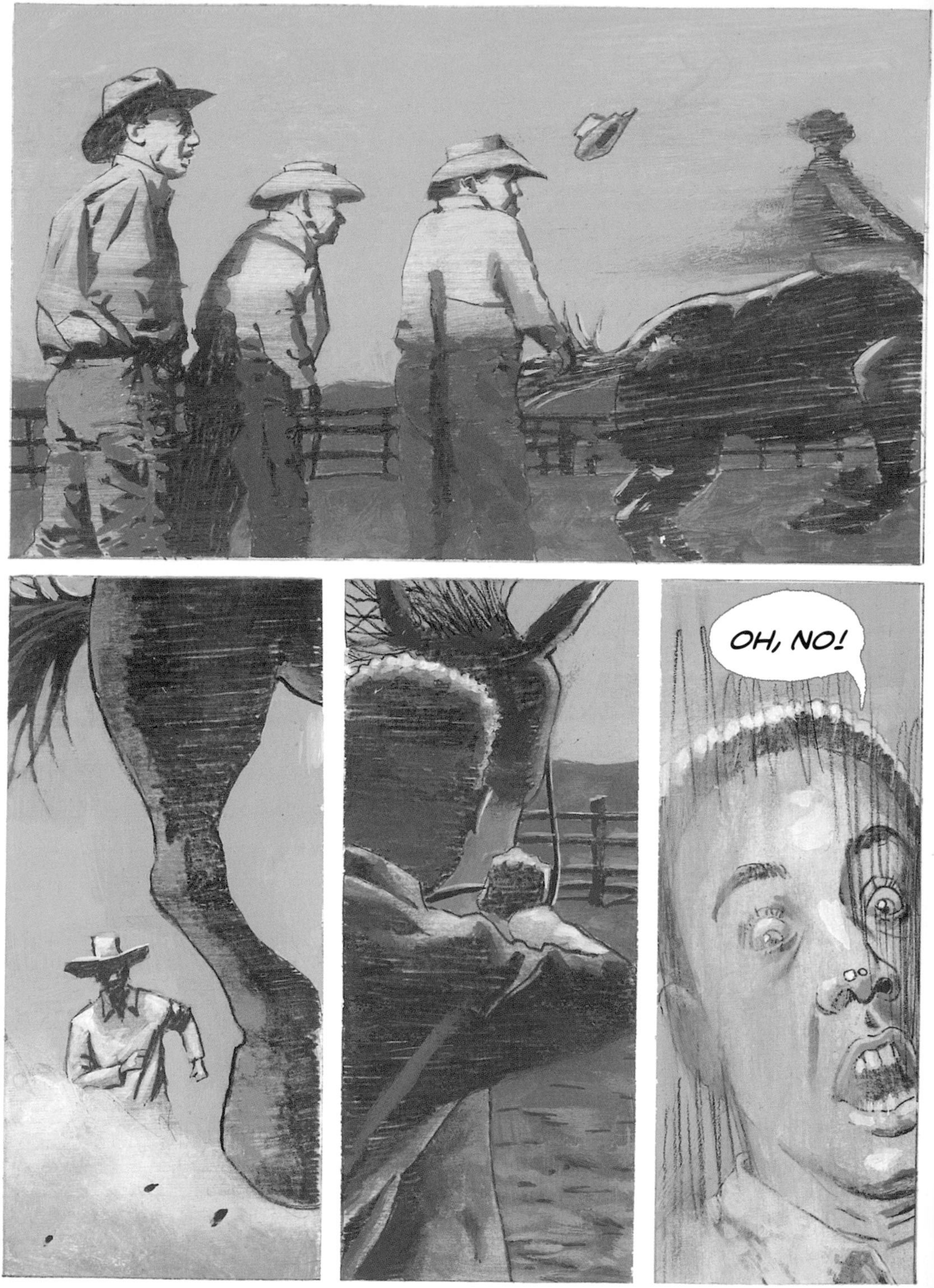
OH, NO!

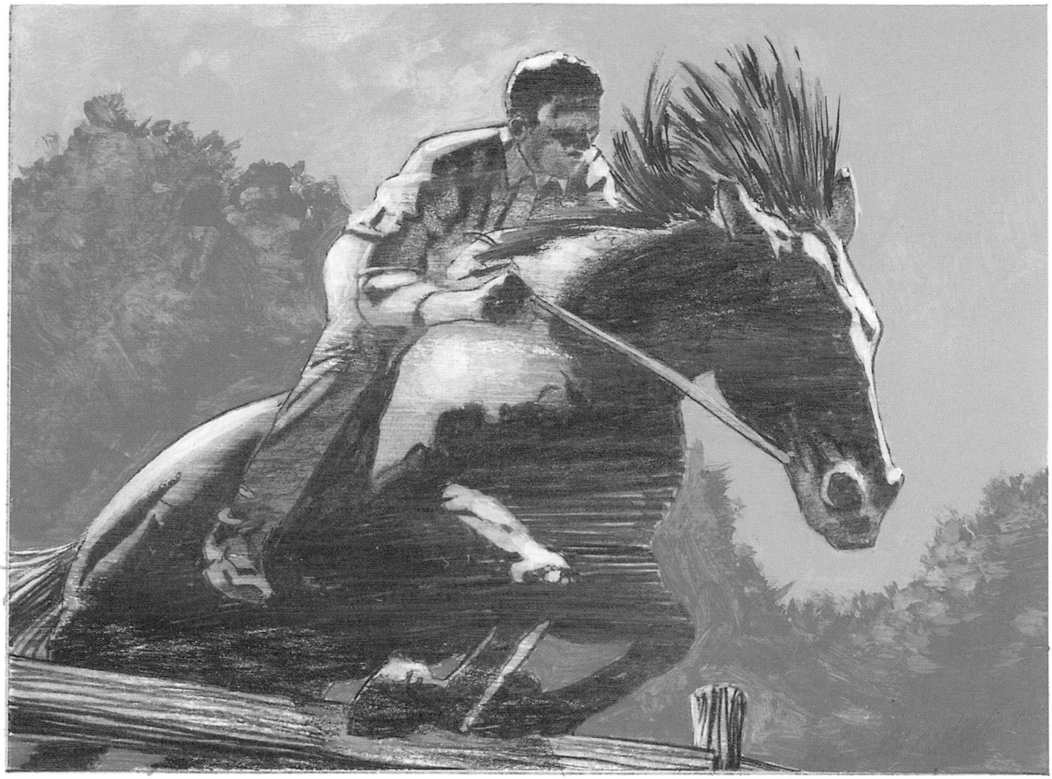

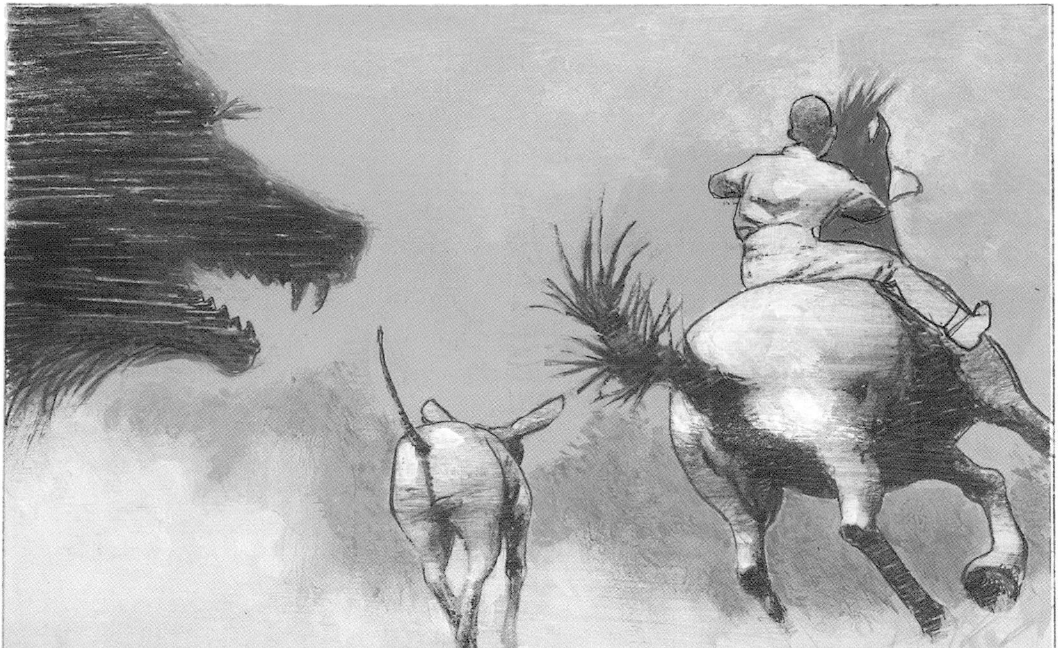

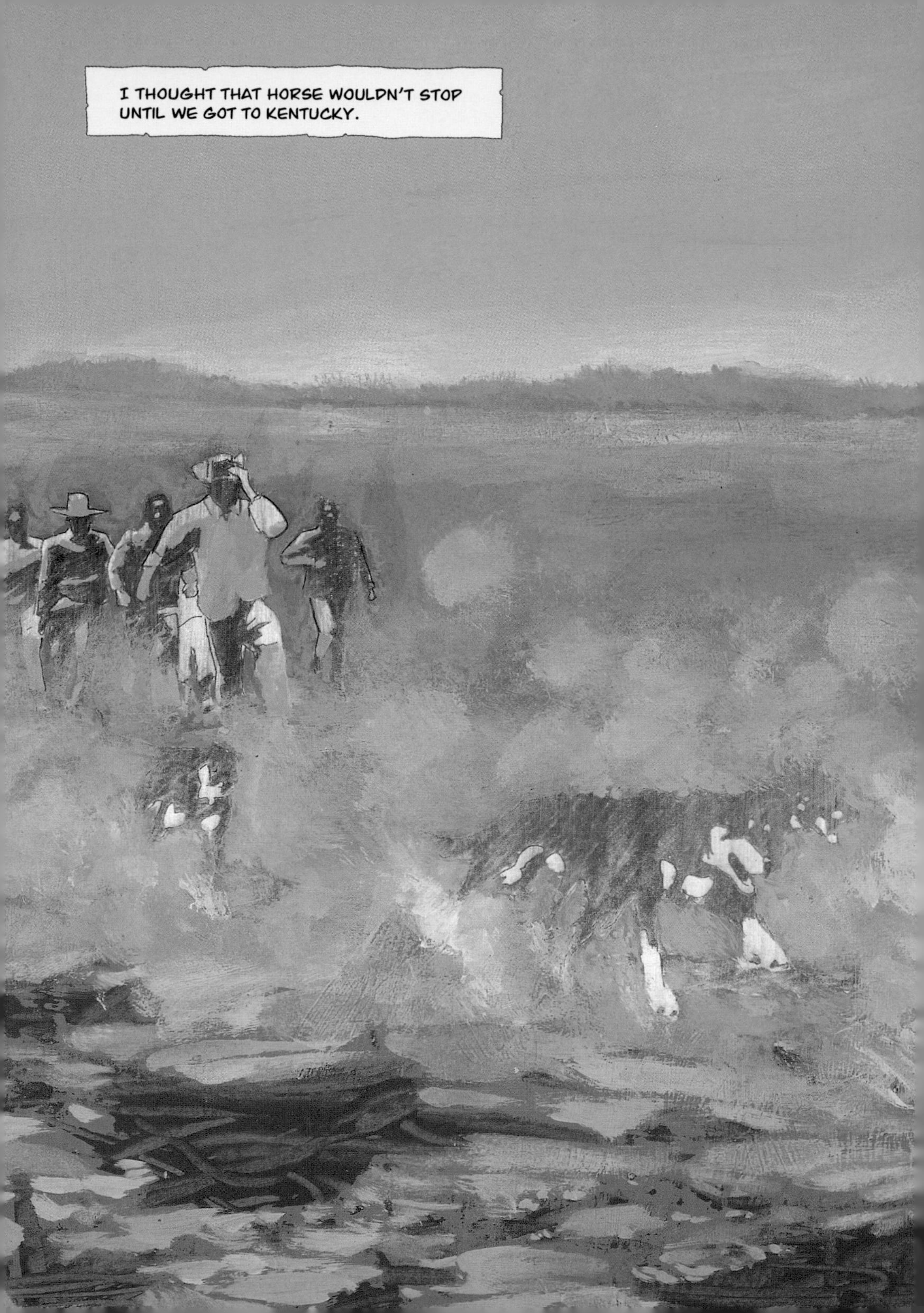
I THOUGHT THAT HORSE WOULDN'T STOP UNTIL WE GOT TO KENTUCKY.

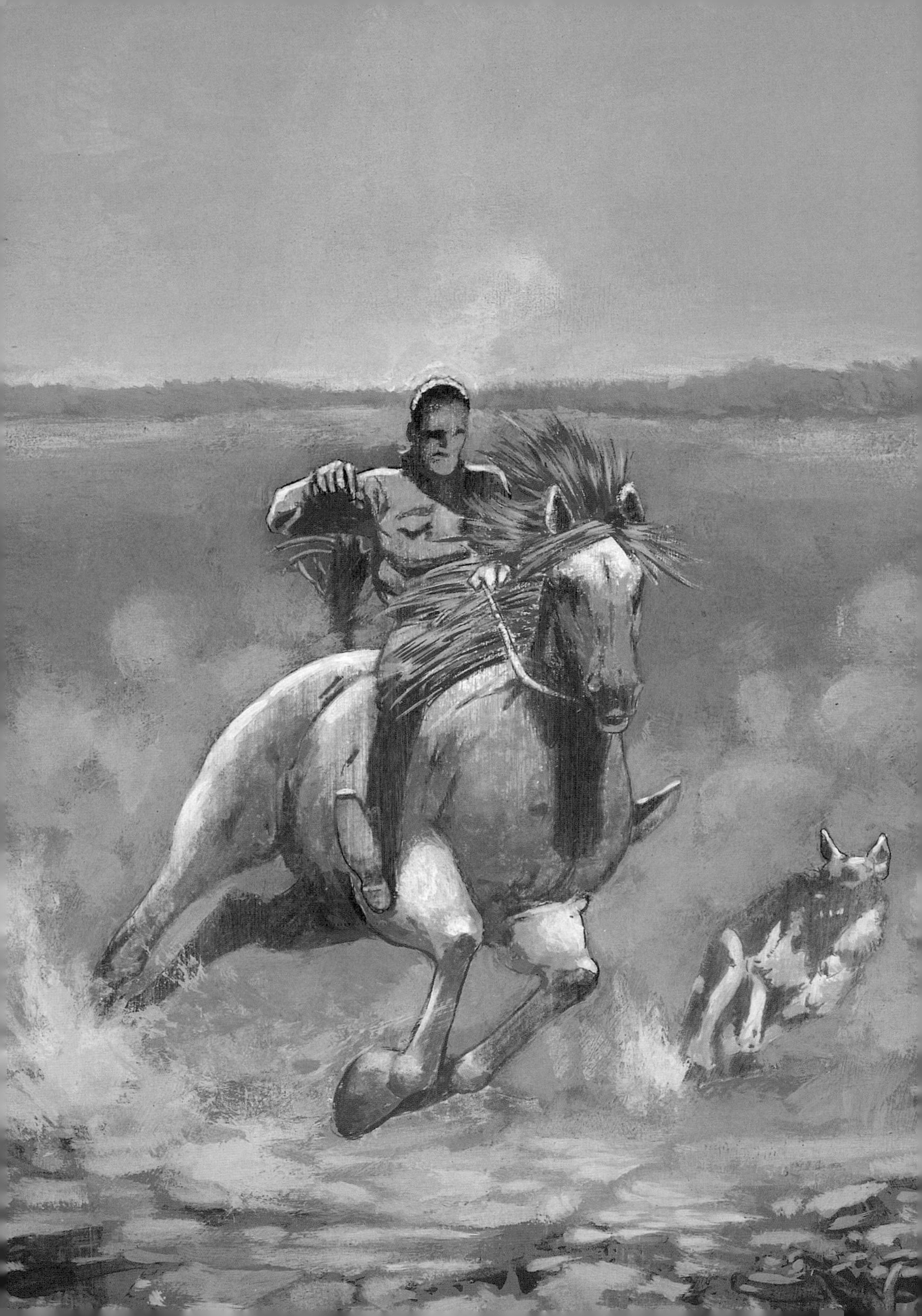

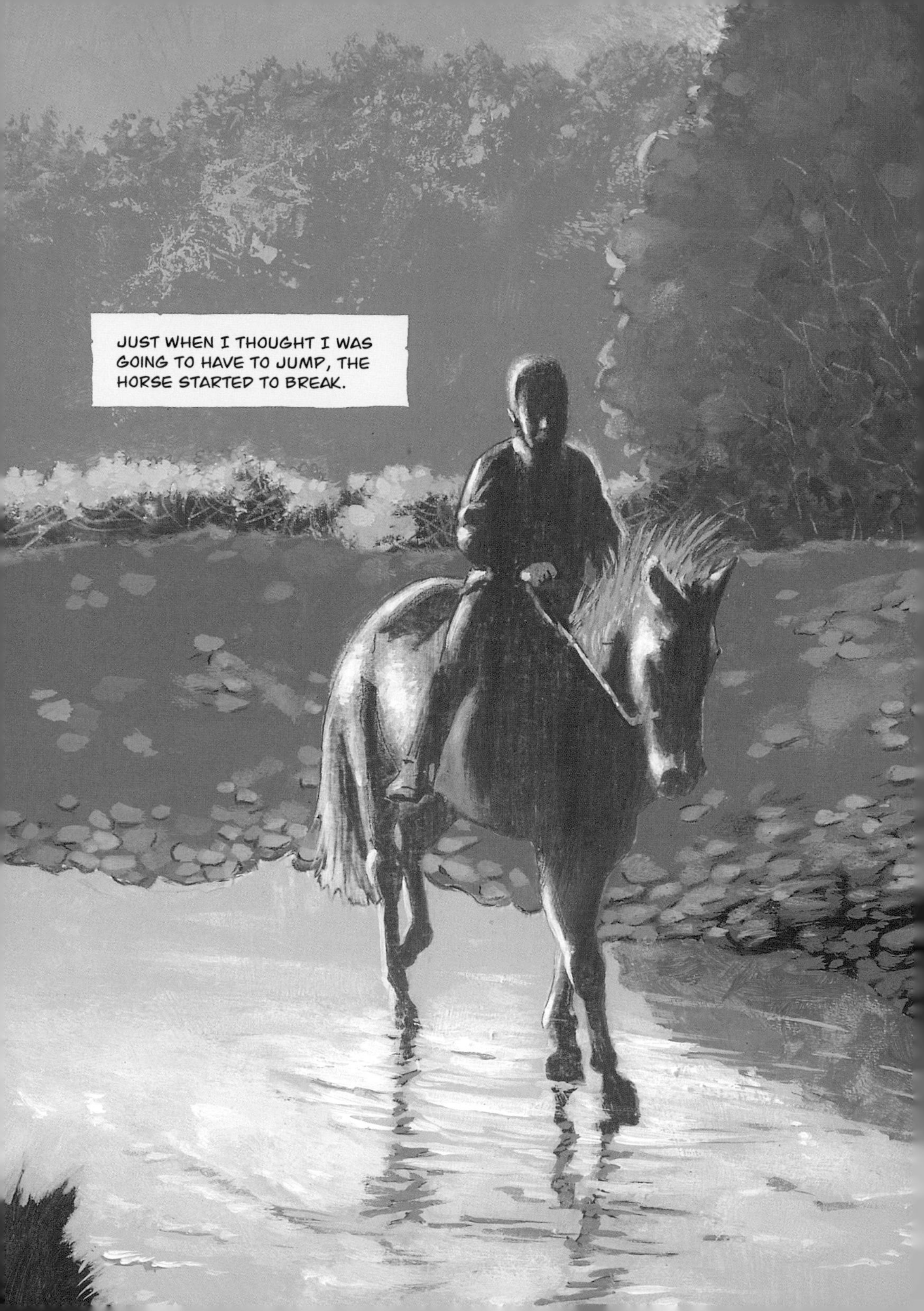
JUST WHEN I THOUGHT I WAS GOING TO HAVE TO JUMP, THE HORSE STARTED TO BREAK.

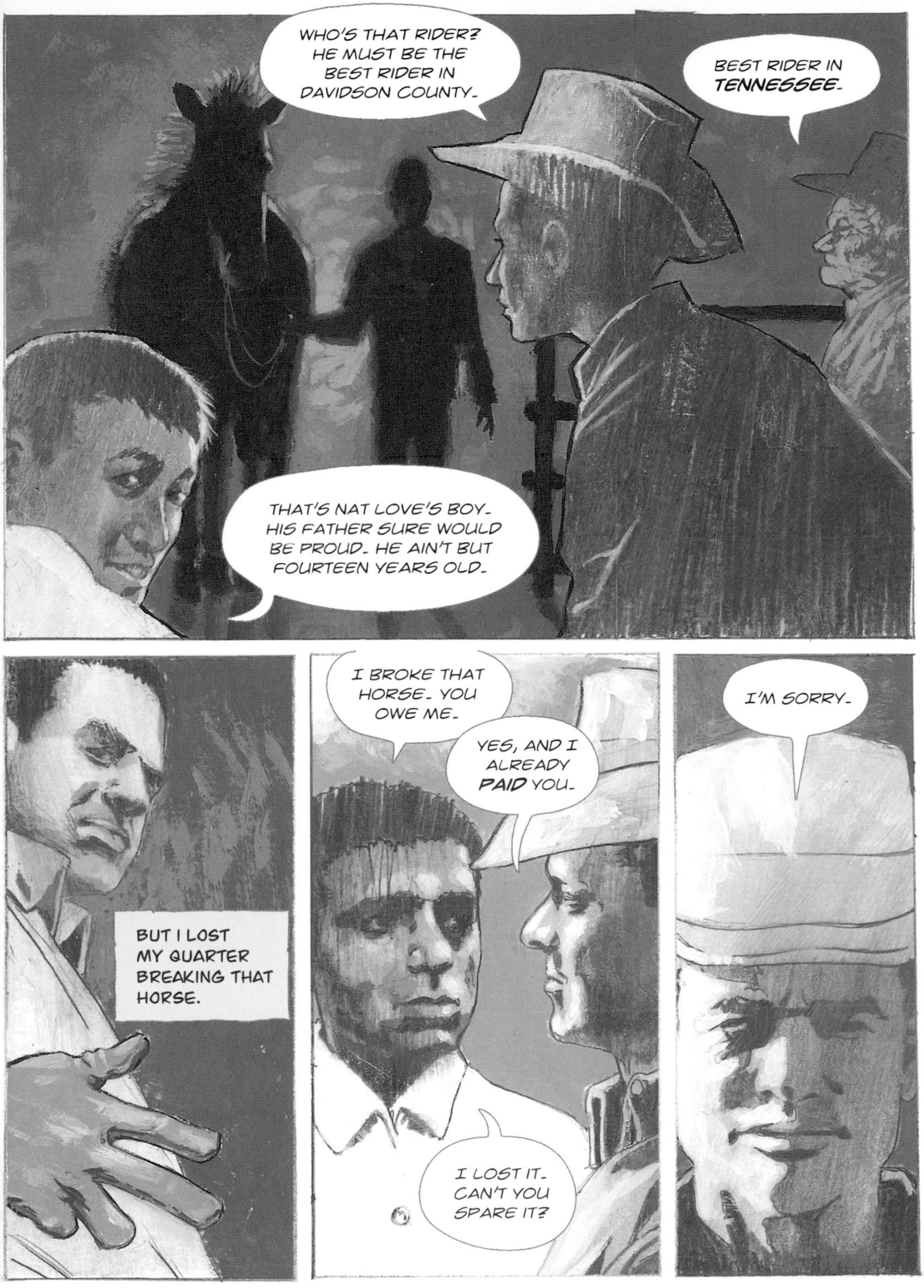
WHO'S THAT RIDER? HE MUST BE THE BEST RIDER IN DAVIDSON COUNTY.
BEST RIDER IN **TENNESSEE**.
THAT'S NAT LOVE'S BOY. HIS FATHER SURE WOULD BE PROUD. HE AIN'T BUT FOURTEEN YEARS OLD.
BUT I LOST MY QUARTER BREAKING THAT HORSE.
I BROKE THAT HORSE. YOU OWE ME.
YES, AND I ALREADY **PAID** YOU.
I LOST IT. CAN'T YOU SPARE IT?
I'M SORRY.

I wasn't too mad at Bill Williams. He was raised to be long on business sense and short on compassion.

It was about this time that I started to get my first ideas about moving out on my own. I kept working and kept thinking.

I finally got lucky on a horse raffle. I turned a 50-cent ticket into 100 dollars. The man running the raffle bought the horse back from me, figuring I needed 50 dollars more than I needed a horse. He was right. He tried to raffle it off again, and I won the raffle again, and somebody else bought the horse for 50 dollars. I think the Lord was trying to tell me something.

I got home and told Mother that I wanted to go west and make my way in life. I gave her half my winnings. I took the other half and bought my first set of new clothes. I looked like a man. I felt like a man. Jordan and my uncle were at home to take care of Mother. I said my good-byes and gave out my last embraces. Then I set out west, toward Kansas. I'd heard good things were happening there. That was February 1869.

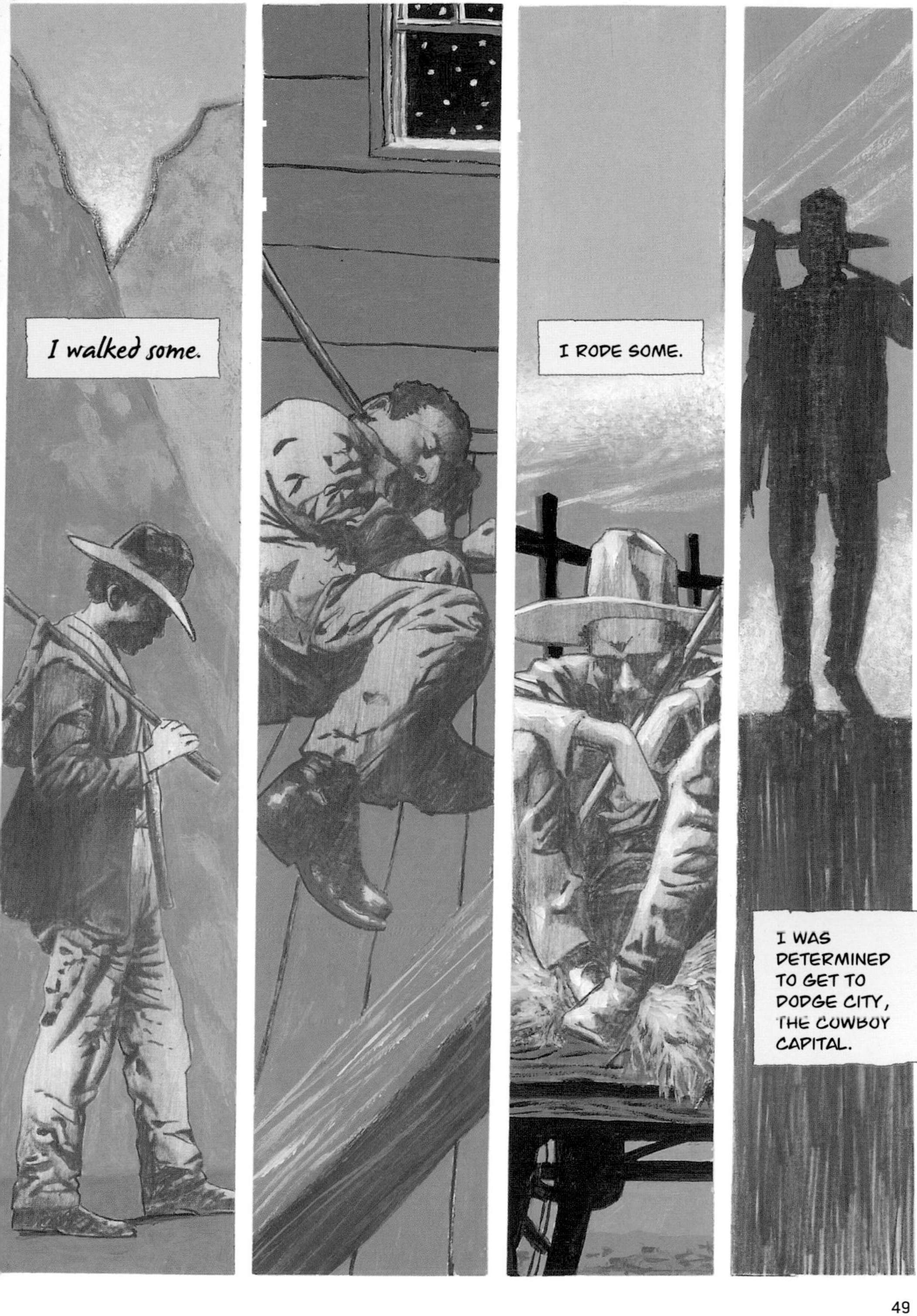
I walked some.
I RODE SOME.
I WAS DETERMINED TO GET TO DODGE CITY, THE COWBOY CAPITAL.

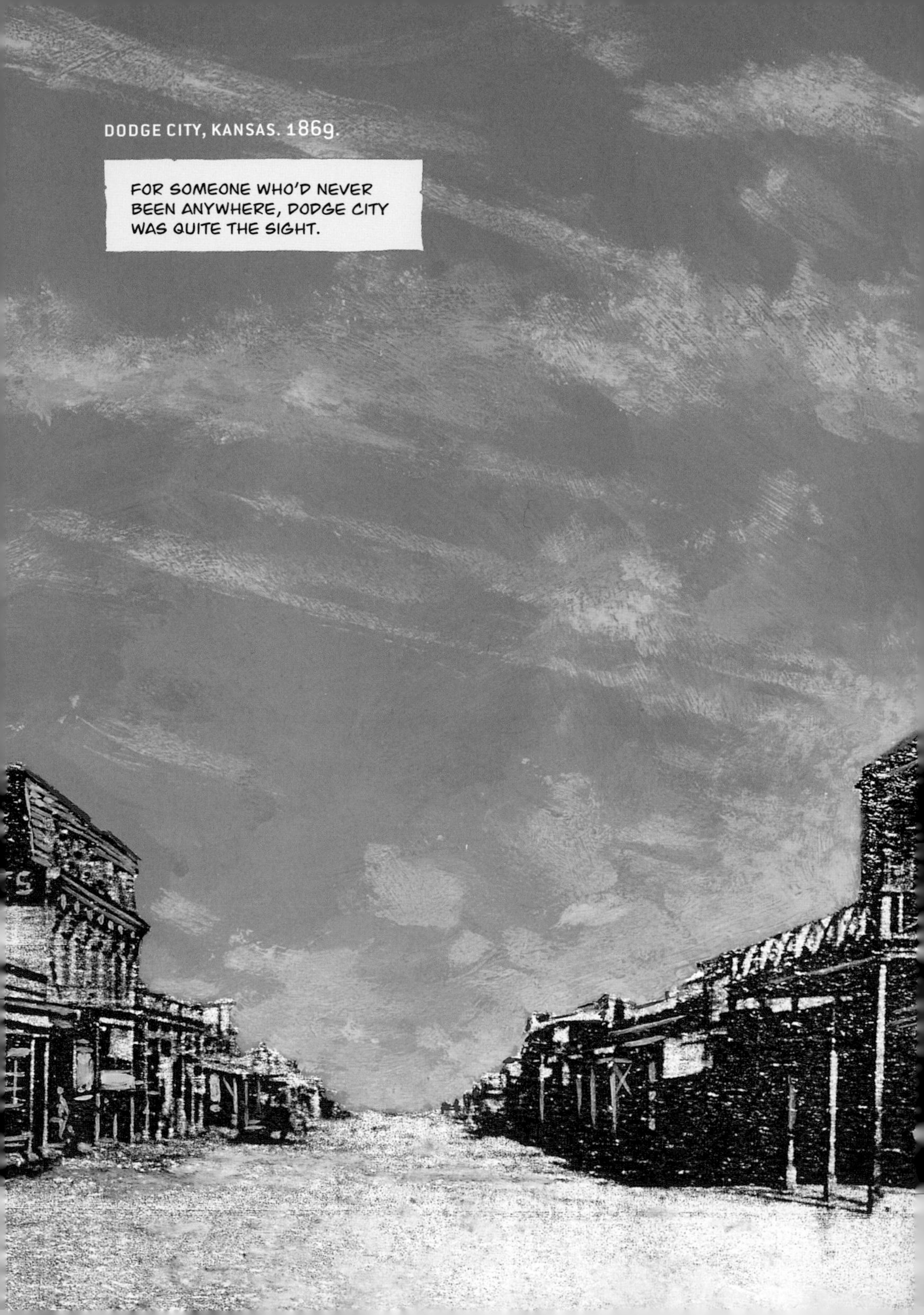
DODGE CITY, KANSAS. 1869.
FOR SOMEONE WHO'D NEVER BEEN ANYWHERE, DODGE CITY WAS QUITE THE SIGHT.

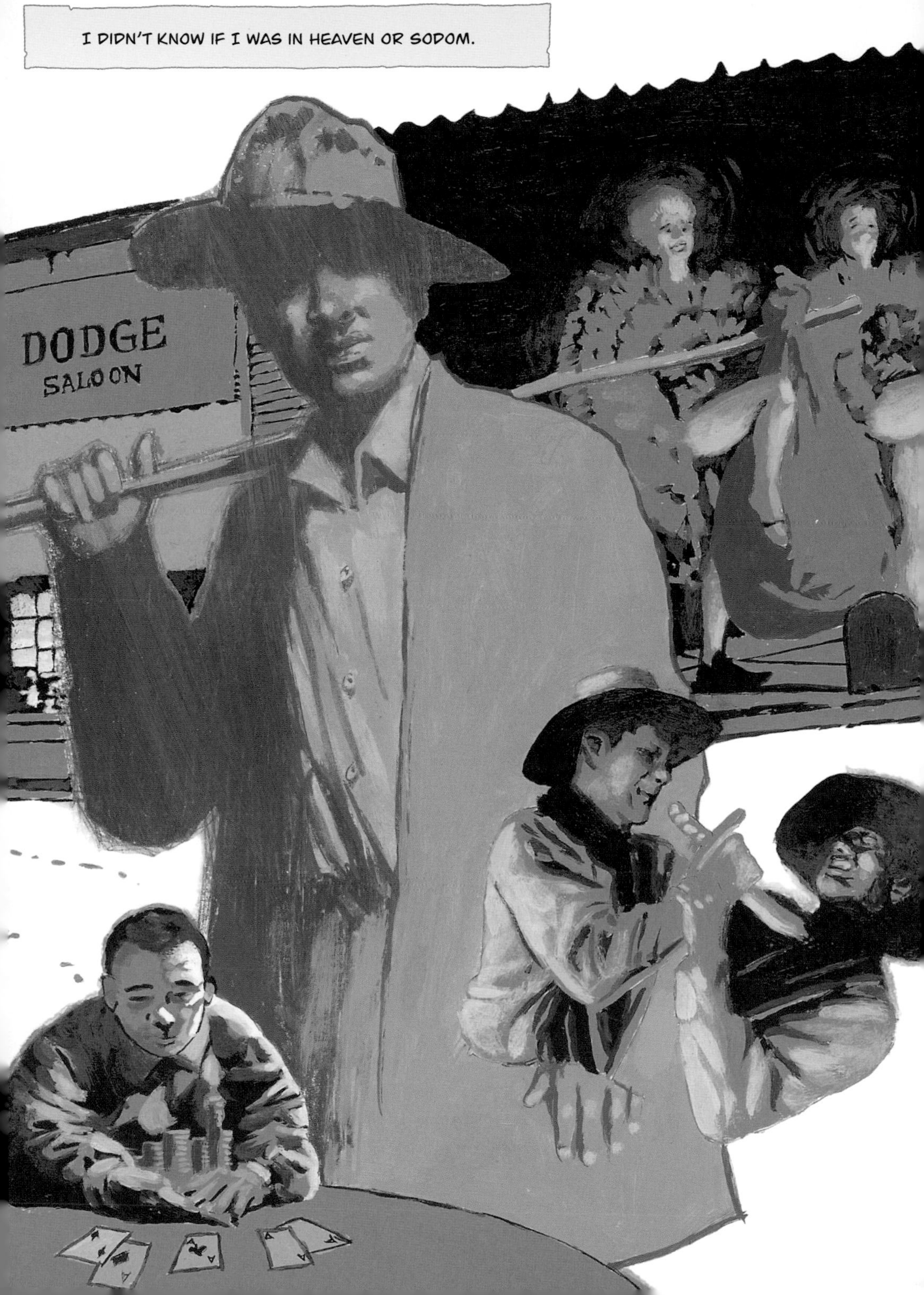
I DIDN'T KNOW IF I WAS IN HEAVEN OR SODOM.
DODGE
SALOON

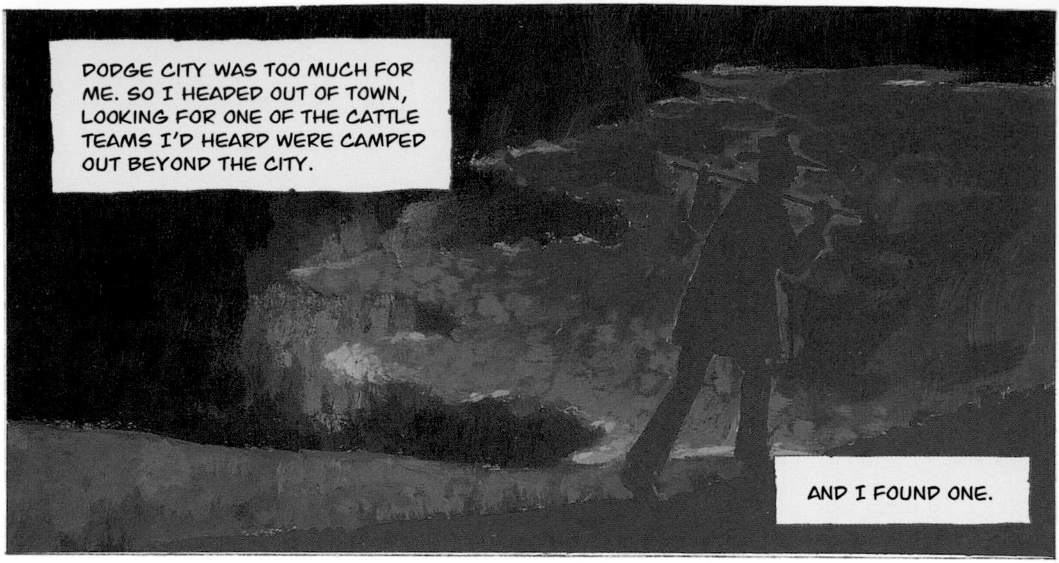
DODGE CITY WAS TOO MUCH FOR ME. SO I HEADED OUT OF TOWN, LOOKING FOR ONE OF THE CATTLE TEAMS I'D HEARD WERE CAMPED OUT BEYOND THE CITY.
AND I FOUND ONE.

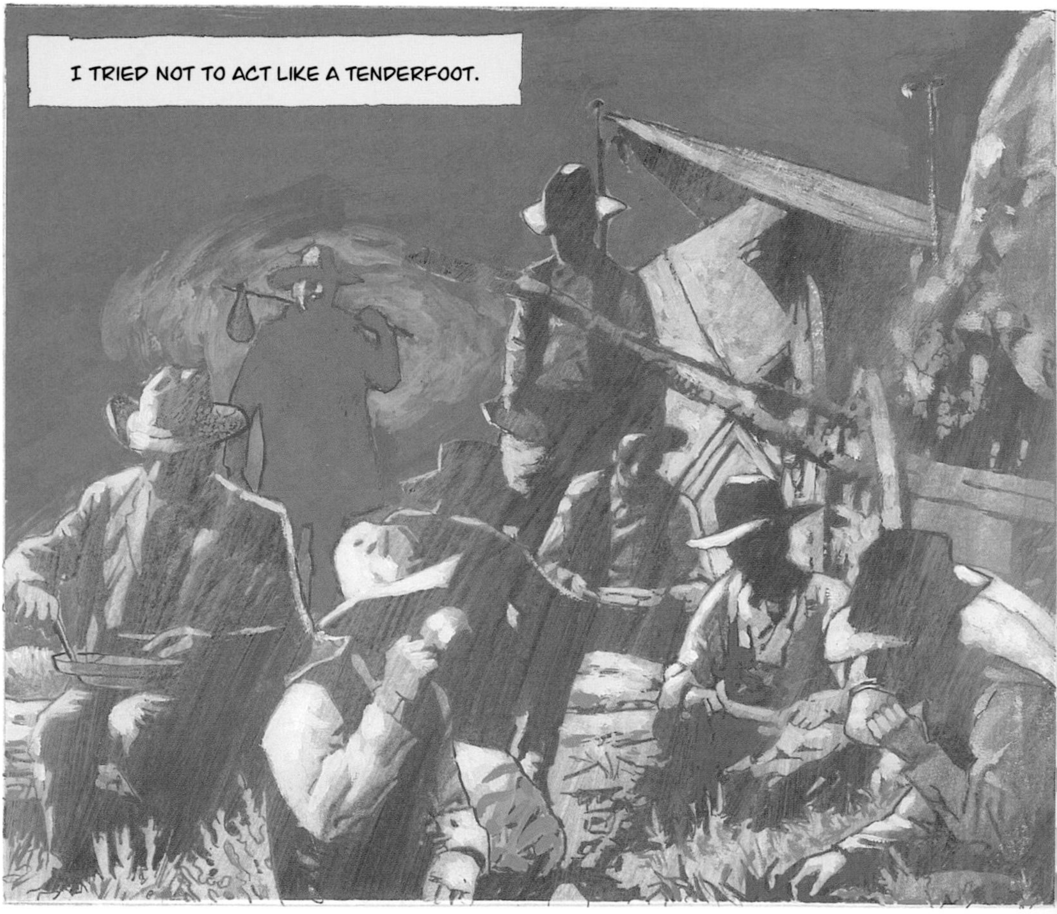
I TRIED NOT TO ACT LIKE A TENDERFOOT.

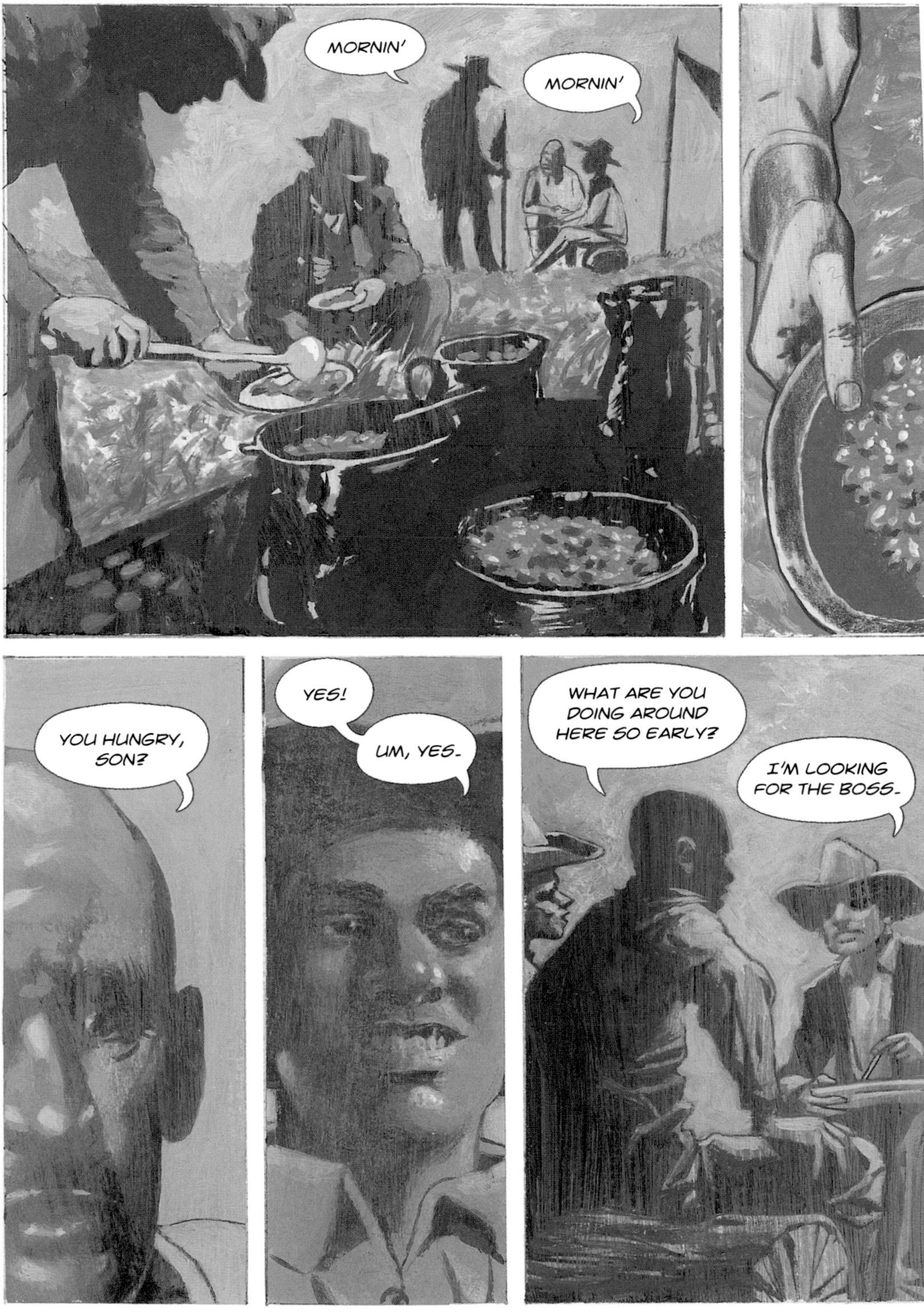
MORNIN'
MORNIN'
YOU HUNGRY, SON?
YES!
UM, YES.
WHAT ARE YOU DOING AROUND HERE SO EARLY?
I'M LOOKING FOR THE BOSS.

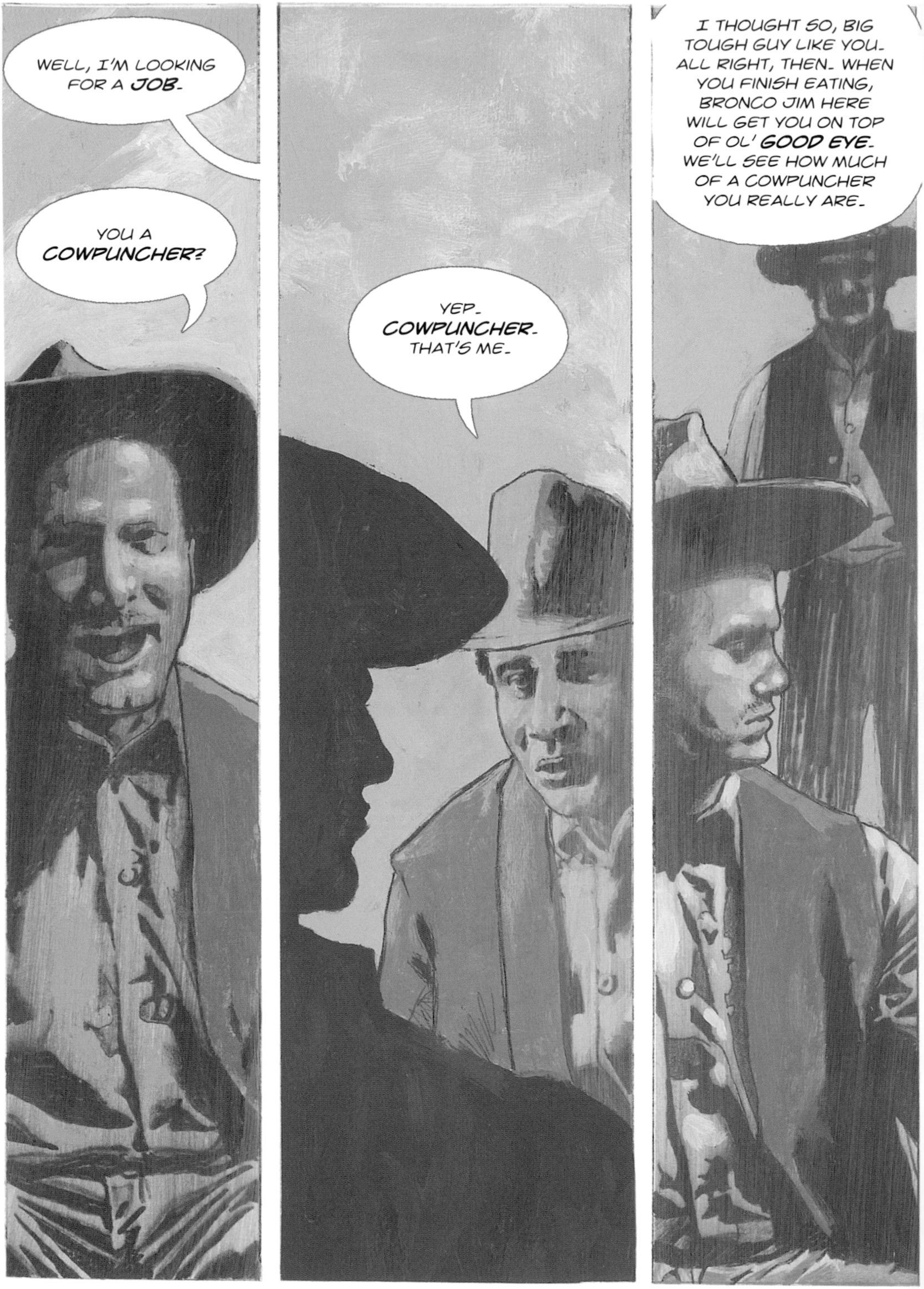
WELL, I'M LOOKING FOR A **JOB**.
YOU A **COWPUNCHER**?
YEP. **COWPUNCHER**. THAT'S ME.
I THOUGHT SO, BIG TOUGH GUY LIKE YOU. ALL RIGHT, THEN. WHEN YOU FINISH EATING, BRONCO JIM HERE WILL GET YOU ON TOP OF OL' **GOOD EYE**. WE'LL SEE HOW MUCH OF A COWPUNCHER YOU REALLY ARE.

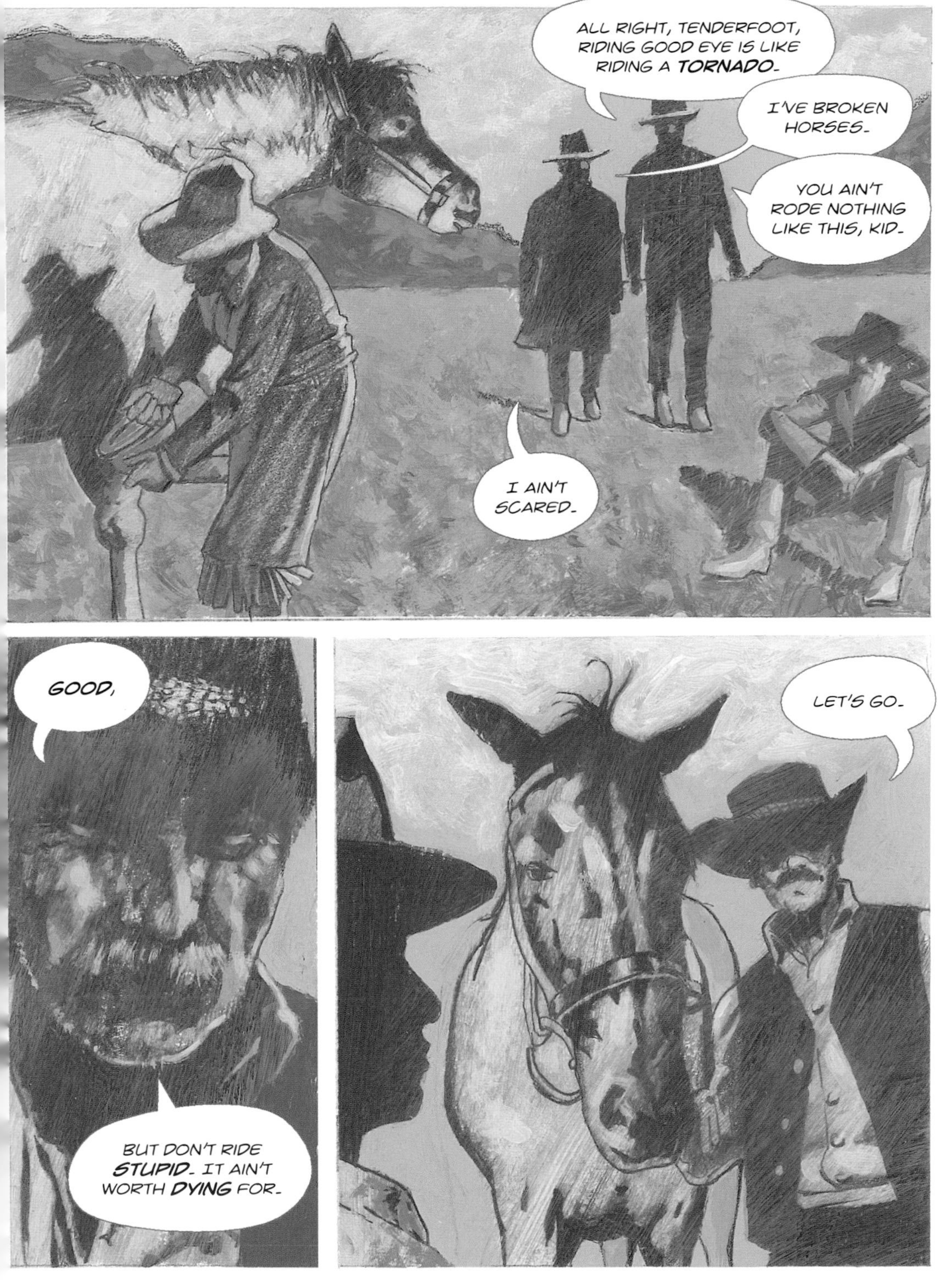
ALL RIGHT, TENDERFOOT, RIDING GOOD EYE IS LIKE RIDING A TORNADO.
I'VE BROKEN HORSES.
YOU AIN'T RODE NOTHING LIKE THIS, KID.
I AIN'T SCARED.
GOOD,
BUT DON'T RIDE STUPID. IT AIN'T WORTH DYING FOR.
LET'S GO.

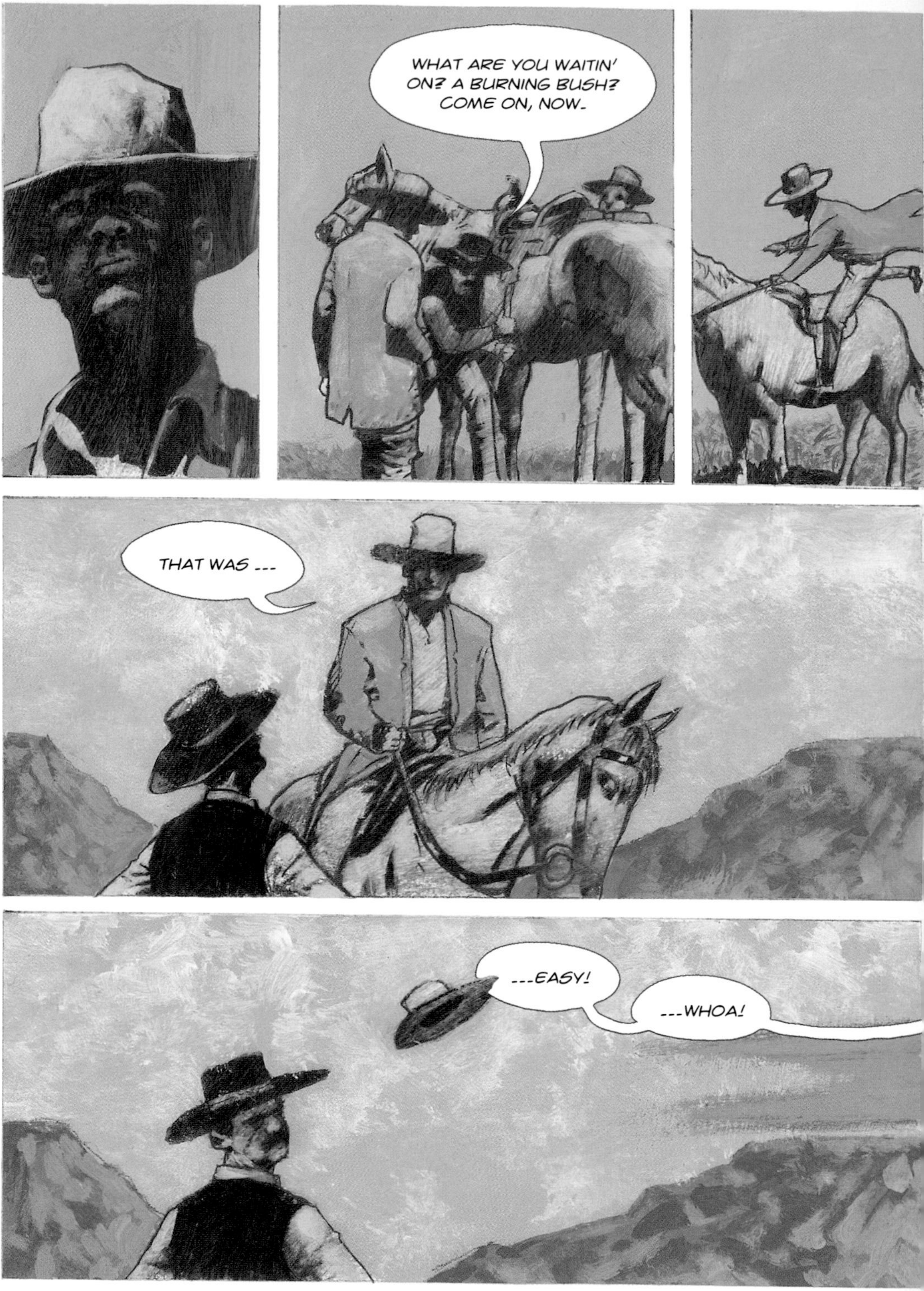
WHAT ARE YOU WAITIN' ON? A BURNING BUSH? COME ON, NOW.
THAT WAS ---
---EASY!
---WHOA!

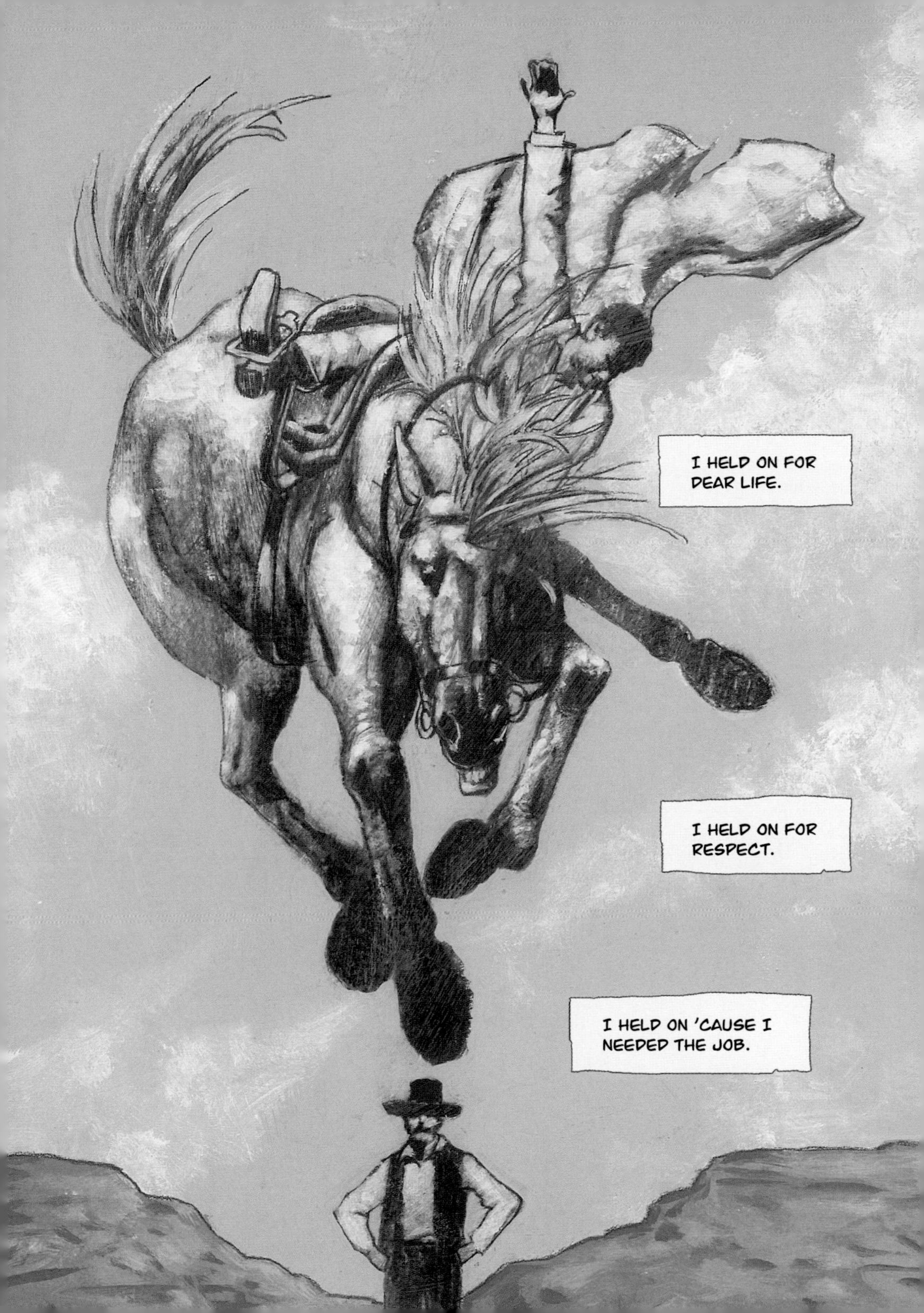
I HELD ON FOR DEAR LIFE.
I HELD ON FOR RESPECT.
I HELD ON 'CAUSE I NEEDED THE JOB.

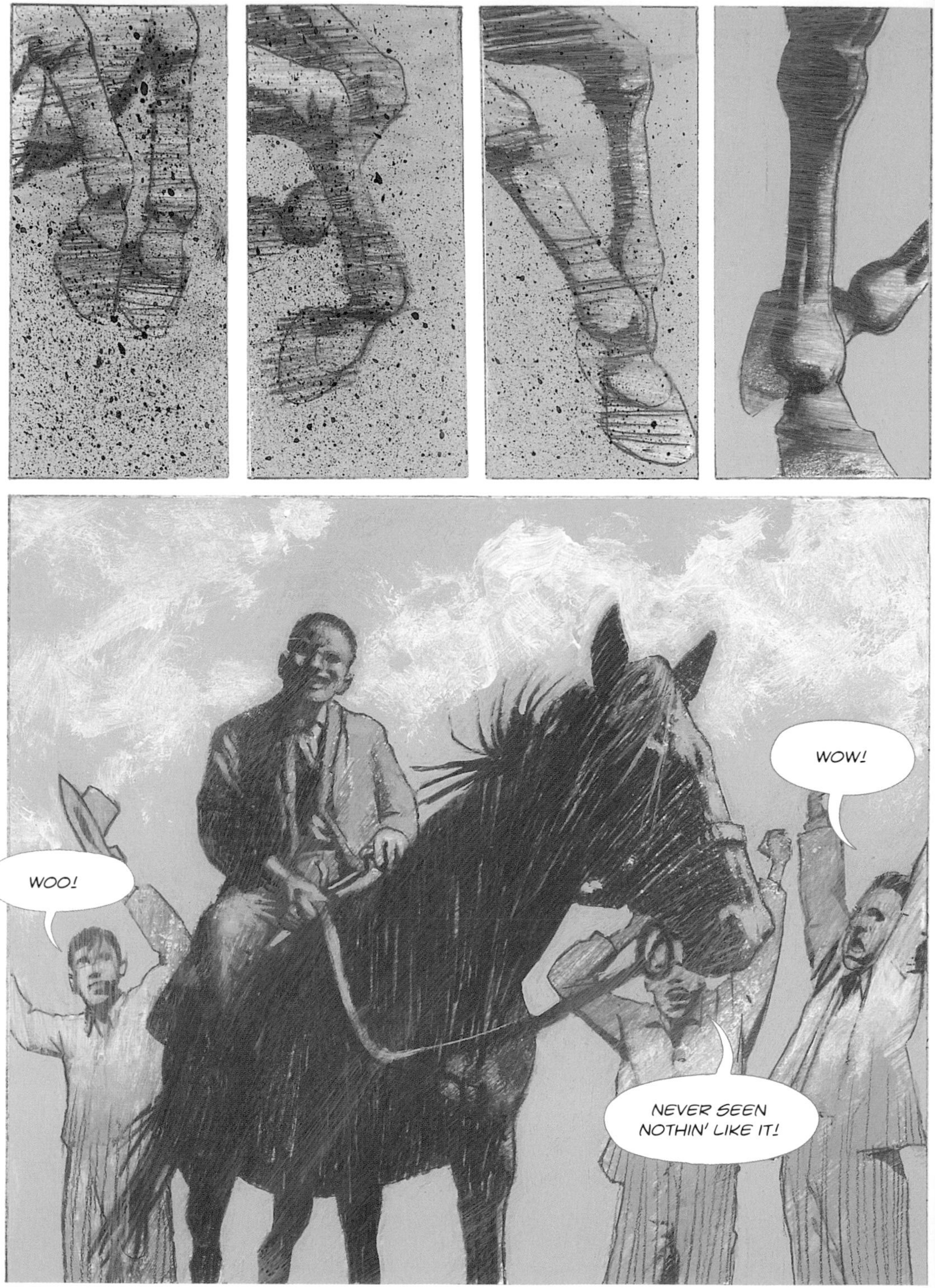
WOO!
WOW!
NEVER SEEN NOTHIN' LIKE IT!

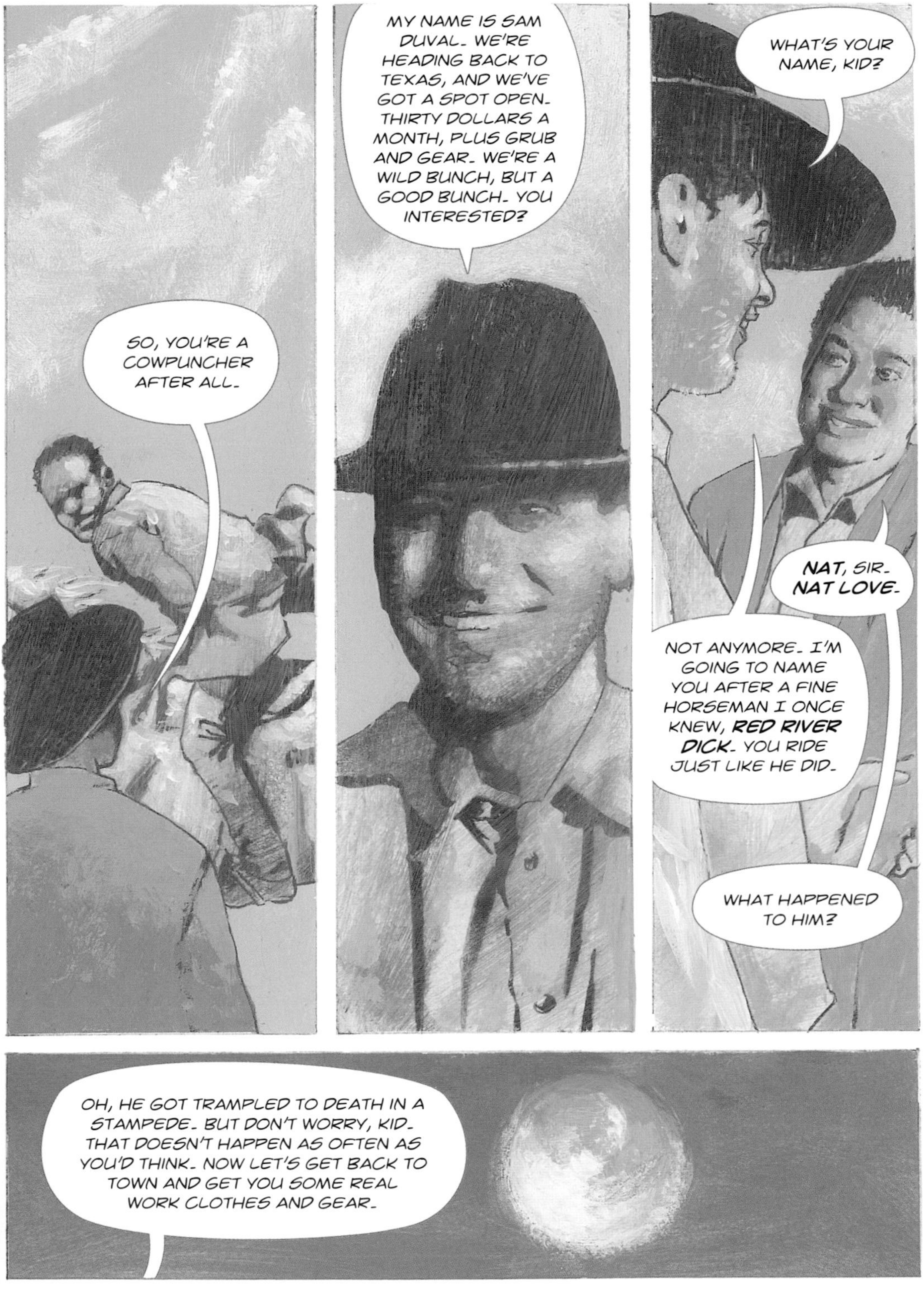
SO, YOU'RE A COWPUNCHER AFTER ALL.
MY NAME IS SAM DUVAL. WE'RE HEADING BACK TO TEXAS, AND WE'VE GOT A SPOT OPEN. THIRTY DOLLARS A MONTH, PLUS GRUB AND GEAR. WE'RE A WILD BUNCH, BUT A GOOD BUNCH. YOU INTERESTED?
WHAT'S YOUR NAME, KID?
NAT, SIR. NAT LOVE.
NOT ANYMORE. I'M GOING TO NAME YOU AFTER A FINE HORSEMAN I ONCE KNEW, RED RIVER DICK. YOU RIDE JUST LIKE HE DID.
WHAT HAPPENED TO HIM?
OH, HE GOT TRAMPLED TO DEATH IN A STAMPEDE. BUT DON'T WORRY, KID. THAT DOESN'T HAPPEN AS OFTEN AS YOU'D THINK. NOW LET'S GET BACK TO TOWN AND GET YOU SOME REAL WORK CLOTHES AND GEAR.

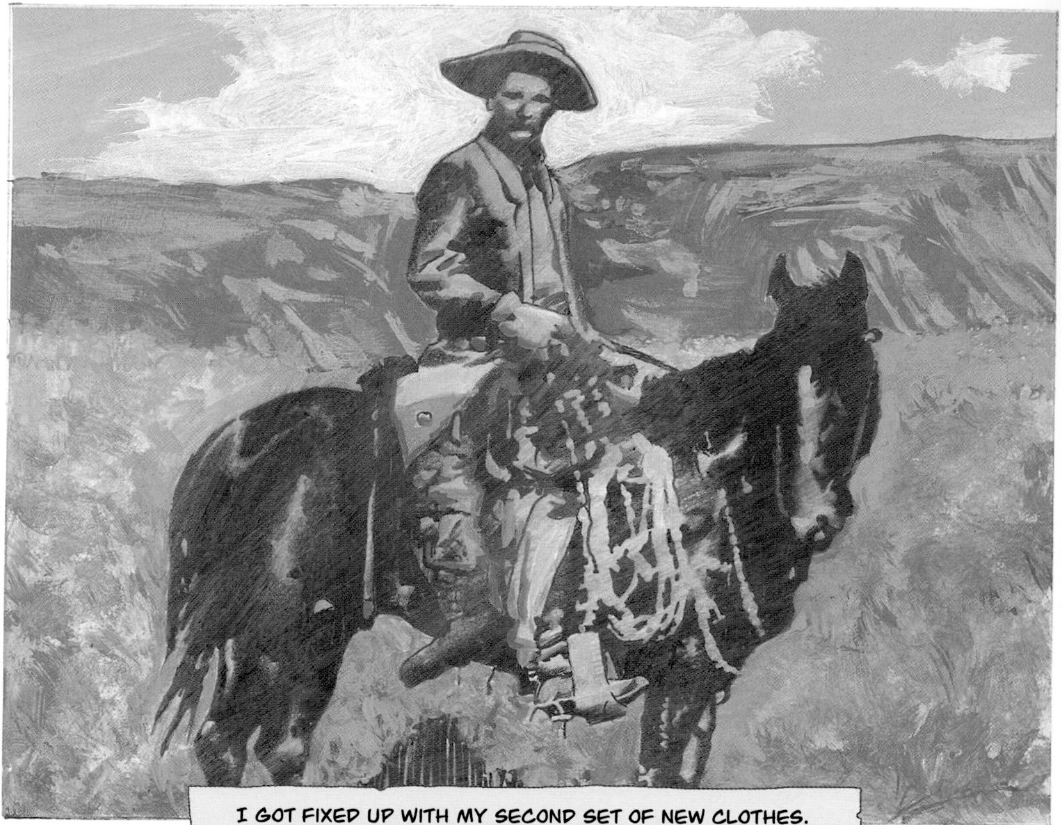
I GOT FIXED UP WITH MY SECOND SET OF NEW CLOTHES.
AND I GOT A GUN. A 45 COLT REVOLVER, TO BE EXACT.

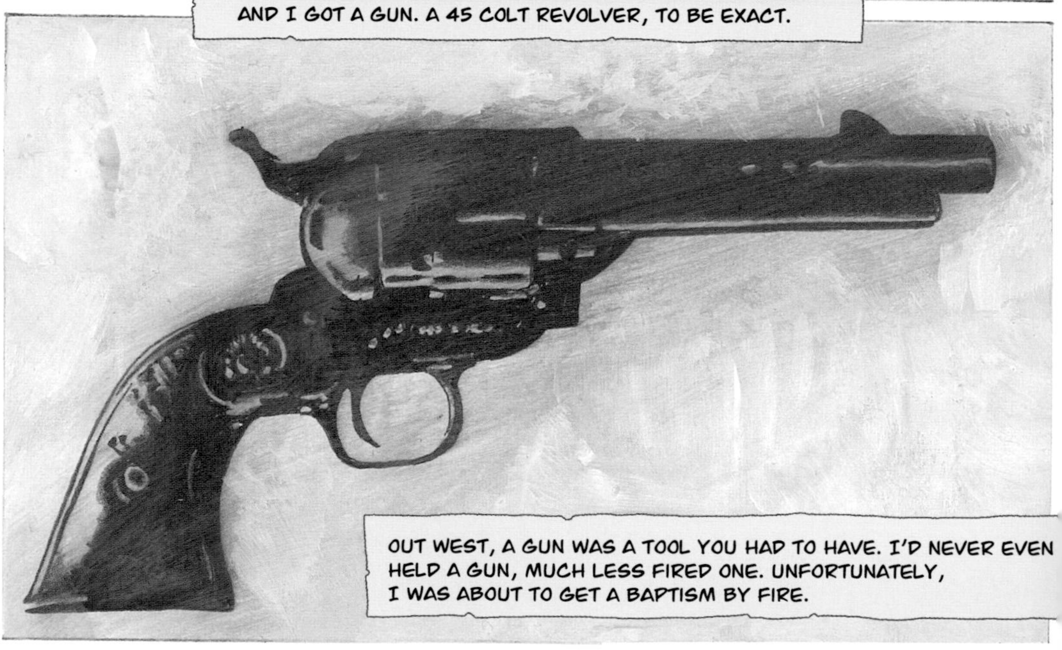
OUT WEST, A GUN WAS A TOOL YOU HAD TO HAVE. I'D NEVER EVEN HELD A GUN, MUCH LESS FIRED ONE. UNFORTUNATELY, I WAS ABOUT TO GET A BAPTISM BY FIRE.

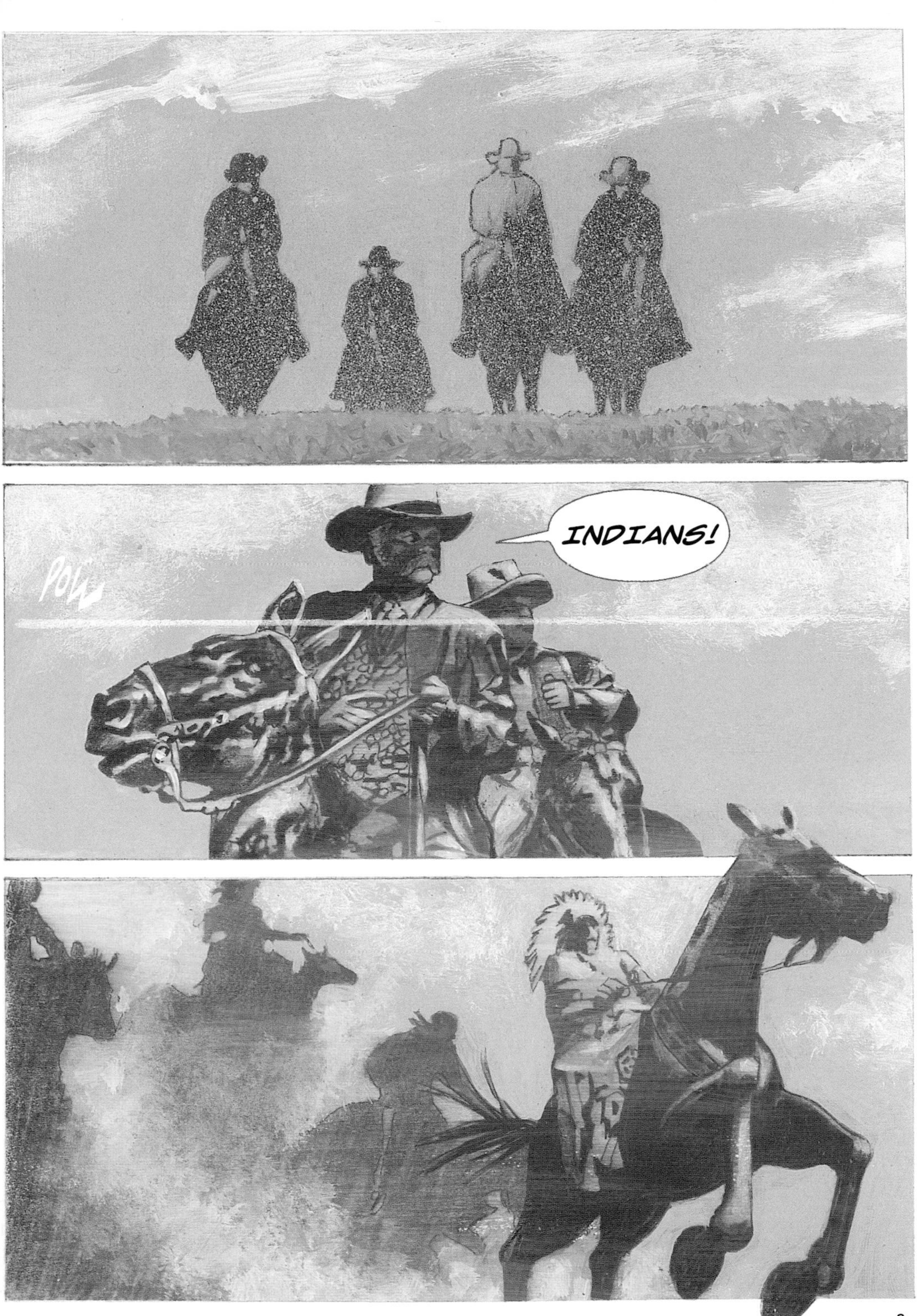
POW
INDIANS!

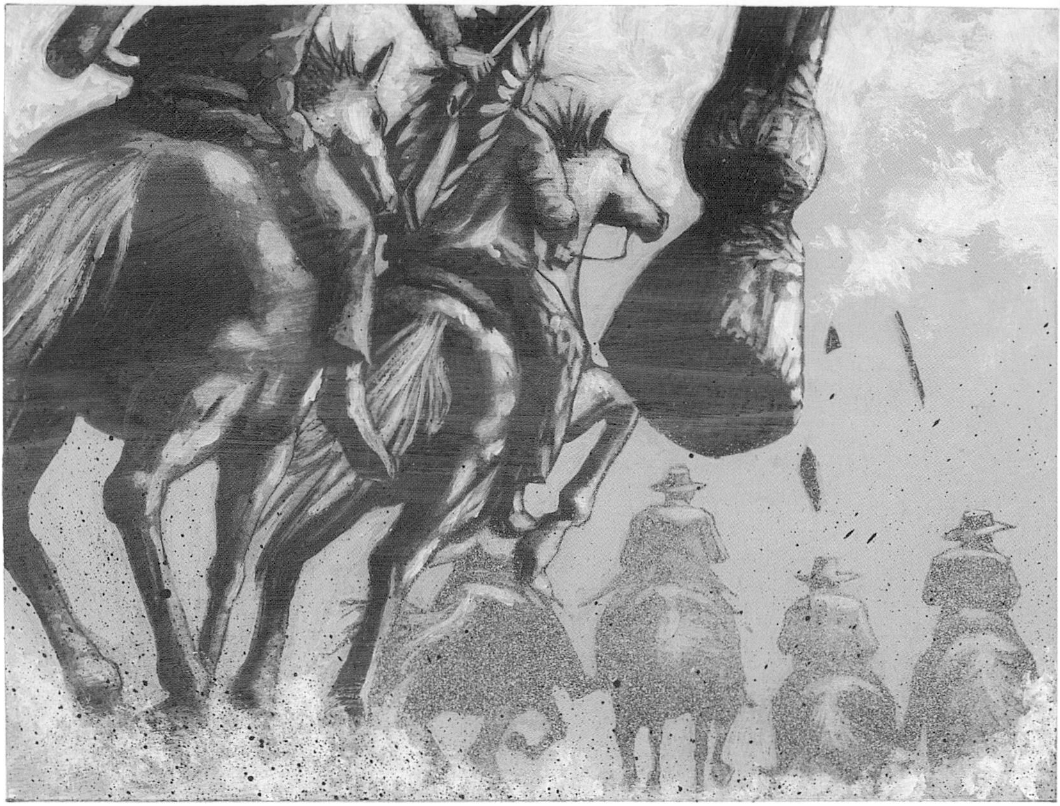

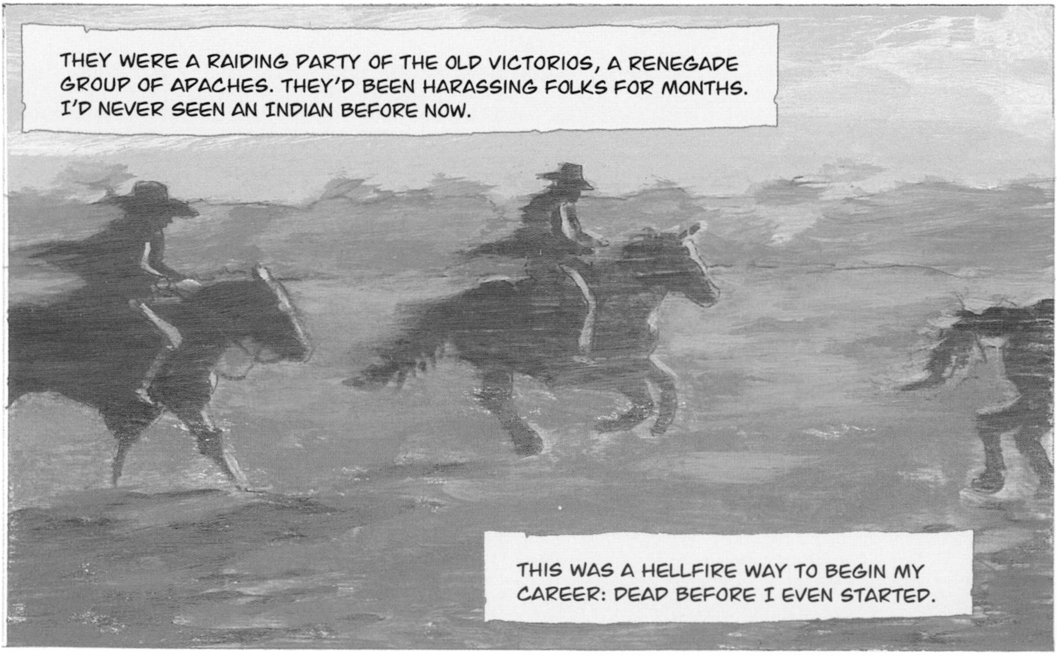
THEY WERE A RAIDING PARTY OF THE OLD VICTORIOS, A RENEGADE GROUP OF APACHES. THEY'D BEEN HARASSING FOLKS FOR MONTHS. I'D NEVER SEEN AN INDIAN BEFORE NOW.
THIS WAS A HELLFIRE WAY TO BEGIN MY CAREER: DEAD BEFORE I EVEN STARTED.

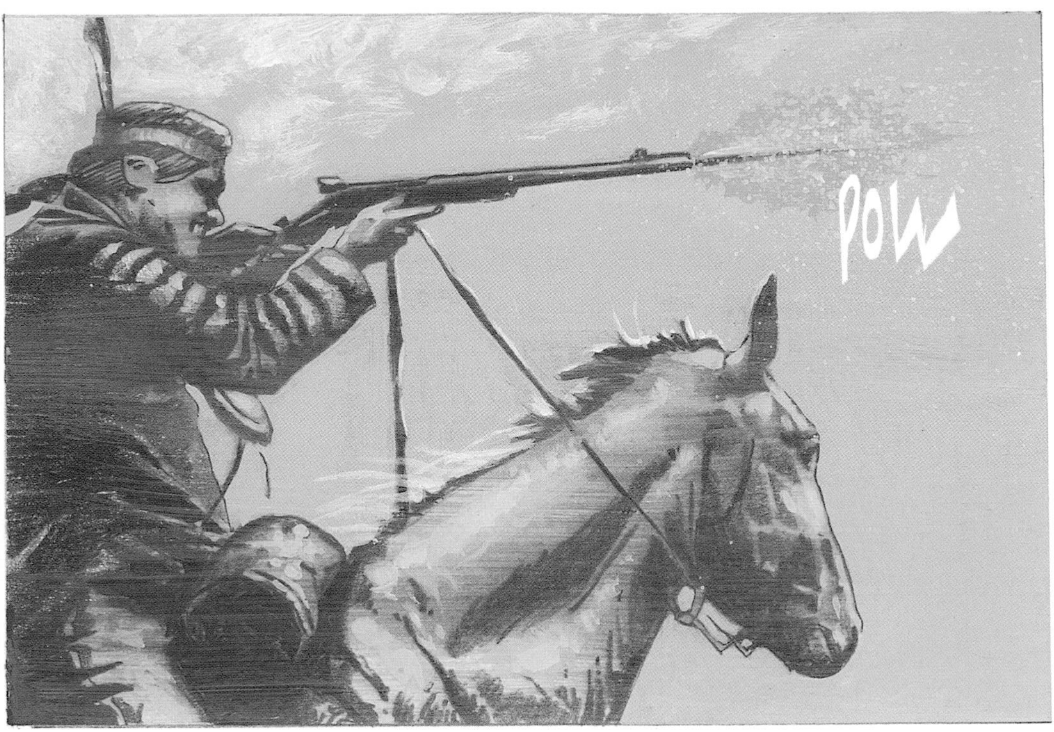
POW

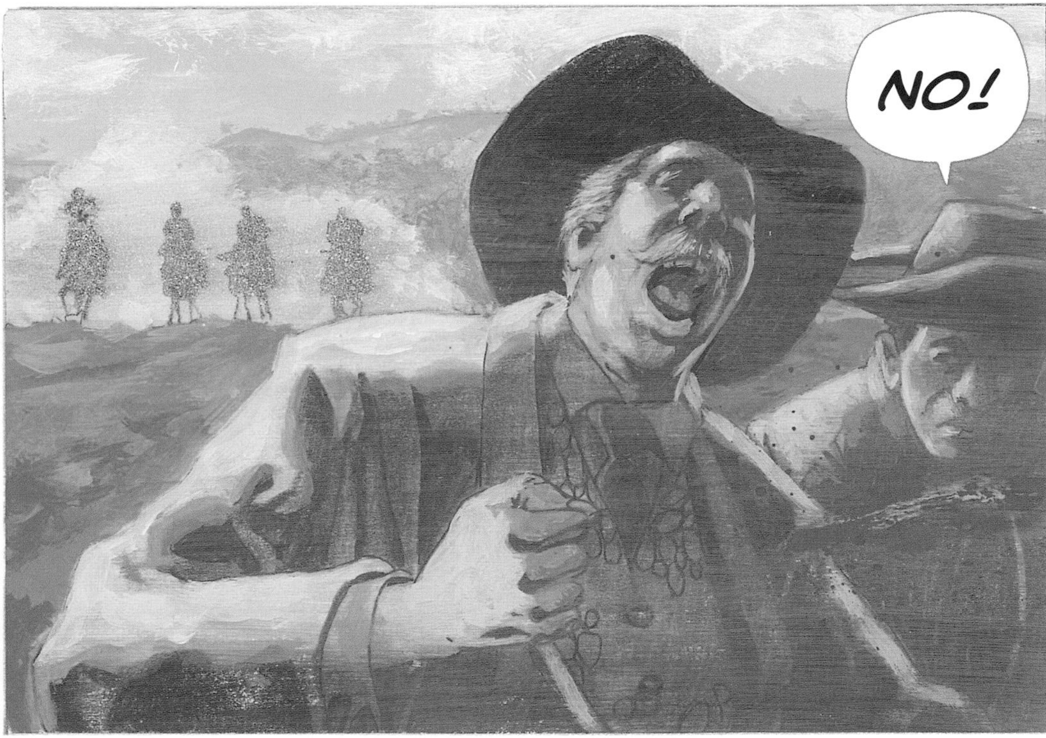
NO!

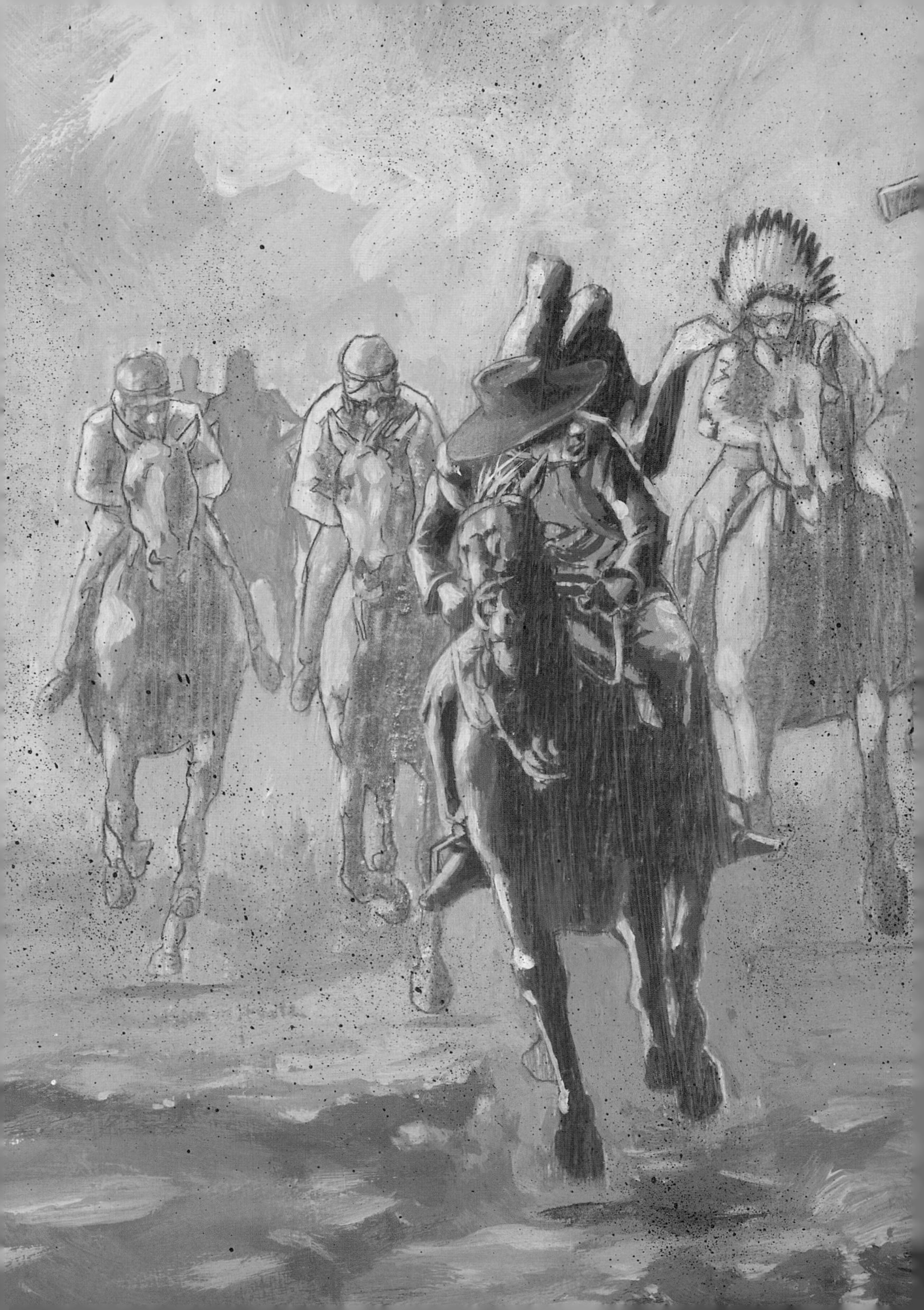

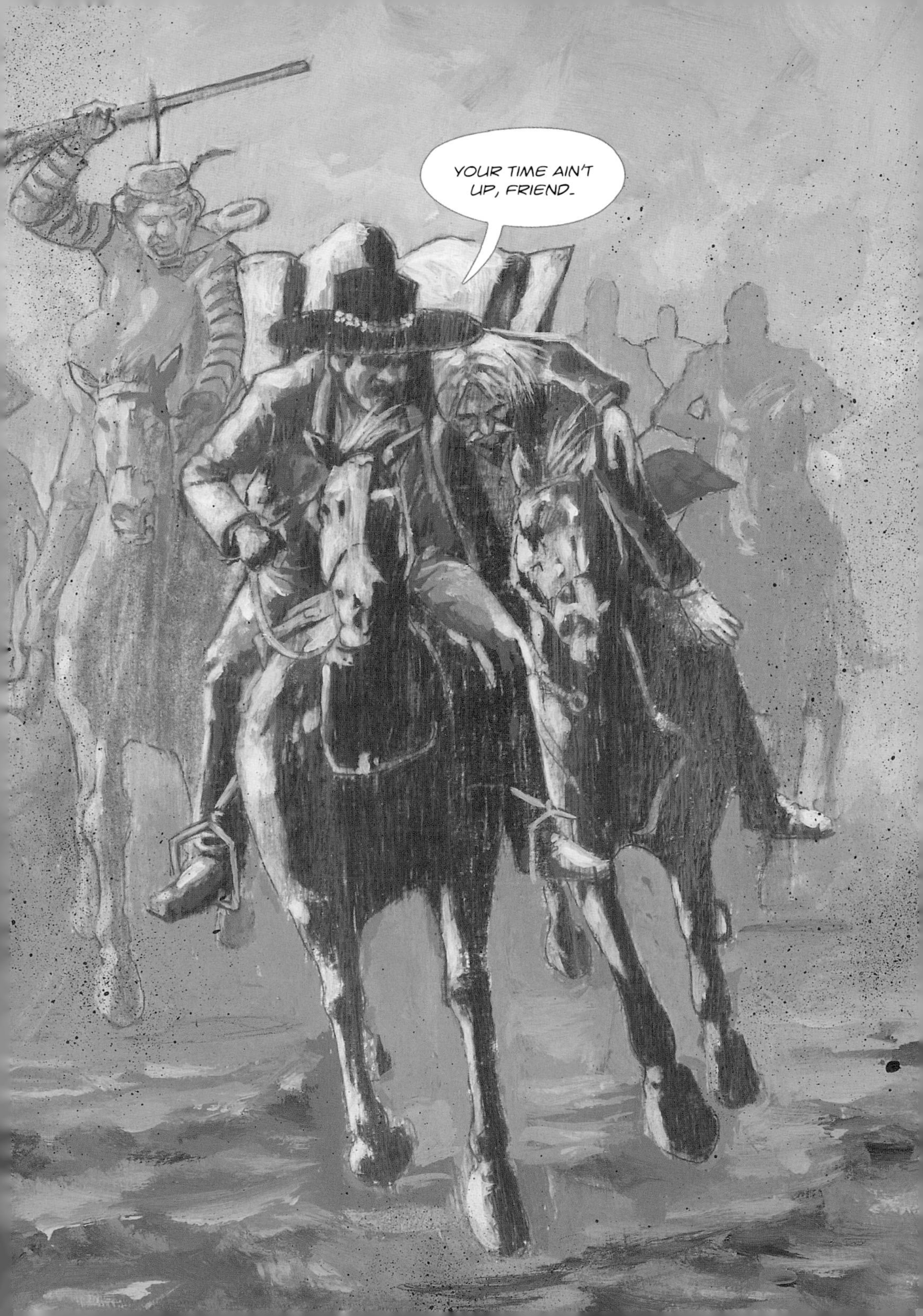
YOUR TIME AIN'T UP, FRIEND.

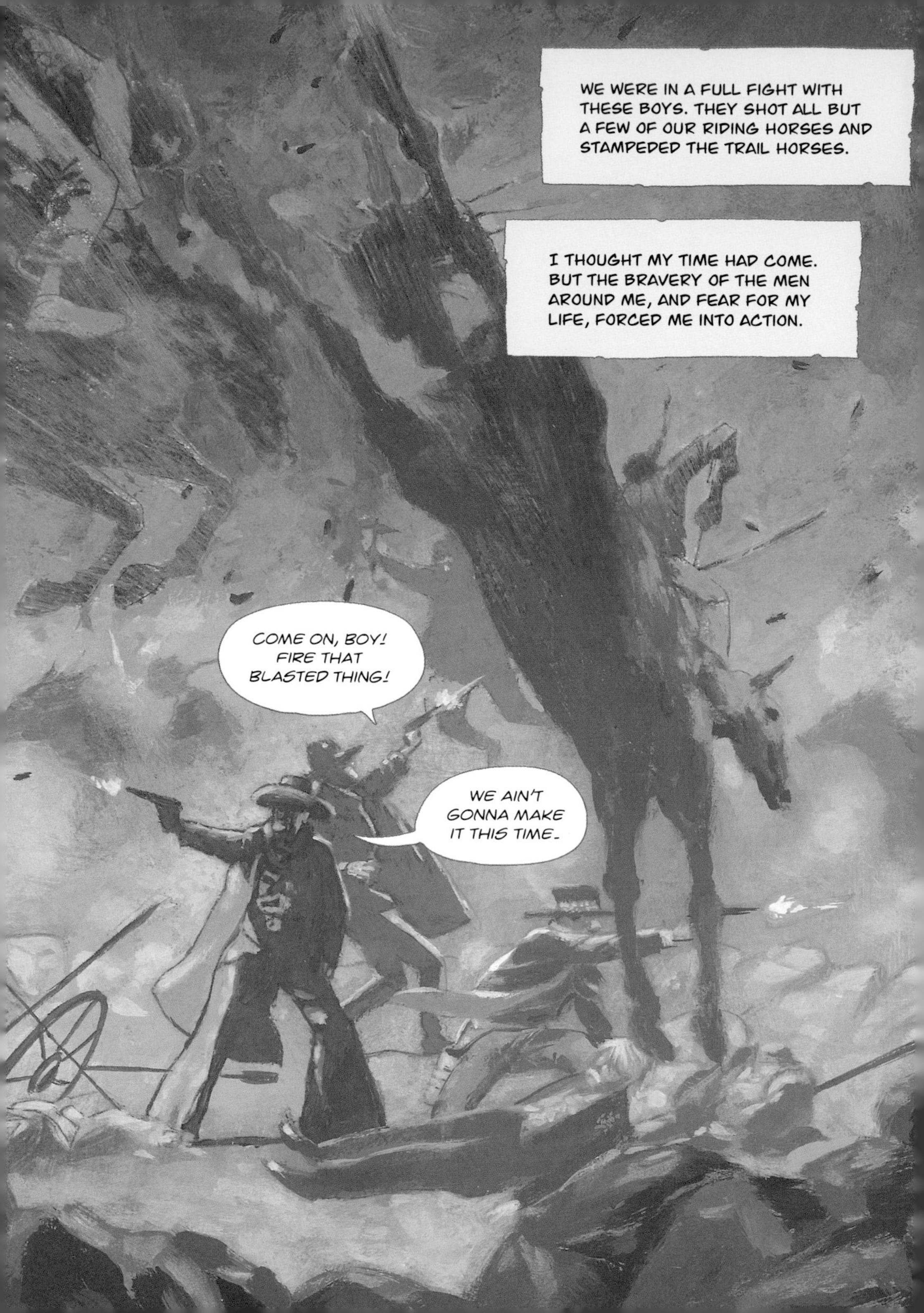
WE WERE IN A FULL FIGHT WITH THESE BOYS. THEY SHOT ALL BUT A FEW OF OUR RIDING HORSES AND STAMPEDED THE TRAIL HORSES.
I THOUGHT MY TIME HAD COME. BUT THE BRAVERY OF THE MEN AROUND ME, AND FEAR FOR MY LIFE, FORCED ME INTO ACTION.
COME ON, BOY! FIRE THAT BLASTED THING!
WE AIN'T GONNA MAKE IT THIS TIME...

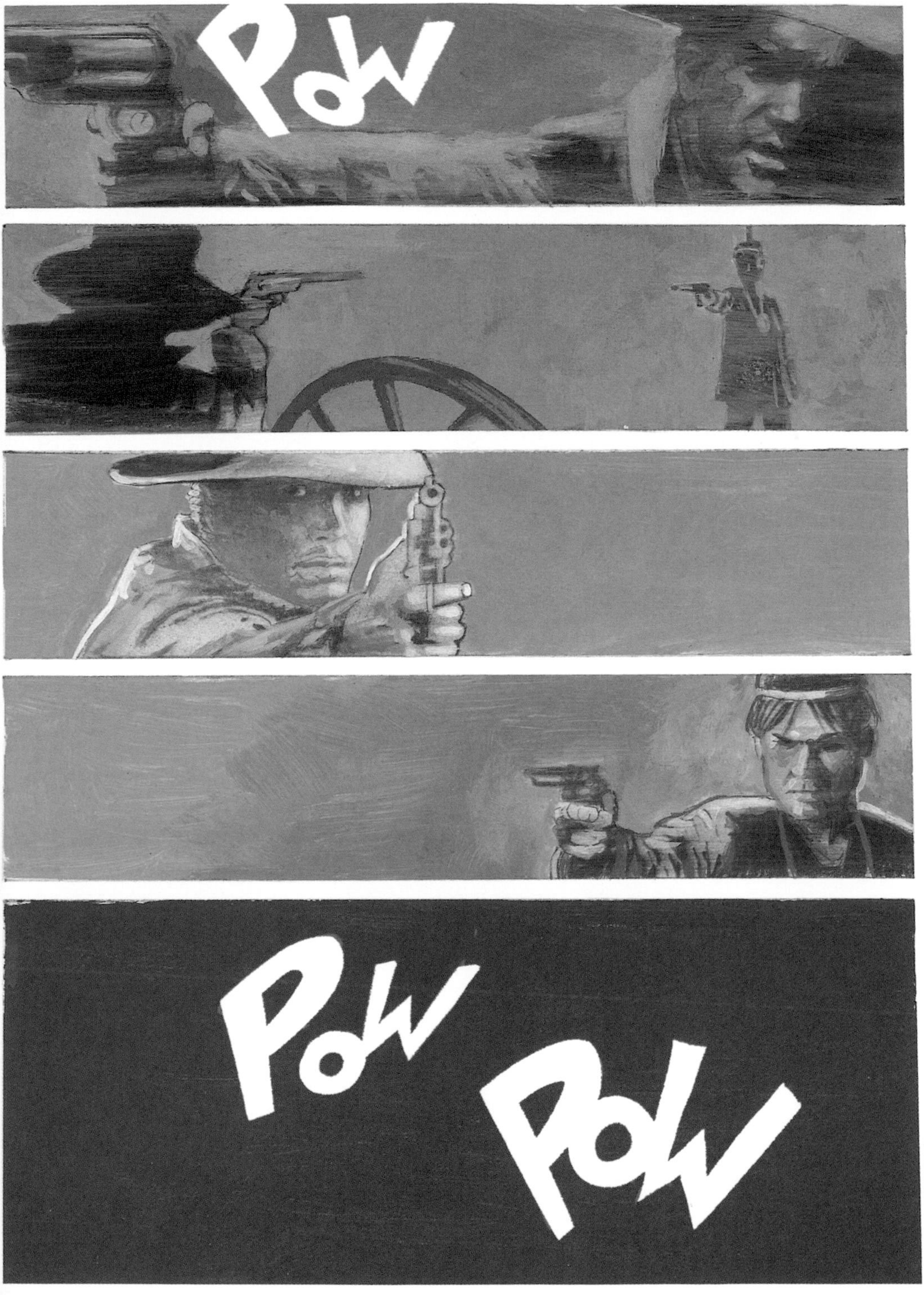
POW
POW
POW

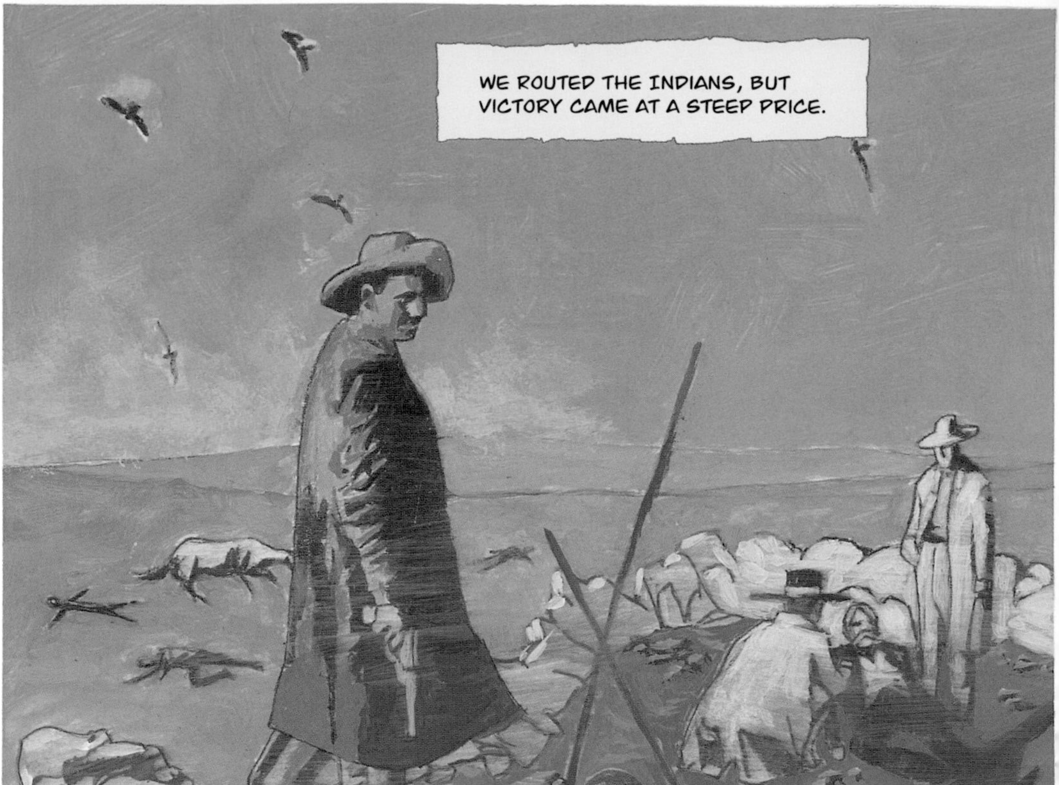
WE ROUTED THE INDIANS, BUT VICTORY CAME AT A STEEP PRICE.

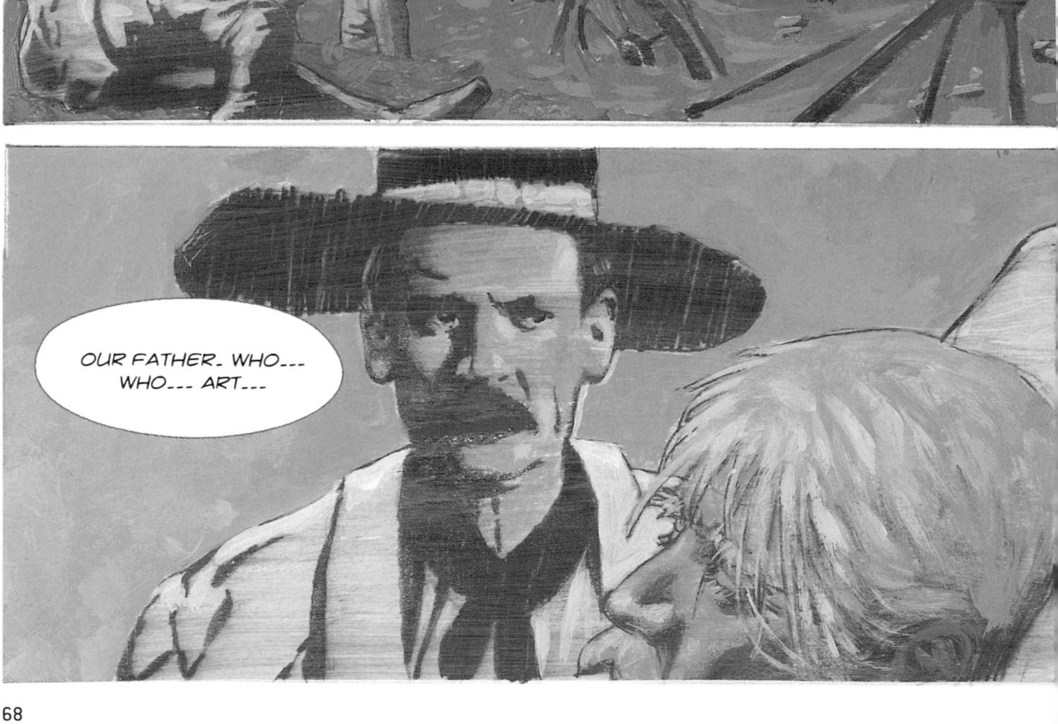
OUR FATHER- WHO--- WHO--- ART---

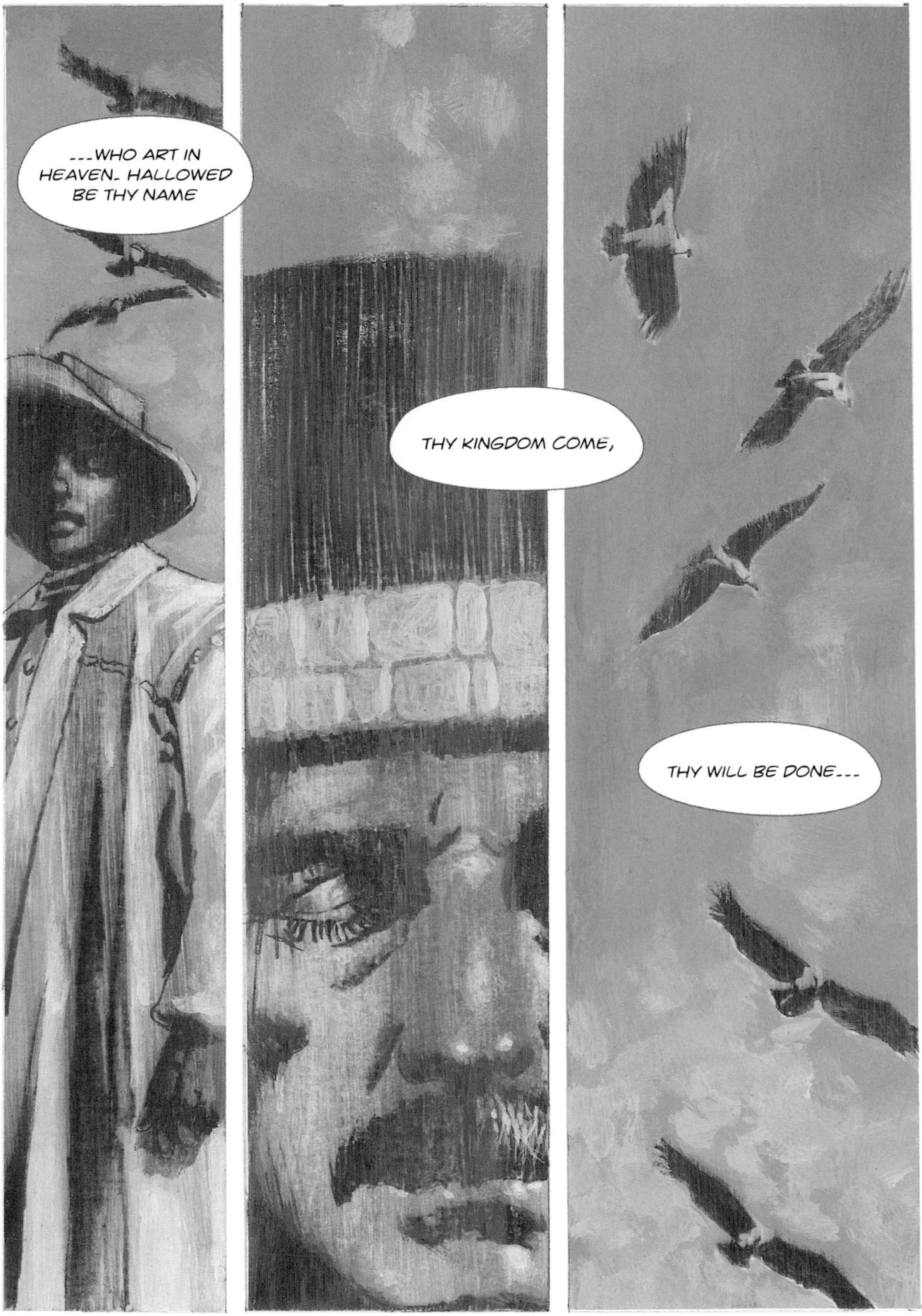
...WHO ART IN HEAVEN. HALLOWED BE THY NAME
THY KINGDOM COME,
THY WILL BE DONE...

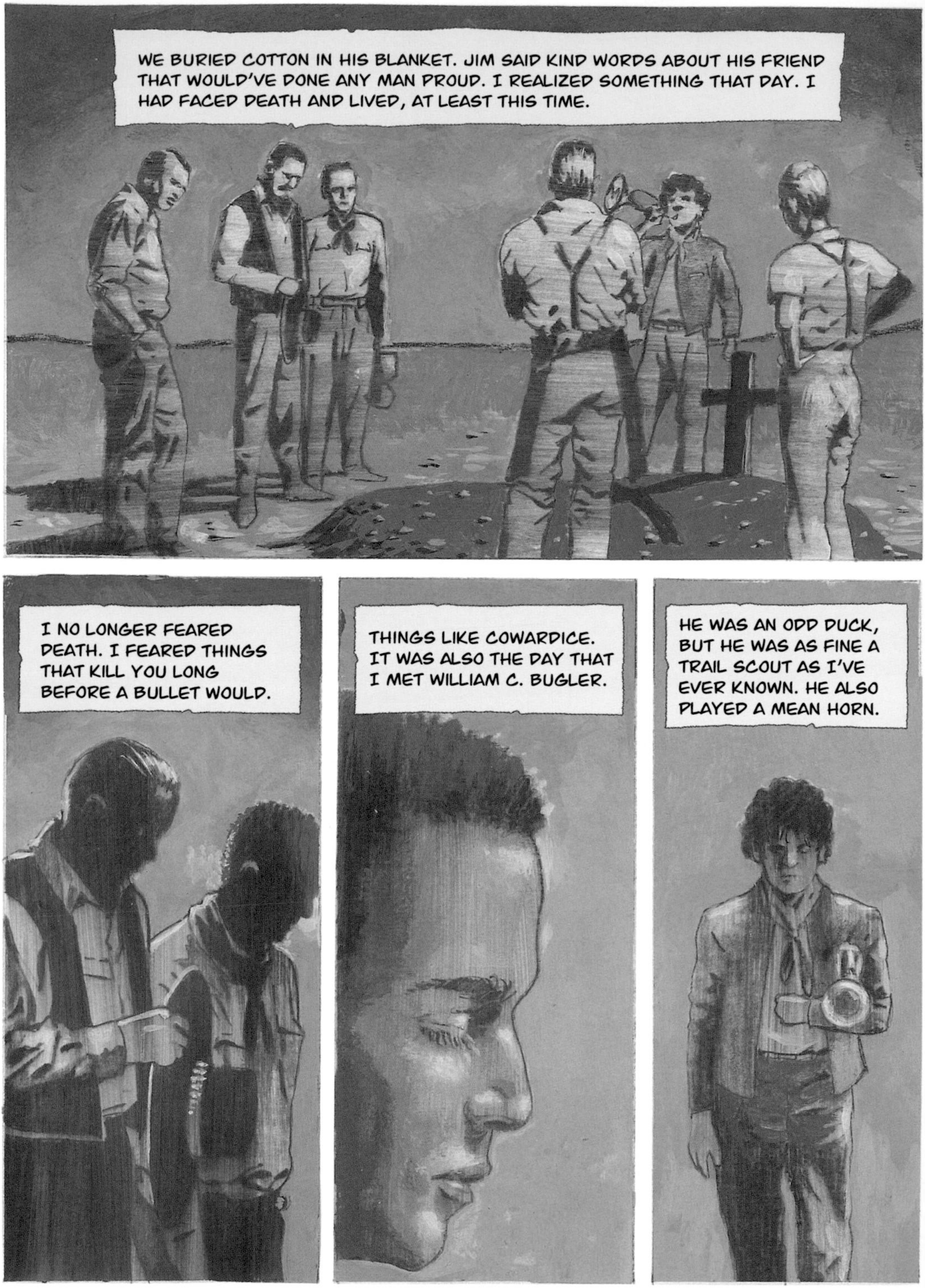
WE BURIED COTTON IN HIS BLANKET. JIM SAID KIND WORDS ABOUT HIS FRIEND THAT WOULD'VE DONE ANY MAN PROUD. I REALIZED SOMETHING THAT DAY. I HAD FACED DEATH AND LIVED, AT LEAST THIS TIME.
I NO LONGER FEARED DEATH. I FEARED THINGS THAT KILL YOU LONG BEFORE A BULLET WOULD.
THINGS LIKE COWARDICE. IT WAS ALSO THE DAY THAT I MET WILLIAM C. BUGLER.
HE WAS AN ODD DUCK, BUT HE WAS AS FINE A TRAIL SCOUT AS I'VE EVER KNOWN. HE ALSO PLAYED A MEAN HORN.

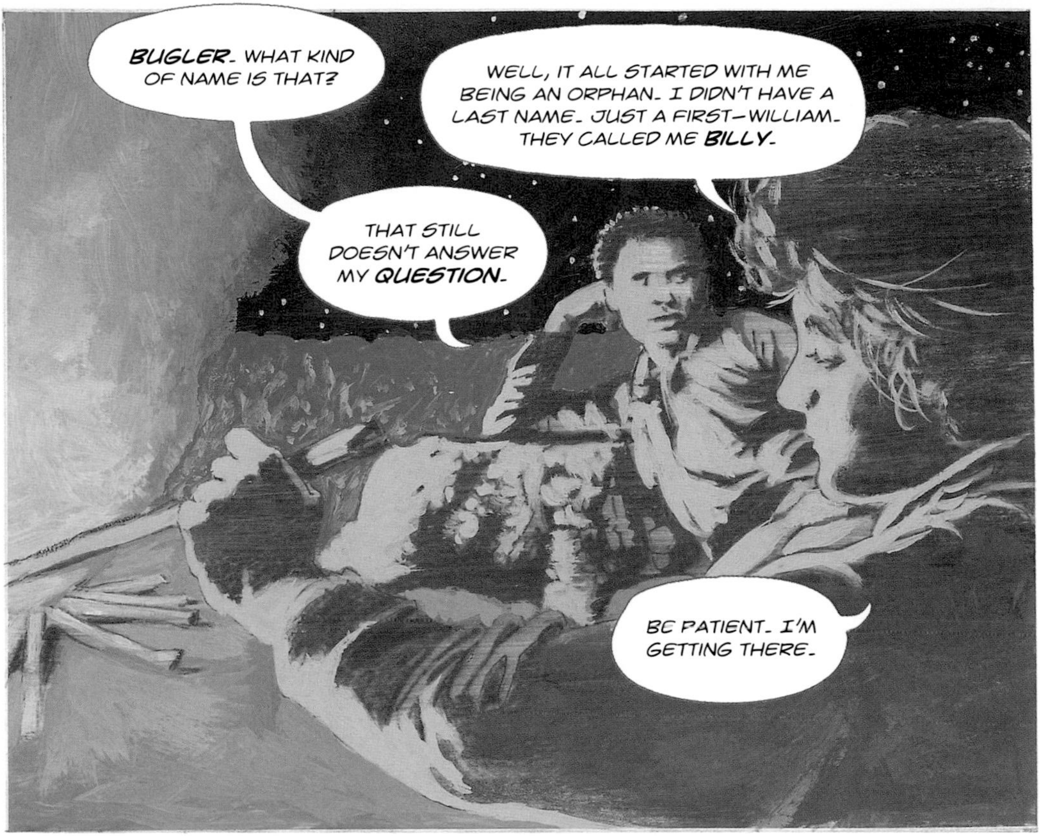
BUGLER. WHAT KIND OF NAME IS THAT?
WELL, IT ALL STARTED WITH ME BEING AN ORPHAN. I DIDN'T HAVE A LAST NAME. JUST A FIRST—WILLIAM. THEY CALLED ME BILLY.
THAT STILL DOESN'T ANSWER MY QUESTION.
BE PATIENT. I'M GETTING THERE.

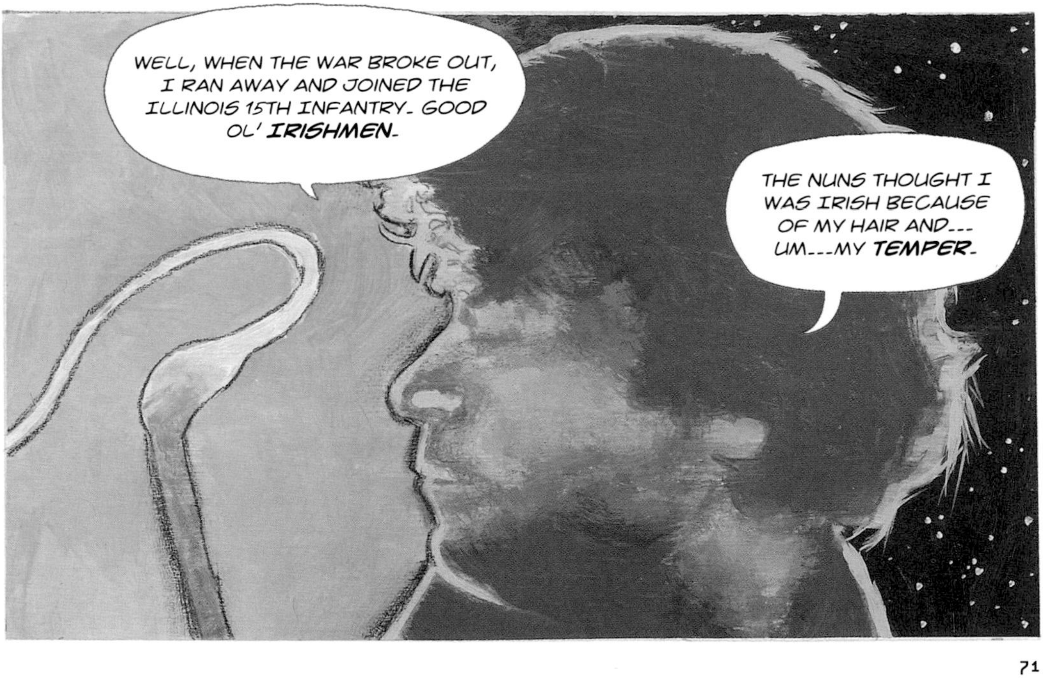
WELL, WHEN THE WAR BROKE OUT, I RAN AWAY AND JOINED THE ILLINOIS 15TH INFANTRY. GOOD OL' IRISHMEN.
THE NUNS THOUGHT I WAS IRISH BECAUSE OF MY HAIR AND... UM...MY TEMPER.

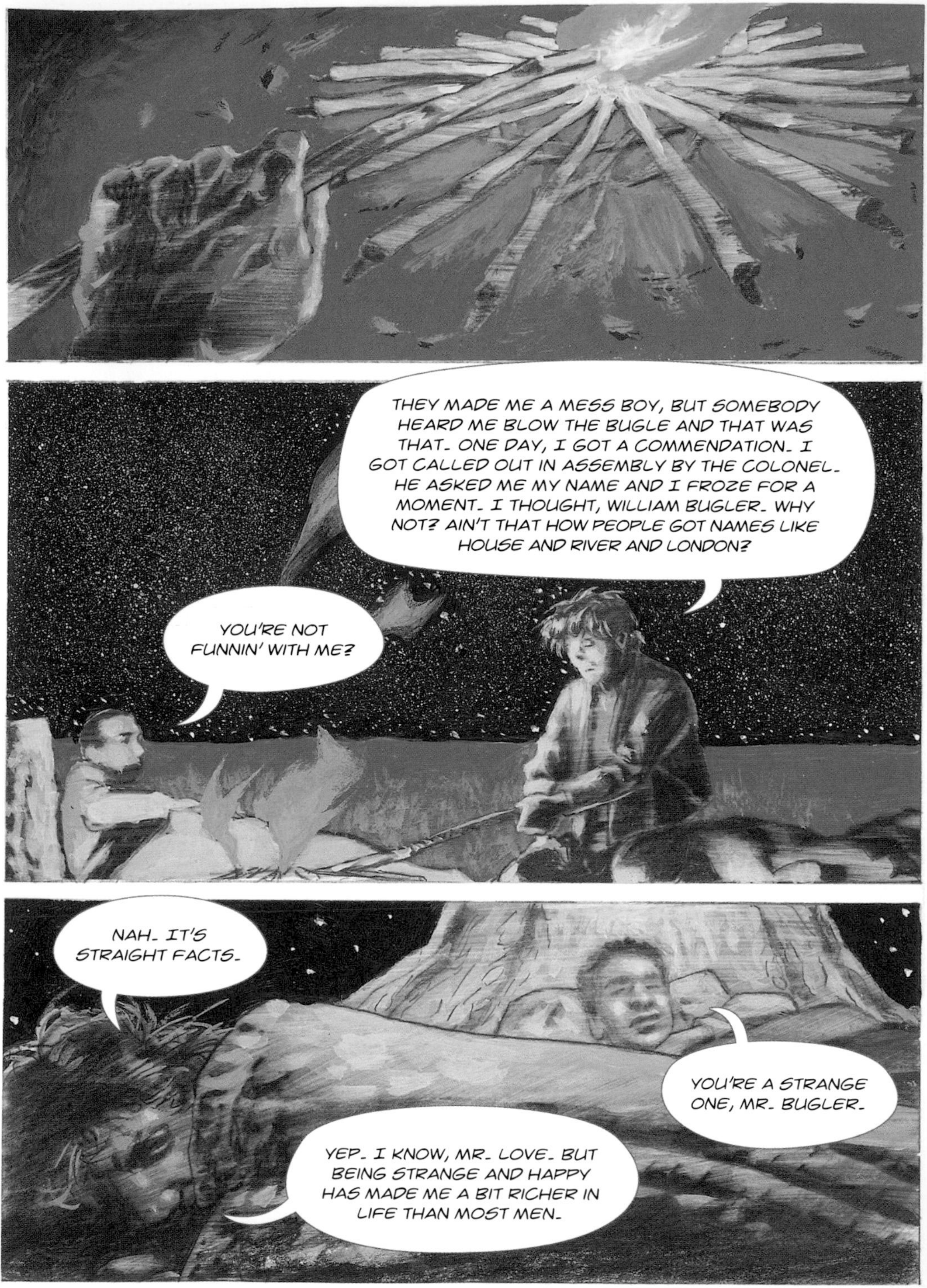
THEY MADE ME A MESS BOY, BUT SOMEBODY HEARD ME BLOW THE BUGLE AND THAT WAS THAT. ONE DAY, I GOT A COMMENDATION. I GOT CALLED OUT IN ASSEMBLY BY THE COLONEL. HE ASKED ME MY NAME AND I FROZE FOR A MOMENT. I THOUGHT, WILLIAM BUGLER. WHY NOT? AIN'T THAT HOW PEOPLE GOT NAMES LIKE HOUSE AND RIVER AND LONDON?
YOU'RE NOT FUNNIN' WITH ME?
NAH. IT'S STRAIGHT FACTS.
YOU'RE A STRANGE ONE, MR. BUGLER.
YEP. I KNOW, MR. LOVE. BUT BEING STRANGE AND HAPPY HAS MADE ME A BIT RICHER IN LIFE THAN MOST MEN.

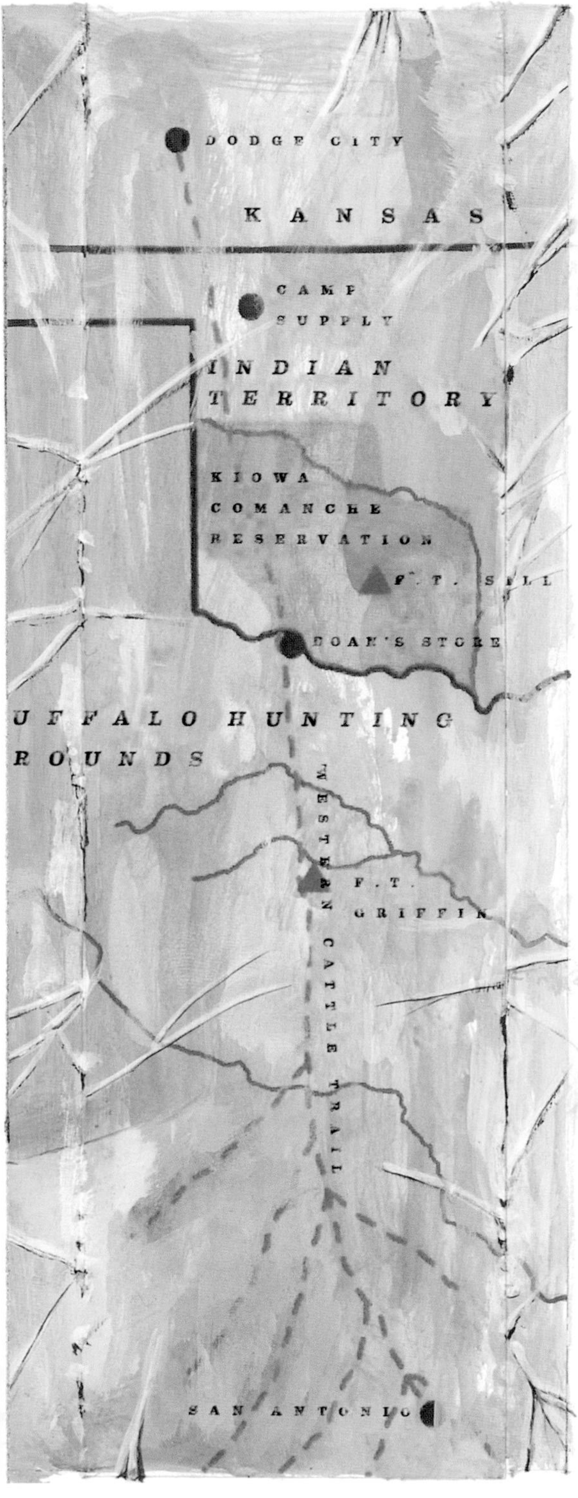
DODGE CITY
KANSAS
CAMP SUPPLY
INDIAN TERRITORY
KIOWA COMANCHE RESERVATION
F.T. SILL
DOAN'S STORE
UFFALO HUNTING ROUNDS
WESTERN CATTLE TRAIL
F.T. GRIFFIN
SAN ANTONIO

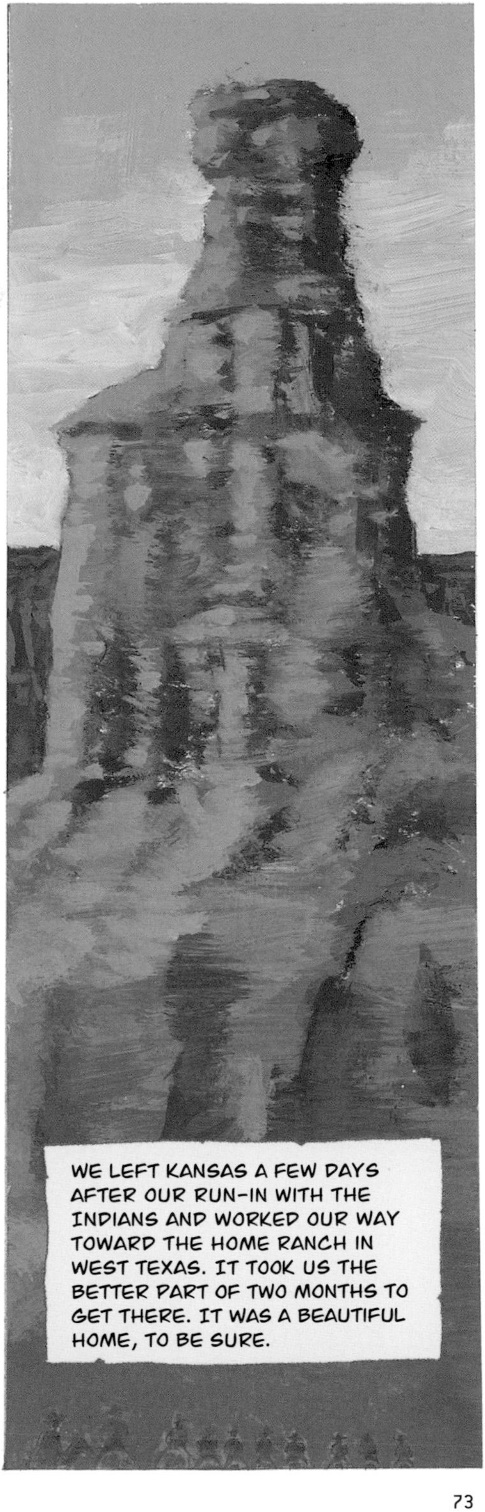
WE LEFT KANSAS A FEW DAYS AFTER OUR RUN-IN WITH THE INDIANS AND WORKED OUR WAY TOWARD THE HOME RANCH IN WEST TEXAS. IT TOOK US THE BETTER PART OF TWO MONTHS TO GET THERE. IT WAS A BEAUTIFUL HOME, TO BE SURE.

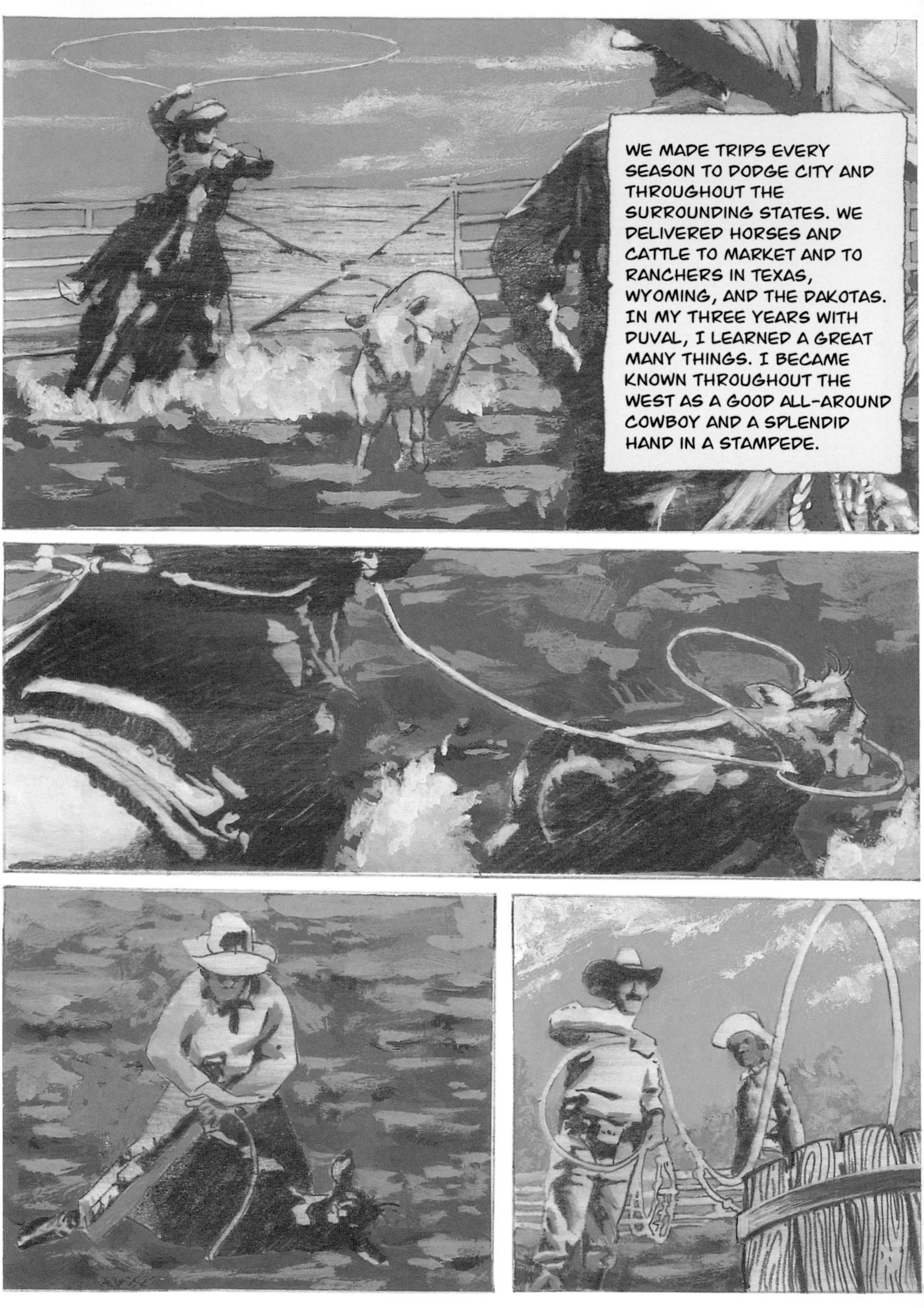
WE MADE TRIPS EVERY SEASON TO DODGE CITY AND THROUGHOUT THE SURROUNDING STATES. WE DELIVERED HORSES AND CATTLE TO MARKET AND TO RANCHERS IN TEXAS, WYOMING, AND THE DAKOTAS. IN MY THREE YEARS WITH DUVAL, I LEARNED A GREAT MANY THINGS. I BECAME KNOWN THROUGHOUT THE WEST AS A GOOD ALL-AROUND COWBOY AND A SPLENDID HAND IN A STAMPEDE.

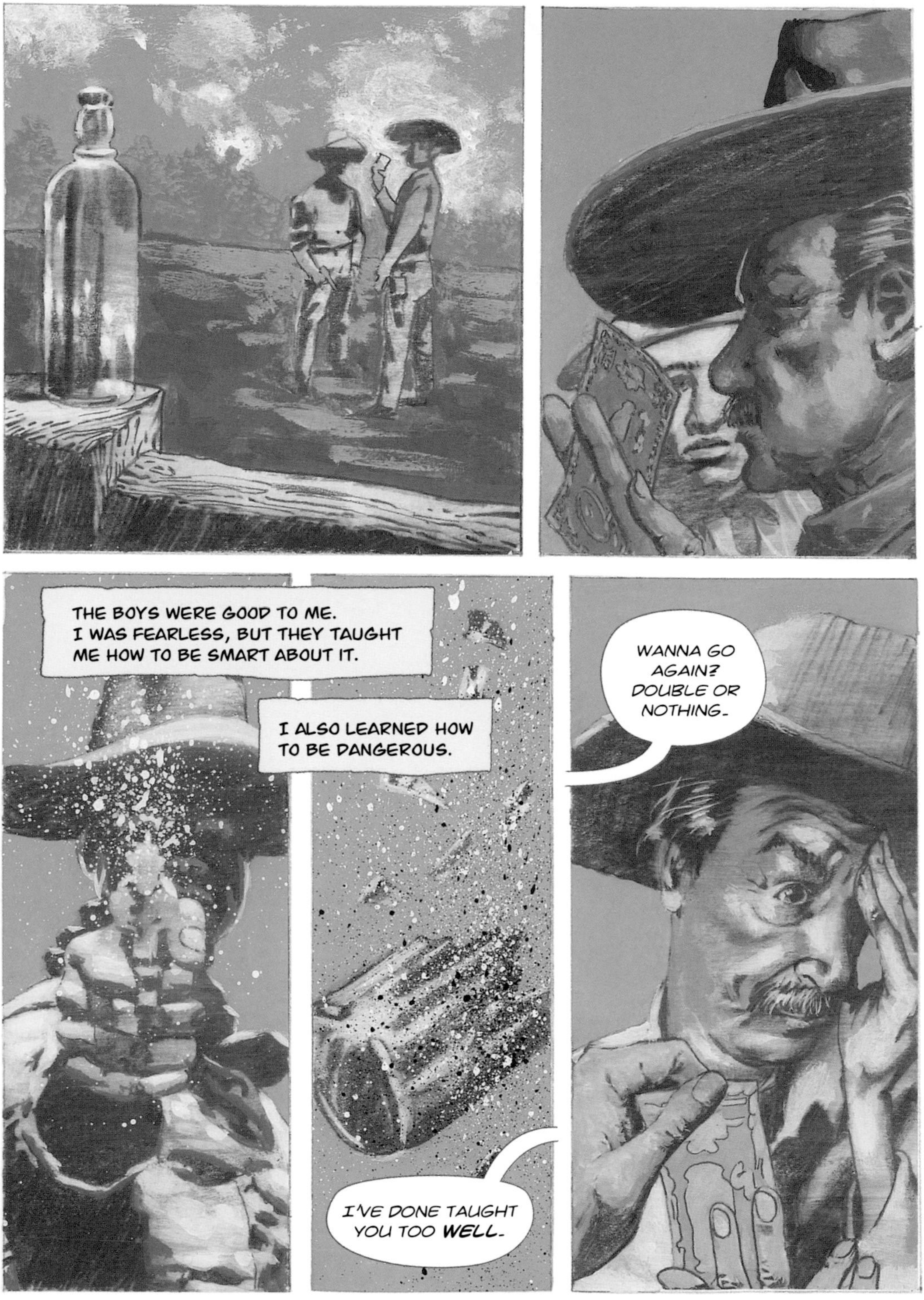
THE BOYS WERE GOOD TO ME. I WAS FEARLESS, BUT THEY TAUGHT ME HOW TO BE SMART ABOUT IT.
I ALSO LEARNED HOW TO BE DANGEROUS.
WANNA GO AGAIN? DOUBLE OR NOTHING.
I'VE DONE TAUGHT YOU TOO **WELL**.

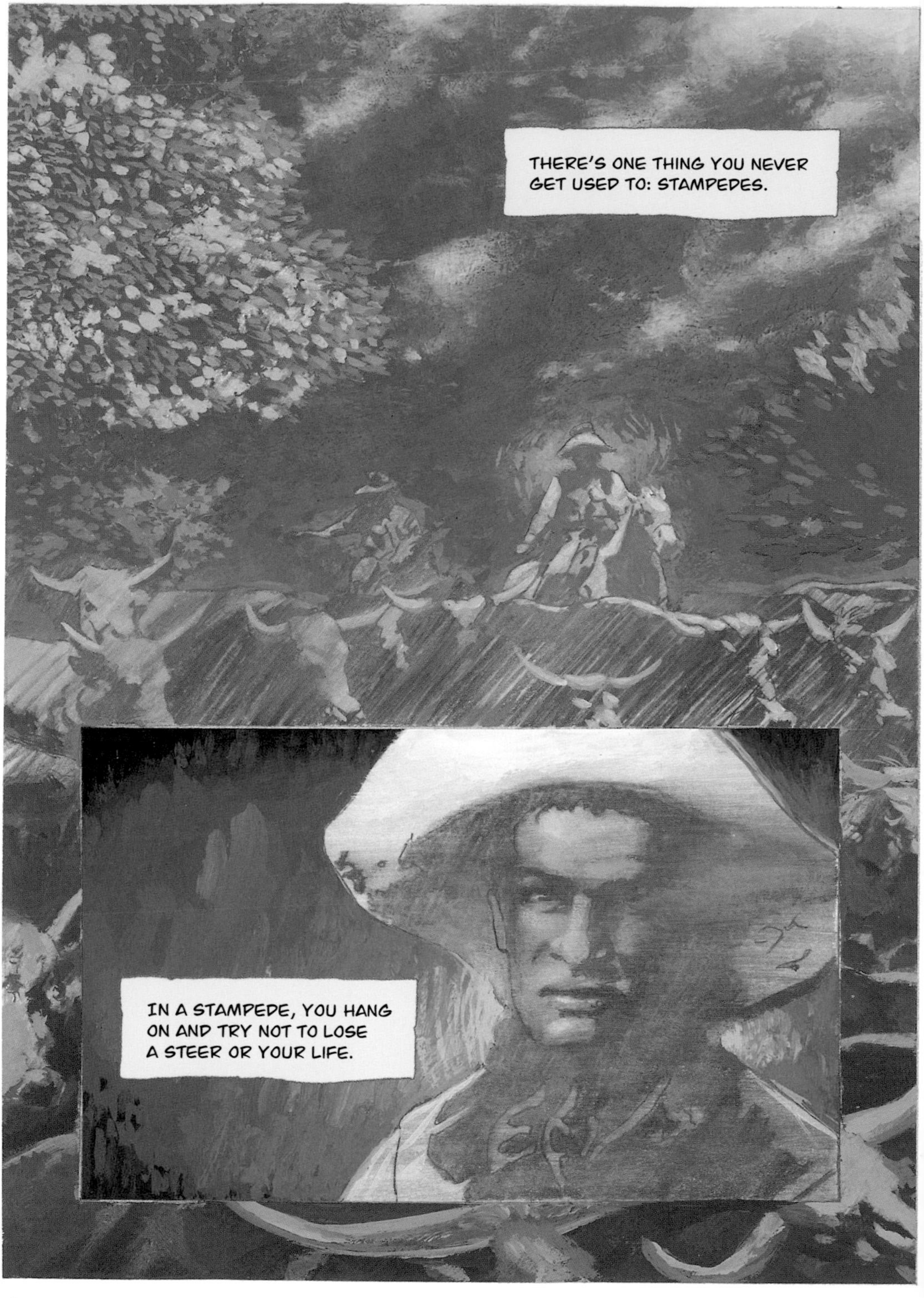
THERE'S ONE THING YOU NEVER GET USED TO: STAMPEDES.
IN A STAMPEDE, YOU HANG ON AND TRY NOT TO LOSE A STEER OR YOUR LIFE.

OCTOBER 1872.

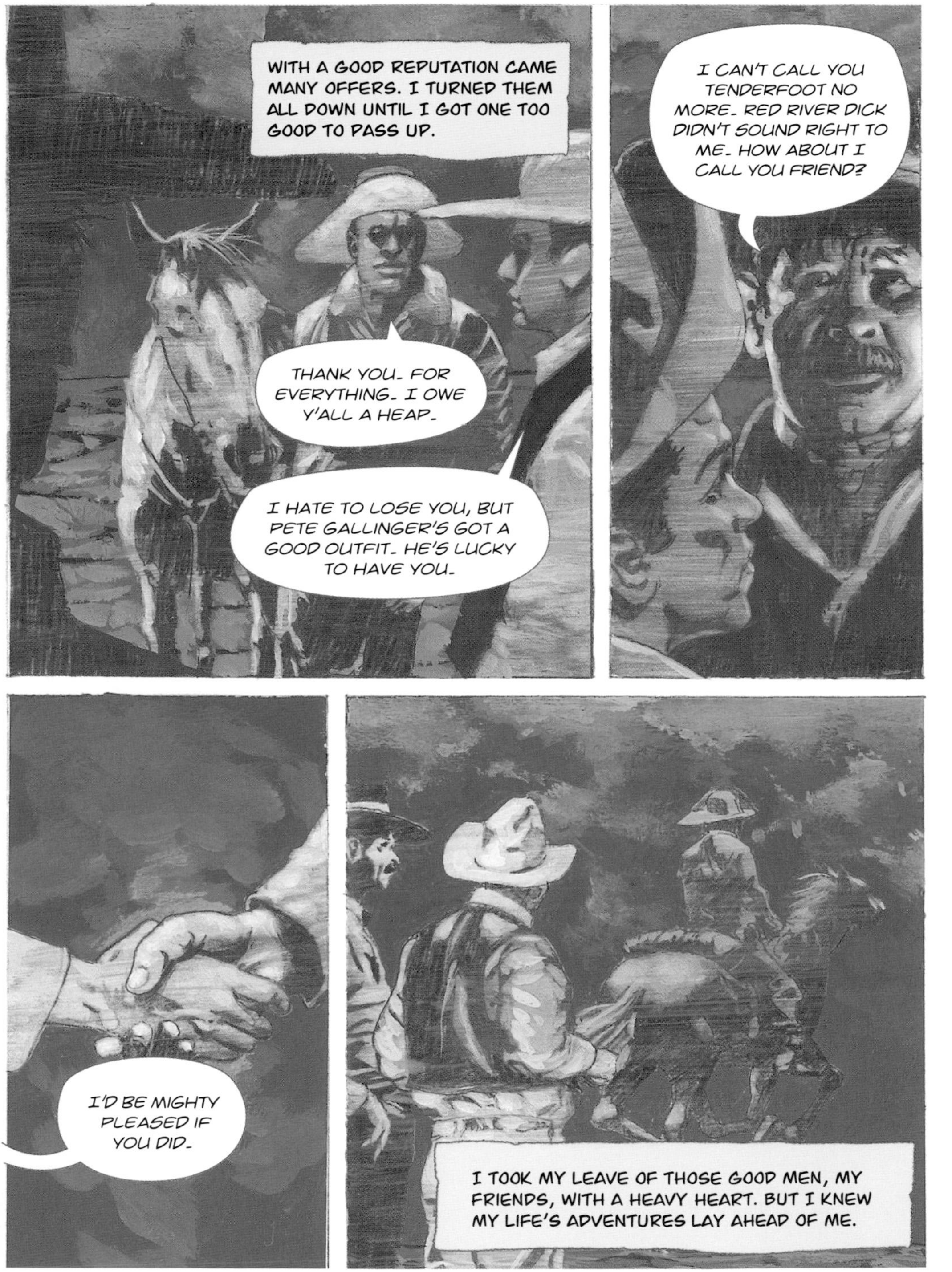

WITH A GOOD REPUTATION CAME MANY OFFERS. I TURNED THEM ALL DOWN UNTIL I GOT ONE TOO GOOD TO PASS UP.
THANK YOU. FOR EVERYTHING. I OWE Y'ALL A HEAP.
I HATE TO LOSE YOU, BUT PETE GALLINGER'S GOT A GOOD OUTFIT. HE'S LUCKY TO HAVE YOU.
I CAN'T CALL YOU TENDERFOOT NO MORE. RED RIVER DICK DIDN'T SOUND RIGHT TO ME. HOW ABOUT I CALL YOU FRIEND?
I'D BE MIGHTY PLEASED IF YOU DID.
I TOOK MY LEAVE OF THOSE GOOD MEN, MY FRIENDS, WITH A HEAVY HEART. BUT I KNEW MY LIFE'S ADVENTURES LAY AHEAD OF ME.

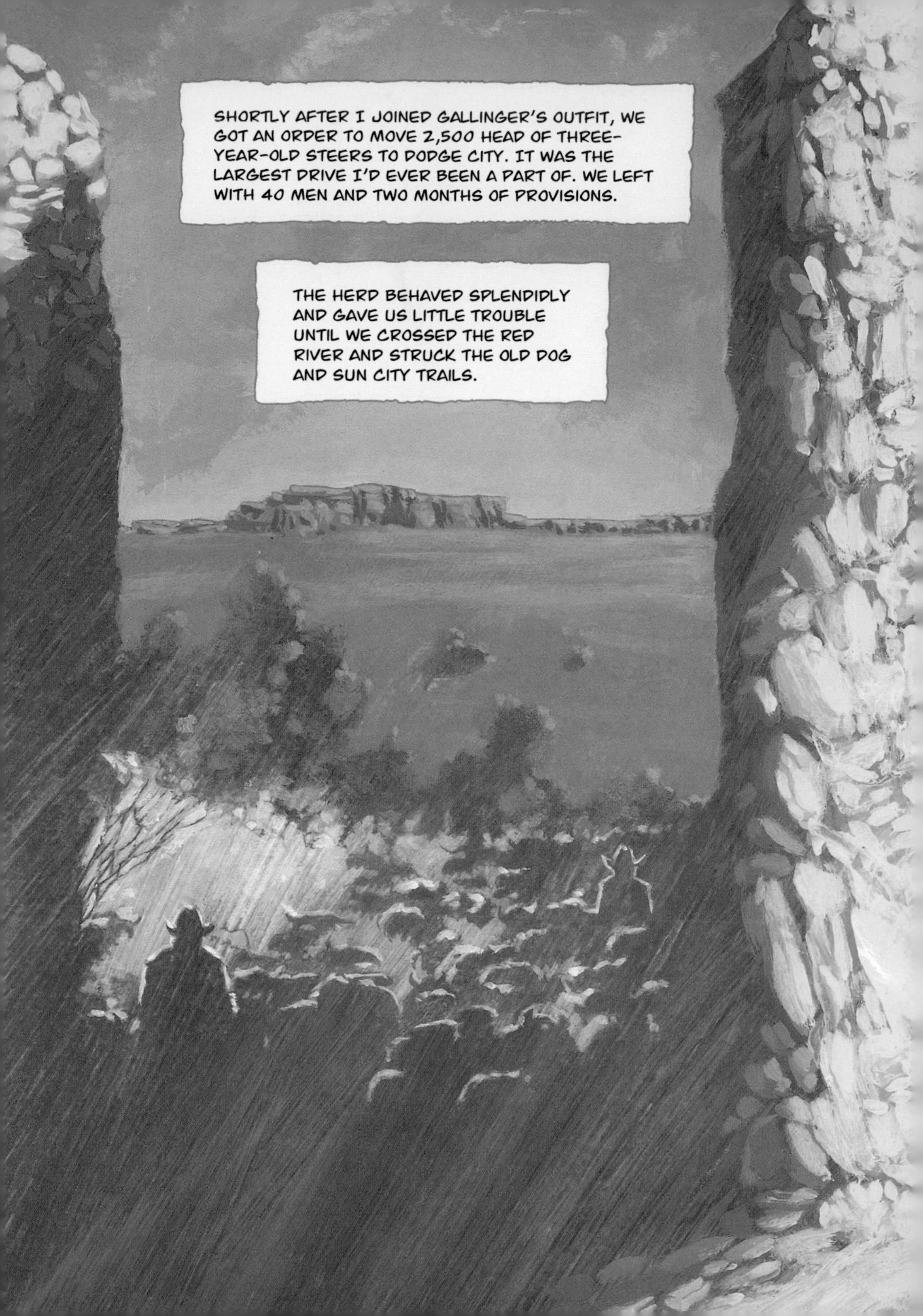
SHORTLY AFTER I JOINED GALLINGER'S OUTFIT, WE GOT AN ORDER TO MOVE 2,500 HEAD OF THREE-YEAR-OLD STEERS TO DODGE CITY. IT WAS THE LARGEST DRIVE I'D EVER BEEN A PART OF. WE LEFT WITH 40 MEN AND TWO MONTHS OF PROVISIONS.
THE HERD BEHAVED SPLENDIDLY AND GAVE US LITTLE TROUBLE UNTIL WE CROSSED THE RED RIVER AND STRUCK THE OLD DOG AND SUN CITY TRAILS.

JUNE 27, 1873. ON THE CHISHOLM TRAIL AT THE OKLAHOMA-KANSAS BORDER.

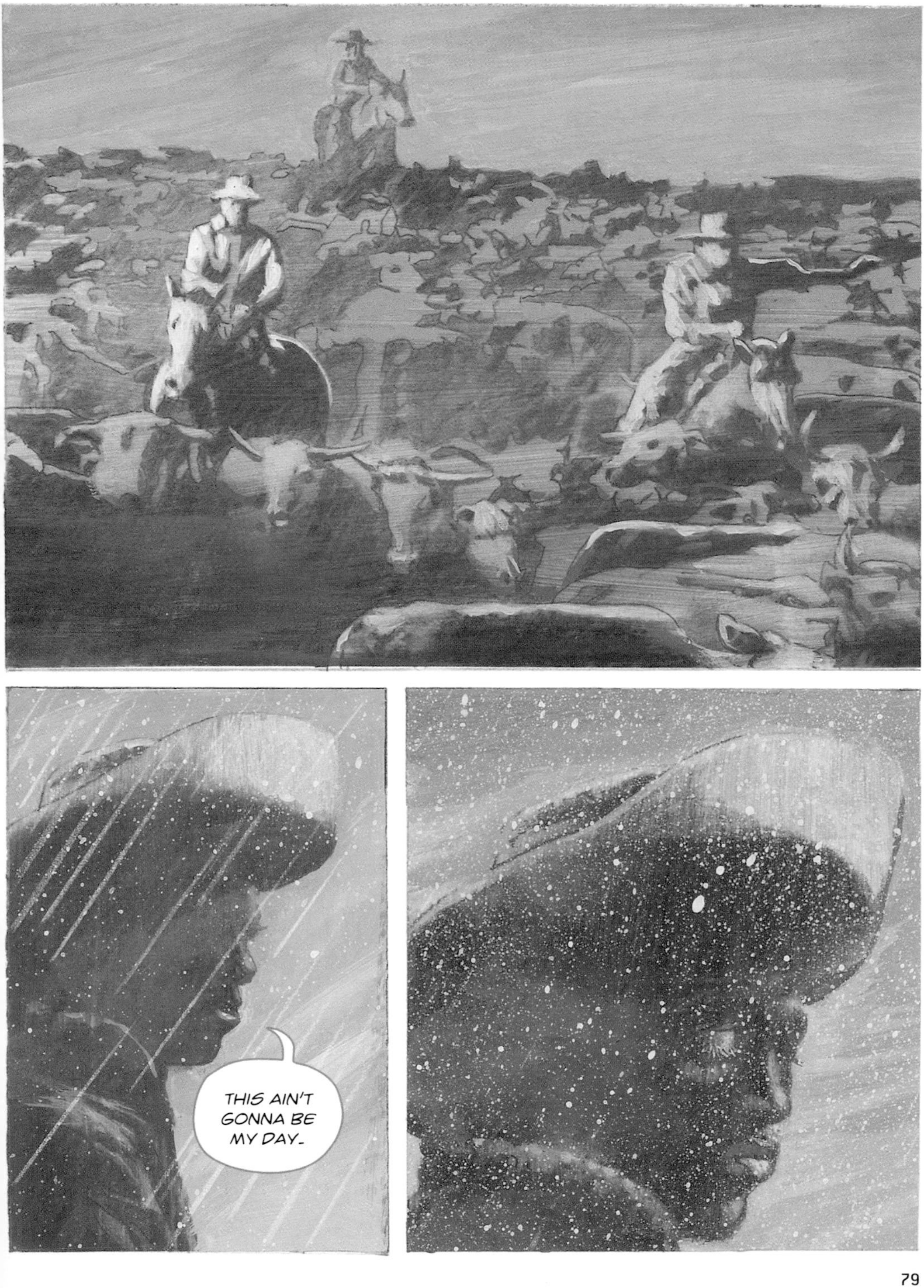
THIS AIN'T GONNA BE MY DAY.

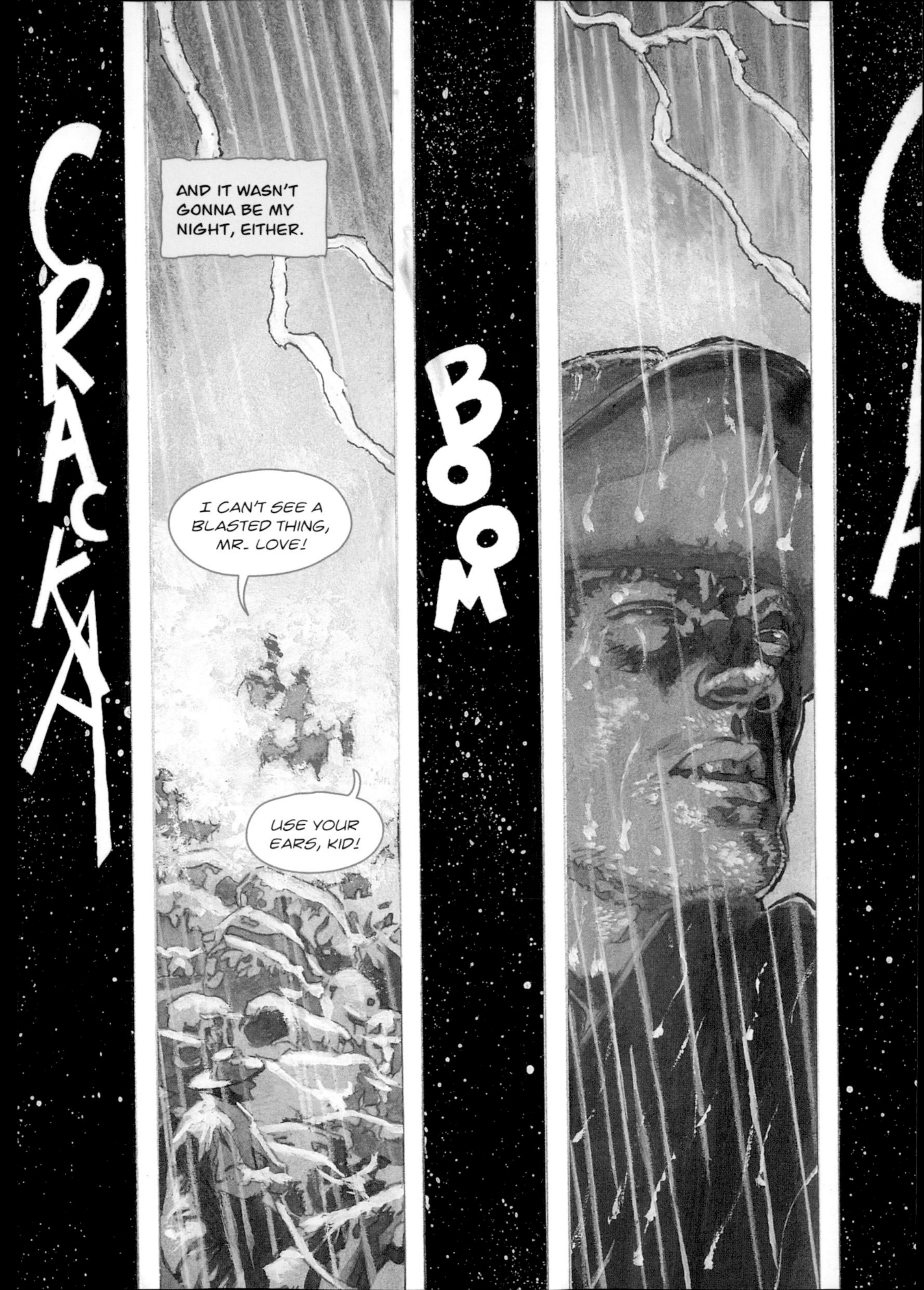
CRACKA
AND IT WASN'T GONNA BE MY NIGHT, EITHER.
I CAN'T SEE A BLASTED THING, MR. LOVE!
USE YOUR EARS, KID!
BOOM

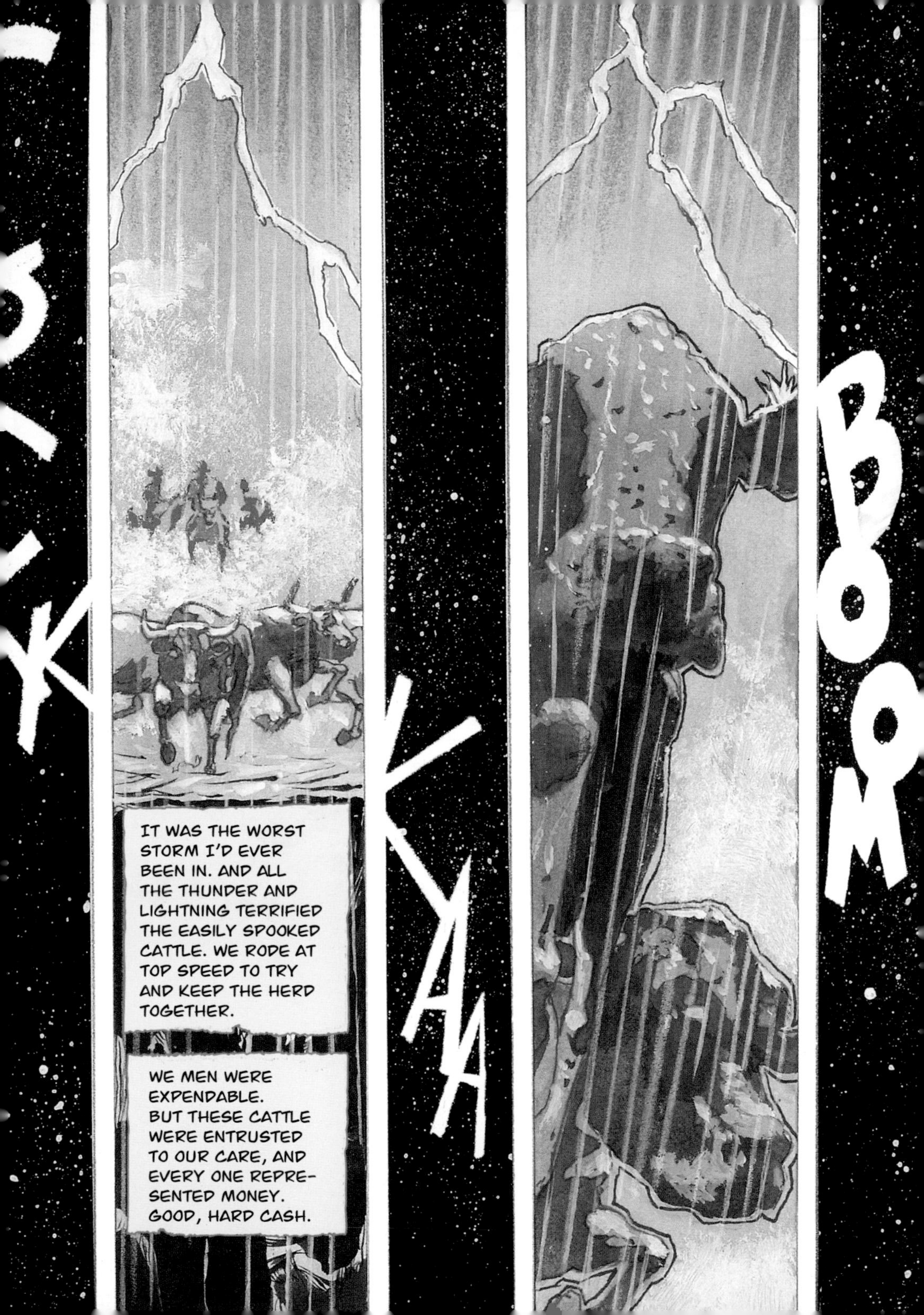
IT WAS THE WORST STORM I'D EVER BEEN IN. AND ALL THE THUNDER AND LIGHTNING TERRIFIED THE EASILY SPOOKED CATTLE. WE RODE AT TOP SPEED TO TRY AND KEEP THE HERD TOGETHER.
WE MEN WERE EXPENDABLE. BUT THESE CATTLE WERE ENTRUSTED TO OUR CARE, AND EVERY ONE REPRESENTED MONEY. GOOD, HARD CASH.
BOOM

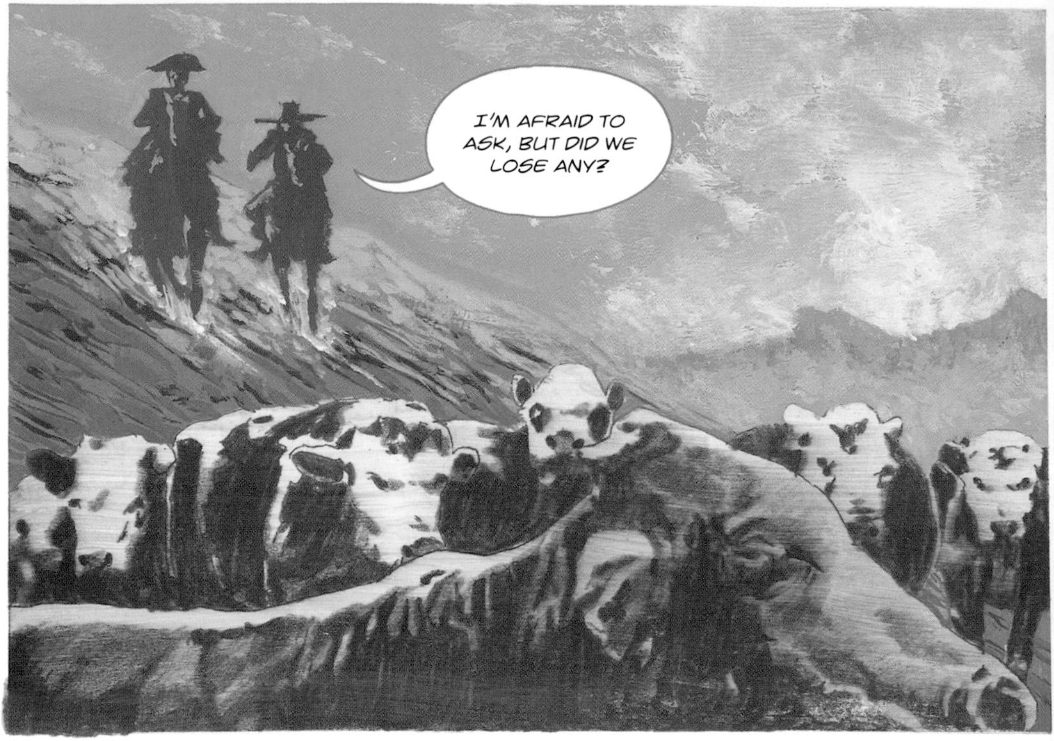
I'M AFRAID TO ASK, BUT DID WE LOSE ANY?

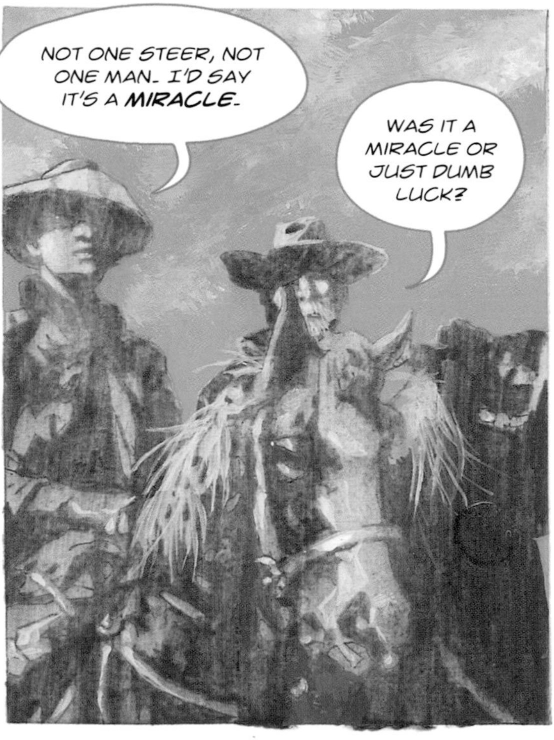
NOT ONE STEER, NOT ONE MAN. I'D SAY IT'S A **MIRACLE**.
WAS IT A MIRACLE OR JUST DUMB LUCK?

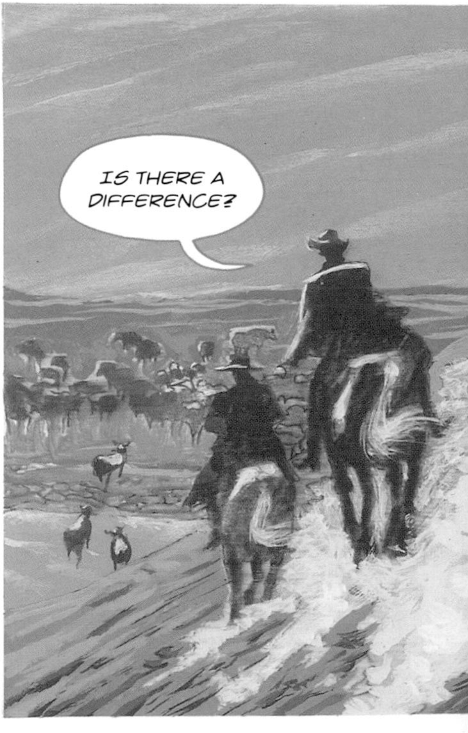
IS THERE A DIFFERENCE?

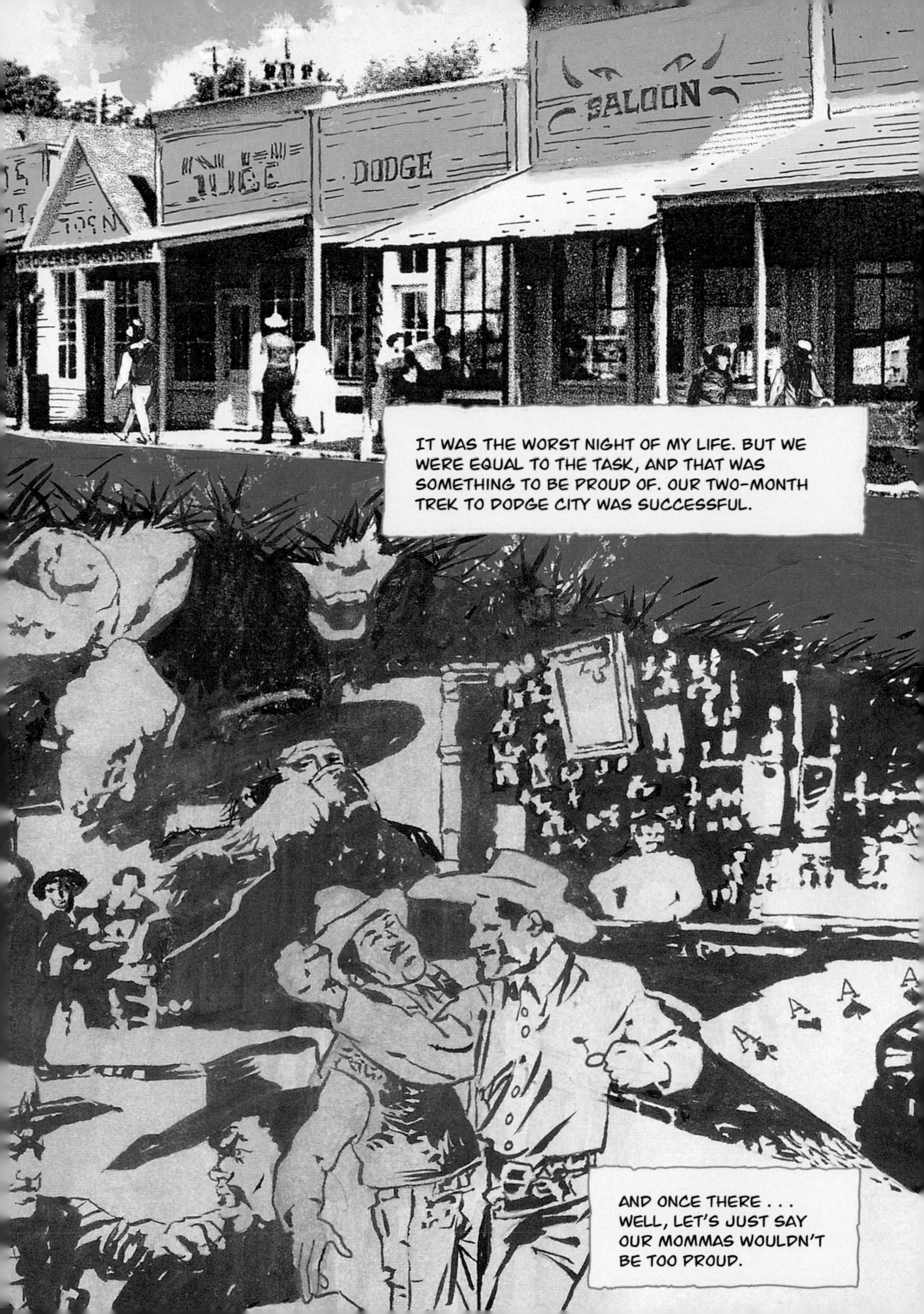
SALOON
DODGE
IT WAS THE WORST NIGHT OF MY LIFE. BUT WE WERE EQUAL TO THE TASK, AND THAT WAS SOMETHING TO BE PROUD OF. OUR TWO-MONTH TREK TO DODGE CITY WAS SUCCESSFUL.
AND ONCE THERE . . . WELL, LET'S JUST SAY OUR MOMMAS WOULDN'T BE TOO PROUD.

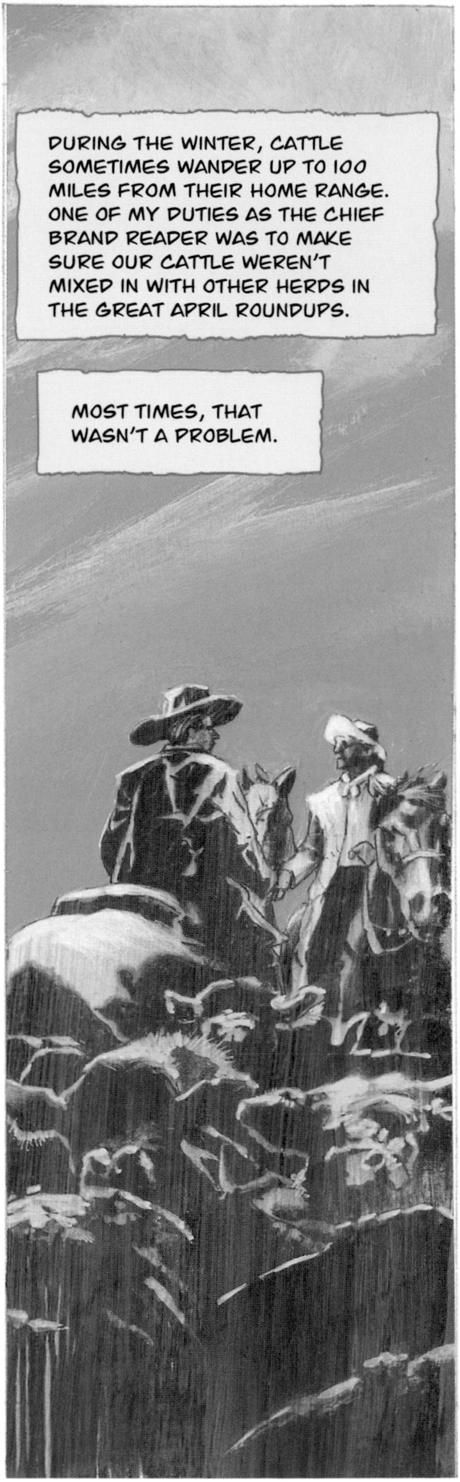
DURING THE WINTER, CATTLE SOMETIMES WANDER UP TO 100 MILES FROM THEIR HOME RANGE. ONE OF MY DUTIES AS THE CHIEF BRAND READER WAS TO MAKE SURE OUR CATTLE WEREN'T MIXED IN WITH OTHER HERDS IN THE GREAT APRIL ROUNDUPS.
MOST TIMES, THAT WASN'T A PROBLEM.

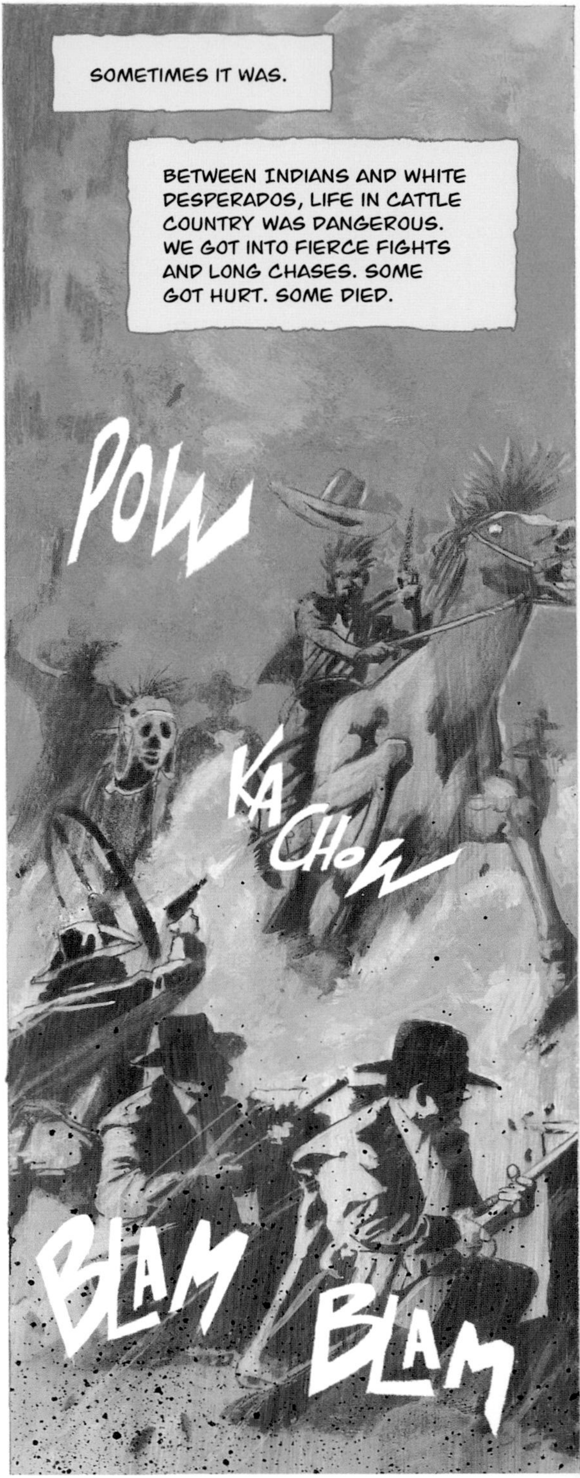
SOMETIMES IT WAS.
BETWEEN INDIANS AND WHITE DESPERADOS, LIFE IN CATTLE COUNTRY WAS DANGEROUS. WE GOT INTO FIERCE FIGHTS AND LONG CHASES. SOME GOT HURT. SOME DIED.
POW
KA CHOW
BLAM
BLAM

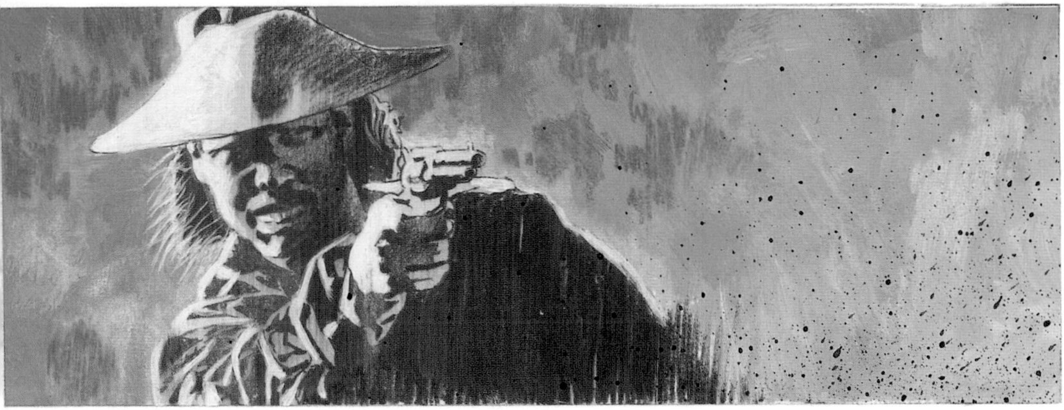

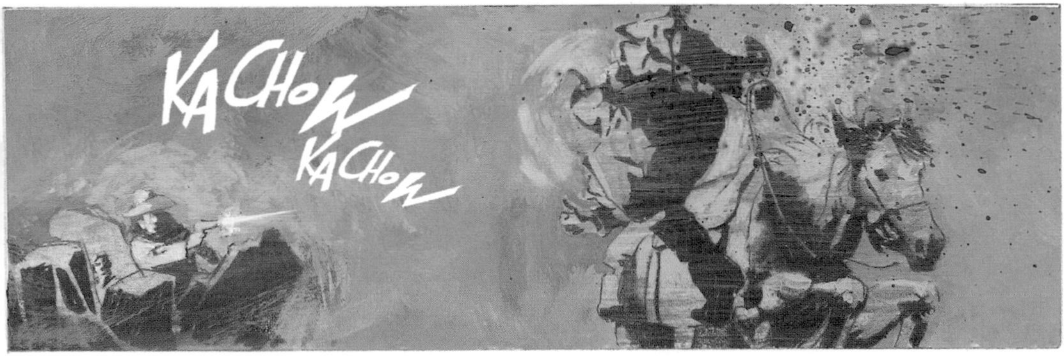
KACHOW
KACHOW

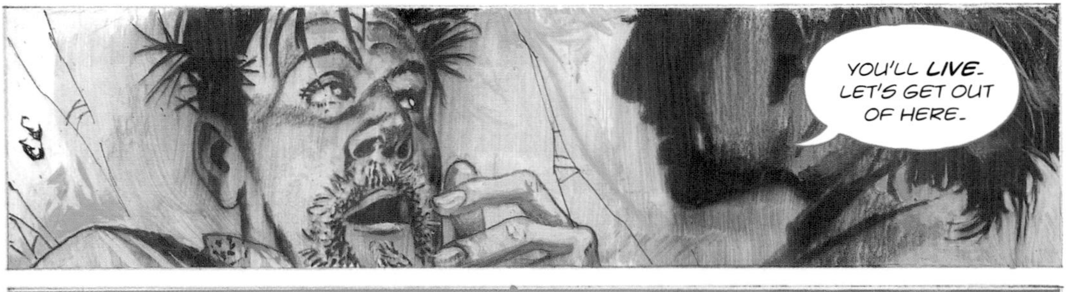
YOU'LL **LIVE**. LET'S GET OUT OF HERE.

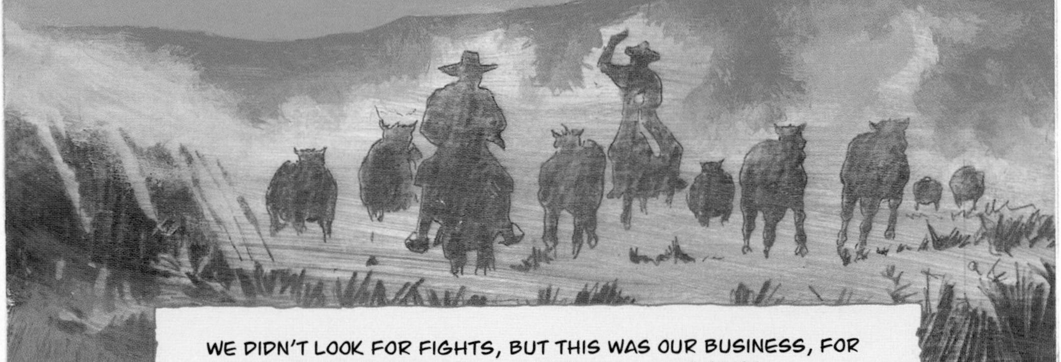
WE DIDN'T LOOK FOR FIGHTS, BUT THIS WAS OUR BUSINESS, FOR WHICH WE WERE PAID GOOD. WE TOOK LIFE AS IT CAME.

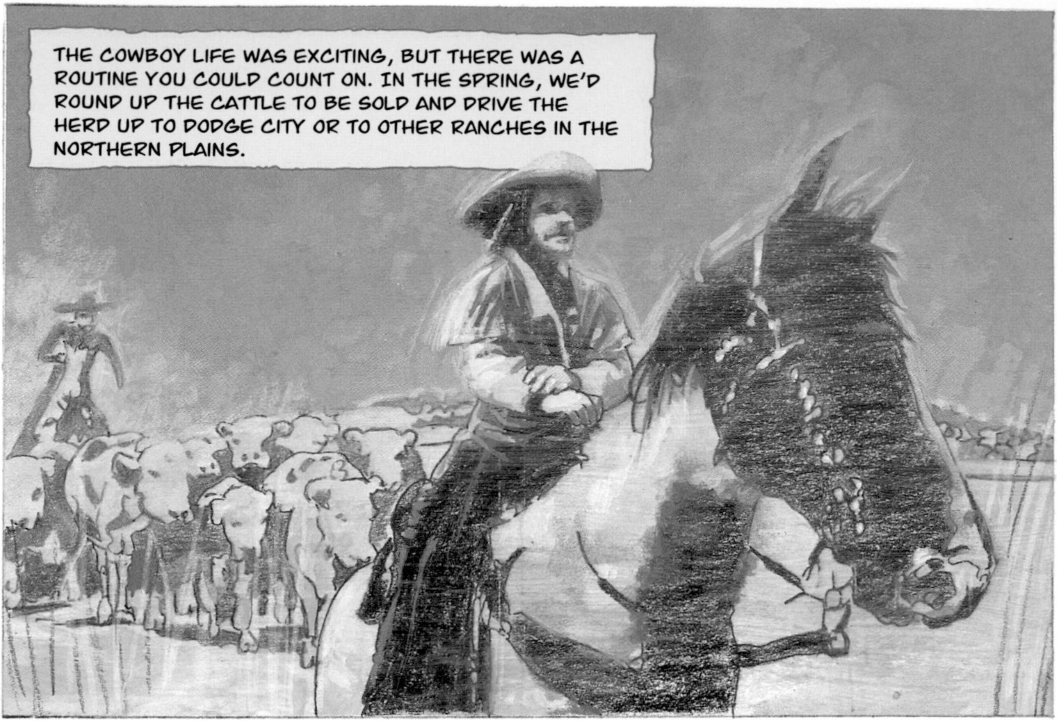
THE COWBOY LIFE WAS EXCITING, BUT THERE WAS A ROUTINE YOU COULD COUNT ON. IN THE SPRING, WE'D ROUND UP THE CATTLE TO BE SOLD AND DRIVE THE HERD UP TO DODGE CITY OR TO OTHER RANCHES IN THE NORTHERN PLAINS.

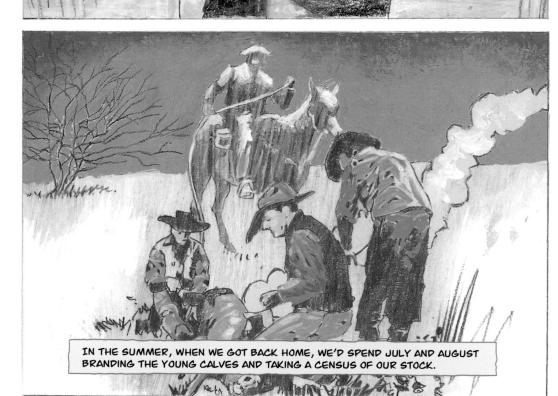

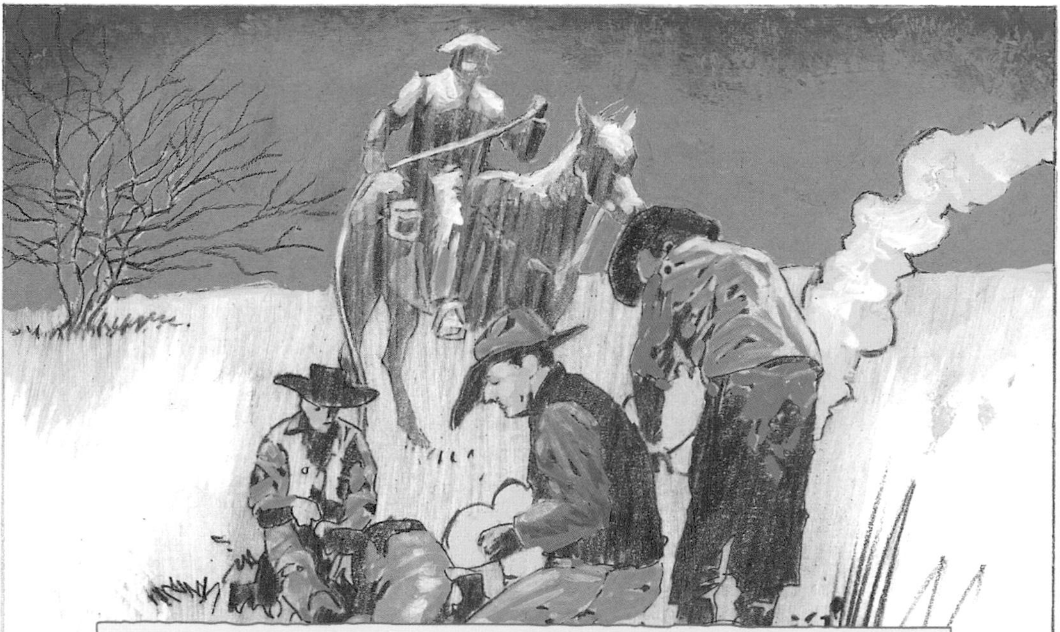
IN THE SUMMER, WHEN WE GOT BACK HOME, WE'D SPEND JULY AND AUGUST BRANDING THE YOUNG CALVES AND TAKING A CENSUS OF OUR STOCK.

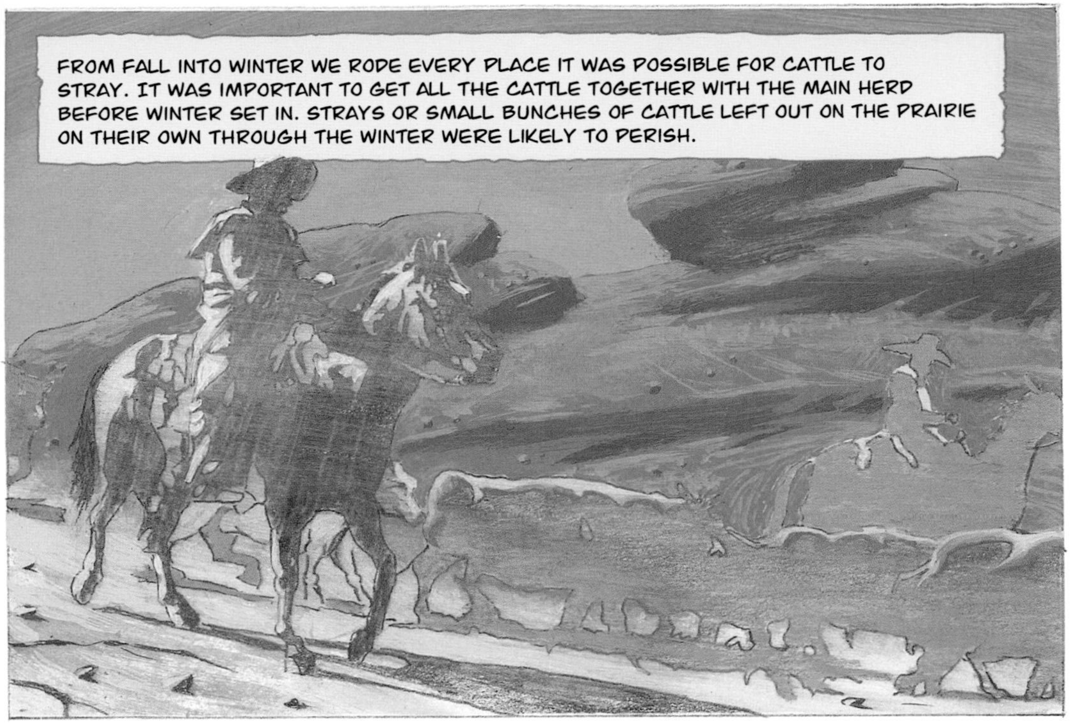
FROM FALL INTO WINTER WE RODE EVERY PLACE IT WAS POSSIBLE FOR CATTLE TO STRAY. IT WAS IMPORTANT TO GET ALL THE CATTLE TOGETHER WITH THE MAIN HERD BEFORE WINTER SET IN. STRAYS OR SMALL BUNCHES OF CATTLE LEFT OUT ON THE PRAIRIE ON THEIR OWN THROUGH THE WINTER WERE LIKELY TO PERISH.

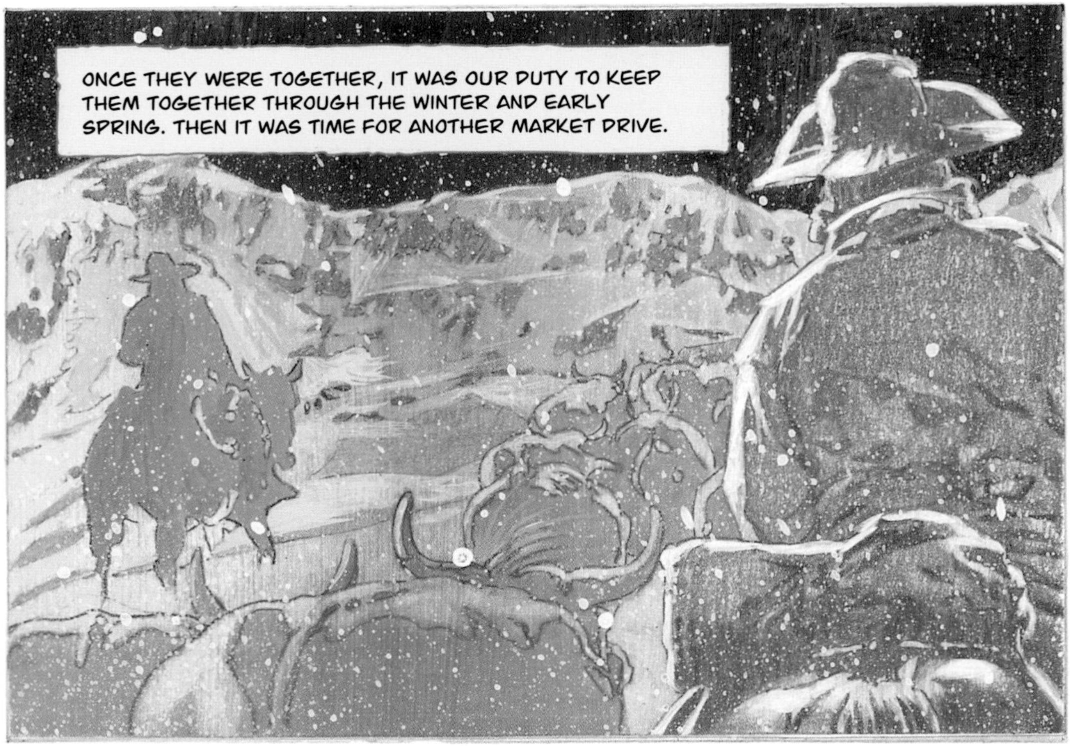
ONCE THEY WERE TOGETHER, IT WAS OUR DUTY TO KEEP THEM TOGETHER THROUGH THE WINTER AND EARLY SPRING. THEN IT WAS TIME FOR ANOTHER MARKET DRIVE.

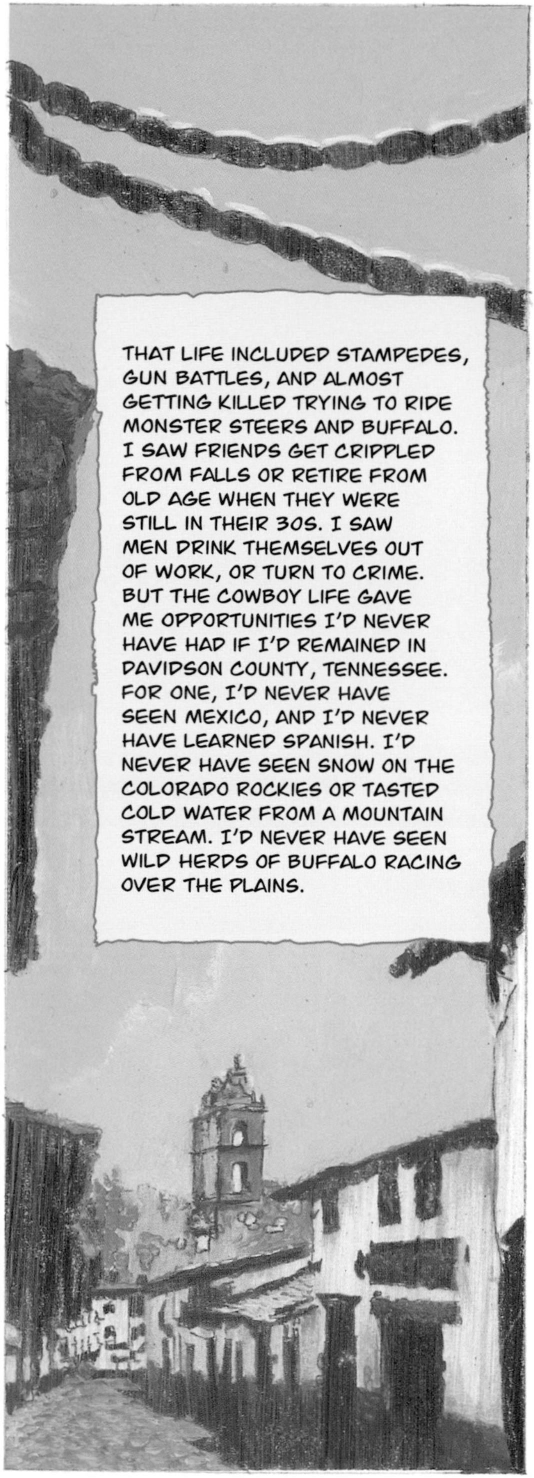
THAT LIFE INCLUDED STAMPEDES, GUN BATTLES, AND ALMOST GETTING KILLED TRYING TO RIDE MONSTER STEERS AND BUFFALO. I SAW FRIENDS GET CRIPPLED FROM FALLS OR RETIRE FROM OLD AGE WHEN THEY WERE STILL IN THEIR 30S. I SAW MEN DRINK THEMSELVES OUT OF WORK, OR TURN TO CRIME. BUT THE COWBOY LIFE GAVE ME OPPORTUNITIES I'D NEVER HAVE HAD IF I'D REMAINED IN DAVIDSON COUNTY, TENNESSEE. FOR ONE, I'D NEVER HAVE SEEN MEXICO, AND I'D NEVER HAVE LEARNED SPANISH. I'D NEVER HAVE SEEN SNOW ON THE COLORADO ROCKIES OR TASTED COLD WATER FROM A MOUNTAIN STREAM. I'D NEVER HAVE SEEN WILD HERDS OF BUFFALO RACING OVER THE PLAINS.

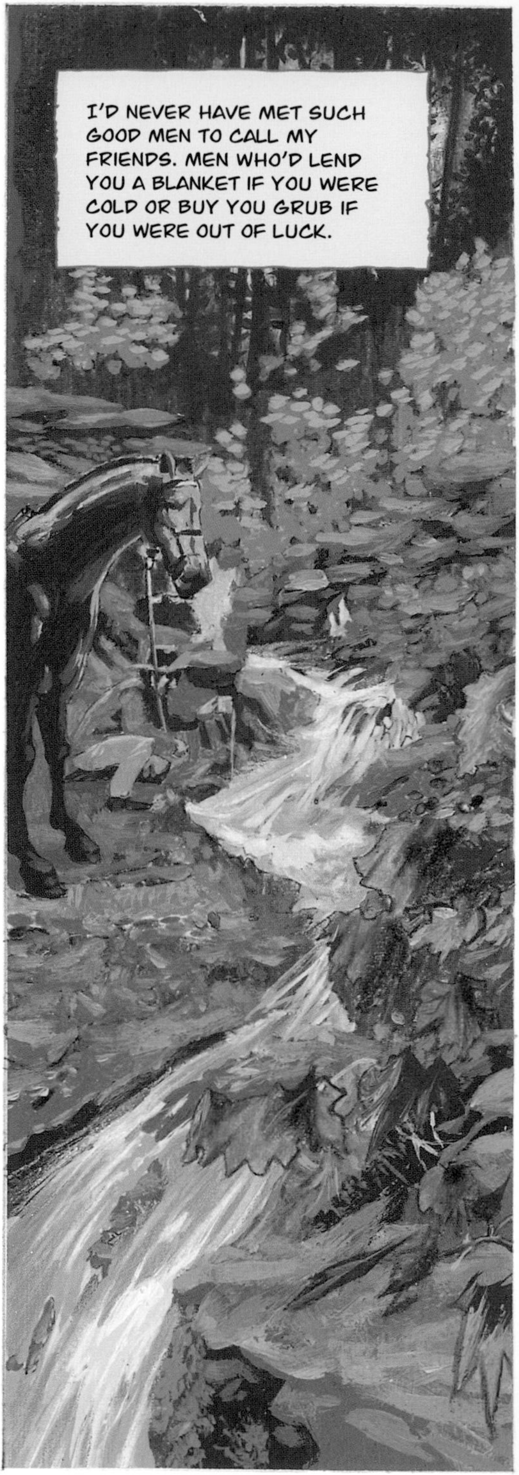
I'D NEVER HAVE MET SUCH GOOD MEN TO CALL MY FRIENDS. MEN WHO'D LEND YOU A BLANKET IF YOU WERE COLD OR BUY YOU GRUB IF YOU WERE OUT OF LUCK.

IN ORDER TO LIVE IN THE OLD WEST, A COWBOY COULDN'T LIVE IN FEAR. I KNEW MANY MEN WHO DIED JUST DOING THEIR JOBS. AND THERE WERE PLENTY OF TIMES I THOUGHT I WAS ONLY A HEARTBEAT AWAY FROM MEETING MY MAKER.

TAKE THE TIME WE PICKED UP 500 FOUR-YEAR-OLD STEERS DOWN ON THE RIO GRANDE AND HEADED NORTH TO A RANCH UP IN NORTHERN WYOMING.

WHEN WE HIT INDIANA TERRITORY, WE SPENT TENSE NIGHTS WITH OUR BOOTS ON AND OUR GUNS AT OUR SIDES. IF WE WEREN'T THINKING ABOUT INDIAN ATTACKS, WE WERE WORRYING ABOUT THE HERD STAMPEDING. I DIDN'T THINK THINGS COULD GET ANY WORSE.

THEY DID.

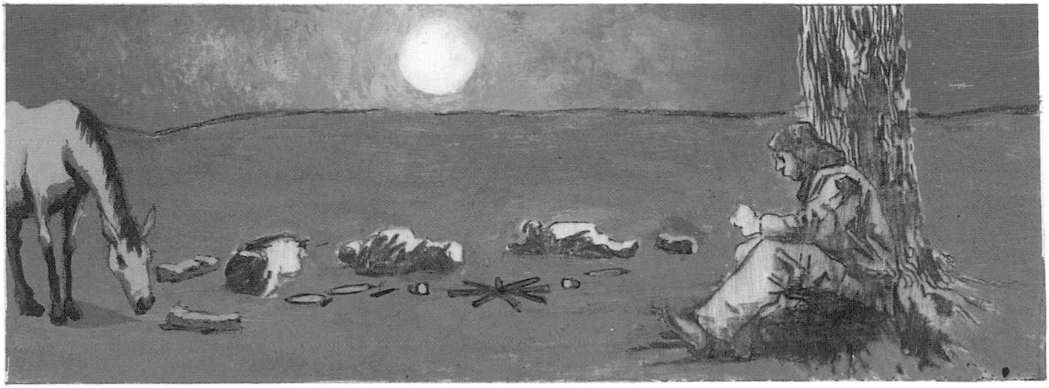

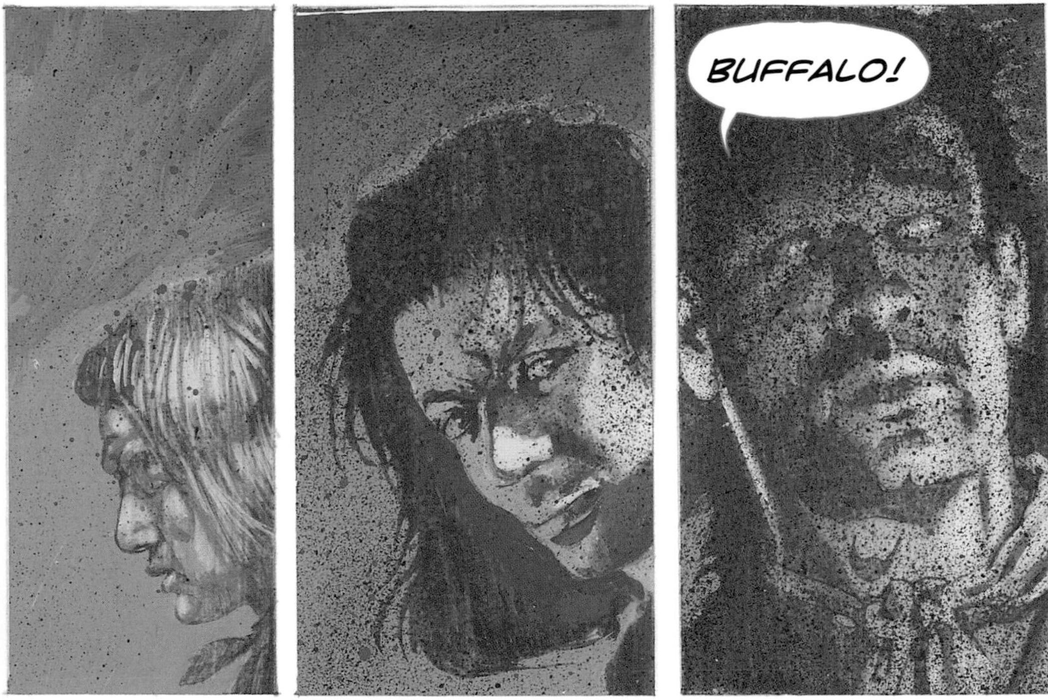
BUFFALO!

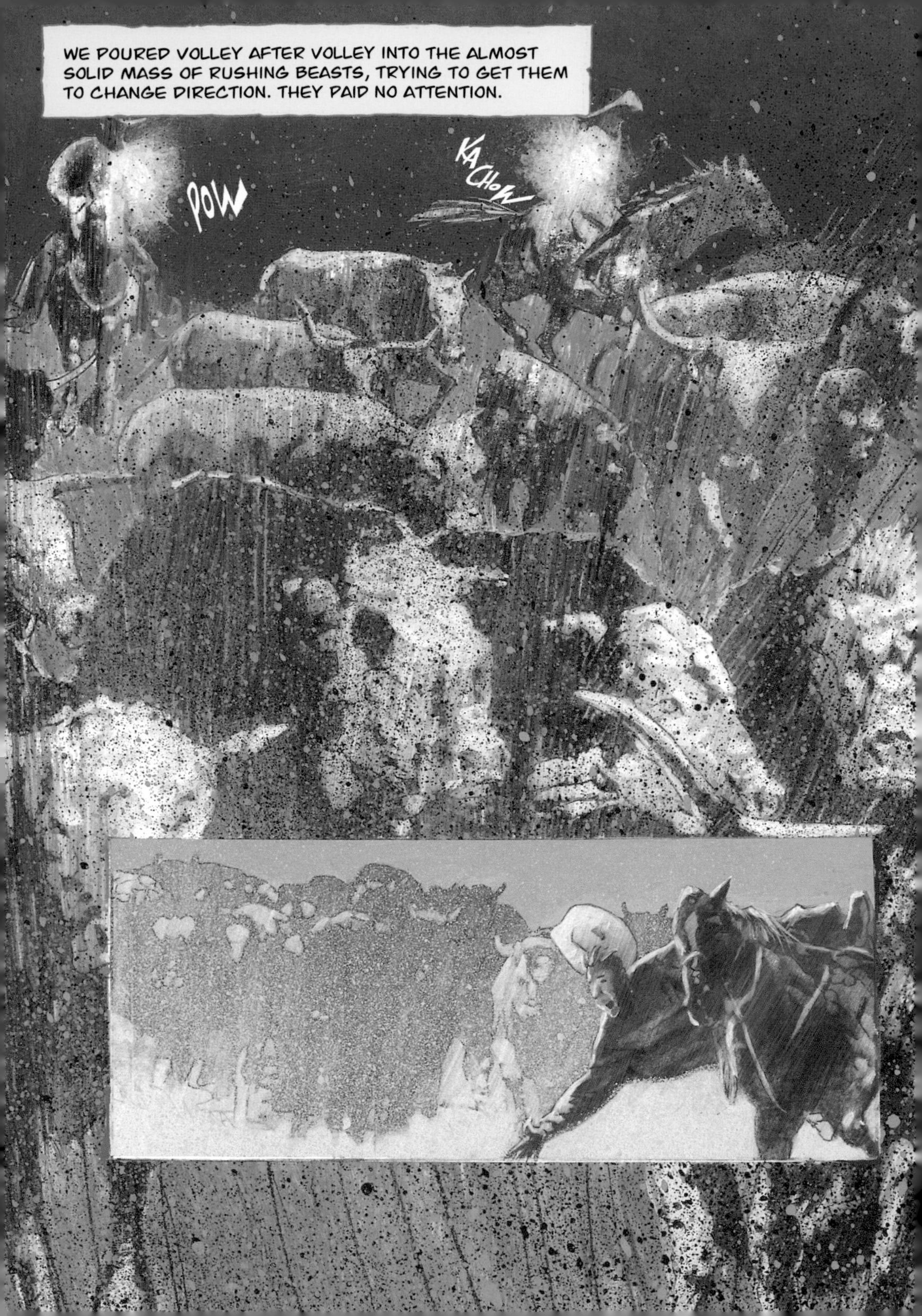
WE POURED VOLLEY AFTER VOLLEY INTO THE ALMOST SOLID MASS OF RUSHING BEASTS, TRYING TO GET THEM TO CHANGE DIRECTION. THEY PAID NO ATTENTION.
POW
KACHOW

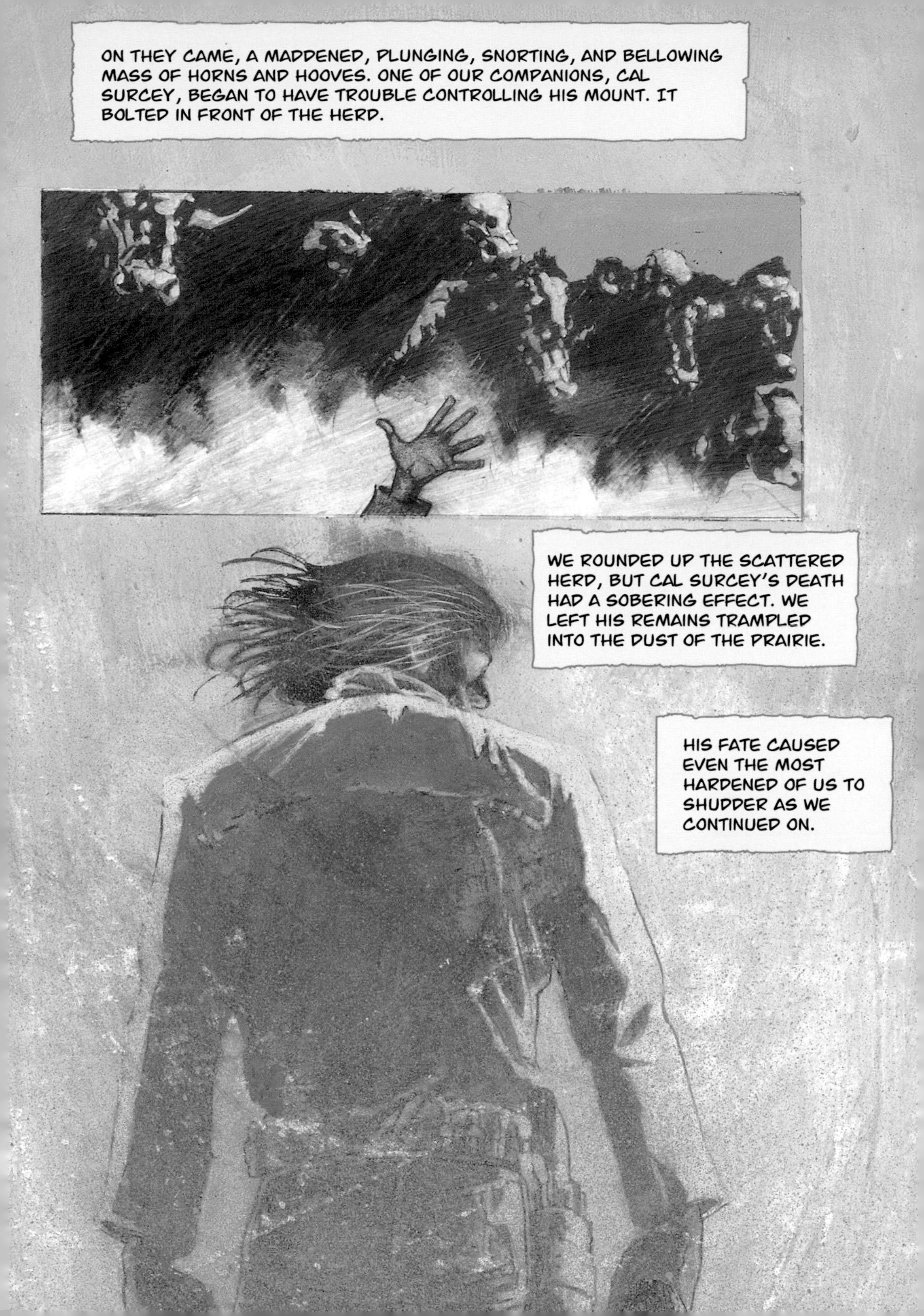
ON THEY CAME, A MADDENED, PLUNGING, SNORTING, AND BELLOWING MASS OF HORNS AND HOOVES. ONE OF OUR COMPANIONS, CAL SURCEY, BEGAN TO HAVE TROUBLE CONTROLLING HIS MOUNT. IT BOLTED IN FRONT OF THE HERD.
WE ROUNDED UP THE SCATTERED HERD, BUT CAL SURCEY'S DEATH HAD A SOBERING EFFECT. WE LEFT HIS REMAINS TRAMPLED INTO THE DUST OF THE PRAIRIE.
HIS FATE CAUSED EVEN THE MOST HARDENED OF US TO SHUDDER AS WE CONTINUED ON.

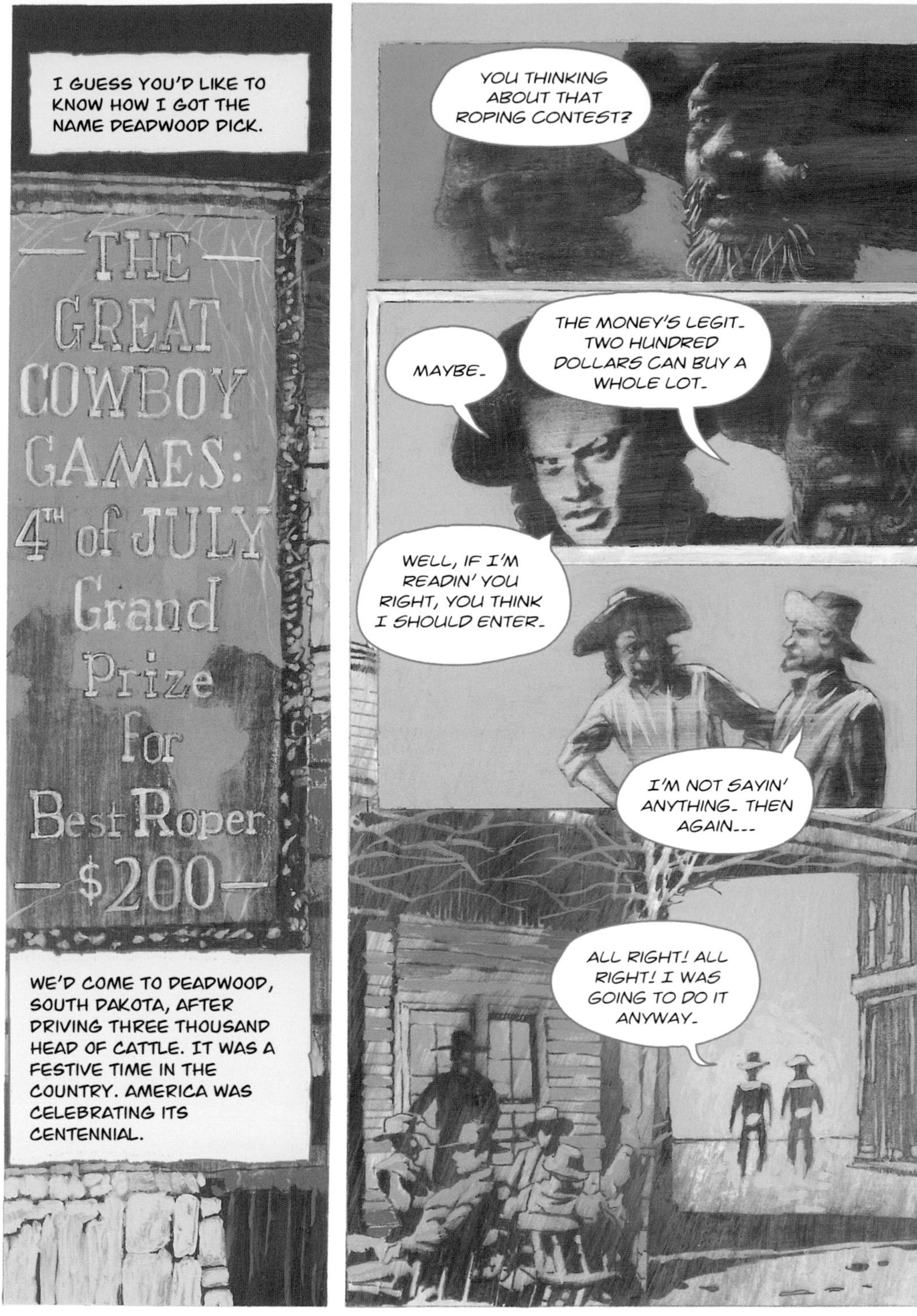
I GUESS YOU'D LIKE TO KNOW HOW I GOT THE NAME DEADWOOD DICK.
THE GREAT COWBOY GAMES: 4TH of JULY Grand Prize For Best Roper $200
WE'D COME TO DEADWOOD, SOUTH DAKOTA, AFTER DRIVING THREE THOUSAND HEAD OF CATTLE. IT WAS A FESTIVE TIME IN THE COUNTRY. AMERICA WAS CELEBRATING ITS CENTENNIAL.
YOU THINKING ABOUT THAT ROPING CONTEST?
MAYBE.
THE MONEY'S LEGIT. TWO HUNDRED DOLLARS CAN BUY A WHOLE LOT.
WELL, IF I'M READIN' YOU RIGHT, YOU THINK I SHOULD ENTER.
I'M NOT SAYIN' ANYTHING. THEN AGAIN...
ALL RIGHT! ALL RIGHT! I WAS GOING TO DO IT ANYWAY.

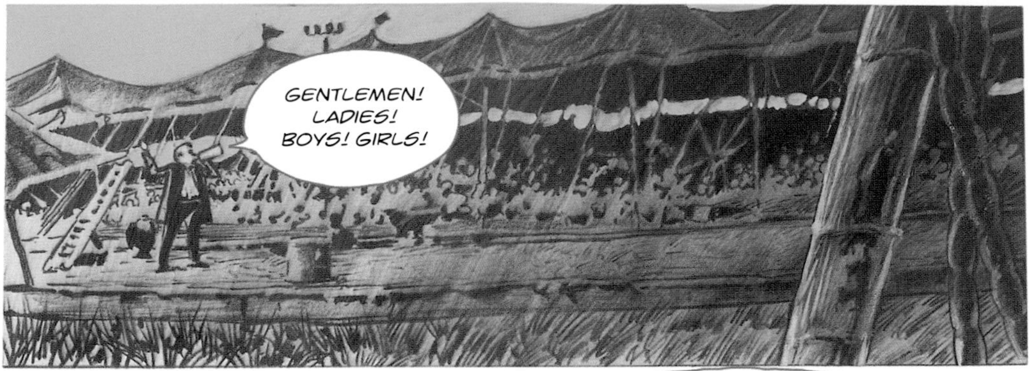
GENTLEMEN! LADIES! BOYS! GIRLS!

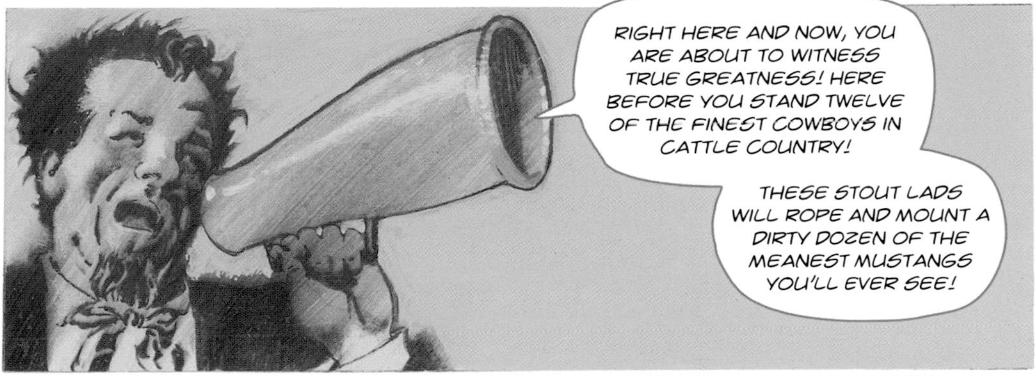
RIGHT HERE AND NOW, YOU ARE ABOUT TO WITNESS TRUE GREATNESS! HERE BEFORE YOU STAND TWELVE OF THE FINEST COWBOYS IN CATTLE COUNTRY!
THESE STOUT LADS WILL ROPE AND MOUNT A DIRTY DOZEN OF THE MEANEST MUSTANGS YOU'LL EVER SEE!

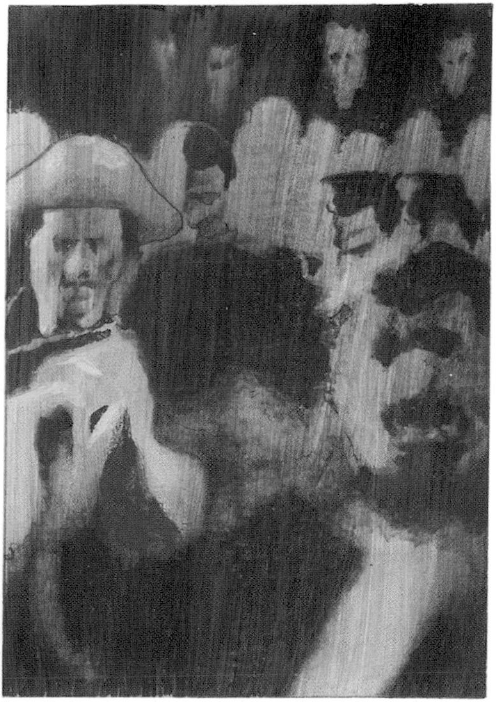

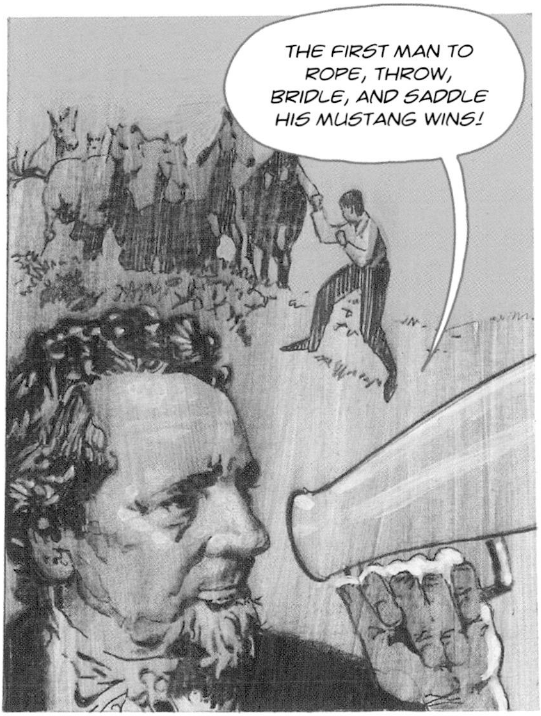
THE FIRST MAN TO ROPE, THROW, BRIDLE, AND SADDLE HIS MUSTANG WINS!

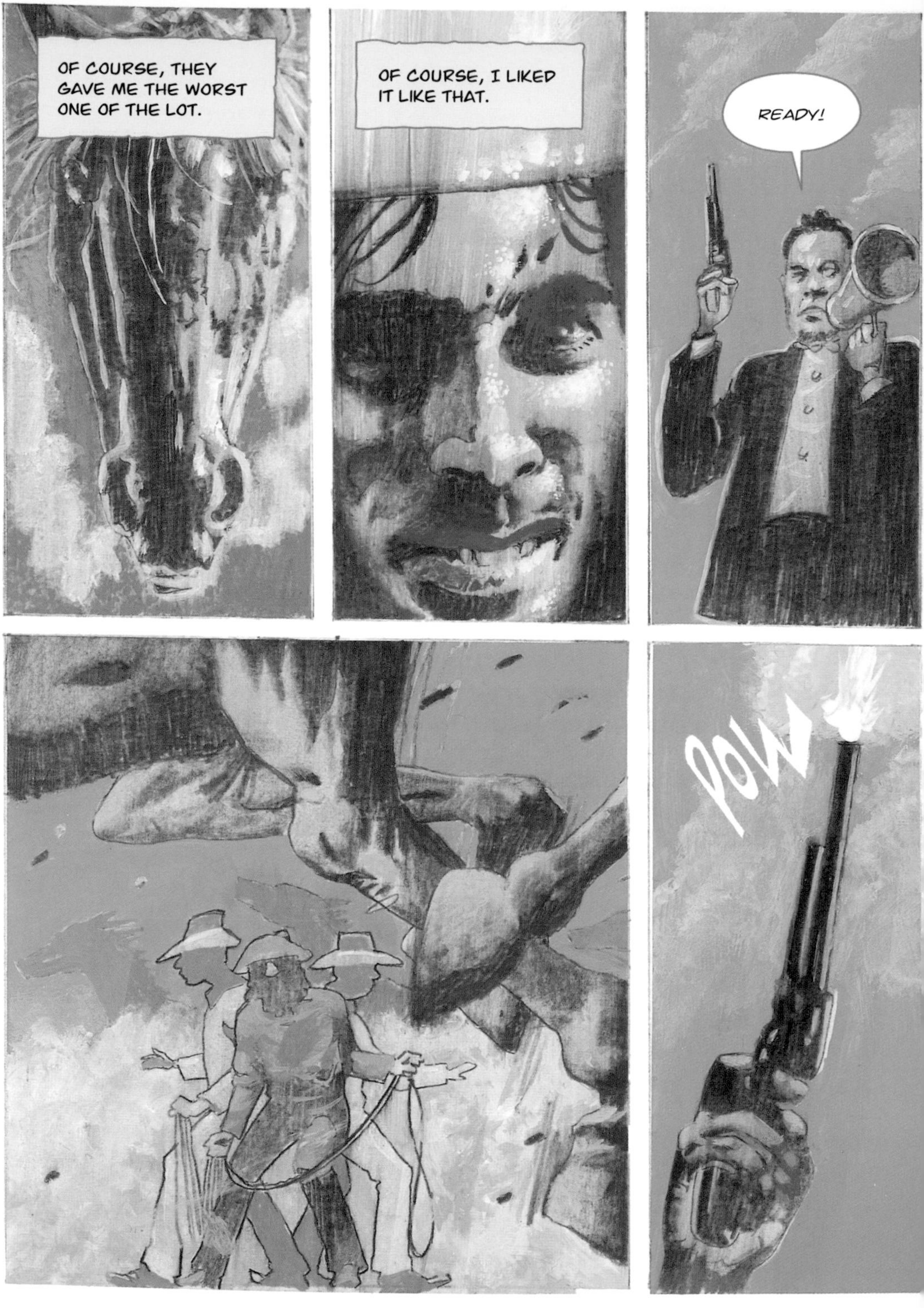
OF COURSE, THEY GAVE ME THE WORST ONE OF THE LOT.
OF COURSE, I LIKED IT LIKE THAT.
READY!
POW

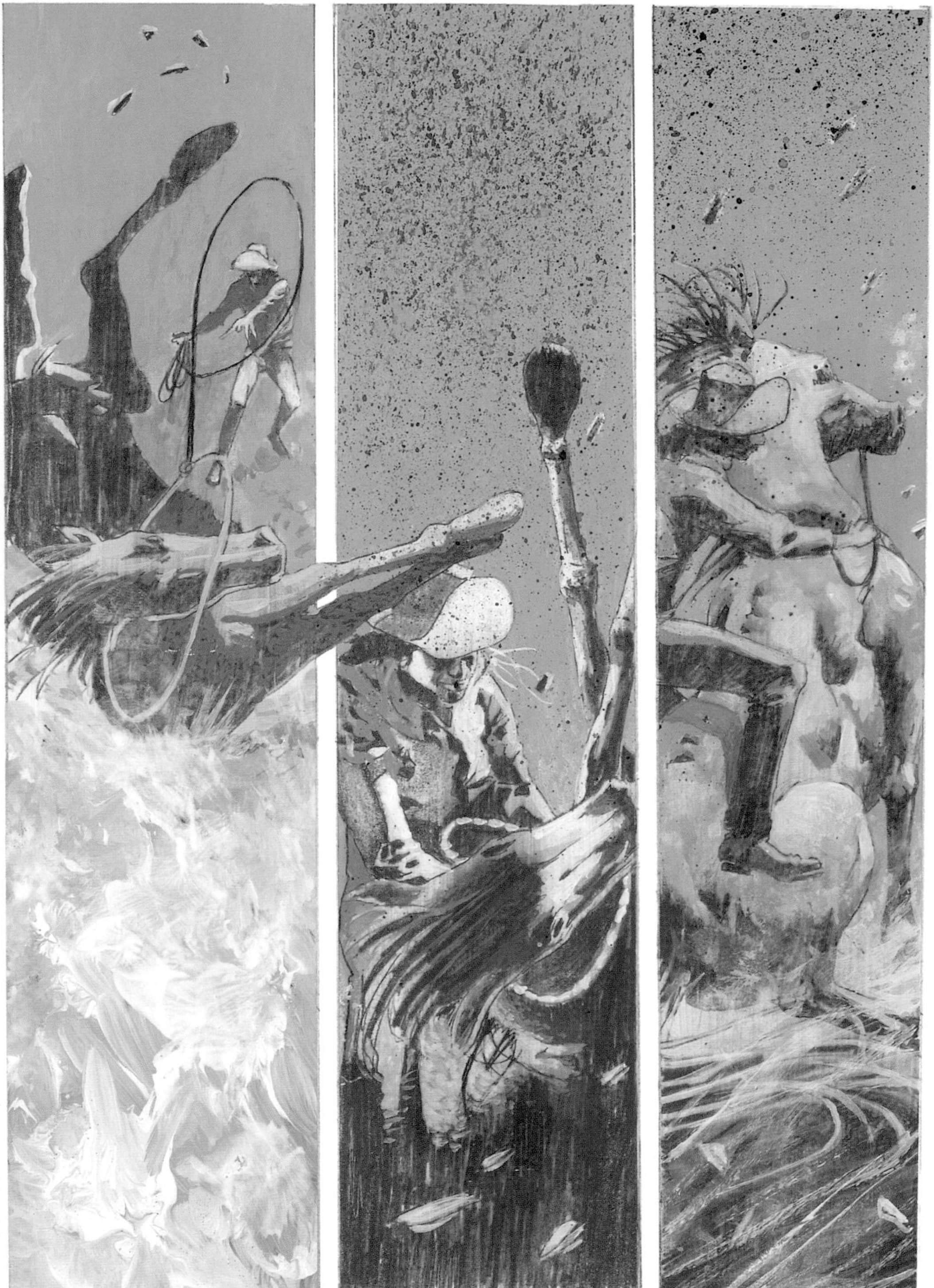

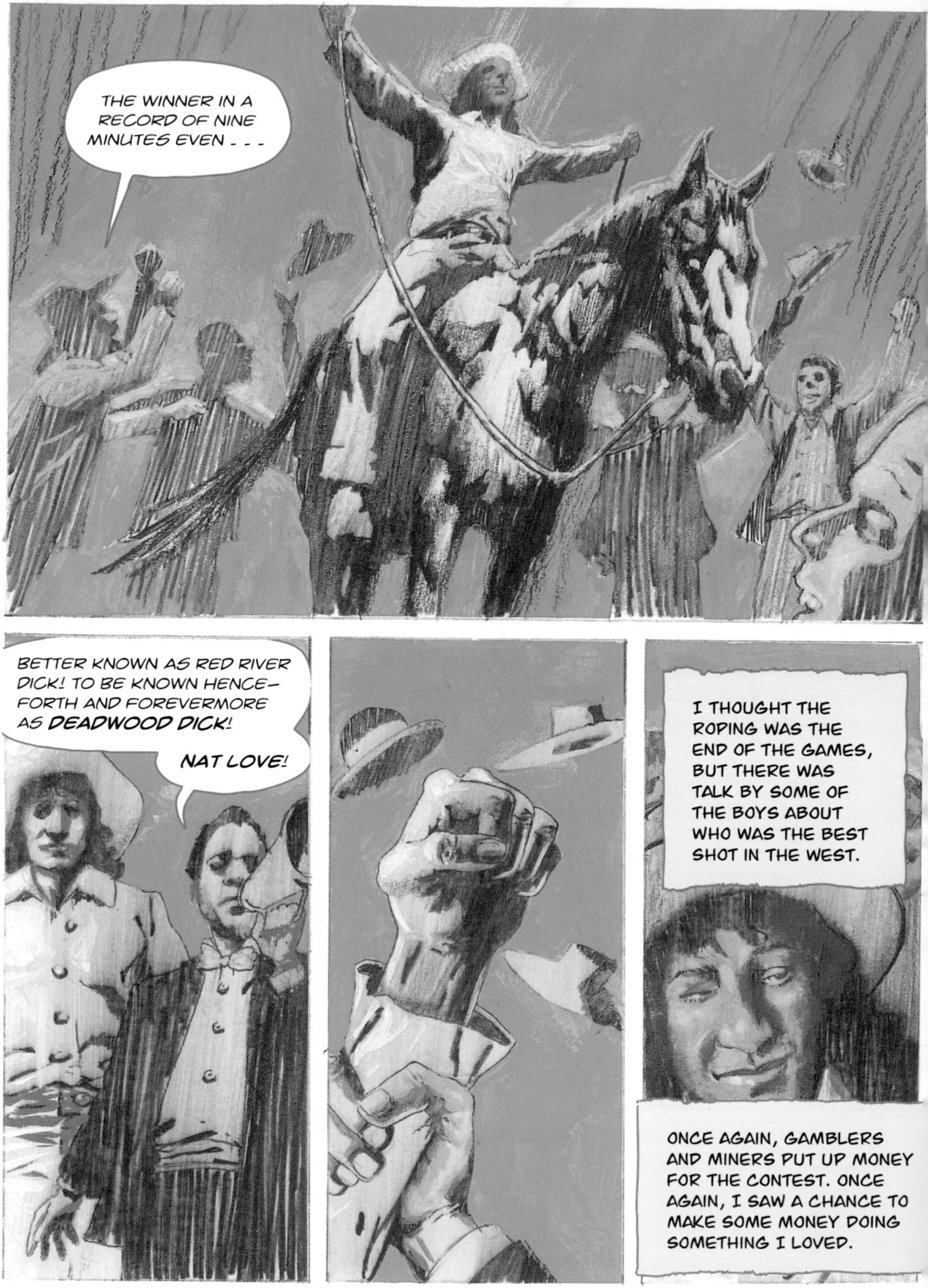
THE WINNER IN A RECORD OF NINE MINUTES EVEN . . .
BETTER KNOWN AS RED RIVER DICK! TO BE KNOWN HENCE-FORTH AND FOREVERMORE AS DEADWOOD DICK!
NAT LOVE!
I THOUGHT THE ROPING WAS THE END OF THE GAMES, BUT THERE WAS TALK BY SOME OF THE BOYS ABOUT WHO WAS THE BEST SHOT IN THE WEST.
ONCE AGAIN, GAMBLERS AND MINERS PUT UP MONEY FOR THE CONTEST. ONCE AGAIN, I SAW A CHANCE TO MAKE SOME MONEY DOING SOMETHING I LOVED.

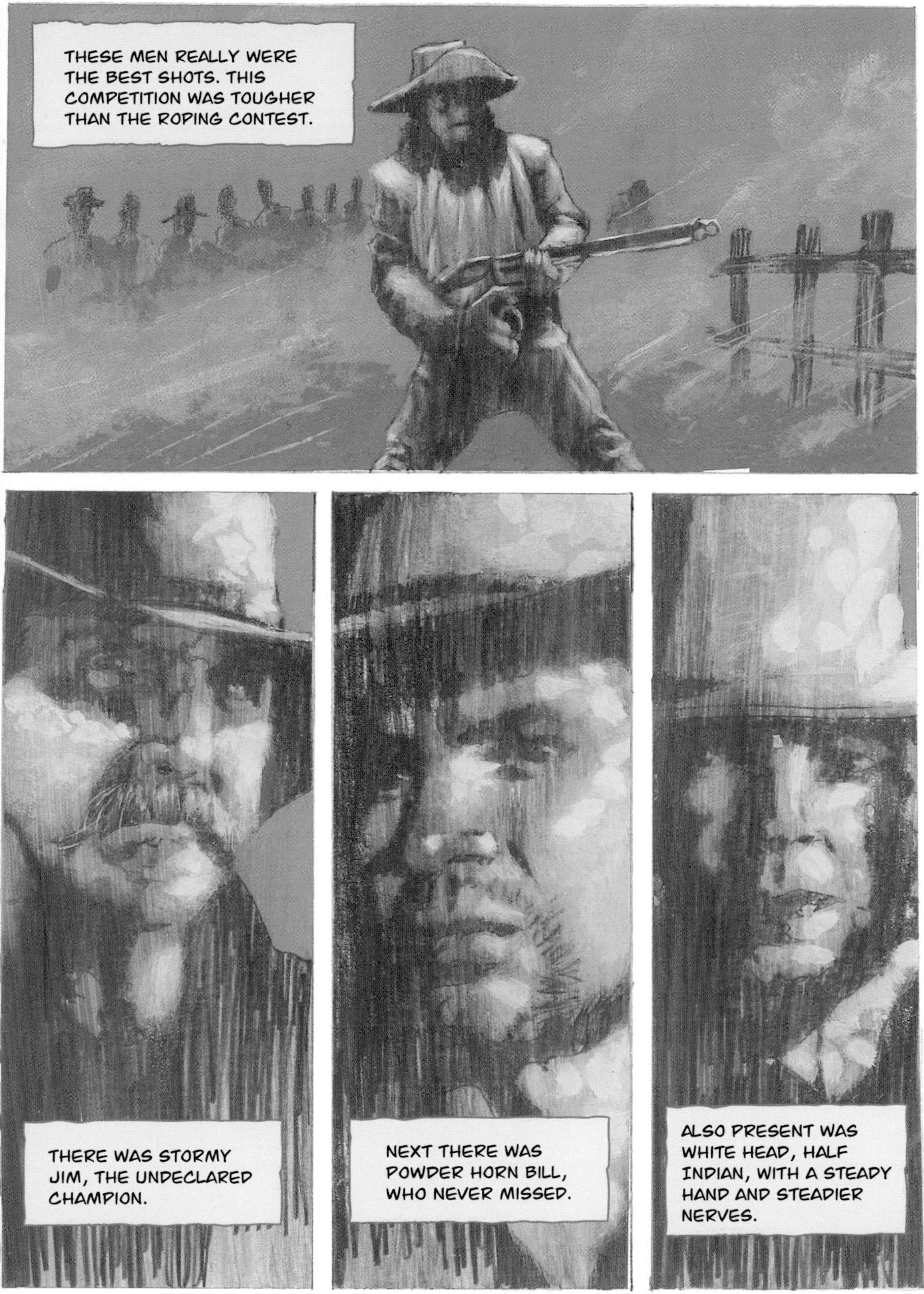
THESE MEN REALLY WERE THE BEST SHOTS. THIS COMPETITION WAS TOUGHER THAN THE ROPING CONTEST.
THERE WAS STORMY JIM, THE UNDECLARED CHAMPION.
NEXT THERE WAS POWDER HORN BILL, WHO NEVER MISSED.
ALSO PRESENT WAS WHITE HEAD, HALF INDIAN, WITH A STEADY HAND AND STEADIER NERVES.

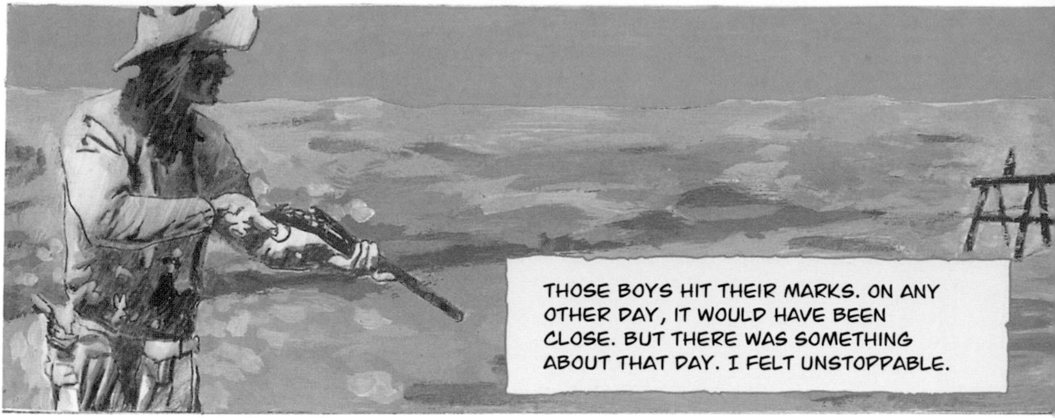
THOSE BOYS HIT THEIR MARKS. ON ANY OTHER DAY, IT WOULD HAVE BEEN CLOSE. BUT THERE WAS SOMETHING ABOUT THAT DAY. I FELT UNSTOPPABLE.

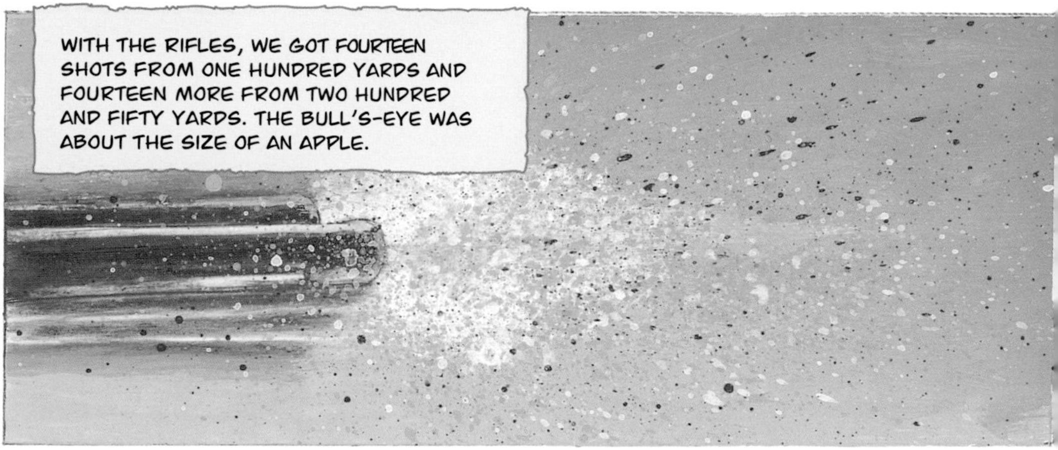
WITH THE RIFLES, WE GOT FOURTEEN SHOTS FROM ONE HUNDRED YARDS AND FOURTEEN MORE FROM TWO HUNDRED AND FIFTY YARDS. THE BULL'S-EYE WAS ABOUT THE SIZE OF AN APPLE.

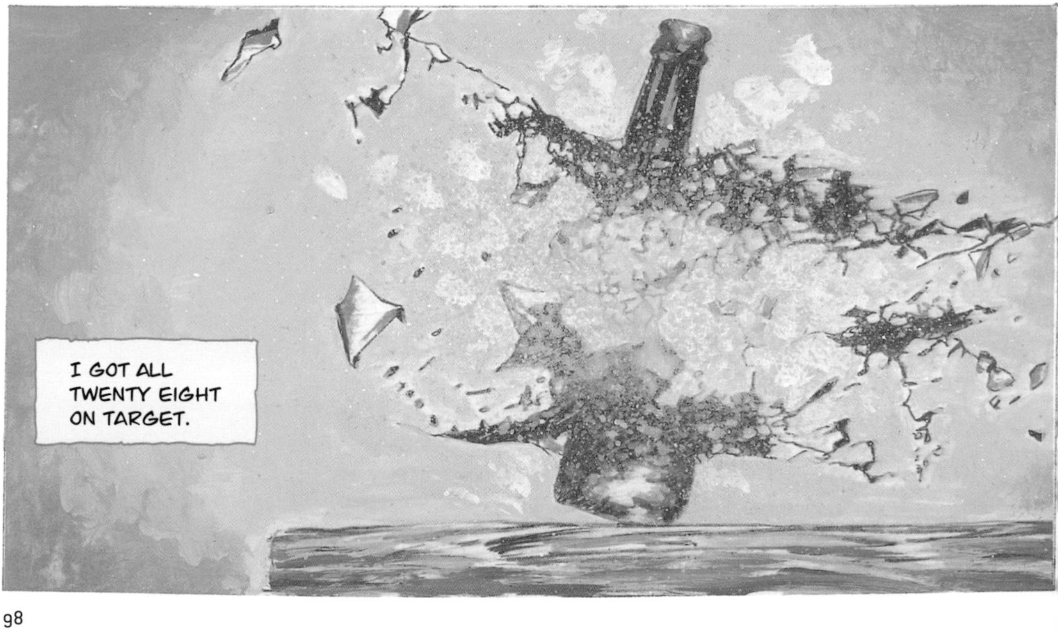
I GOT ALL TWENTY EIGHT ON TARGET.

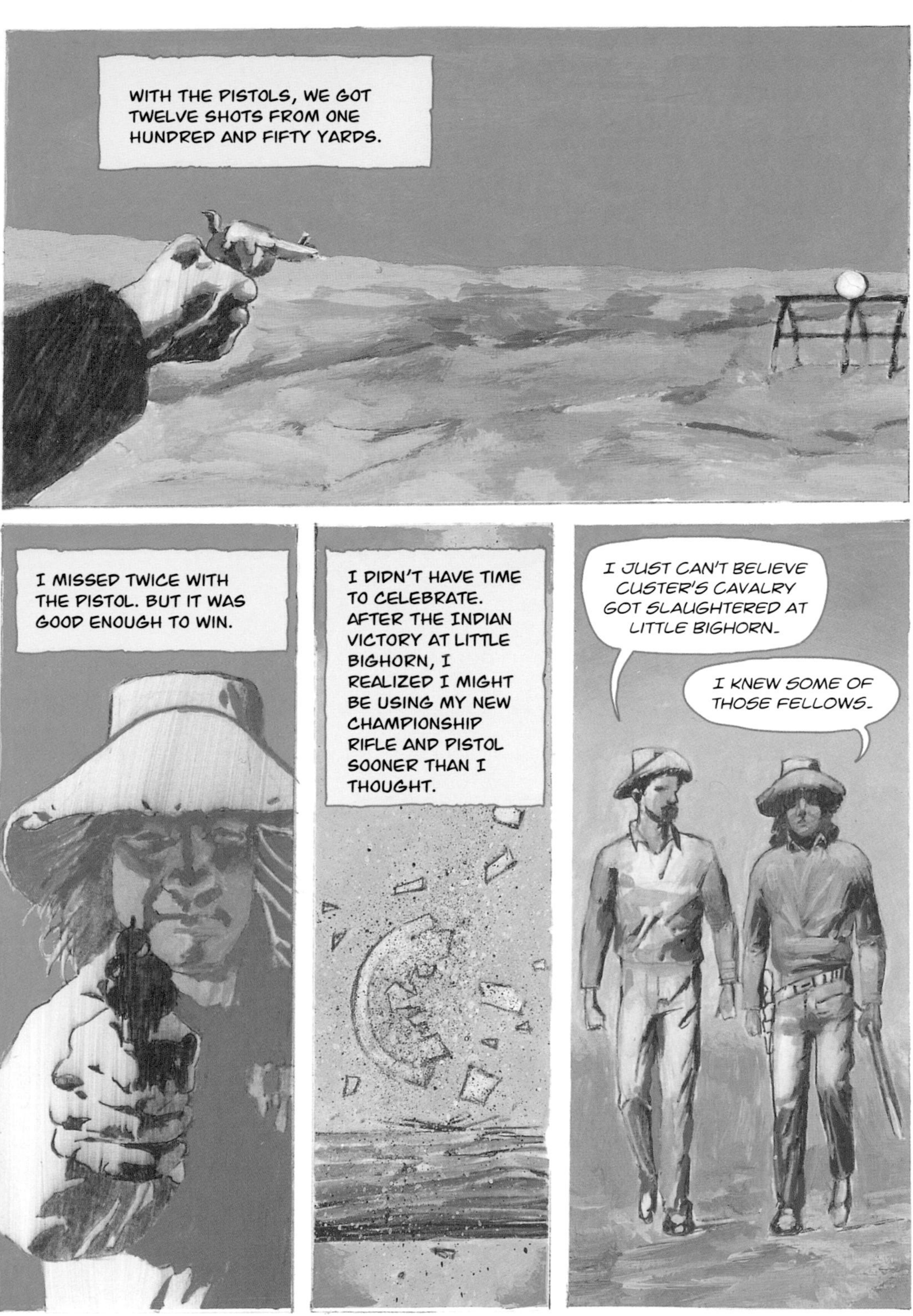
WITH THE PISTOLS, WE GOT TWELVE SHOTS FROM ONE HUNDRED AND FIFTY YARDS.
I MISSED TWICE WITH THE PISTOL. BUT IT WAS GOOD ENOUGH TO WIN.
I DIDN'T HAVE TIME TO CELEBRATE. AFTER THE INDIAN VICTORY AT LITTLE BIGHORN, I REALIZED I MIGHT BE USING MY NEW CHAMPIONSHIP RIFLE AND PISTOL SOONER THAN I THOUGHT.
I JUST CAN'T BELIEVE CUSTER'S CAVALRY GOT SLAUGHTERED AT LITTLE BIGHORN.
I KNEW SOME OF THOSE FELLOWS.

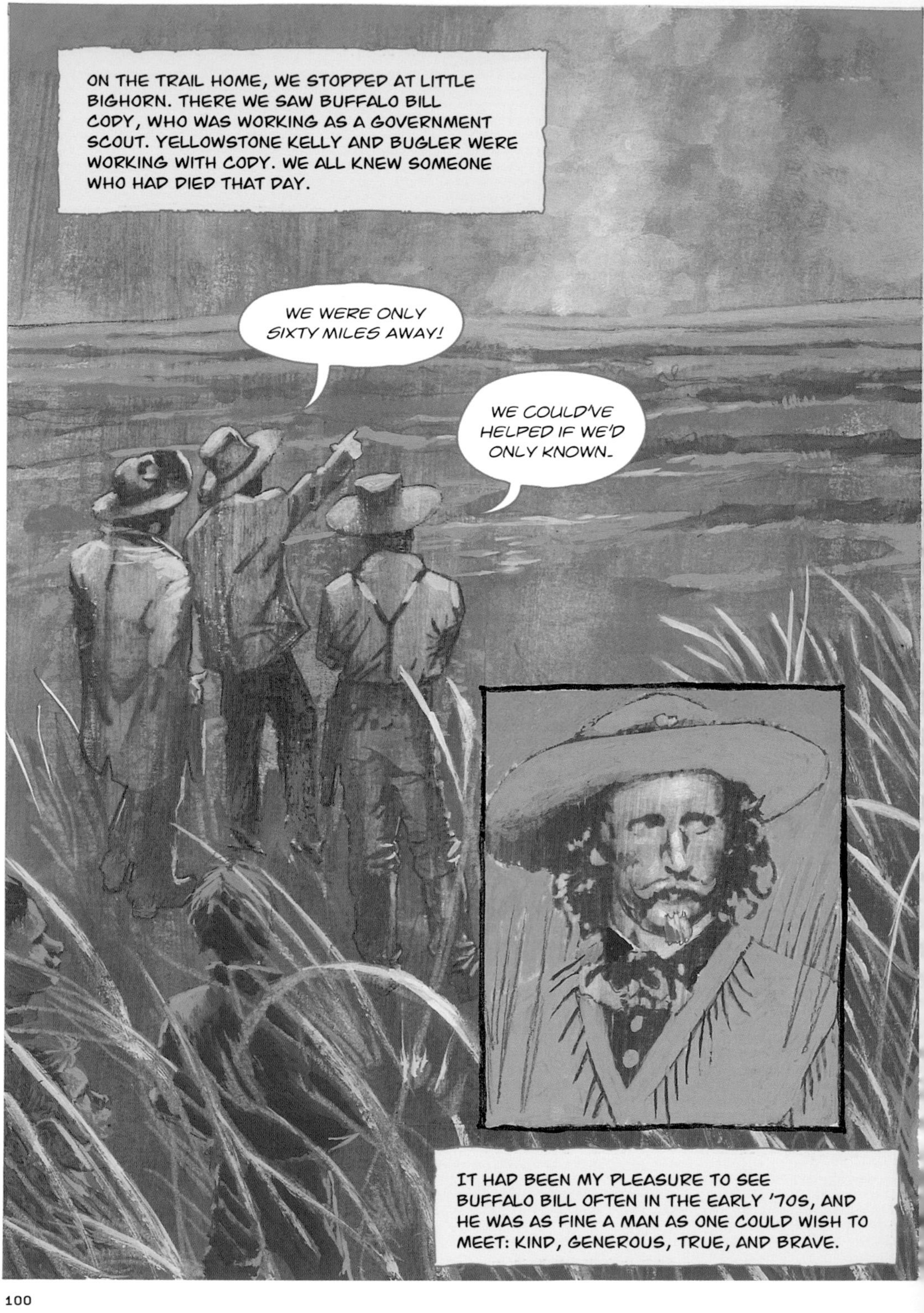
ON THE TRAIL HOME, WE STOPPED AT LITTLE BIGHORN. THERE WE SAW BUFFALO BILL CODY, WHO WAS WORKING AS A GOVERNMENT SCOUT. YELLOWSTONE KELLY AND BUGLER WERE WORKING WITH CODY. WE ALL KNEW SOMEONE WHO HAD DIED THAT DAY.
WE WERE ONLY SIXTY MILES AWAY!
WE COULD'VE HELPED IF WE'D ONLY KNOWN...
IT HAD BEEN MY PLEASURE TO SEE BUFFALO BILL OFTEN IN THE EARLY '70S, AND HE WAS AS FINE A MAN AS ONE COULD WISH TO MEET: KIND, GENEROUS, TRUE, AND BRAVE.

It took us two months to make it from Deadwood back to the home ranch in Arizona. Thankfully, it was an uneventful trip. Well, really, the events turned out in the number of folks along the way who had heard about my exploits.

Arriving home, I was given enough salutes of whoops, hollers, and gun blasts to wake the devil. People told me that they were not surprised by my success, but they were happy nonetheless that I had brought home the records.

After a good rest, we were back riding the range again, getting our herds in good condition for winter. But three months after my greatest triumph came a day when I thought for sure I was going to meet my maker.

OCTOBER 4, 1876. TWENTY MILES FROM THE GALLINGER RANCH.

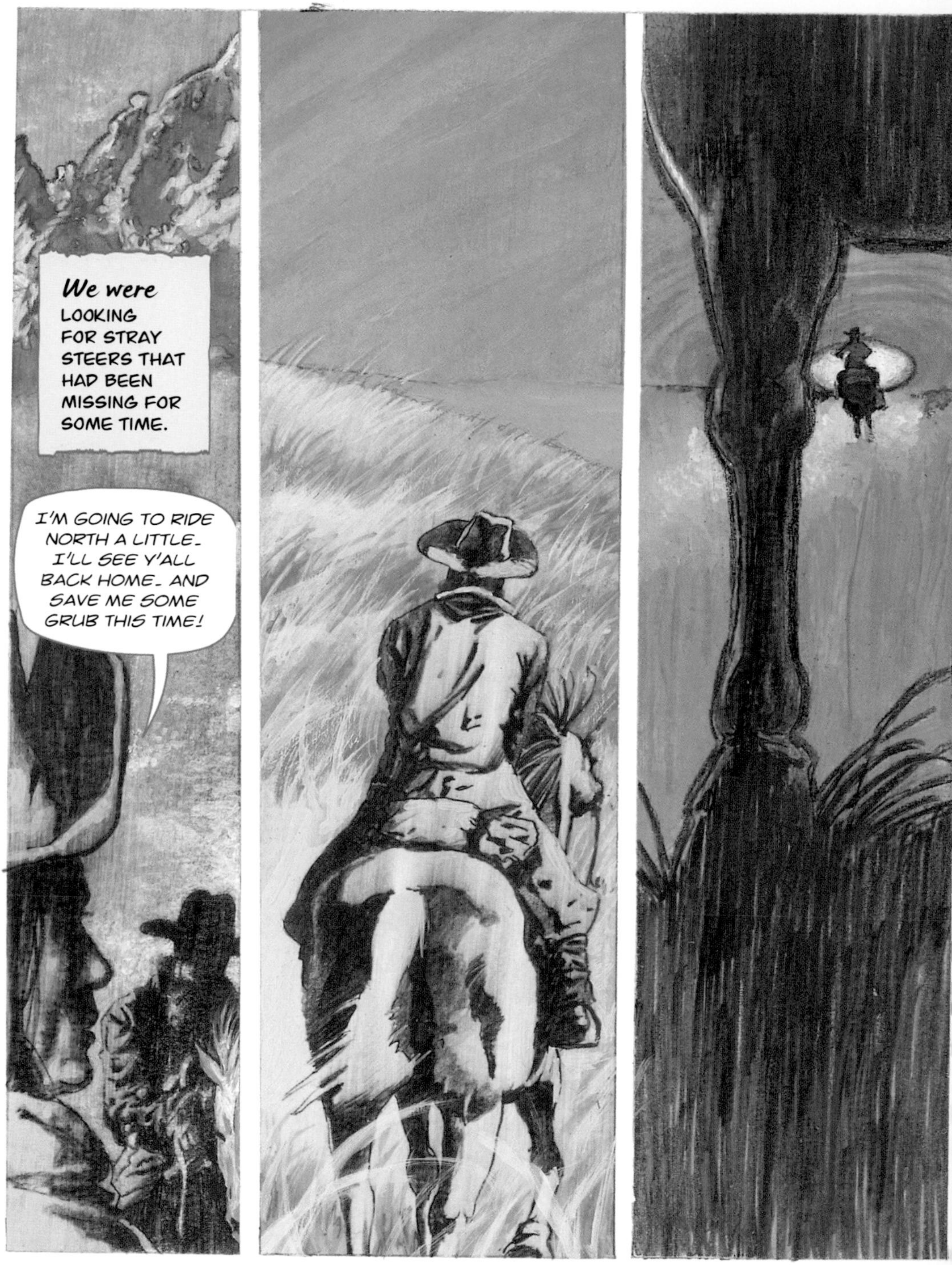

We were LOOKING FOR STRAY STEERS THAT HAD BEEN MISSING FOR SOME TIME.
I'M GOING TO RIDE NORTH A LITTLE. I'LL SEE Y'ALL BACK HOME. AND SAVE ME SOME GRUB THIS TIME!

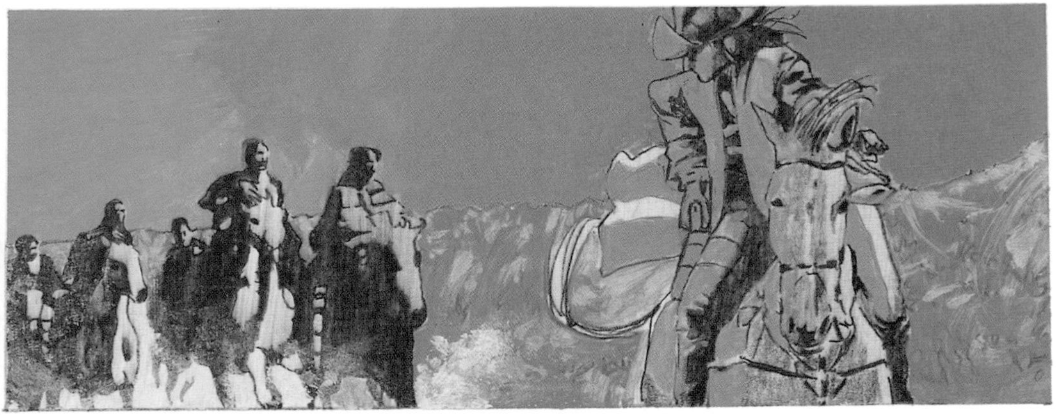

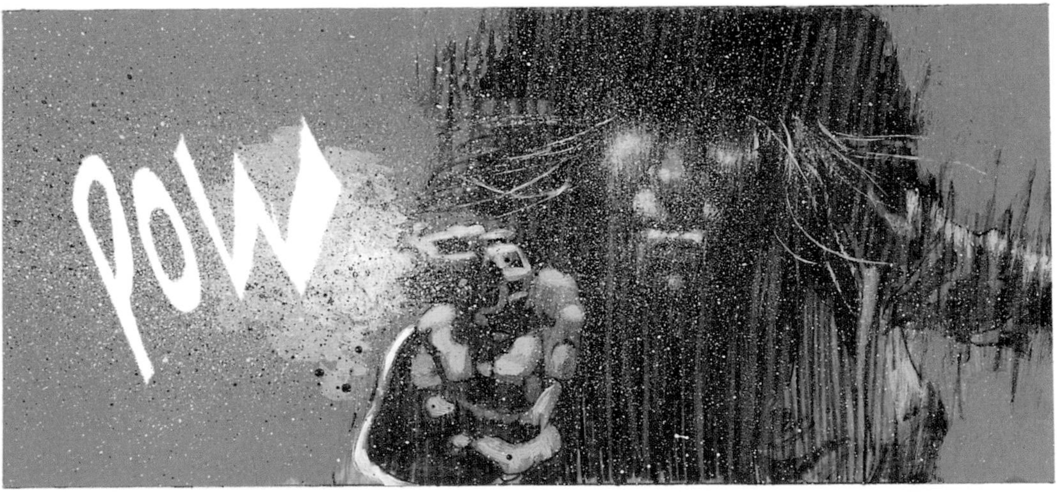
POW

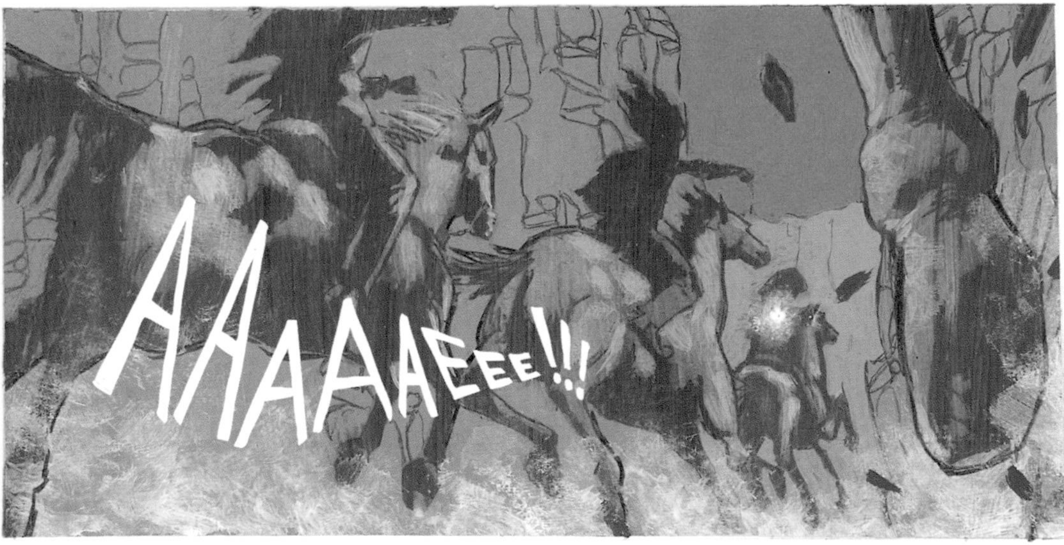
AAAAAEEE!!!

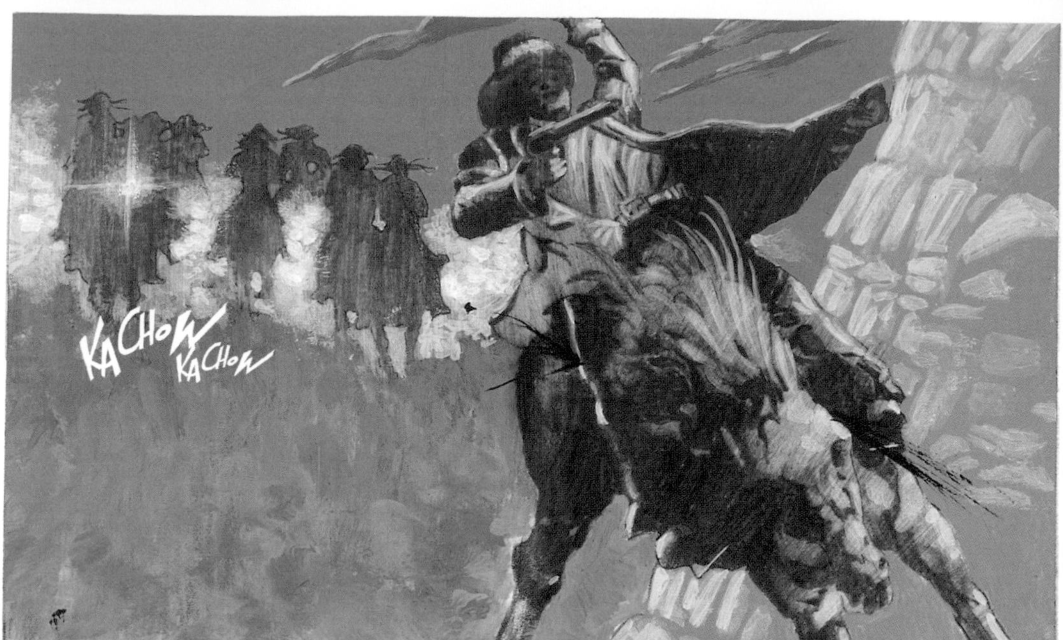
KACHOW
KACHOW

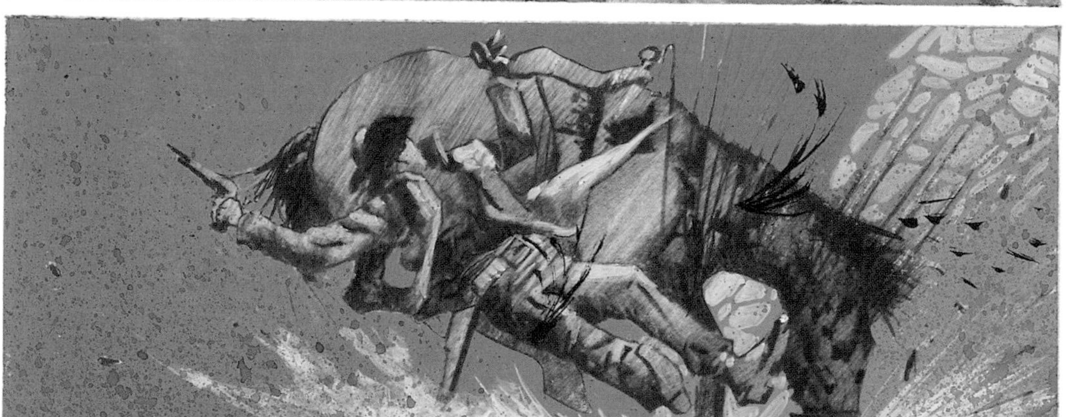

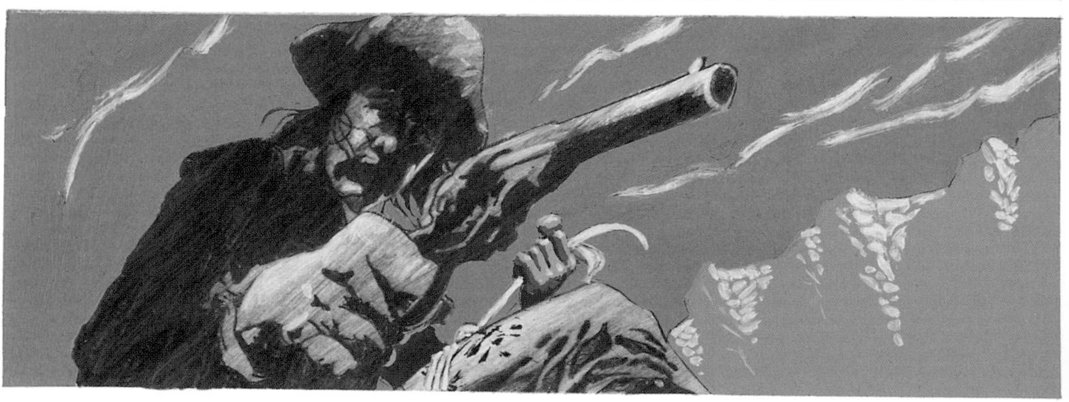

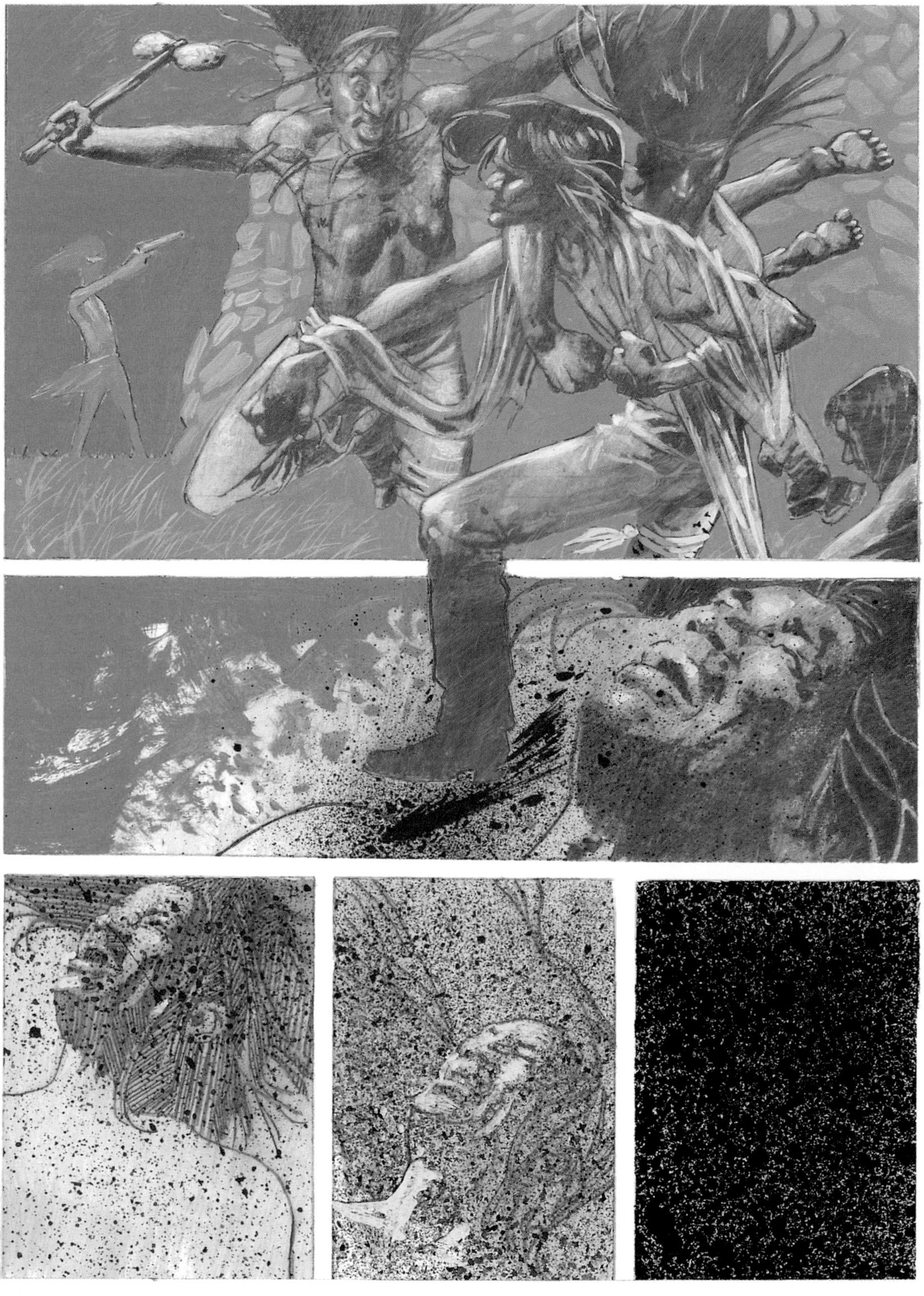

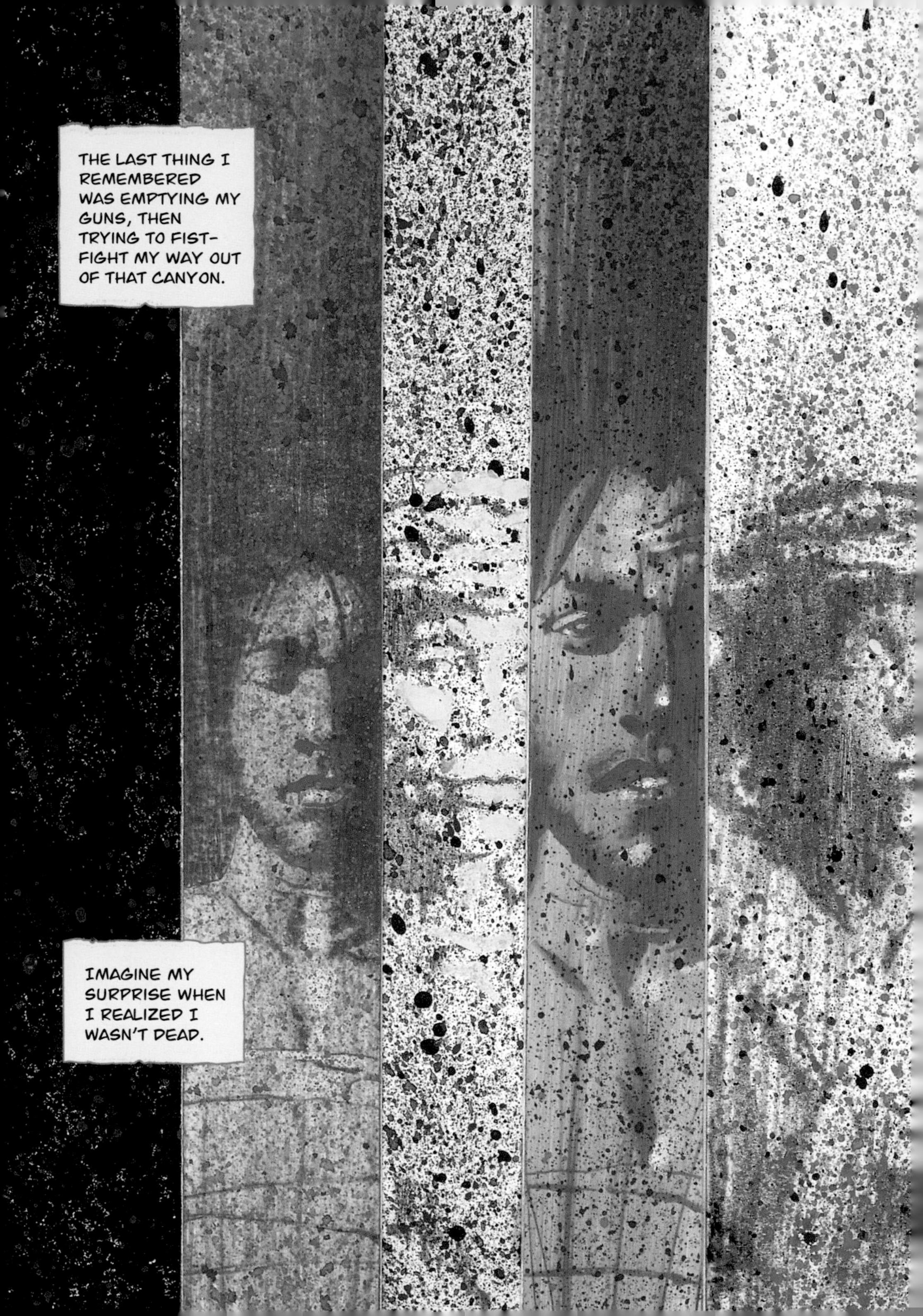
THE LAST THING I REMEMBERED WAS EMPTYING MY GUNS, THEN TRYING TO FIST-FIGHT MY WAY OUT OF THAT CANYON.
IMAGINE MY SURPRISE WHEN I REALIZED I WASN'T DEAD.

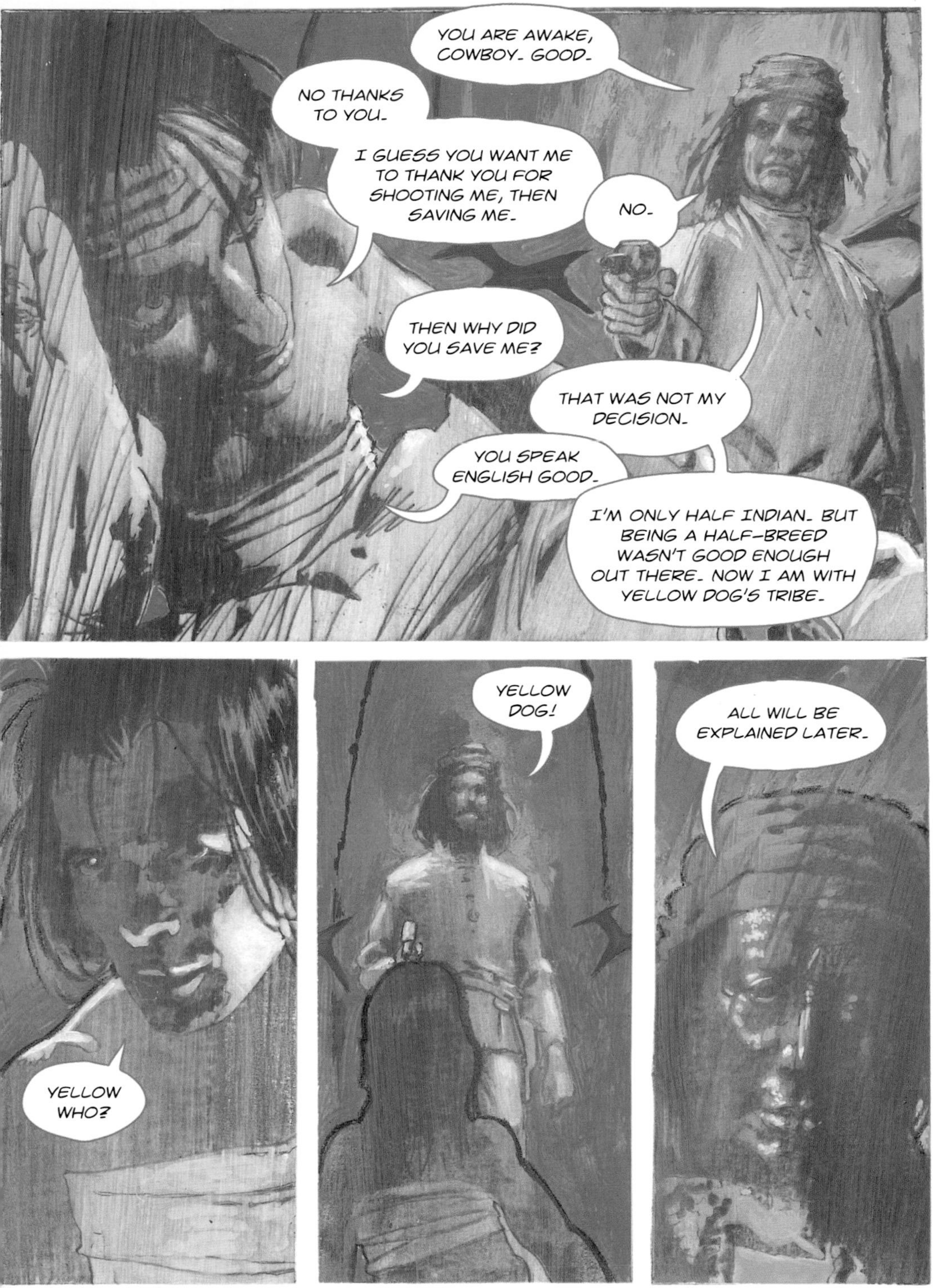
YOU ARE AWAKE, COWBOY. GOOD.
NO THANKS TO YOU.
I GUESS YOU WANT ME TO THANK YOU FOR SHOOTING ME, THEN SAVING ME.
NO.
THEN WHY DID YOU SAVE ME?
THAT WAS NOT MY DECISION.
YOU SPEAK ENGLISH GOOD.
I'M ONLY HALF INDIAN. BUT BEING A HALF-BREED WASN'T GOOD ENOUGH OUT THERE. NOW I AM WITH YELLOW DOG'S TRIBE.
YELLOW WHO?
YELLOW DOG!
ALL WILL BE EXPLAINED LATER.

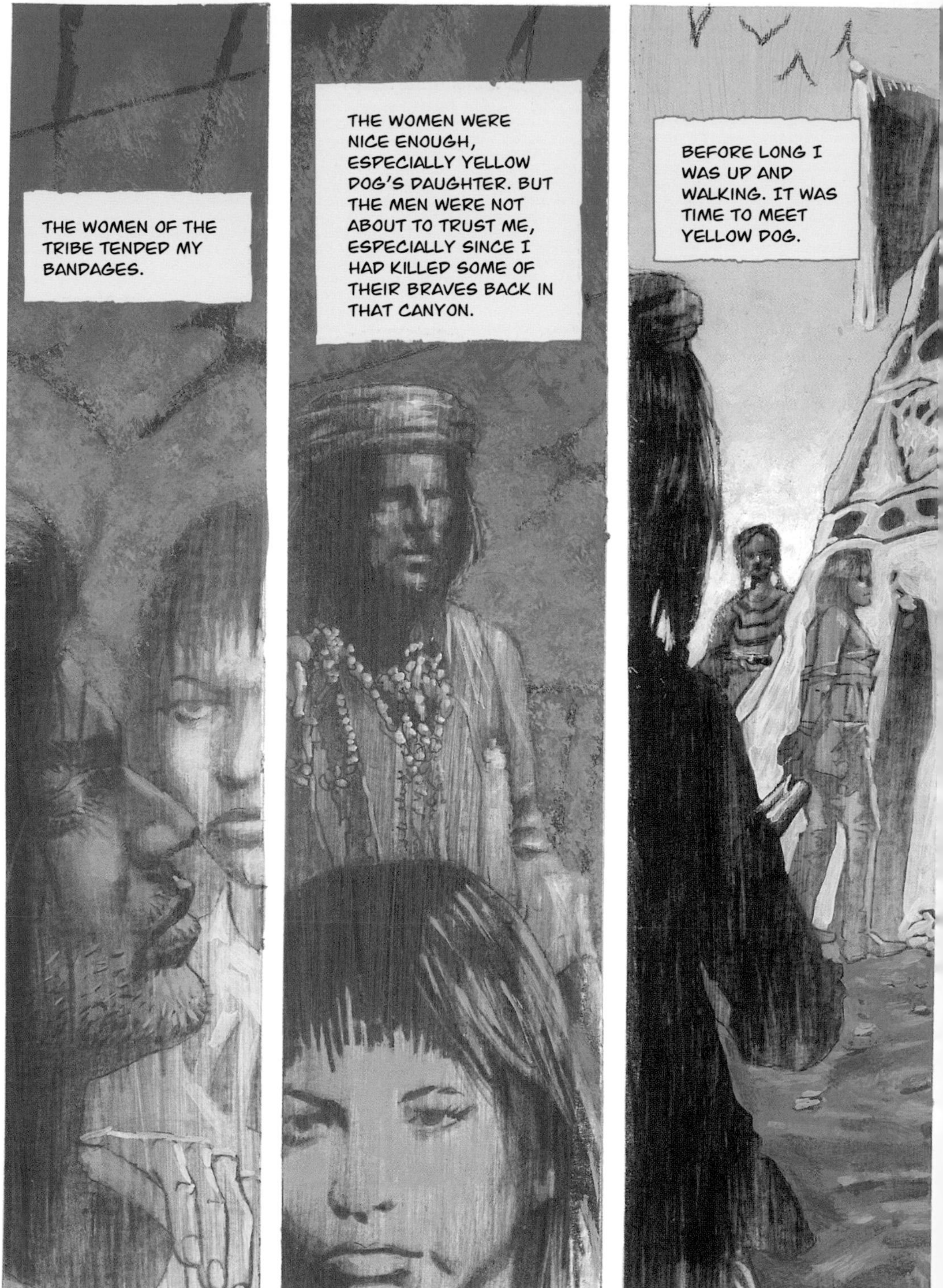
THE WOMEN OF THE TRIBE TENDED MY BANDAGES.
THE WOMEN WERE NICE ENOUGH, ESPECIALLY YELLOW DOG'S DAUGHTER. BUT THE MEN WERE NOT ABOUT TO TRUST ME, ESPECIALLY SINCE I HAD KILLED SOME OF THEIR BRAVES BACK IN THAT CANYON.
BEFORE LONG I WAS UP AND WALKING. IT WAS TIME TO MEET YELLOW DOG.

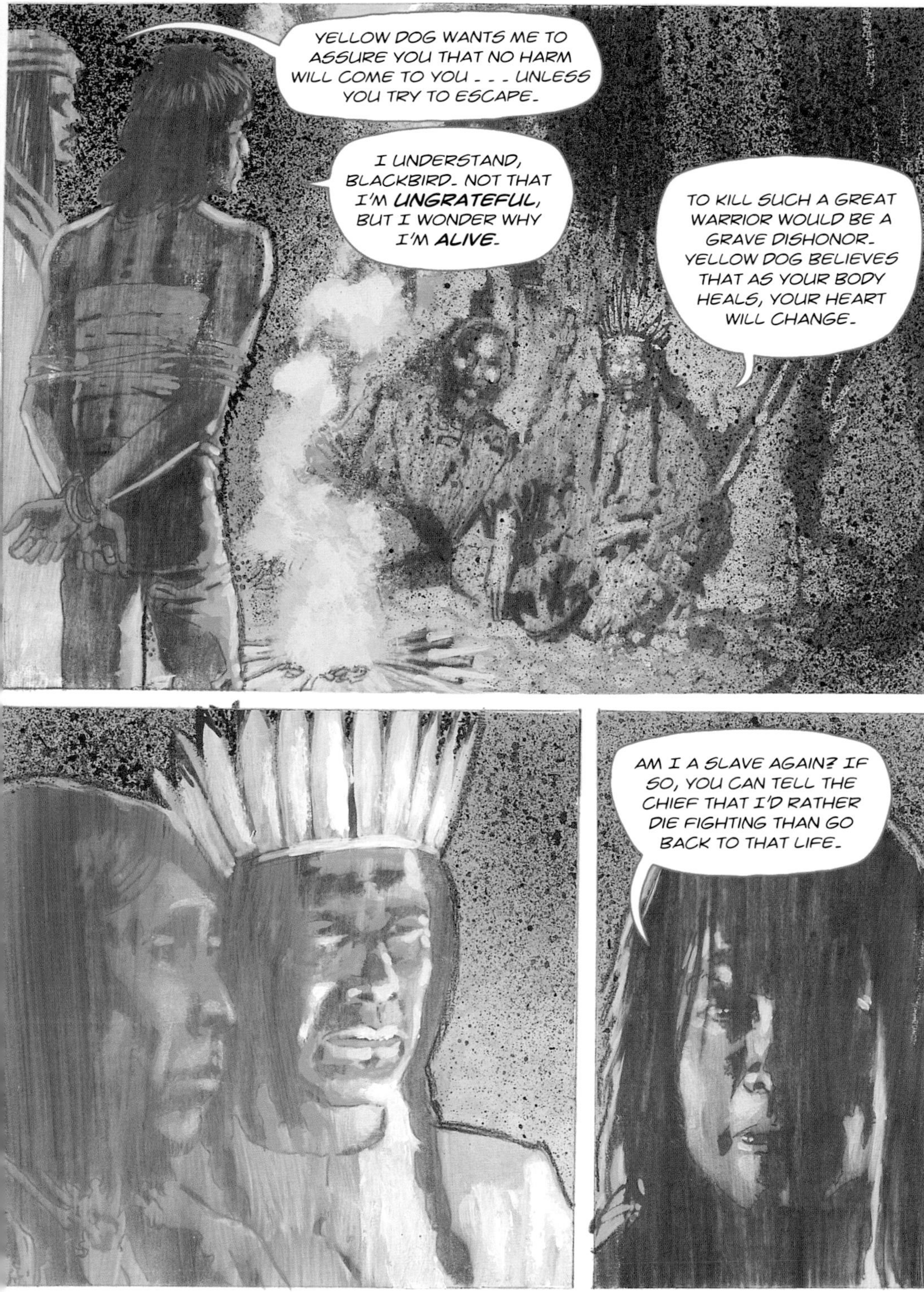
YELLOW DOG WANTS ME TO ASSURE YOU THAT NO HARM WILL COME TO YOU . . . UNLESS YOU TRY TO ESCAPE.
I UNDERSTAND, BLACKBIRD. NOT THAT I'M **UNGRATEFUL**, BUT I WONDER WHY I'M **ALIVE**.
TO KILL SUCH A GREAT WARRIOR WOULD BE A GRAVE DISHONOR. YELLOW DOG BELIEVES THAT AS YOUR BODY HEALS, YOUR HEART WILL CHANGE.
AM I A SLAVE AGAIN? IF SO, YOU CAN TELL THE CHIEF THAT I'D RATHER DIE FIGHTING THAN GO BACK TO THAT LIFE.

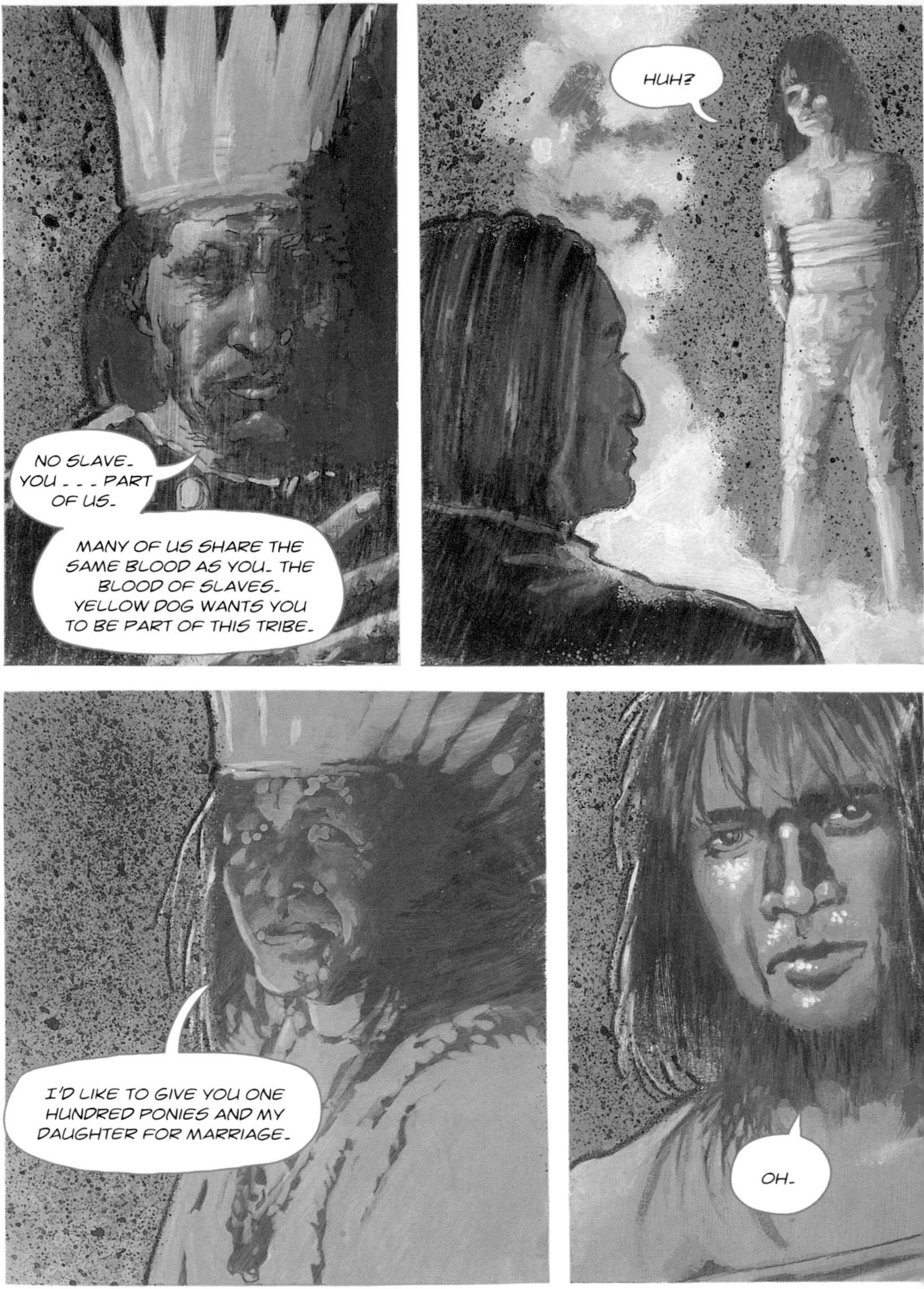
NO SLAVE. YOU . . . PART OF US.
MANY OF US SHARE THE SAME BLOOD AS YOU. THE BLOOD OF SLAVES. YELLOW DOG WANTS YOU TO BE PART OF THIS TRIBE.
HUH?
I'D LIKE TO GIVE YOU ONE HUNDRED PONIES AND MY DAUGHTER FOR MARRIAGE.
OH.

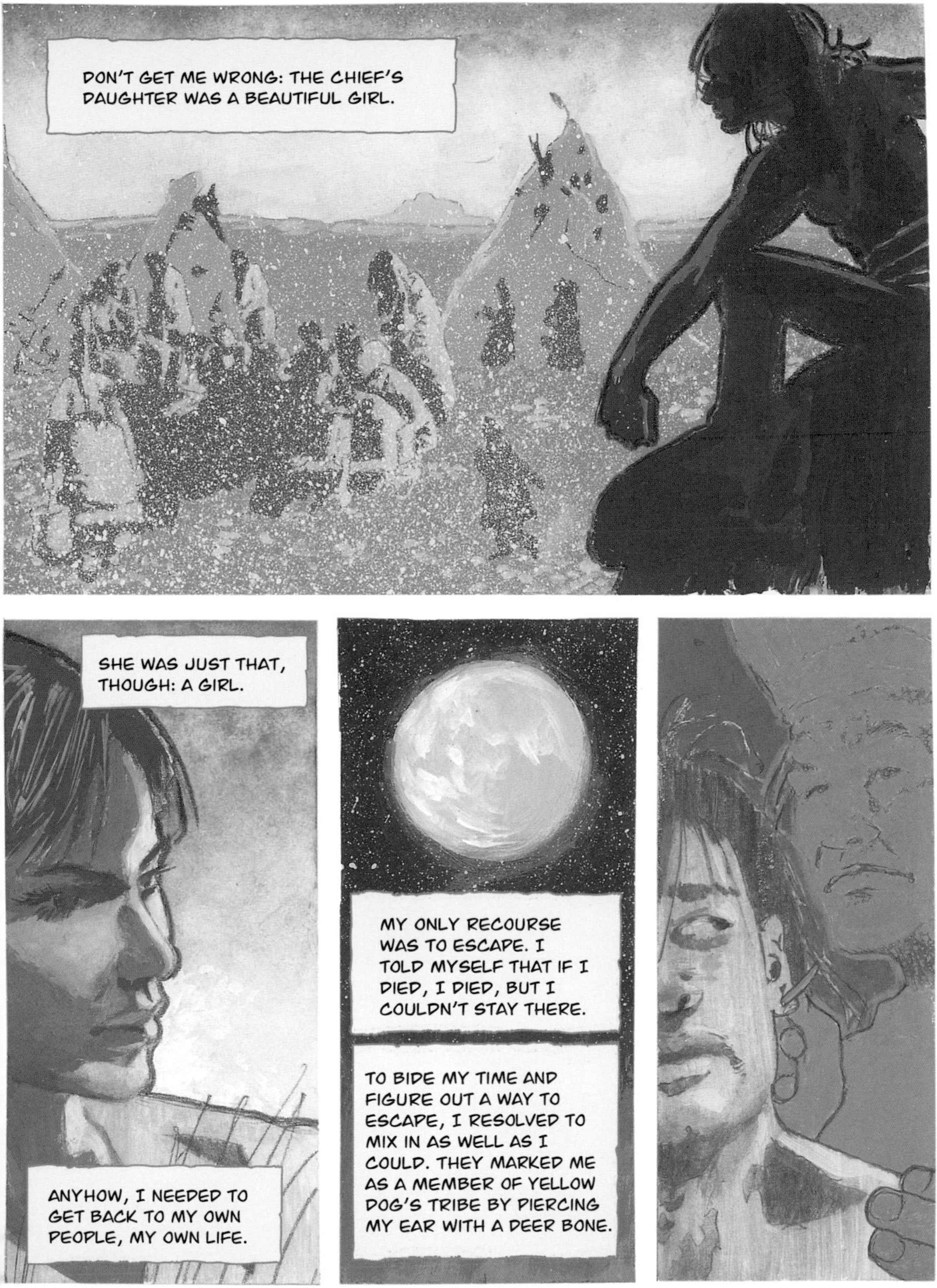
DON'T GET ME WRONG: THE CHIEF'S DAUGHTER WAS A BEAUTIFUL GIRL.
SHE WAS JUST THAT, THOUGH: A GIRL.
ANYHOW, I NEEDED TO GET BACK TO MY OWN PEOPLE, MY OWN LIFE.
MY ONLY RECOURSE WAS TO ESCAPE. I TOLD MYSELF THAT IF I DIED, I DIED, BUT I COULDN'T STAY THERE.
TO BIDE MY TIME AND FIGURE OUT A WAY TO ESCAPE, I RESOLVED TO MIX IN AS WELL AS I COULD. THEY MARKED ME AS A MEMBER OF YELLOW DOG'S TRIBE BY PIERCING MY EAR WITH A DEER BONE.

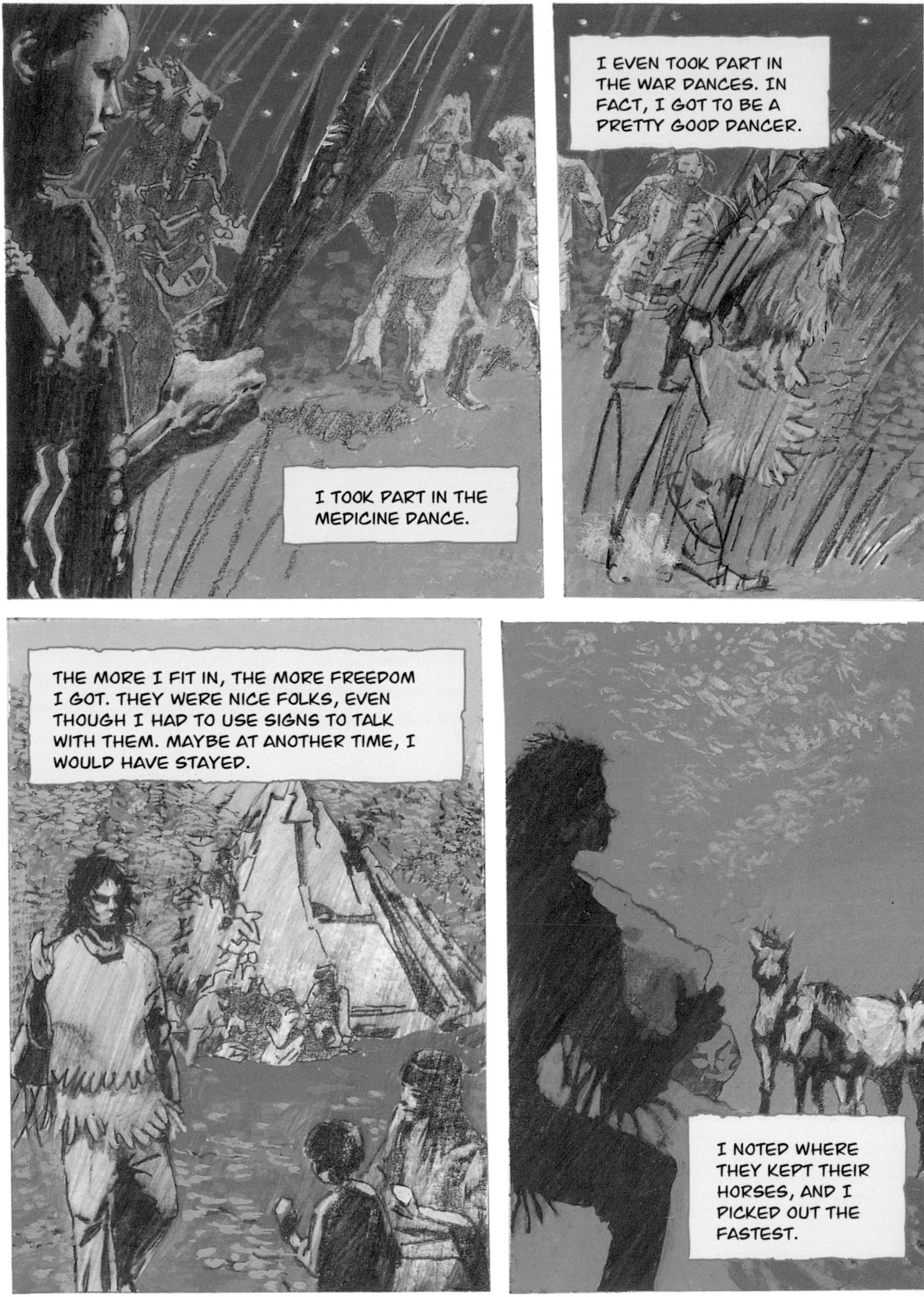
I TOOK PART IN THE MEDICINE DANCE.
I EVEN TOOK PART IN THE WAR DANCES. IN FACT, I GOT TO BE A PRETTY GOOD DANCER.
THE MORE I FIT IN, THE MORE FREEDOM I GOT. THEY WERE NICE FOLKS, EVEN THOUGH I HAD TO USE SIGNS TO TALK WITH THEM. MAYBE AT ANOTHER TIME, I WOULD HAVE STAYED.
I NOTED WHERE THEY KEPT THEIR HORSES, AND I PICKED OUT THE FASTEST.

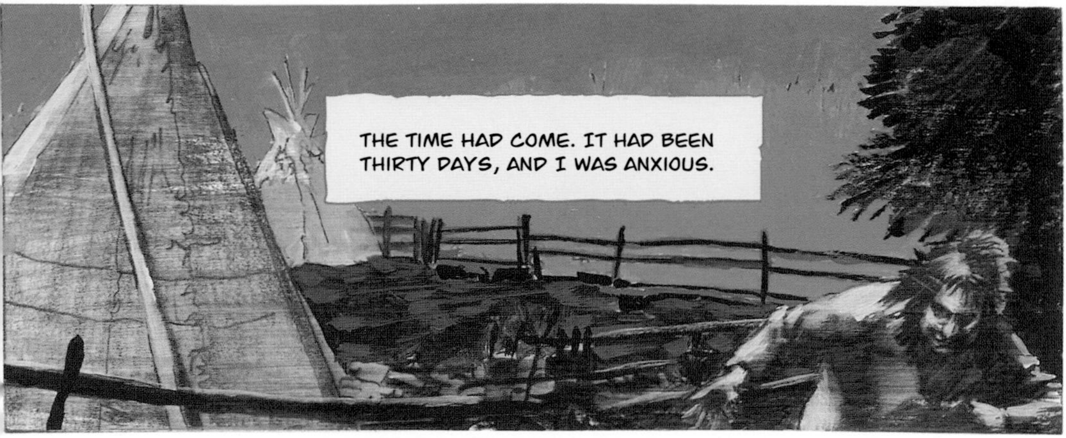
THE TIME HAD COME. IT HAD BEEN THIRTY DAYS, AND I WAS ANXIOUS.

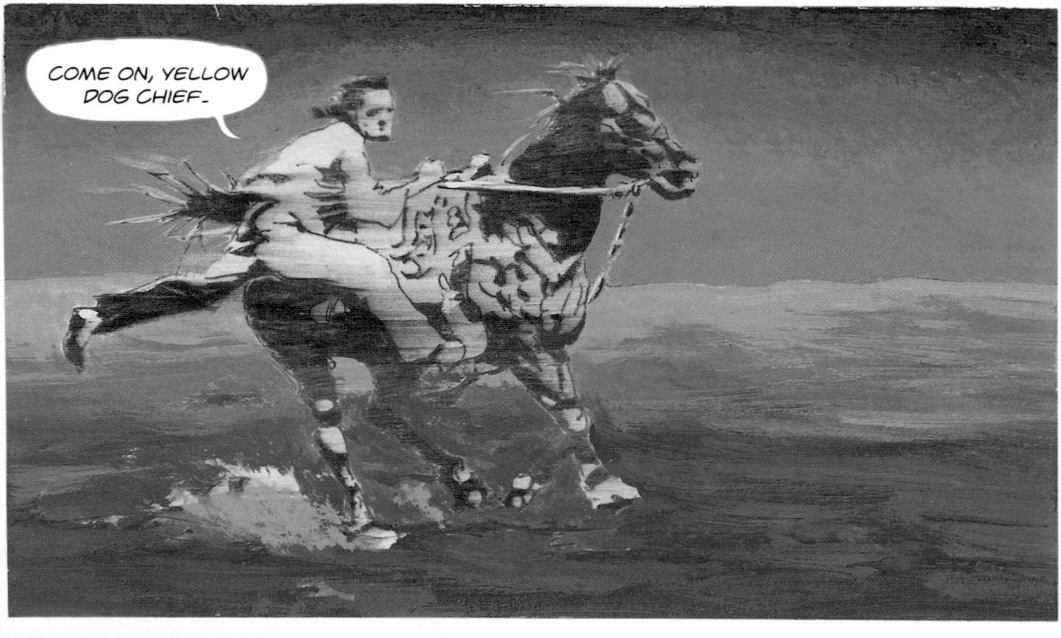
COME ON, YELLOW DOG CHIEF.

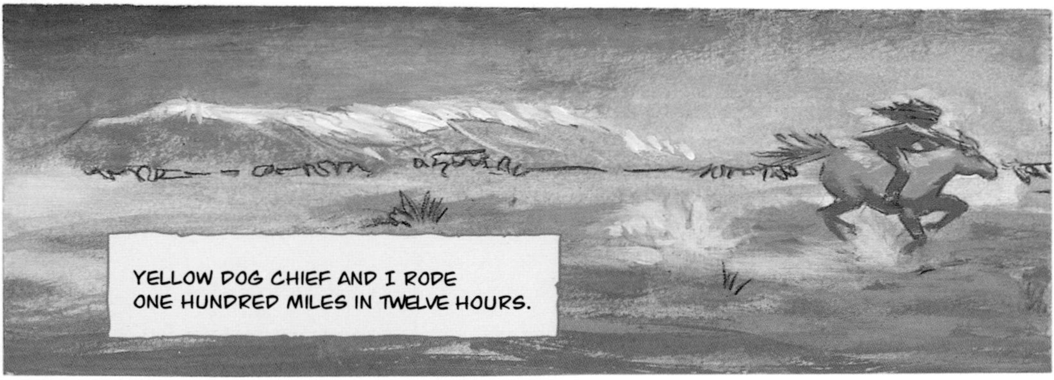
YELLOW DOG CHIEF AND I RODE ONE HUNDRED MILES IN TWELVE HOURS.

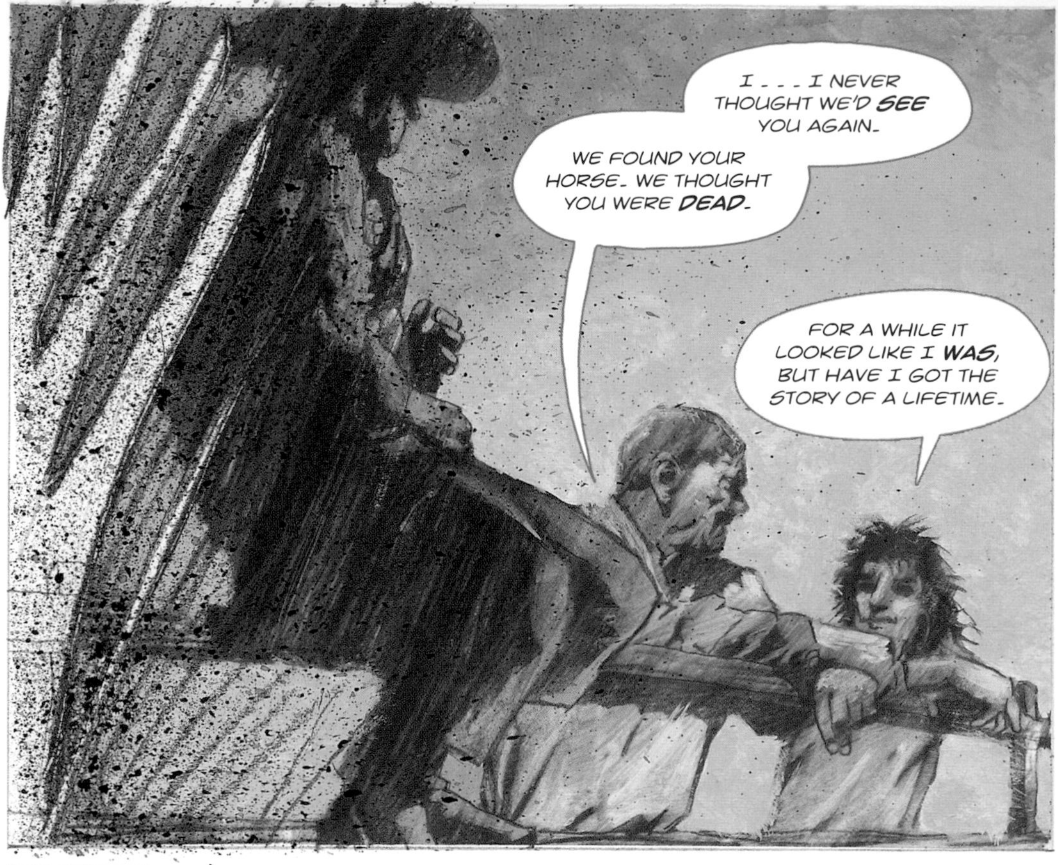
I . . . I NEVER THOUGHT WE'D SEE YOU AGAIN.
WE FOUND YOUR HORSE. WE THOUGHT YOU WERE DEAD.
FOR A WHILE IT LOOKED LIKE I WAS, BUT HAVE I GOT THE STORY OF A LIFETIME.

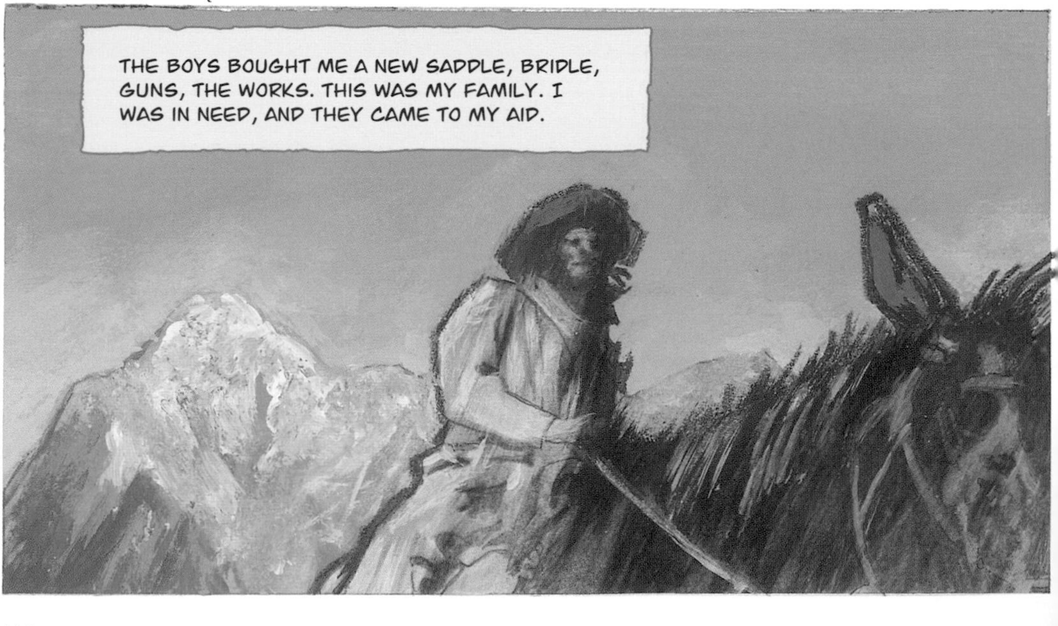
THE BOYS BOUGHT ME A NEW SADDLE, BRIDLE, GUNS, THE WORKS. THIS WAS MY FAMILY. I WAS IN NEED, AND THEY CAME TO MY AID.

One of their bullets had caught me in the leg, another in my breast just over my heart. My nose had been nearly cut off, and also one of my fingers. Those Indians are certainly wonderful doctors. They covered my wounds with some kind of salve made from herbs. The wounds healed in a surprisingly short time.

I kept Yellow Dog Chief as my playing horse. I didn't ride him too hard, except for an occasional race. As for the real Yellow Dog, I never did see him or his tribe again. I had been in tough scrapes with Indians, rustlers, and outlaws. But the closest I ever came to dying was fighting Yellow Dog. I wish I could have met him under better circumstances.

I did meet other great men in my lifetime, though. In fact, two of them, Bat and Jim Masterson, kept me from being put in federal prison.

SPRING 1877. OLD FORT DODGE, KANSAS.

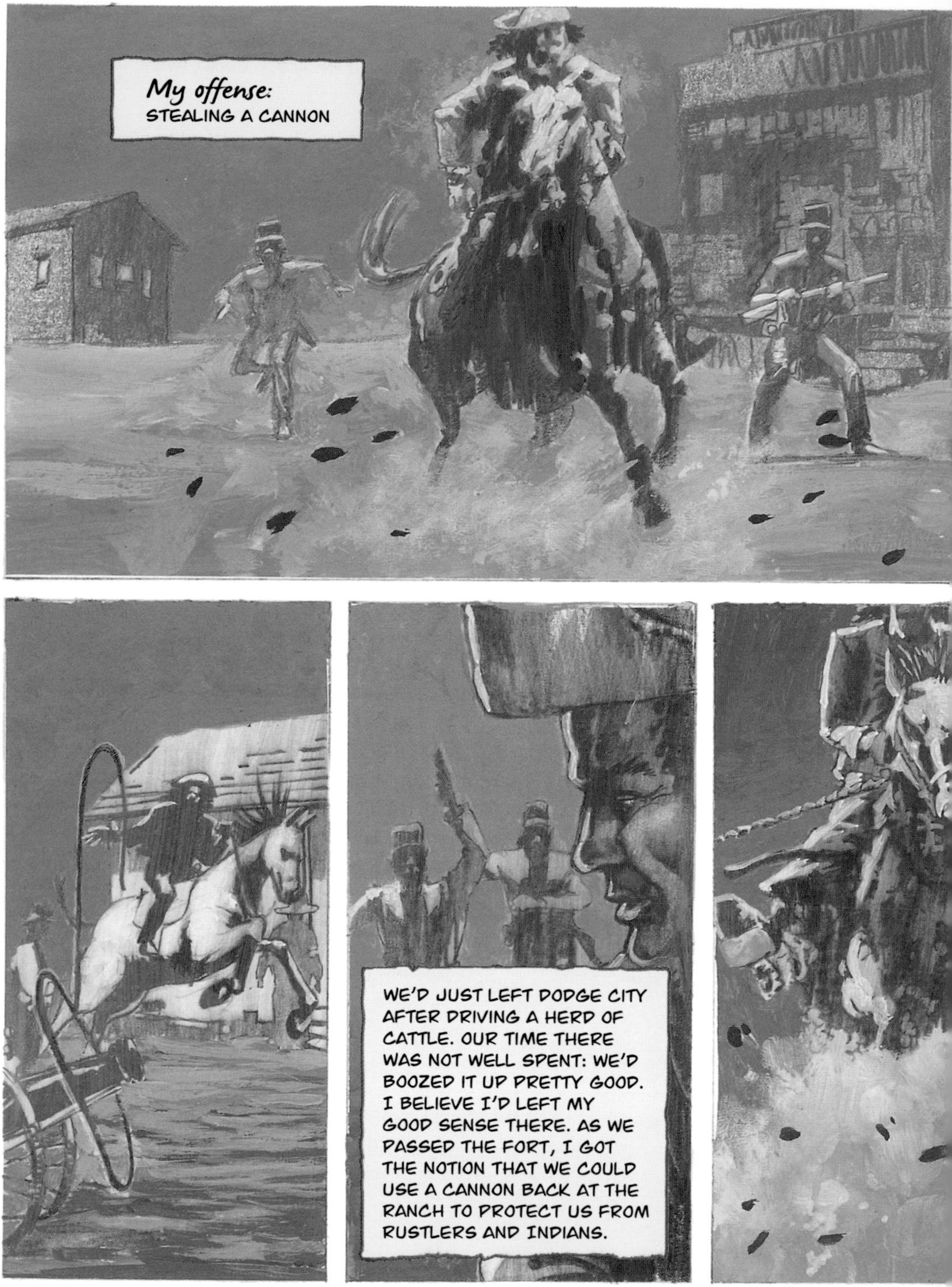
My offense:
STEALING A CANNON
WE'D JUST LEFT DODGE CITY AFTER DRIVING A HERD OF CATTLE. OUR TIME THERE WAS NOT WELL SPENT: WE'D BOOZED IT UP PRETTY GOOD. I BELIEVE I'D LEFT MY GOOD SENSE THERE. AS WE PASSED THE FORT, I GOT THE NOTION THAT WE COULD USE A CANNON BACK AT THE RANCH TO PROTECT US FROM RUSTLERS AND INDIANS.

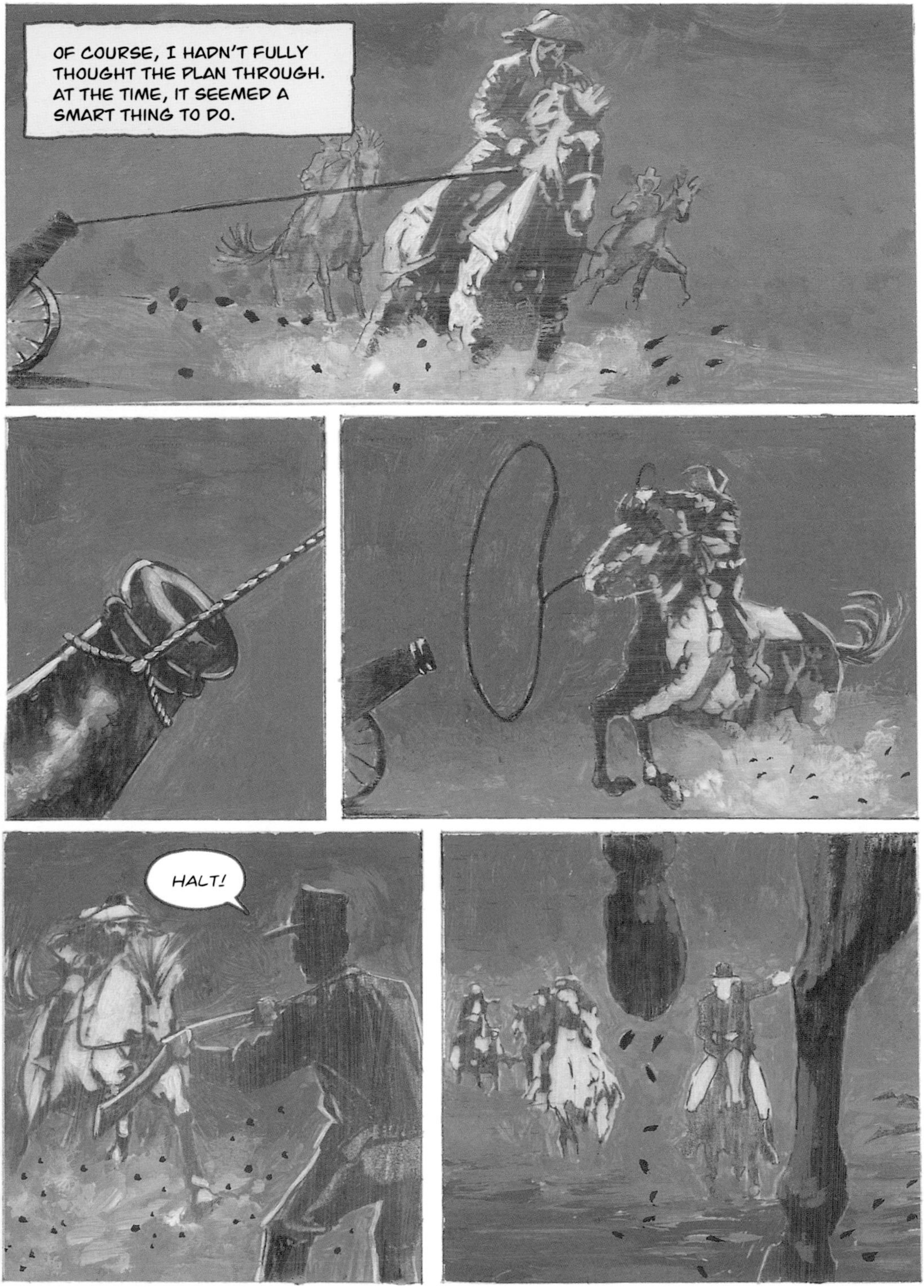
OF COURSE, I HADN'T FULLY THOUGHT THE PLAN THROUGH. AT THE TIME, IT SEEMED A SMART THING TO DO.
HALT!

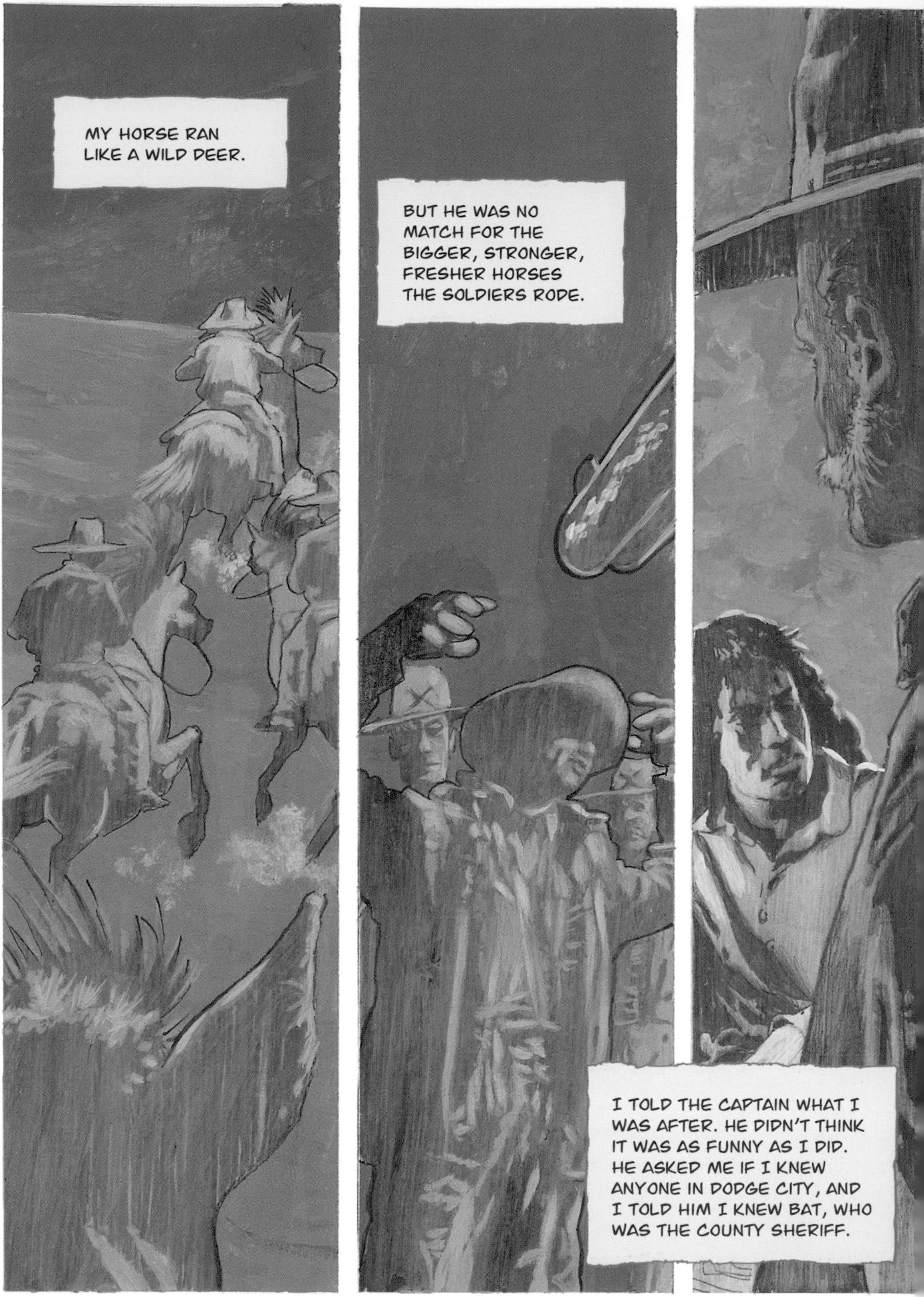
MY HORSE RAN LIKE A WILD DEER.
BUT HE WAS NO MATCH FOR THE BIGGER, STRONGER, FRESHER HORSES THE SOLDIERS RODE.
I TOLD THE CAPTAIN WHAT I WAS AFTER. HE DIDN'T THINK IT WAS AS FUNNY AS I DID. HE ASKED ME IF I KNEW ANYONE IN DODGE CITY, AND I TOLD HIM I KNEW BAT, WHO WAS THE COUNTY SHERIFF.

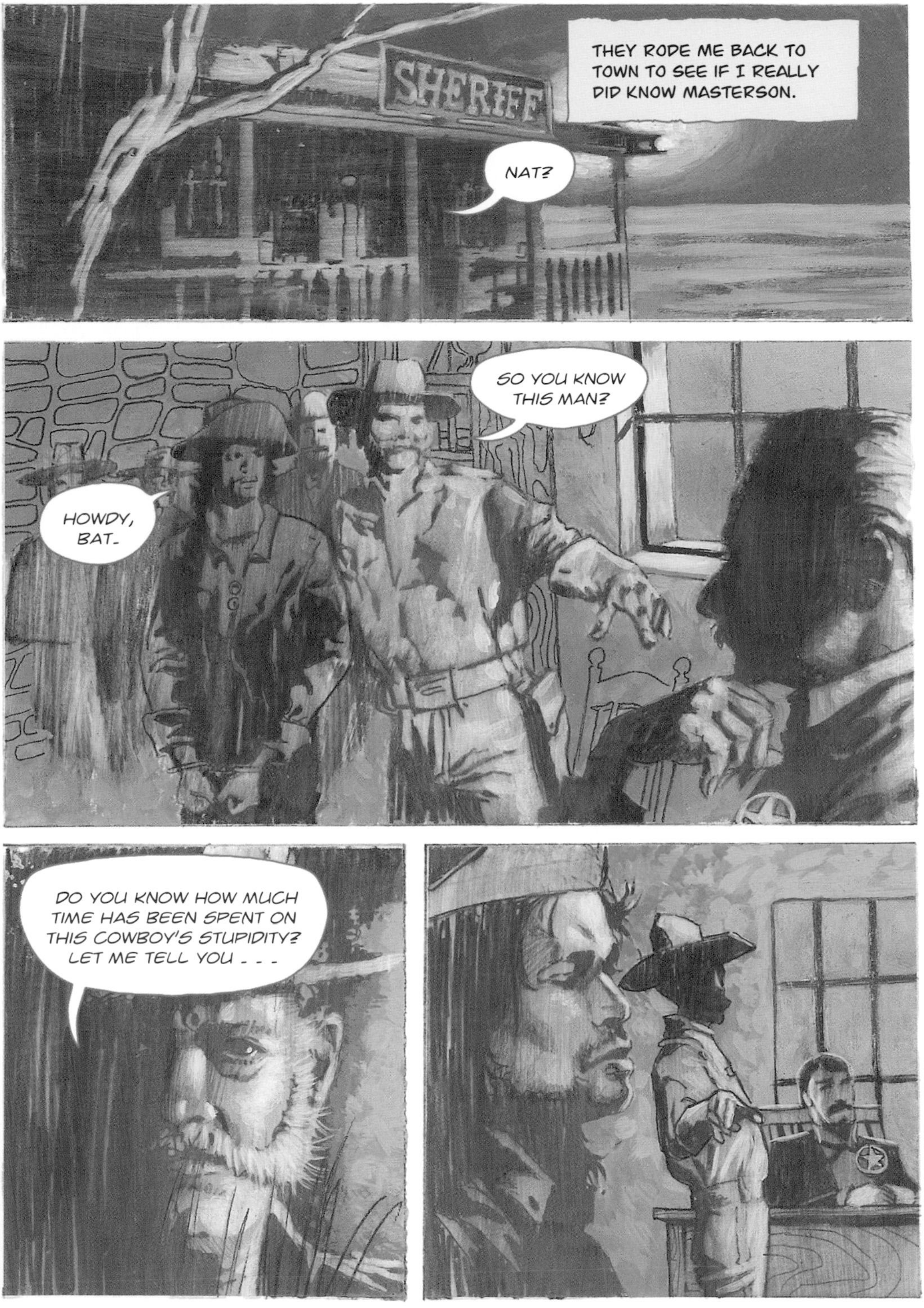
THEY RODE ME BACK TO TOWN TO SEE IF I REALLY DID KNOW MASTERSON.
SHERIFF
NAT?
SO YOU KNOW THIS MAN?
HOWDY, BAT.
DO YOU KNOW HOW MUCH TIME HAS BEEN SPENT ON THIS COWBOY'S STUPIDITY? LET ME TELL YOU . . .

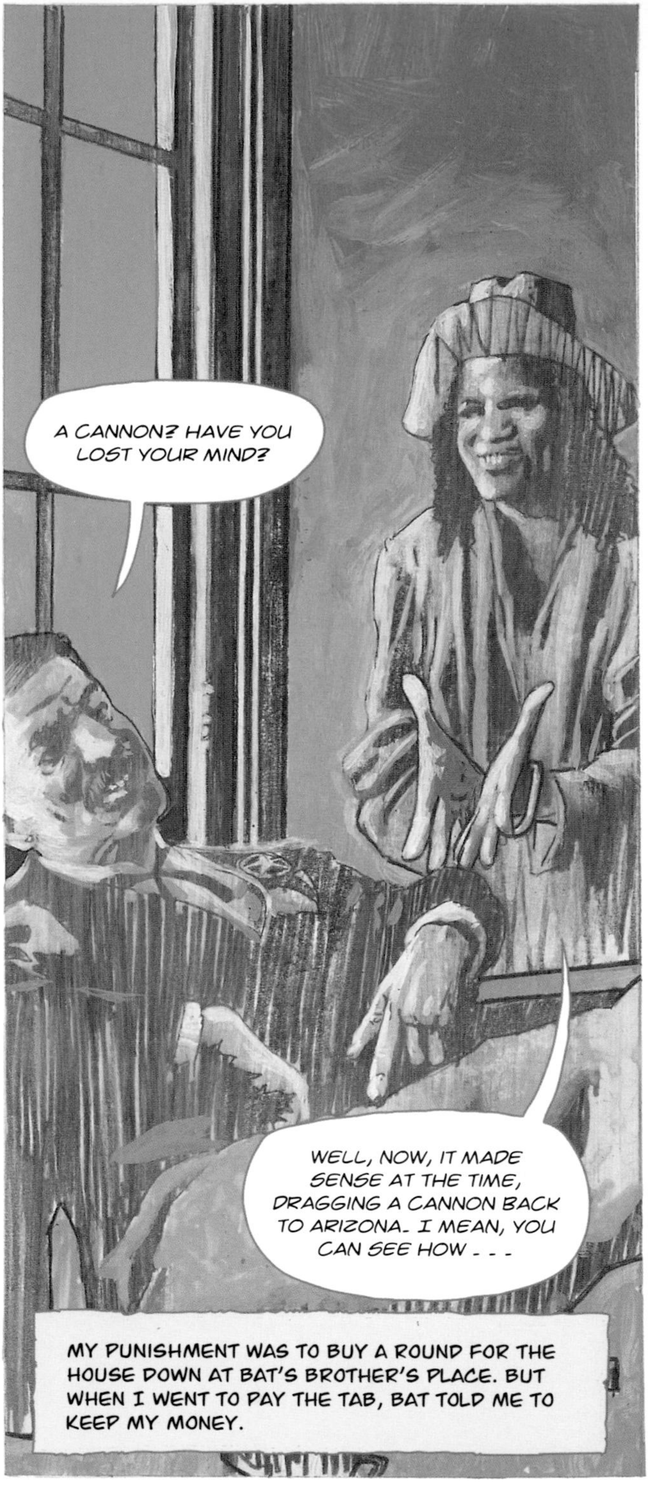
A CANNON? HAVE YOU LOST YOUR MIND?
WELL, NOW, IT MADE SENSE AT THE TIME, DRAGGING A CANNON BACK TO ARIZONA. I MEAN, YOU CAN SEE HOW . . .
MY PUNISHMENT WAS TO BUY A ROUND FOR THE HOUSE DOWN AT BAT'S BROTHER'S PLACE. BUT WHEN I WENT TO PAY THE TAB, BAT TOLD ME TO KEEP MY MONEY.
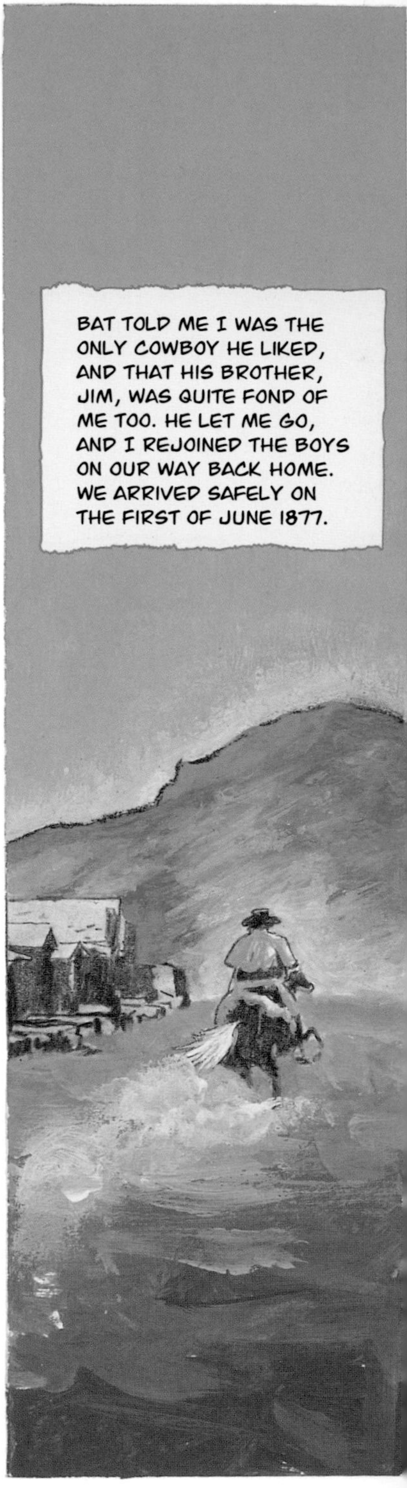
BAT TOLD ME I WAS THE ONLY COWBOY HE LIKED, AND THAT HIS BROTHER, JIM, WAS QUITE FOND OF ME TOO. HE LET ME GO, AND I REJOINED THE BOYS ON OUR WAY BACK HOME. WE ARRIVED SAFELY ON THE FIRST OF JUNE 1877.

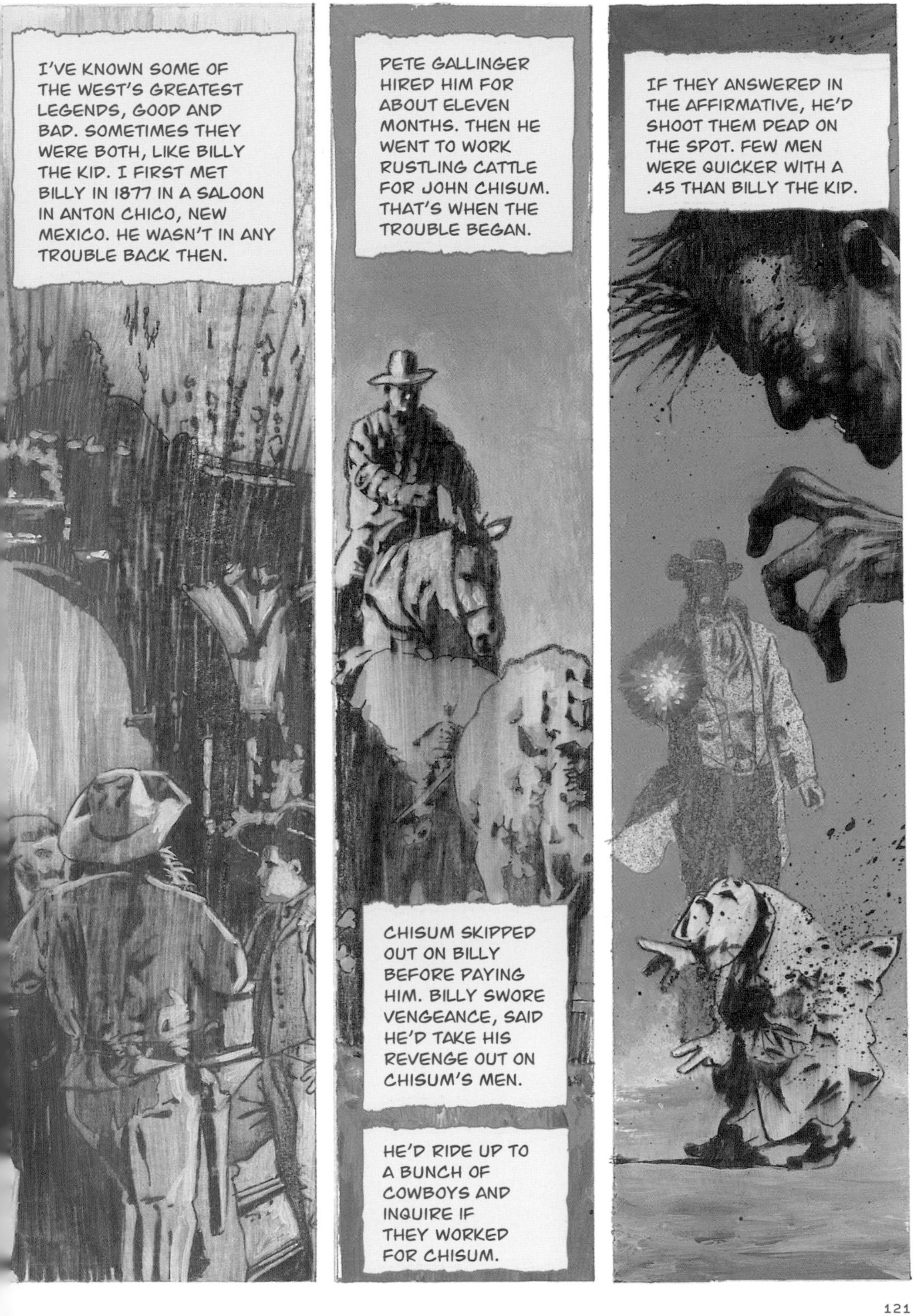
I'VE KNOWN SOME OF THE WEST'S GREATEST LEGENDS, GOOD AND BAD. SOMETIMES THEY WERE BOTH, LIKE BILLY THE KID. I FIRST MET BILLY IN 1877 IN A SALOON IN ANTON CHICO, NEW MEXICO. HE WASN'T IN ANY TROUBLE BACK THEN.
PETE GALLINGER HIRED HIM FOR ABOUT ELEVEN MONTHS. THEN HE WENT TO WORK RUSTLING CATTLE FOR JOHN CHISUM. THAT'S WHEN THE TROUBLE BEGAN.
CHISUM SKIPPED OUT ON BILLY BEFORE PAYING HIM. BILLY SWORE VENGEANCE, SAID HE'D TAKE HIS REVENGE OUT ON CHISUM'S MEN.
HE'D RIDE UP TO A BUNCH OF COWBOYS AND INQUIRE IF THEY WORKED FOR CHISUM.
IF THEY ANSWERED IN THE AFFIRMATIVE, HE'D SHOOT THEM DEAD ON THE SPOT. FEW MEN WERE QUICKER WITH A .45 THAN BILLY THE KID.

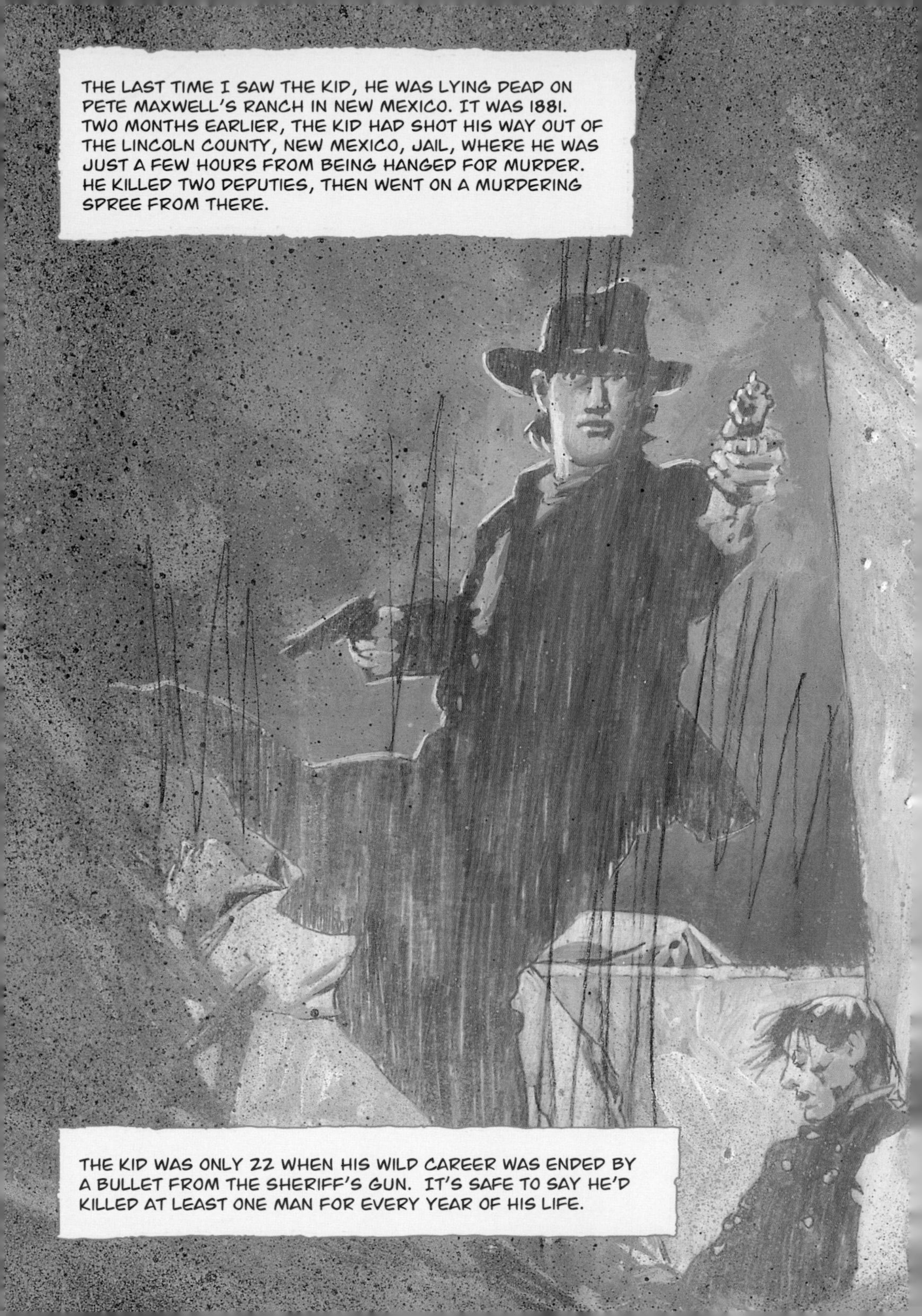
THE LAST TIME I SAW THE KID, HE WAS LYING DEAD ON PETE MAXWELL'S RANCH IN NEW MEXICO. IT WAS 1881. TWO MONTHS EARLIER, THE KID HAD SHOT HIS WAY OUT OF THE LINCOLN COUNTY, NEW MEXICO, JAIL, WHERE HE WAS JUST A FEW HOURS FROM BEING HANGED FOR MURDER. HE KILLED TWO DEPUTIES, THEN WENT ON A MURDERING SPREE FROM THERE.
THE KID WAS ONLY 22 WHEN HIS WILD CAREER WAS ENDED BY A BULLET FROM THE SHERIFF'S GUN. IT'S SAFE TO SAY HE'D KILLED AT LEAST ONE MAN FOR EVERY YEAR OF HIS LIFE.

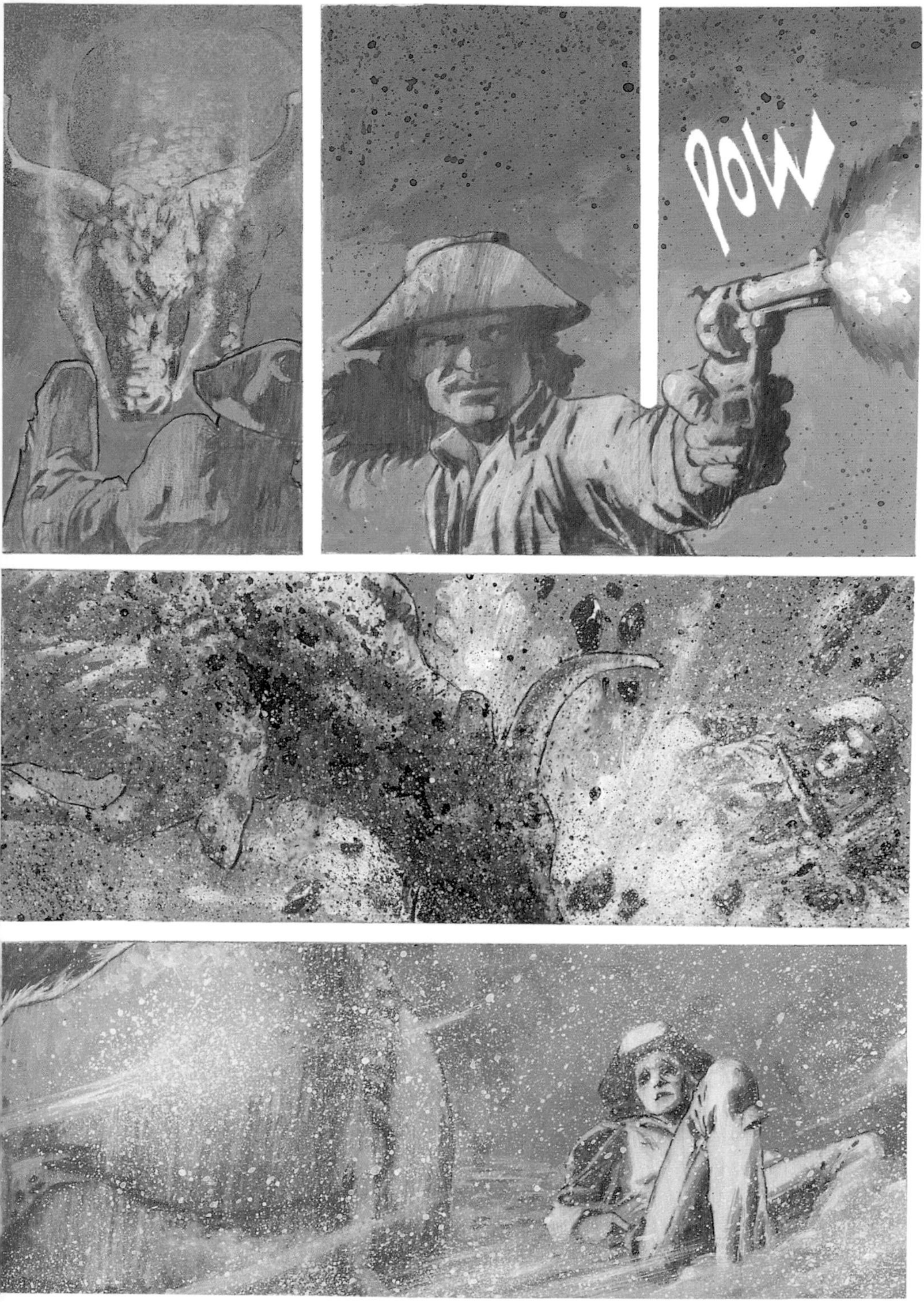
POW

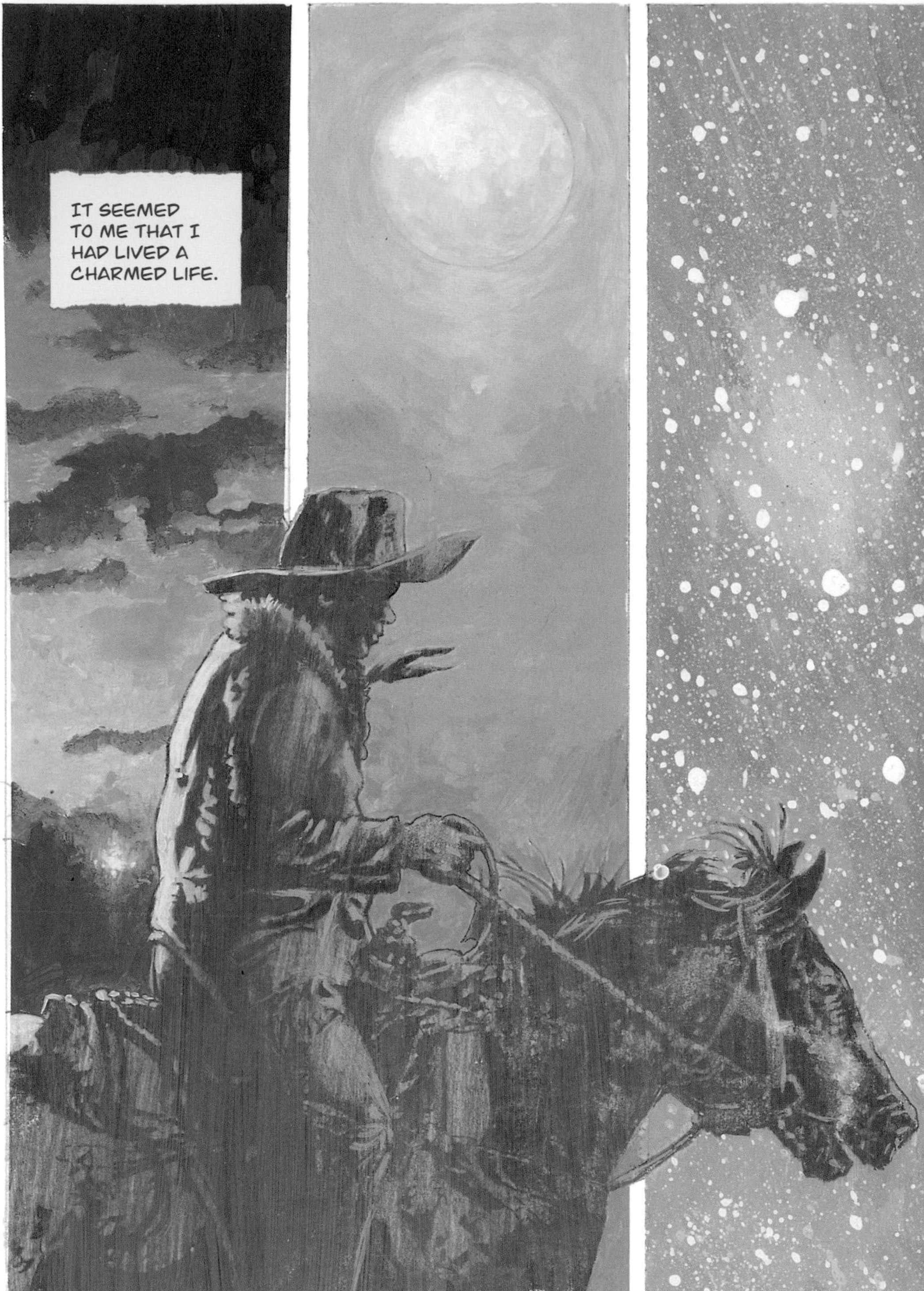
IT SEEMED TO ME THAT I HAD LIVED A CHARMED LIFE.

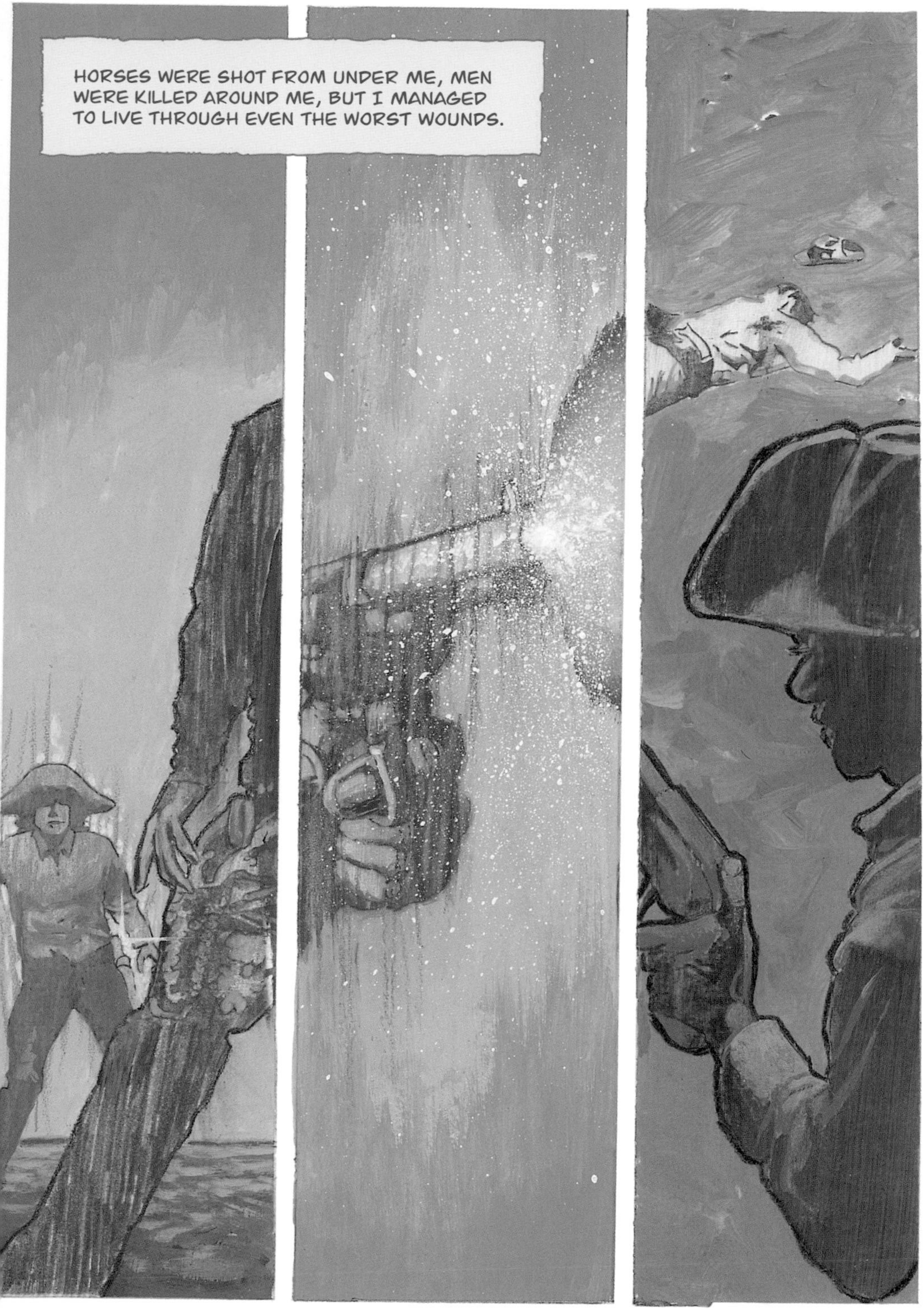
HORSES WERE SHOT FROM UNDER ME, MEN WERE KILLED AROUND ME, BUT I MANAGED TO LIVE THROUGH EVEN THE WORST WOUNDS.

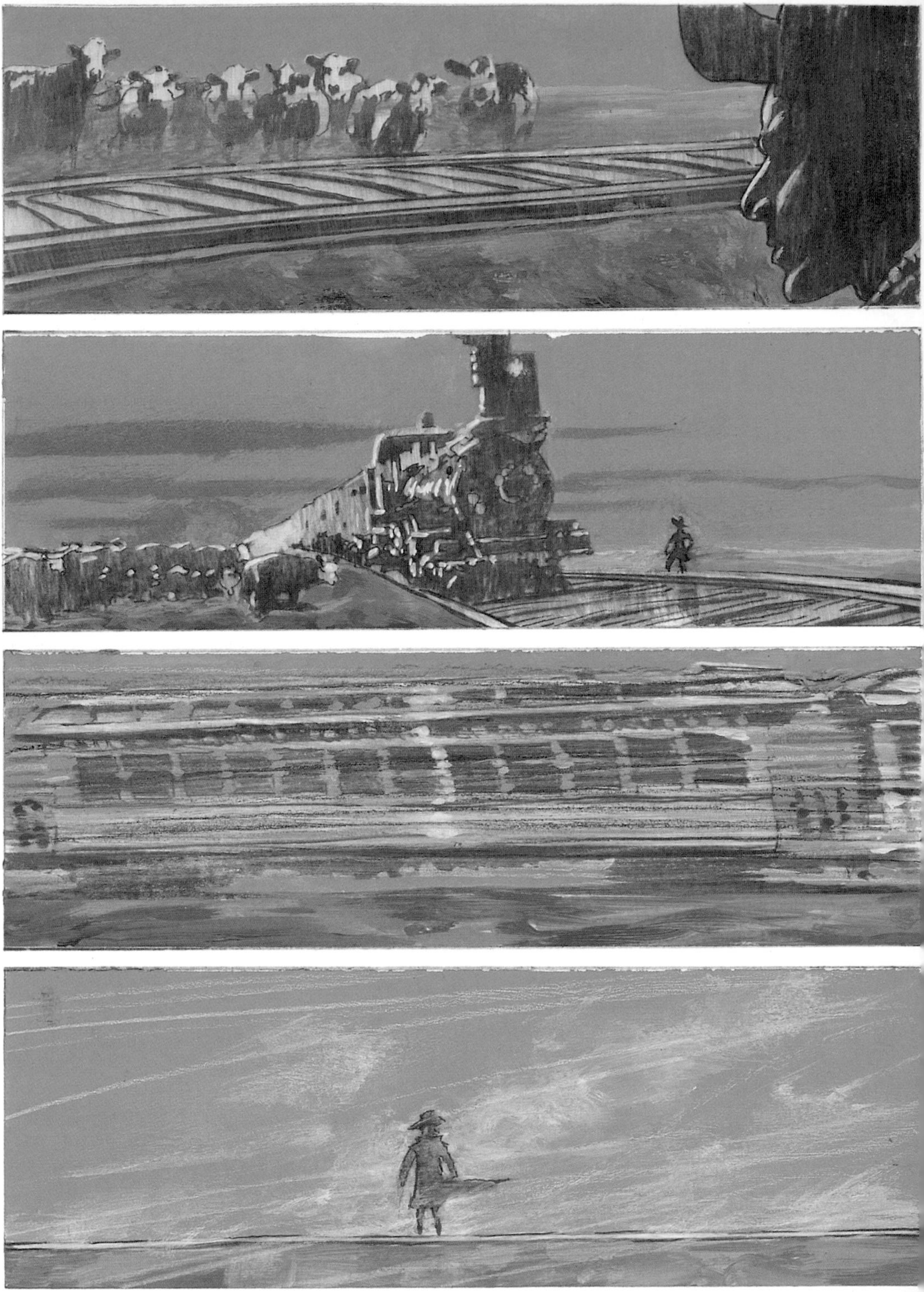

During my long experience in cattle country I had traveled every known trail and over immense stretches of land where there was no sign of a trail—nothing but an expanse of prairie, bare except for the buffalo grass and here and there a lone tree. The long stretches of grazing land rolled away in billows of hill and gully, like the waves of the ocean.

The great buffalo slaughter commenced in the West in 1874. By 1877, buffalo had become so scarce that it was a rare occasion when you came across a herd of more than fifty animals.

With the march of progress, the West was modernized by the railroad. We cowboys were no longer called upon to follow the long-horned steers and mustangs on the trail. There was a new order to things, and we were not a part of it.

In 1889, I bid farewell to the life I had lived for twenty years.

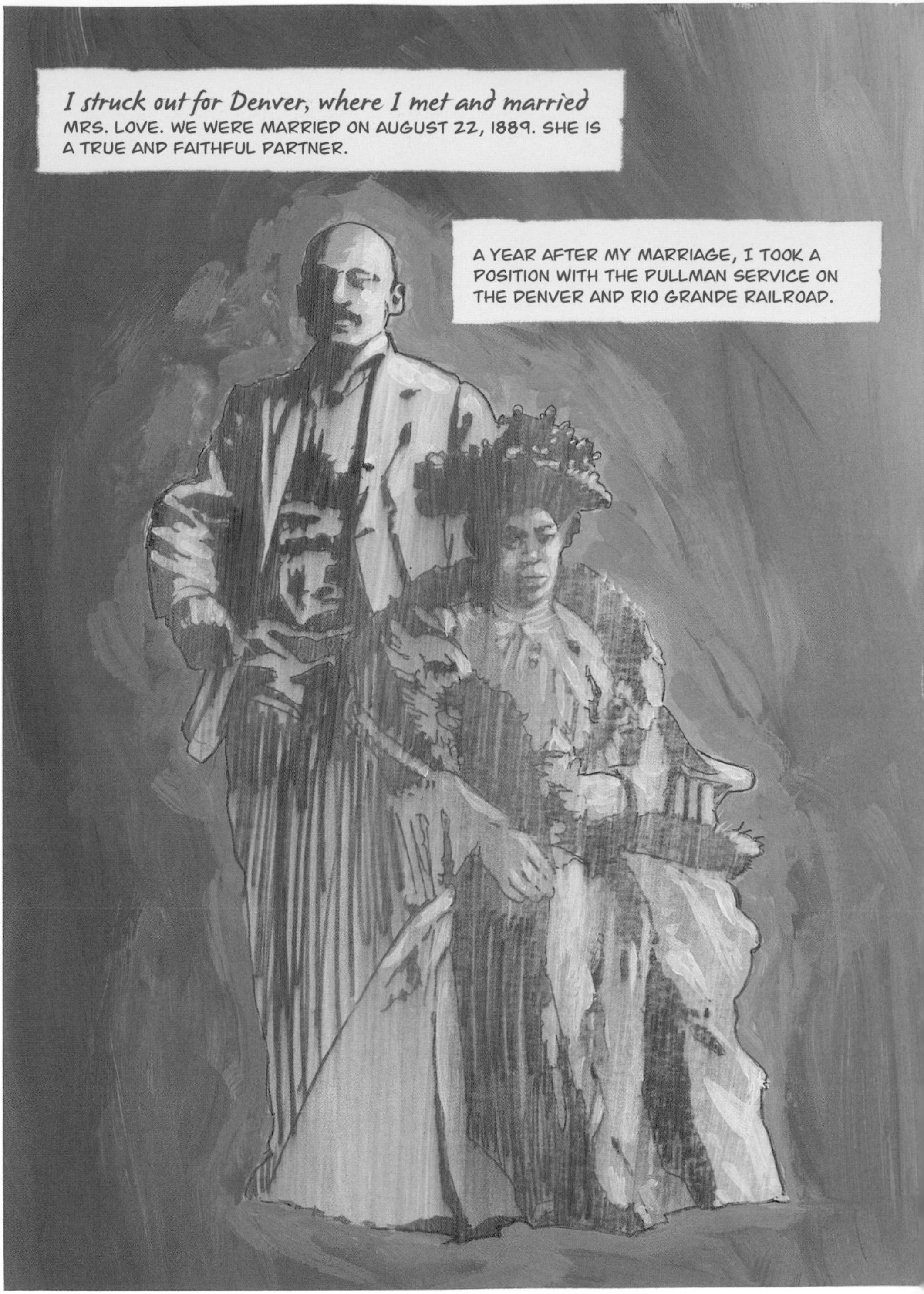
I struck out for Denver, where I met and married MRS. LOVE. WE WERE MARRIED ON AUGUST 22, 1889. SHE IS A TRUE AND FAITHFUL PARTNER.
A YEAR AFTER MY MARRIAGE, I TOOK A POSITION WITH THE PULLMAN SERVICE ON THE DENVER AND RIO GRANDE RAILROAD.

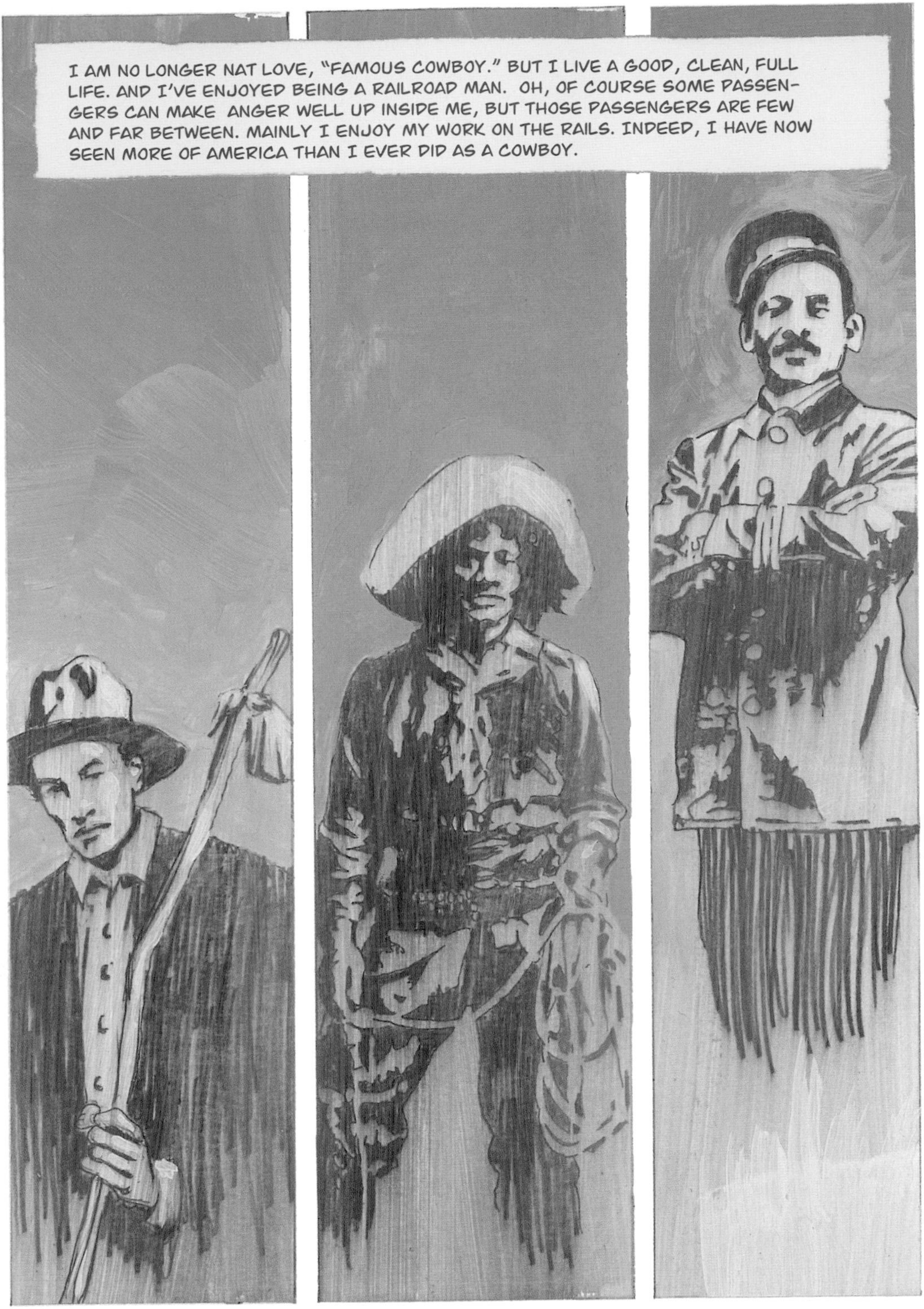
I AM NO LONGER NAT LOVE, "FAMOUS COWBOY." BUT I LIVE A GOOD, CLEAN, FULL LIFE. AND I'VE ENJOYED BEING A RAILROAD MAN. OH, OF COURSE SOME PASSENGERS CAN MAKE ANGER WELL UP INSIDE ME, BUT THOSE PASSENGERS ARE FEW AND FAR BETWEEN. MAINLY I ENJOY MY WORK ON THE RAILS. INDEED, I HAVE NOW SEEN MORE OF AMERICA THAN I EVER DID AS A COWBOY.

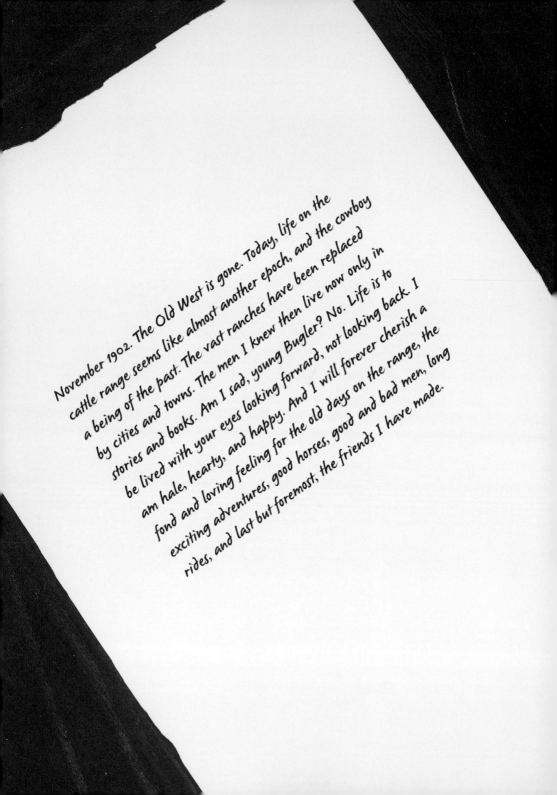

November 1902. The Old West is gone. Today, life on the cattle range seems like almost another epoch, and the cowboy a being of the past. The vast ranches have been replaced by cities and towns. The men I knew then live now only in stories and books. Am I sad, young Bugler? No. Life is to be lived with your eyes looking forward, not looking back. I am hale, hearty, and happy. And I will forever cherish a fond and loving feeling for the old days on the range, the exciting adventures, good horses, good and bad men, long rides, and last but foremost, the friends I have made.

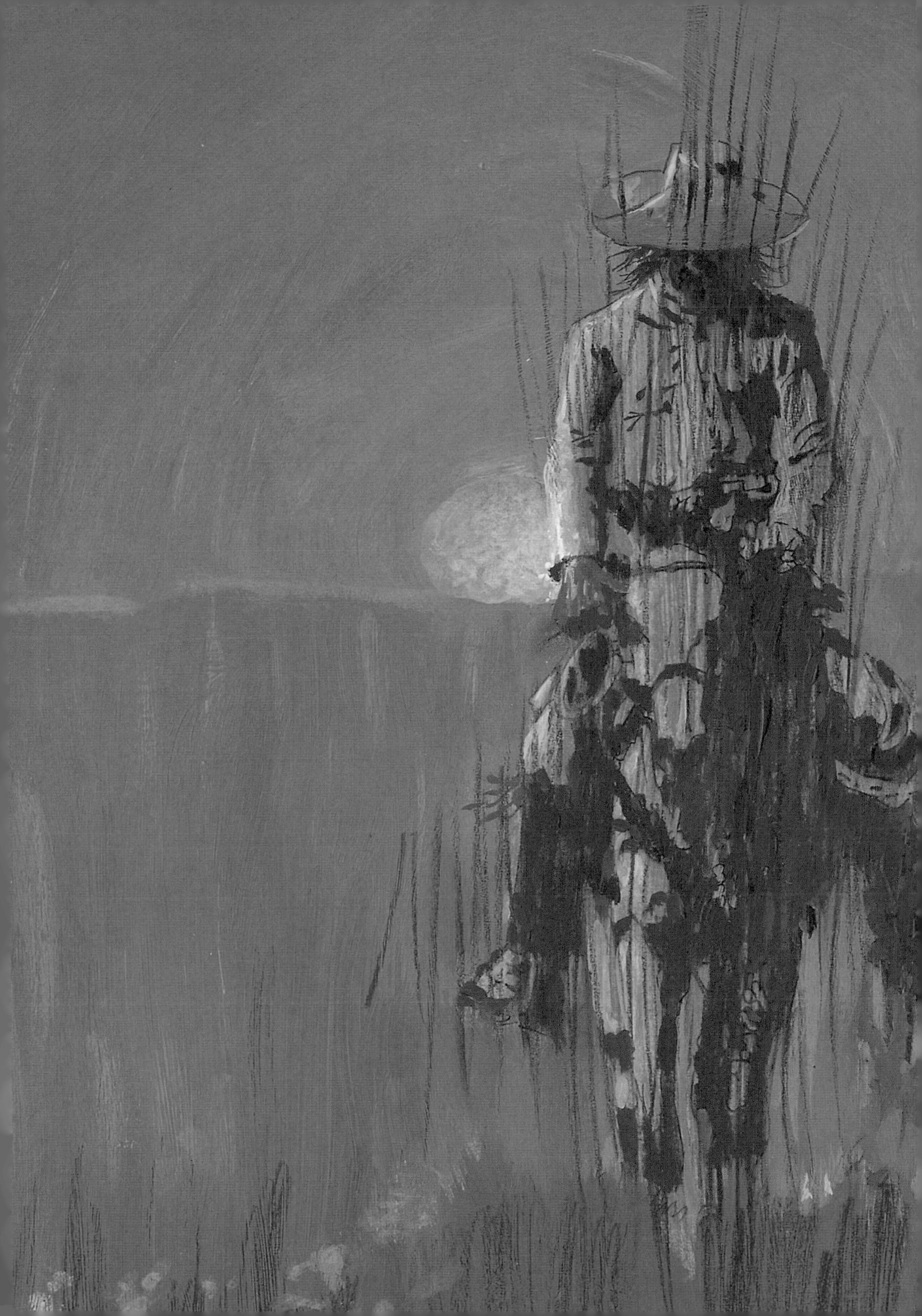

A Note from the Authors

When we set out to write *Best Shot in the West*,
our intent was to bring to life on these pages a truly marvelous
figure of the Old West. Since the publication of his autobiography,
*The Life and Adventures of Nat Love Better Known in the Cattle Country
as "Deadwood Dick,"* Nat Love's life has been picked at, sorted out,
shaken, stirred, examined, discussed, and evaluated by historians
and critics trying to separate mythology from reality. This mattered
little to us. Our goal was simple: Nat Love deserves
a book worthy of his remarkable life.

While a great deal of *Best Shot in the West* follows the
adventures described in Love's autobiography, some aspects of this
graphic novel have been dramatized, such as the invention of Bugler
and Nat's inspiration for writing the original autobiography.

A Note from the Artist

Illustrating the McKissacks' wonderful story has been
an exciting time for me. The time frame—the Old West—was
fascinating to research and paint. In the process, I not only became
friends with the amazing Nat Love, I found a wealth of stories of
Old West African Americans, Native Americans, Asian Americans, and
every other American that would make exciting books on their own. I
hope someday I'll get to illustrate some of them as well.